Anthony Quinn was born in Liverpool in 1964. From 1998 to 2013 he was the film critic for the *Independent*. His novels include *The Rescue Man*, which won the 2009 Authors' Club Best First Novel Award; *Half of the Human Race*; *The Streets*, which was shortlisted for the 2013 Walter Scott Prize; *Curtain Call*, soon to be a feature film starring Ian McKellen and Gemma Arterton; *Freya*, *Eureka*, *Our Friends in Berlin* and *London, Burning*. He also wrote the recent Liverpool memoir *Klopp*.

'A gripping mystery ... Sweeping across centuries in its three interlinked sections, it summons the past effortlessly, as a vehicle for a plot that is both intricate and immaculately constructed ... Quinn's most ambitious book to date and decidedly his best' Alex Preston, *Observer*

'A witty and affecting saga ... It delights in exploring tiny, unexpected quirks of character and broad brushstrokes of greater emotion alike, and never fails to entertain' Alexander Larman, *Spectator*

'Quinn displays an impressive range of expression: the mannered, epistolary style of the early chapters gives way to touches of Victorian gothic, and then to crisp contemporary prose' Kimberley Long, *Financial Times*

'A deft, century-hopping novel ... delights in the granular details of an era, as well as a thorough knowledge of its broad sweep' Imogen Hermes Gowar, *Guardian*

'There is a delicious mystery at the heart of this novel' *Daily Mail*

'Quinn is an intelligent analyst of the uncertainties of love and art' *Sunday Times*

'Pleasurable ... The novel is a triptych, each part standing alone and quickly establishing its particular note and colour by means of language, carefully chosen detail and a sprinkling of familiar names' *Times Literary Supplement*

'Quinn is an accomplished writer at ease with the idioms of the past ... He is also a subtle creator of character ... opens up timeless themes of family, success and love' Michael Prodger, *New Statesman*

'[A] beguiling new novel about the mysteries of creativity from master storyteller Anthony Quinn ... Every sentence he produces is a joy' *Metro*

'[A] stylish literary triptych ... Quinn is a fine writer with an instinctive understanding of the pitfalls of the bohemian life' *Mail on Sunday*

'Truly magnificent ... each part is separate and distinct, involving and compassionate, yet all are mysteriously connected ... Period details sparkle in this elegant prose ... This is Quinn's masterpiece' Sue Gaisford, *Tablet*

'One of my favourite writers ... a breathtakingly ambitious novel that nails the small personal triumphs and tragedies of each woman's life' Sarra Manning, *Red*

'Poignant, involving, beautiful and thoroughly entertaining ... Quinn's best and most ambitious novel yet dances through three centuries, entwines the worlds of theatre and art in a thoroughly seductive embrace, and brings all his considerable gifts into play ... This is a novel packed with pleasures' Christobel Kent, *Perspective Magazine*

MOLLY
&
THE CAPTAIN

Anthony Quinn

abacus
books

ABACUS

First published in Great Britain in 2022 by Abacus
This paperback edition published in Great Britain in 2023 by Abacus

1 3 5 7 9 10 8 6 4 2

A CIP catalogue record for this book
is available from the British Library.

Paperback ISBN 978-0-349-14429-0

Typeset in Caslon by M Rules
Printed and bound in Great Britain by
Clays Ltd, Elcograf S.p.A.

Papers used by Abacus are from well-managed forests
and other responsible sources.

MIX
Supporting
responsible forestry
FSC® C104740

Abacus
An imprint of
Little, Brown Book Group
Carmelite House
50 Victoria Embankment
London EC4Y 0DZ

An Hachette UK Company
www.hachette.co.uk

www.littlebrown.co.uk

*To Grace and George
and Gabriel*

Fame is rot; daughters are the thing.

J. M. BARRIE

Merrymounts

September 5th, 1785

Mr Lowther called at the house again. He stayed for an hour &
behaved with a Civility I had thought beyond him. When we
had first met him at the Rooms he was much distracted — today
confessed he seldom enjoyed a large company save when obliged
to perform. Pa remarked, 'But sir, you are always performing' —
which of course he intended as mischief but Mr Lowther took him
to mean his Professional life as violinist — So he spoke of his work
with the orchestra &c.

Molly & I later prevail'd on him to accompany Ma on the piano
forte. On taking his leave Mr Lowther made a deep bow & paid
her compliments on the fineness of her playing. Pa has since been
pleased to call him 'old Slyboots'.

September 10th, 1785

Bath appears to be in a permanent state of Commotion. Though I
should always chuse to live in a large town the din of carriages & the
cries of traders on Milsom-street seem to grow louder by the day. So
vexed was I by the Noise that in the forenoon I had to take my book
& seek the quiet of the back parlour — Still restless I persuaded
Molly to join me for an outing & we rode as far as Bennington Hall.
We stopt & watched the swallows all flocking together in the sky
ready for their long journey south. They chattered away on high,
cajoling one another. How comes about this great Migration? How

3

does this flighty mass of creatures settle upon the question of when to go — or where?

My dear Susan — I should have written to you before, but waited till I could finish the little sketch here enclosed. I am afraid it is a poor thing, but since you were so good as to sit those long hours I felt obliged to make an end of it. I know you will be mindful of my feelings, but do give an honest Opinion. Pa as you know has devoted himself to instructing us from an early age in painting & drawing — He means to ensure Molly & I may do something for Bread in case an accident should befall us. He believes this a better way than making fine trumpery of his daughters & enlisting us in the 'wild goose chace' — the Pursuit of a Husband.

Molly would be happy as a cicada to find some eligible Gentleman — at the Rooms last week she quite fatigued herself with dancing. I have cautioned her against too bold a display of Spirits, tho' I see no real harm in it. The unmarried daughters of Bath vastly outnumber the men of fortune & while that remains so she might do as she pleases. You enquired in your last as to the Musician — I had forgot you met Mr John Lowther on your visit — & am pleased to say our acquaintance continues most agreeably. Of his Accomplishments one cannot doubt — maestro of the violin, composer &c — yet I confess myself more charmed by the graciousness of his Manner, & by his pleasant Countenance. Even Pa, who naturally considers talk of Gentlemen a lot of chaff & disdains them for all but one part (that is their Purse) — even he concedes that Mr Lowther is 'd——m'd clever' & 'not a bad Fiddler'.

I should be glad to hear that you have met with a sensible worthy man. You reported an outing to Brighton yet say almost nothing of the gaieties there — I dare say you attended a Ball or a Concert in all that time! Please to tell me when you write & spare no detail of your adventures, for we are very dull here. Pa left yesterday for London on business at the Royal Academy, & the house always is quieter in his absence. Molly & Ma beg to be remembered to their dear cousin, as do I —

Yours truly & affectionately,
Laura

October 15th, 1785

Today a letter from Pa in London. He is returned to his lodgings in Norfolk-street now that the Decorating is finished. He writes that the press of business has thwarted him in completing his commissions & will delay his return. He is troubled in partickular by 'a Coxcomb' who has twice failed to meet appointments for sitting — thus has he lost a whole morning in waiting — 'I would fain kick the fellow's a——se down the stairs & have done with him, but élas the commission is too valuable to forgo so must I grin & shrug & accept the Gentleman's compliments'. To the side of this he has drawn a Caricature of a man tumbling down a stair, propelled by a large buckled Shoe.

October 21st, 1785

Newton brought the carriage around & took me to Widcombe Hill with easel & a plan of employment. Here I pass'd the afternoon in trying to draw the scudding clouds overhead & the shimmering movement of the poplar leaves in the wind.

Landskip painting Pa esteems highest of all — he does

'phizmongering', that is Faces, solely for Bread — & I endeavour to learn from his example. He has allowed me even to borrow his own paints & Palette, as though his Genius might be extracted from a mere handling of them. Would that it were! — then might I emulate the lightsome touch, the feathery brush-strokes & brilliancies of light for which the Merrymount name is renowned. Alas, cleaving to his lessons does not render the result of any greater consequence than an untutored student's — mere aping of technique is no guarantee of Beauty or Verisimilitude. On occasion I flatter'd myself that some stroke of chalk could be called an Effect, for it seemed to Conjure a fleeting likeness of Nature — & it pleased my eye. But these felicities owed more to Chance I think than the careful exercise of Skill, for when I attempted to reproduce such Effects my hand failed me. I should like to please him but 'tis folly to suppose I should make a Livelihood. These ruminations have left me low in spirits.

October 26th, 1785

We met Mr Lowther again at the Rooms & enjoyed a half-hour of his good manners. Indeed, I could not conceive a stronger impression of his estimable nature, his knowledge of the world, & his sound judgement. He asked after Ma & Pa with a deference I found very attractive in a man whose own standing in Society is considerable. When Molly was distracted by another friend of hers he took leave to pay me a partickular compliment, viz. he had been hoping to see my face there today & in that very instant — this said with smiles — marked my entrance into the Rooms. I dare to wonder if his addresses betoken more than simple amiability. I can determine nothing at present. If his heart does suffer agitation he makes convincing disguise of it.

Afternoon with Molly on a walk to Bathampton Down. Quite fair when we set out, wearing stout boots & stopping often to marvel at the autumn motley, the maples & beeches with their beautiful golden-russet tinges. We stepped through the little grove where Pa once painted us as girls — I wonder if there was ever an Englishman who painted his Family so often? He holds that his Landskips are his most accomplished work but that his favourites are 'Portrait of the Painter's Daughters' & the earlier 'The Merrymount Sisters at Night' — which we all know as 'Molly & the Captain'. Visitors to the house are apt to comment upon the latter, such is its renown as a Conversation-piece. It was painted in the year of I think 1763, when I was eleven & Molly nine, as we stood in the Drawing room amid the encroaching dark of the evening (Pa still likes to paint at night). Molly's dress is silver, mine Naples yellow. He was most partickular as to how we should pose — with her right hand Molly reaches towards the candle, a brightness in her gaze, while I, the sensible older sister, hold a restraining arm across, lest the flame should burn her fingers. I remember a Commotion very late one evening when Ma rushed in to scold him & deplore the hour he had kept us till.

He laughed & promised to reward us for our Patience tho' I cannot now recall what form our reward took. In truth, we already had everything we wanted.

November 9th, 1785

According to his Letter Ma rec'd today Pa returns at the end of the week. We had a jolly coze about a party for his Birthday on the 28th & agreed that the one best capable of arranging such a thing was Pa himself — tho' rise to the occasion we must. I caught a cold when we were walking & am confined within doors. Molly laughs to hear my voice through a Block'd nose, & she is a lively mimick — 'O bisery, a code in the Head!' &c.

November 14th, 1785

When Pa saw my sketches from Widcombe Hill I expected no enthusiastic response — nor did I receive one. He is never much dispos'd to flattery. Yet I did detect a gleam of Curiosity in his eye, more than he has hitherto express'd, as he bent low to examine some bit of cross-hatching. He then said, to my surprize, 'You have more of the artist than half those that get money by it' — & explained that with a brisk instruction in colour I had it quite within my power to essay Drapery & Landskip backgrounds. This branch of painting, employed by many portrait painters, is unlikely to bring Fame, he said, but 'if 'twere well done it may earn a Fortune'.

November [1785]

'Tis melancholy to see the two large oaks stripped bare, their leaves papering the ground. The trees seem to look down at their naked selves, like forlorn lunatic creatures who have cast off their undercloaths.

November 28th, 1785

We had fifty here, perhaps more, for Pa's birthday. Sally & the two girls had made the House gay with flowers & lighted dozens of candles in every room. Plates of cold ham, duck & chicken were laid out, with wine & sherry to drink. The furniture had been removed from the large Dining room to make way for the dancing. It had been my intention to ask Mr Lowther if his Quartet would provide the music but Molly had already secured his agreement. The parish Curate Mr Gunton seemed eager to engage me — we have a slight acquaintance from Church — but I was careful not to catch his eye. I fear I may have been rude, for when he stepped towards me I turned away to converse with my aunt & uncle Daventry. (I am not certain that Mr G—— is quite a gentleman, & his face is so very plain.) I could have wished to speak longer with Mr Lowther but he was for the most part occupied with his fiddling. When finally he did approach he begged my pardon for being so occupied & said that of course we should dance together. He asked me why I was known in the Family as the Captain, & I explained that Pa bestow'd the name when I was a girl on account of my tendency to direct others. (I am no longer so domineering.) Pa has always had a love of such nicknames — his own Wife he calls 'Queen Mab' or 'Mabs' or 'Queenie' (her name is Miranda). I forbore to disclose Pa's name for him, but Mr Lowther's thoughts were in any case running on other Business. Knowing Pa's predilection for Musicians — he prefers their Company & has painted a half-dozen in his time — he asked me whether I thought Pa would look favourably on a request to paint his Portrait. Trying to conceal my surprize I replied that he was busy with Commissions & due to return to London forthwith — but if it pleased him I would mention his petition. He smiled & thanked me. In truth, I am confounded by this forwardness & now inclin'd to wonder if this has been his private Object all along — Not to court me at all but to ingratiate himself with 'the finest Face painter in England'.

Later when Molly & I talked of the evening (she too had danced with Mr Lowther) I tried to ascertain whether he had repeated any of this Business to her. I could see from her puzzl'd Expression that she was entirely ignorant of it. I retired to bed in miserable spirits.

My dear Susan,

I am now settled at Pa's lodgings after a journey from Bath that was not more than usually uncomfortable. At my window I hear each day a prodigious rattling & clattering of carriages, carts, horses &c from the Strand — it starts up from dawn & grows louder through the forenoon. The House here is commodious, on four floors, the uppermost one in which Pa works & instructs his students. I count myself among them. He still believes me capable of drapery painting, that is providing the background to the canvases of Portrait painters. Alas I have no great confidence, tho' I devote a few hours each day to the undertaking. Now that Molly has given up I feel it behoves one of us in the event of misfortune to have, as my naval uncle would say, a shot in the locker. Moreover I have made myself useful in unexpected ways. The other day Pa, requiring lead-white, porte-crayons &c asked for the footman to be sent off to purchase them; but Cook said the boy was afraid to peep into the street lest he be press'd for Sea service. I heard shouts of D——m'd knave &c but still the boy would not go. So instead I did his errand, & reported to Pa that no press had got me. — 'Aye,' he said, '& if they had you'd make a braver tar than that blockhead.'

I had kept watch at Milsom-street for a letter from Mr Lowther but none came before I left. His compliments I fear I have mistaken & what I first construed as interest was a mere overflow of charm. Or perhaps I was his go-between — He wants to have his Portrait done, & supposed I might recommend him. When I raised the matter Pa said he had not imagined Musicians to be so 'well-breeched'. I replied, quietly, that Mr L—— might be hoping for it as a Token of friendship.

At that he laughed & said that the Gentleman must think very highly of himself. Later he directed me to send a short message to 'our friend' the Musician; upon it he had written three lines — 50 guineas for a head — 80 guineas for a half-length — 150 guineas for a full-length. Thus I am placed in what is commonly called a cleft-stick, either to disoblige Pa if I refuse to send it or to offend Mr L—— if I do.

Of course it suits my father to be blunt. Such behaviour in Bath I had plentiful opportunity to observe & while it caused us mortification I understood it as a Natural emanation of Character. He has a generous heart but a rough tongue, & in company he is apt to be rowdy, intemperate, thoughtless. He is not one to trim his words. His love of Comedy will outrun his Civility & he would fain play the joker than allow others to be comfortable. He remains in many ways the wild Suffolk lad he once was, unwilling to be tamed, by his Family or anyone else. I hardly need say this entire Business is entre nous. Next week Molly & Ma arrive here for Christmas, so the House will be full. Pa is, as once I overheard a guest at Milsom-street say, 'vehemently hospitable', tho' at present he is agonized by Gout & shouts at the servants. Thus will I relish the more my visit to you at Rye in the New Year, when I may at last hope for some Peace & Quiet. I remain, dear coz, most affectionately yours,

Laura

December 12th, 1785

A very odd encounter this morning. I was in the lower parlour engross'd in a drawing when a knock came at the door. I called for the boy to attend to it but rec'd no answer — perchance still in hiding from the Press — no maidservant about either & Cook too deaf to hear it so I went up to the Hall myself. Opening the door I found there a Lady, not young, well-drest, once beautiful I think, but faded, who asked if Mr Merrymount was at home. Her voice was low & pleasant on the ear. I told her that he was out all day on Business & invited her to leave her card. At that she smiled — as though to say she had no such thing — gave me a Curious look & thanked me for my trouble. She was retreating down the step when I asked her —'What name should I give?' — at which she seemed to falter & paused —'Mrs Vavasor', she replied, & with a charming bow departed. I wondered if I had heard the name before. Pa's acquaintance in London is wide, his clients many & various, & the appearance of one unknown to me could scarcely be thought remarkable. But there was about this Lady something that struck me as mysterious, either in her self-possession or in her elegant but careless attire — I could not decide. The impression of her countenance remained with me all day & Pa was hardly through the door before I informed him of Mrs Vavasor's calling. I marked his Expression as I said the name, but if it caused him discomfort he hid it well, replying with only mild surprize that he didn't know the Lady was in Town. I asked who she was. 'Why, you have never heard of Mrs Vavasor?' he cried. She, he was pleased to tell me, is the greatest Actress of her day, a Notable personage & a friend to the Quality. I can only say her Renown has yet to reach Milsom-street. He enquired as to our converse (briefly told) & seemed rather vexed that he should have been away when she called.

December [1785]

It being unseasonably mild when Molly arrived yesterday we went for a walk along the Strand & into the Temple, where the Lawyers flap around in their gowns like great black crows. When we pass'd a gathering of them I saw how close they put their heads together while they talked as though they feared to be overheard. Or were they merely deaf? We descended to the River & watched the little tugs & skiffs plying across the water. A mist had descended, & we lost sight of the Southern bank.

Molly said that Bath holds itself in very high esteem & yet has no inkling of its paltriness compar'd with London. —'The crowds who frequent the Rooms would be shocked to know of what little consequence they are in a single one of the Drawing rooms of St James or Piccadilly.' But I said that it should be a lesson for everyone that we are a perfect Nothing beyond our own circle — that our concerns are of vanishing interest even to those who live in the neighbouring house. I suppose that such a lesson would take most people a lifetime to absorb.

I enquired with pretended carelessness as to Mr Lowther. Molly said that he had called twice before they left for London, & still made no mention of the Portrait business. I did not send Pa's list of his fees to Mr L—— after all. It seemed ungracious, even if his Vanity merited it.

January 11th, 1786, Rye

Accommodated neath the roof of my Wootton cousins for almost a week I have greatly taken to the Sussex life, the long walks by the sea, the pleasant little harbour, & the strange salt air with its promise of health. This morning a gull perched on my bedroom sill & looked down its great enquiring beak at me as if to ask — Is Breakfast served? The town itself, with its winding, crooked streets & pretty cottages seems to me a happy spot. The welcome from the family has been all I could wish. Uncle Henry is a jolly red-faced country gentleman, shoots nearly every day & drinks flip every evening. Aunt Clara is like Ma, comely, pale-complexion'd, a little severe but good-humoured withal. He dotes upon her.

Susan's brothers Charles & Frederick are more amiable than they were as schoolboys — The former is in the employ of a building merchant, the latter studies to be a Doctor.

Susan, two years younger than I, seems quite as sanguine as ever tho' she appears to entertain no significant prospects of Marriage. She is busy with her Charitable work & visiting the local poor, occupies her hours of leisure with sewing, reading &c — never seems to chafe at the lack of Society about her. I cannot pretend such a life would satisfy me, & yet I envy her this contentment with her lot. She is proof that a narrow orbit of acquaintance does not necessarily beget a narrowness of mind. She listened carefully to my account of Mr Lowther's behaviour. 'I dare say he has conceived a partiality for you,' she began. 'His attentions have been too persistent to argue otherwise. Perhaps he was persuaded to withdraw out of a consciousness of your superiority to him.' Superiority in what regard? I asked. Susan considered. 'In temperament, in manners, in social standing, & quite probably in intellect. Many a man would,' she added. I blushed & laughed at the compliment, tho' even if all that were true I would never disdain Mr L—'s overtures, for even in his Pride I could not help but admire him.

January 17th, 1786

To Hastings in the carriage with Susan. We arrived wind-whipp'd & frozen. I had brought with me chalks & paper but my hands were blue with cold & could not hold steady to draw. We walked for an hour on the shingle, our bonnets tied firmly beneath as the wind got up an almighty howl & snatch'd our voices away.

We stopt occasionally to gaze out to Sea & watch the breakers thunder towards us. The roar was majestic & terrible. On the horizon, smudg'd with grey, a single tiny fishing boat was tossed about on the swell & I thought once more of our narrow life & its Insignificance. I remarked to Susan on the emptiness of the

Scene — we had not passed another soul as we walked. 'Do you wonder?' said she. 'No sensible person would take a constitutional in such weather!' Then to a tea-room on the Parade, where we took shelter at last from the wild buffeting.

January 30th, 1786

Today arrived back at Milsom-street after nearly two months away. I perceived something amiss from the moment I entered the house, weary & travel-worn — I could not say exactly what, but Sally did not catch my eye on greeting & Ma appeared somewhat distracted as she enquired as to my journey &c. 'Is Molly ill?' I said, imagining the worst. Ma shook her head & told me I should rest for the afternoon. I retired to my bed-chamber & was dozing there when Ma came on tip-toe into the room & sat on the bed. She said there was News that might grieve me — I asked her to tell it — & she looked at me with a Face that mingled kindness & pity. 'Molly is to be married,' she began (my immediate sensation was of joy) & continued —'to Mr Lowther.' I was astonished & for a moment lost the power of speech. How could this be? Ma hurried on with an account of Mr L——'s courtship, apparently conducted in secrecy during the weeks I was away in London, tho' I think it must have begun at an earlier date, perhaps at the Party in November, I cannot say. He proposed to her two weeks ago, while I was at Rye, & Molly accepted. 'What did Pa say?' I asked — my hand trembles as I write this — 'He believes the fellow a sneaking dissembler,' she said, 'but since Molly is determined upon having him there is nothing to be done.' Old Slyboots — Pa knew his Man. I was quite composed throughout our converse, but once Ma had gone I gave way to tears & much bitter lament. I remained thus in my bed-chamber for the rest of the evening.

January 31st, 1786

Pa came to me this morning & spoke as gently & feelingly as Ma had done, tho' now I could not refrain from weeping. He said Mr L— was a 'blackguard' who had used me very badly, but of course he cannot speak as candidly to the man who is soon to be his Son-in-law. The situation is impossible. Pa looked pained & said he knew not how the fellow had glozed his way into the affections of Molly but that to him the direst calamity of all would be to see his daughters estranged.

'You have been too dear to one another to be sundered by his ignoble scheming. Molly is wild & headstrong but assuredly she did not purpose to do you ill. You have good understanding; I know you will come to forgive her.'

Will I? I think it will not be soon.

February [1786]

The mood at home has been lowering & I fear I am the cause. I keep away from Molly as much as I can but come the hour of dinner we are obliged to face one another. I want to be civil but my countenance betrays the wretched hours I have spent brooding. Pa keeps up a jolly run of talk withal, & Ma looks on nervously as we sit in silence across the table. This evening Molly visited my chamber & across her own drawn features I could read the unhappiness there. She owned that it affected her grievously to see me miserable on her account, to which I replied that it could be little wondered at. I might have borne Mr L——'s throwing me off for anyone else. But that my own sister should have connived at it cut me to the heart — At which she broke out that no such connivance could be laid to her charge, that Mr L——'s addresses to her had come without warning or invitation.

Ought she to have rebuffed him simply because his original

preference had been for me? I replied with some haughtiness that I could not vouch for her Conscience, but for myself 'twould be impossible to brook such treatment of my own kin. At that her face crumpled & tears poured down so piteously I was minded to forswear my indignation & pet her as I used to when we were girls.

But I could not, I was too distraught, & we parted in misery. I wish I had never set eyes upon that man.

February 21st, 1786, London

I am now once more settled at Norfolk-street. A relief to us all, I believe. The domestic uproar occasioned by Molly's engagement became too much to bear & I begged Pa to allow me to resume my residence here. He agreed very willingly. He removes to London more often now that his Commissions have multiplied. At first I felt too sick at heart to be in Company & kept to my chamber, reading & thinking. But today I resolved not to mope & putting on my thick-sol'd boots I walked through the West End & thence into May Fair, where so many of Pa's clients reside. The grand houses seemed to frown as I peered in their windows.

There was a frost about & once or twice I slipped, but did not fall. The queer pinched faces of London folk much impress'd me. On Bond-street I bought a woollen shawl, which sits about my shoulders as I write these lines. 'Tis odd how a few hours of activity can lift the spirits. A stroll in the City has not the healthful benefits of a Country Walk, but I think surpasses it for interest.

Pa troubled again with Gout but still manages to work.

I rec'd yesterday a letter from Molly but find I have no inclination to answer it.

I was tramping through the morning crowds at Covent Garden when I passed a Lady whose face I thought familiar. In a hurry I retraced my steps & plucked at her arm — a momentary Expression of alarm crossed her features (she perhaps mistook me for a strumpet on the prowl) till of a sudden she recognised me & smiling said — 'Why, Miss Merrymount, is it not?' I returned the smile, & blush'd, for I could not recall her name — knew her only as the Lady who had called at the house in December. She must have perceived this, & said, 'Mrs Vavasor, at your service.' The thoroughfare on which we stood was busy so I asked her if she would have tea with me at Norfolk-street, & she consented right away. 'My father told me you are an Actress,' I said once we were settled, 'of great Esteem,' I added quickly. Mrs Vavasor looked at me with laughing eyes & said, 'Aye, if an Actress can be said to possess such a thing . . . 'Tis not esteemed a nice profession at all.' As she spoke I took the chance to study her — She is fine-featured, with dark olive eyes & nut-brown hair, not tall, with a neat waist & pretty legs. But more striking to me was her easy & natural Manner, enhanced by a charming laugh. Indeed her laughter has two different registers — the one that sounds like the tinkling of a bell, the other deeper, bawdier — & sounds like a man. I asked her about her acquaintance with Pa, to which she replied they had met at Drury-lane when she was playing in 'The Way of the World' — 'My employer, Mr Sheridan, introduced us over a Supper at his rooms, & very civil & humorous I found him — You are fortunate indeed to have such a Father!' She owned she had been here but a week ago & had hoped to meet me, but Pa had said I was a little indisposed. 'You are recovered now?' she continued. I told her I was quite well. We talked for an hour or more. As she was taking her leave I said that Pa would be vexed to have missed her — 'Then in recompense allow me to invite you both to Drury-lane for an evening, that is, if you should care to see me on a stage?' I replied, truthfully, that nothing would give me keener pleasure.

When she had gone I dashed up to my chamber & made a quick sketch of Mrs Vavasor's head while she was still fresh in my Memory.

Norfolk-street, Strand
March 17th, 1786

Dearest Susan —I must tell you of our outing to the Drury-lane Theatre to see 'Twelfth Night'. Mrs Vavasor, whose acquaintance I lately made, sent around tickets to Norfolk-street as she had promised. Pa seemed bemused that we should share her invitation but did not stand on ceremony & laughed out loud when he saw that sherry & cake had been laid on for us in the Box. 'Lizzie (as he calls her) has conceived a liking of you, I fancy — I never get so much as the ship's biscuit when I attend.' I was stupefied at the size of the Theatre, by the noise & bustle from the pit right up to the gallery, wherefrom a hundred faces at a time seemed to loom in the candlelight. I had seen the play once at Bath & remembered the Plot, but in all other partickulars this was quite different — the vast chandeliers, the gilded ceiling, the luxurious sets, the quality of the music & overtopping them all the Majesty of Mrs Vavasor as Viola. Never did I see such a performance in which humour & lightness were married so cleverly to pathos of expression.

Her voice is all harmony, the delivery so cleverly managed that when she spoke in the guise of 'Cesario' she beguiled us entirely. She looked uncommonly pretty in man's Cloaths. The applause she won at the end of the play rang to all corners & very well deserved it was.

But this was by no means the end to the night's entertainment, for Mrs V—— had sent her maid to invite us to her Dressing-room — such a place I had not visited. Imagine, dear coz, a maze of stairs & gloomy passages that lead to a general Dressing-room where a candle & mirror are assigned to each actor; around them flit stage-hands, hairdressers, lighting men, scene-shifters, assorted helpers, even nursemaids who have tended an actress's children — like a little household unto itself. Mrs V—— had her own room away from this where Pa & I were obliged to watch as she with the aid of her Dresser divested herself of the costume & the paint from her face — Pa not at all embarrassed but of course I blushed to see such a thing, even with a screen betwixt us. When she emerged to receive us she told the maid to lay the Table — & next moment a servant carried in a tray of cold meats, bread, bottles of ale &c from the tavern next door. We took our supper & talked past midnight of Shakespeare, the stage & the 'devilish' Business of acting. Mrs V—— tho' tired from her performance was graciousness itself & talked to me as if I were quite as wise as herself about the Theatre, tho' my ignorance must have been apparent. Such a jolly evening I never had.

Let me have a letter from you soon, & make my best compliments to your family.

Yours most affectionately,
Laura

March 26th, 1786

I tormented myself this week by endeavouring to write a letter to Mr Lowther, in which I asked him, candidly, if he believed his conduct towards me befitted that of a gentleman. It was only with this distance of months that I felt calm enough to address him so. Yet when I read it through I found its tone so plaintive in its grievances & doubts that I saw that it would do more harm than good.

The man had already shown himself a blackguard — why should I give him further opportunity to despise me? The letter is now black cinders in the grate.

I then wrote a short letter to Mrs Vavasor thanking her for the hospitality we rec'd at Drury-lane, expecting no prompt reply — yet to my surprize she wrote to ask if I would oblige her with my company this afternoon for a walk in the Green Park. She greeted me warmly & we commenced a stroll. 'Twas a day we felt the spring slowly advance, the wind a little brisk & yet amber rays of sunshine peeped through the mass of clouds. Mrs V—— said I should call her Lizzie, as Pa does, & told me of her Life — Born in Bristol of Irish stock, raised in a theatrical family & from an early age toured the North country — York, Sheffield, Hull, Newcastle, Edinburgh &c — before moving to London aged two & twenty. I asked her if her husband still lived. 'I never had a husband,' she replied — The 'Mrs' she was advised to put before her name by her Mother, who perceived the dangers attending an Actress without protection. She did once have a child, she said — but the father abandoned her & the child died in infancy. Though she did not say so I knew from Pa her performances at Covent Garden had won many friends & admirers —Would she take the chance if Marriage offered? She was thoughtful for a moment.— 'Aye, but such a prospect recedes by the year. I am seven & thirty, close to an age when men's interest quickly wanes.' I am three & thirty, I replied, & cannot pretend myself to have many pretensions in that regard. She looked at me, with some astonishment, said she would not have guessed my age above thirty. 'But your sister is soon to be married, I believe?' As we talked of this I could not remain quite composed & she behaved with great sympathy on hearing the story of Molly & Mr L——. She urged that however disgraceful the latter's conduct I ought not to throw off a beloved sister on his account. 'To forgive demands humility,' said she, 'the hardest of all virtues to master — but also the sweetest.' I thought this wise, &

privately resolved to make Mrs V—— my friend and, if she would allow it, my confidante.

April 9th, 1786

Ma has written to me in distress. It seems there has been a sad revival of Molly's old troubles — as a girl she was subject to delirious fits of a severity that obliged her to keep within doors. Afterwards she would have only a vague notion of these nervous disorders, & she soon returned to the lively & good-hearted girl we knew. As she passed into Womanhood the fits receded in frequency & finally ceased altogether, so we believed. But these last weeks our Molly has been laid low by the Distemper once more. Ma called in the Doctor who following an examination advised her to rest, since when a little calm has been restored — but the fear persists that her Affliction has not been cured, only allayed. I talked over the matter with Pa, also much distressed. He conjectures that the sudden onset of her illness may be traced to the coming Event of her nuptials — 'There is nothing like Marriage to play havoc with a woman's humours,' he says. I asked him if Mr L—— had been apprised of Molly's condition — I mean its true Nature— & he thought not. Perhaps this would give him cause to reconsider their union, I ventured. 'In that case let him be informed of it immediately,' Pa muttered.

In her letter Ma begs me to return home, which I am reluctant to do. But if Molly really is ill I fear I must.

April 22nd, 1786, Bath

Since Pa & I returned to Milsom-street ten days ago we have been greatly relieved to find an improvement in Molly's Health & spirits. Her appearance on first entering her bed-chamber startled me — Her face feverish & pale against the pillow & a trembling agitation in her limbs recalled every aspect of the old Distemper. The Doctor believed it to be an Ague — Pa thought not, & directed Sally to administer cooling draughts & a dose of James's Powder to settle Molly's fits. By degrees we saw a slow improvement, she began to take a little broth while sitting up in bed & talked to us quite calmly again. I think she was pleased to see me, my frowns reserved only for her well-being.

This evening Mr Lowther came to the house & I heard him conferring privately with Pa in the Library — Later he went up to see Molly. All seems to be well. If he did not know of Molly's volatile condition before he surely does now. I had it from Ma that Pa suggested putting off their Marriage till later in the year but Mr L— would not hear of it.

Friday, June 9th, 1786

On this day my sister Molly was married to Mr Lowther at the Abbey Church of Bath. May God bless her & keep her.

[First section of Laura Merrymount's journal ends here]

October 1787, Cavendish-square

Lizzie came again in the forenoon to sit for me. I keep Pa's precepts foremost in mind — viz. to be well aware of the different Effects which one part of a Picture has upon another, & how the Eye may be fooled as to the appearance of size &c if ever the Painter is tempted to overlay his own 'bundle of trumpery' —

It is not the Painter's business to invent, says Pa, only to tell the Truth.

While I worked away Lizzie talked about the trials of her recent Northern tour. The playhouses in Scotland, Yorkshire &c had been most of them full when she performed, yet the manager of the Company had taken a dislike to her — she knew not why — & had bilked her of £100, money she has calculated to be at least half of her earnings.

She has engaged a lawyer to pursue the payment but thus far has rec'd no word. This in itself is a troublesome expence she said & would be entirely unnecessary if Mr S—— had paid her what was owed. Then she burst out —'I am sick of everything under the sun.' I was startled, never having seen her in such a vexed mood. We were silent for some moments until I said that if money was short I would most willingly help release her from any debts. — At that she looked at me strangely & said, 'You think I have told you this as a way to appeal to your Charity?' A heat had come to her Face & I quickly replied that I wished only to be of assistance, but she cut me short — 'I have not grovelled for a thing in my life, & never will,' she said with great haughtiness — & at that she rose & without bothering to change swept out of the room.

Again I was most astonished, so unlike her did this behaviour seem. Some hours later she returned here & earnestly begged my pardon — 'I am out of sorts, my dear girl, & ought not to have spoken so roughly.' I said that I had not meant to give offence — that I merely wished to be of service — at which she became tearful & said that I was the kindest person she knew & please to forget her churlishness. I asked her what the matter was, but she shook her head & claimed an indisposition — Her Sleep has been lately disturbed & made her low-spirited.

We talked a little more, but she was still distracted & soon left the house, this time at least with a civil Farewell.

October 22nd, 1787

Still alarmed by Lizzie's outburst I consulted Pa. He has met the gentleman with whom she shares a house — 'tis said they are married, but Pa believes not. The 'husband' is one Mr Boyce, a lawyer from Bristol, who is known to have ambitions for Parliament. — And that is why the fellow will never marry her, says Pa — Lizzie may be the font of all happiness to a man, but one gift she can never bestow is Respectability.

I am minded to enquire about her domestic arrangements — Could they be related to her anxieties about Money? I suppose such curiosity might be thought impertinent, & I fear to provoke Lizzie again.

October 27th, 1787

To Covent Garden where Pa procured a Family Box to see Lizzie in 'The Double-Dealer'. She played Lady Touchwood, a dissolute, jealous Woman, with admirable skill, tho' coloured with an arrogance I did not like — I would fain not see her play a heartless schemer. Yet there was something else in her that gave me pause — a certain hesitancy in her Comportment, an unsteadiness as might afflict someone under the influence of drink, or an opiate. Was she ill? At the interval Molly took me aside & whispered — 'Is Mrs V— with child?' I said I thought not, tho' during the next Act I observed Lizzie in the light of this conjecture & was inclined to think Molly right —a faint roundness seemed to shadow that graceful figure & gave me to wonder if this might be the cause of her fatigue.

Afterwards at Supper we were gay & talked of Lizzie very fondly, but Molly kept silent on the Subject & so did I.

November 1st, 1787

Lizzie here for the Portrait — I asked her if I might paint in the spectacles she wears for reading — 'To put them on my Face?' she asked. No, this idea did not please her, for wearing the spectacles 'was not in her regular Fashion'. I considered that carrying a Child was hardly in her regular Fashion either, but said nothing. We agreed that she would hold the spectacles in her lap, at the foot of the picture. We had been together two hours or more when I asked her, innocently, if she had been indisposed when she took to the stage last Saturday.— No, she replied, seeming puzzl'd, & I was obliged to own to her what Molly had conjectured. Lizzie returned a look I had oft seen on stage — knowing, with a touch of rue — & confirmed that we had guessed aright. She is content, for she had always hoped to be a Mother, & she laughed as I clapp'd my hands — 'Pray tell no-one,' she said, 'for the Announcement shall not be soon.' I ventured to ask if the news had pleased Mr Boyce? — 'He will be informed in due course.' I was astounded by this — That she had not yet told him! Pa had guessed their Marriage (if indeed it be) was an eccentric one, but this exceeds the measure.

November 4th, 1787

The revelations of recent days have led me to ponder the knotty business of Marriage —As a girl it seemed to me an enviable state & one I would rejoice to attain for myself; yet it seems impossible now to ignore the burden of unhappiness & disappointment that Marriage so often brings in its train. One surely cannot exist in a state of constant intimacy without ever wishing oneself alone. My own Father & Mother have been wed six & thirty years & have loved us as truly as any parents did — but do they reflect with satisfaction on their time as man & wife? I cannot pretend they have been well-suited. Pa is of a hearty gregarious temperament, his humours too quick & unruly for one as shy & placid as Ma — She would prefer a life away from the 'madding crowd' — she dislikes London — while Pa regards Company as his lifeblood & seeks out diversion the year round. Perhaps Lizzie's seeming indifference to Mr Boyce springs from natural wariness — her own parents were grievously unhappy together & she confessed herself relieved when the father abandoned them (she has two sisters). Only Uncle Henry & Aunt Clara to my mind have found true contentment together —& that might be explained by the former's frequent absences from the house.

November 19th, 1787

Pa's patient tutelage notwithstanding, I have made little progress in my career as drapery painter. The agent Mr Goodall on first inspecting the work was certain of attracting clients. I duly took heart from his confidence —Pa himself echoed the encouragement, & all looked set fair. But now Mr G—— reports that his expectations of 'immediate employment' were misplaced. It seems that his clients are less inclined to hire a woman for such work, even when the rates proposed are more favourable than a man's. I asked him why this should be — He shrugged. I would have thought my father's Name alone might have secured a commission, but the agent replied that the Principle — the Prejudice, I might say— held firm. 'If the business were offered in the name of Merrymount & son the prospect would be bright — "& daughter" I fear is not an affinity likely to open purses.'

December 13th, 1787

Lizzie has removed from Queen-street where she had lodgings with Mr Boyce. Relations between them finally broke down once the news of her pregnancy became known. It seems that Mr B—— is not the father at all but a certain Lord Rothwell, a favourite of the Prince. Now scandal pursues her & her Character is mocked in the windows of the Print-shops — Mr Gillray makes great sport of her in his latest drawings. When Pa & I saw her this week at the Haymarket in Cibber's comedy ('She Would and She Would Not') the audience was hostile — shouts & curses from the pit. Lizzie, playing Hippolita, gave as good as she got.

She would always make a bow towards them when in male costume — now she turned her back & bowed the other way, as if to say Kiss my a——e! Pa gave a loud laugh & cried 'Bravo!' I laughed too, tho' I doubted the prudence of her saucy gesture —the Public is a beast to bait at your peril.

December 15th, 1787

I visited her at her new lodgings at Clerkenwell-close — a small cottage, smoky, somewhat cold. I thought she would be mortified to read her name bandied in the Press but she seems indifferent to it — something almost regal in her equanimity. She regards these scurrilous attacks on her as mere 'teazing', says she has known much worse. (Of course, this coolness of temper may be a show.) I asked her about her new protector Lord R—— to which she replied — 'If the press were to be believed I have bestowed my favours on half the aristocracy of London.' With some apprehension I referred to her anxieties about money — the scoundrel manager has yet to pay her —but she assured me that Lord R—— had taken her finances in hand & her debts were discharged. 'I am more grateful to him than I can say,' she said later.

How I admire Lizzie's courage — cast out by her lover, harassed by creditors, ridiculed by pamphleteers, without a husband for the child that is to come — yet nothing will defeat her. Would that I had as much vigour in meeting adversity, 'To take arms against a sea of troubles' — alas, when troubles come I am apt to shrink away, to hide my face from the world. To think Pa used to call me 'Captain' — his imperious daughter!

Cavendish-sq, London
December 20th, 1787

My dear Susan — I rec'd yours & am glad to know all is well with you & the family. Today marks a twelve-month since

we removed from Bath to London — I think we are here
permanently settled, tho' the house is not beloved by all. Ma
finds it too large to manage & quarrels with the servants —she
believes them idle & dishonest, 'like all London folk' — &
lives in constant fear of house-breakers. Pa's assurances that
we are safe —'safe as a mouse in a cheese'—bring her no
comfort. The light & airy rooms suit him very well, however.
He has never found a more congenial place in which to paint
or to show, & used the garden to advantage in the Summer.
I have been endeavouring to help him. So numerous are his
Commissions that he requires on occasion a Landskip painter,
& who might do that job better than the very Person he taught
himself? It went slow at first, for I dread to furnish him with
inferior work, but indeed he seems very satisfied — He has
more confidence in me than I have in myself.

Last week we dined at Mr & Mrs Lowther's, in Soho. They
keep a very grand house — servants, a cook, a Carriage —
which indicates either that Mr L— has a head for business
or else there is a deal more money in Music than I ever
supposed. I thought the partridge at dinner a little tough.
I would scruple to say that Mr L— has improved with
acquaintance —he behaves as though the unpleasantness of last
year was but a minor inconvenience — tho' at least with Molly
I am reconciled. Ma is very tender towards both; Pa keeps
his own Counsel. I have watched him gaze across the table at
his son-in-law & wonder what he might be thinking. Later
Molly showed us the Harp which Pa had given them on their
Wedding — she was briefly persuaded to twang upon it.

My friend Mrs Vavasor has been infamously abused in the
periodicals. The scandal of her pregnancy & ejection from the
house she had shared with her husband have made a Feast of
gossip on which London continues to graze. We have lately
seen her twice on stage. The first time she was subjected to the

provocations of the Pit — jeering & shouts of 'gamester' &c — against which she defended herself with great wit & vigour. Some in the audience admired her for it, & the next time we saw her she was cheered to the echo. Such are the whims of the Public. It would please me to introduce you to Mrs V—— when you visit us — I have good hopes you will like her as much as I do.

I enclose a little Drawing of the Garden here along with Compliments of this happy season to you & the family — I am, dear coz, most affectionately yours,

Laura

January 14th, 1788

An argument has arisen over a painting — one might say The Painting — of Molly & myself, viz 'The Merrymount Sisters at Night'. It presently hangs in the Hallway, just as it did at Milsomstreet for twenty years or more. Perhaps it is the most famous Portrait Pa has ever done — it is certainly the most beloved. Now reports come from Goodall his agent that a Gentleman wishes to purchase it — I know not who, or how he came to see it, for the thing was only twice exhibited in our lifetime, years ago. Pa has never put it up for sale — & would never — but the offer for it is exceptional — 350 guineas. Goodall urges him to sell, & to our amazement so does Ma, for the sum is prodigious. Pa has dismissed the matter out of hand — his attachment to the Portrait is so strong it seems unlikely he will yield.

Today Goodall returns to the house & brings a new offer — 400 guineas. When Ma heard of this she again remonstrated with Pa, saying only a mad man would refuse it. She added that they are already in possession of two other Portraits of 'the girls', both of them as fine as 'Molly & the Captain'. He disagreed — the Painting was strictly not for sale, at any price, & so the dispute rages on, with Ma & Goodall making common cause against Pa's intransigence. Later, when we spoke in private, I asked him why he so determinedly refuses the sale — if the 400 guineas were offered for some other painting he would surely accept it. Pa replied, 'Perhaps so. But this Painting is part of your inheritance. Were I even inclined to I could not in all conscience sell the thing —for I regard it as yours & Molly's.' I thanked him, with all my heart, & silently prayed that we would be worthy trustees of it.

January 27th, 1788

I have returned to the Portrait of Lizzie that I set aside last year, & must now endeavour to finish it —her figure softens more each day that passes, & she herself complains that her Cloaths begin to strain at the seams. I assure her that she is beautiful still, only 'tis beauty of a different order —riper, like a Rubens. Yesterday Pa happened to come into the room where we sat & looked most amused by our cozy companionship — Much joking & teazing. He said, 'I wonder if there lives another Actress in the country who can claim the Honour of being painted by a father & his daughter.' I was much embarrass'd by this & after he had gone I begged Lizzie's pardon — said that the high company with whom Pa associates is apt to make him conceited. He did not mean to speak amiss.

Lizzie seemed not to understand his offence & I was obliged to continue — The Honour of which he boasted did not pertain to the Actress, I said, but to the father & daughter who had been allowed to paint her. But Lizzie laughed this off in her familiar way & said what a 'singular girl' I was.

February 10th, 1788

Yesterday I was with her in her Dressing-room at Drury-lane when there came a knock at the door & a smart well-mannered gentleman entered — Lizzie introduced him as Lord Rothwell. He spoke to her quietly & with respect (I had imagined such a fellow would boom), enquired as to Lizzie's health & expressed a hope that she would agree to dine with him soon. Before he left she explained to Lord R— that I was the daughter of the 'famous' Wm Merrymount, at which he owned to being an admirer & would I be so kind as to convey his compliments &c to my father. I thanked him, & he left. Now if this is really the same Lord whose name has been intimately associated with Lizzie's I confess my astonishment, for while there was graciousness on his part I discerned no history between them above a friendly acquaintance. But Lizzie assured me that this man is her protector & the father of her child. Perhaps then it is my mistake to have believed that Passion should be the ruling principle in chusing one's mate; instead, one should look to the virtues of good sense, reliability & an open hand when entering the marriage market. I remember Cousin Susan telling me as much years ago, but I was headstrong then & thought I knew better.

February 29th, 1788

I felt great apprehension before revealing to Pa the finished Portrait of Lizzie, & not merely because I consider the thing so deeply inferior to his own. I dreaded to hear him find fault in a hand that he himself has tutored — if 'twere so then my venture into Face-painting is gone to smash, for who is more able to teach this branch of Art than Wm Merrymount? But show him I must. His countenance is wont to reveal nothing at first, & I waited in an agony of doubt. Then he nodded several times —smiled, as though to signal his approbation, & asked me how many pictures in total I

32

had finished. I replied that there were nineteen or twenty sketches, four oils of Heads & five Landskips. He said that if all the work was of this calibre (pointing to Lizzie's Portrait) it would incline him to show it in a gallery —He would speak with Goodall about it. I thanked him, tho' felt alarmed. I have not yet self-esteem sufficient to face the Public gaze —the only Arbiter I hoped to please was Pa.

March 4th, 1788

Now he announces that, having consulted with Goodall, an exhibition of my Paintings is to be held —not in a gallery but here, at Cavendish-sq. I felt bound to object to the presumption of this. I protested that only my Name — that is, my kinship with him — could justify such a thing. My work is not yet worthy of exhibition —I should be laugh'd at at every Tea Table in London. But he was not persuaded, believes this to be mere pusillanimity on my part — 'If your work were only in the common Fan-mount stile I own it would not be worth the candle. But there is accomplishment here & much else to delight the eye. Besides, this happens to be my Show-room, & I am d——md if I mayn't show what I please!'

I cannot think Goodall (if indeed he was consulted) would approve this. He would not be swayed, as Pa is, by the sentiments of family. But I fear that once my father has fastened upon a scheme he will not easily let it go.

Cavendish-sq, London
March 12th, 1788

Dearest Susan — I take this spare moment to dash off a line to you. The grand plan to show my work proceeds apace, & I am helplessly swept along in its wake. The house is full from noon to night of Canvas-stretchers, Frame-makers, Picture-hangers,

Nail-bangers & sundry other jobbers preparing the large & small Show-rooms in readiness for the exh. At night I can barely sleep for worry of the Disaster that may follow. As you know, I was quite content to paint on in obscurity, to be that flower 'born to blush unseen' — for I never have conceived a desire for Fame. But Pa is determined to thrust my pictures before the Public gaze. He at least believes in them, & I am thankful that the Merrymount name will attract a crowd, even tho' all the interest be in his name rather than mine.

Mrs Vavasor, her 'bulge' now quite visible, delighted us again this week at Covent Garden in an old comedy, 'The Wonder: A Woman Keeps a Secret'. (It is by Susanna Centlivre — her play 'The Busie Body' we have also seen.) The great house was full & warmly applauded her on first appearing, & again at the end. The scandal of her broken marriage still lingers, & the papers continue to abuse her in the vilest language, but Mrs V—— carries on in spite of them. I shall endeavour to introduce you to our remarkable friend, dear coz — I beg you to attend this little show of mine, or should I say of Pa's, since it is all his doing. The opening is set for a day in April. I will write again once it is settled.

Remember me to your mother & father, & believe me affectionately yours,

Laura

April 4th, 1788

Susan arrived here yesterday & very glad I was of her company in my agitation. I never had a better confidante, so patient & wise in counsel. When I owned to her my terror of the coming exh. she argued that on the contrary it ought to be an occasion of delight—'We are so little noticed in general that when attention comes our way 'tis an

34

obligation as much as a pleasure to savour it.' I saw the good sense in this. We went for diversion to Mr Mendham's in Bond-street where I bought two pairs of satin gloves, one for each of us. Then we walked in the Green Park — saw the horse-chestnuts budding & listened to the larks singing.

For a full two hours I quite forgot the forthcoming Event.

April 5th, 1788

Strange it is how an evening awaited so long & with such dread may come to seem almost a Mirage the next day. Visitors began to arrive after noon & were most of them greeted personally by Pa. In the evening carriages came to the door, the lamps were lit & the guests were served punch & port wine. The house had seldom been so full — the ground floor so crowded that we had to open Pa's Painting-room to accommodate the numbers. I rec'd some compliments on the pictures. Lizzie came straight from the theatre with a company of friends & made a gracious toast to me —I introduced her to Susan & was pleased to watch them talk in a convivial way together. I thought Pa would give an address but he did not, & I was relieved. The agent Goodall lurked about the rooms all evening, occupying guests with his glozing talk. I was desirous to know what had been sold but did not engage him.

April 9th, 1788

I am fortunate to have my cousin here —Without her gentle & philosophical counsel I should have collapsed under the strain of nervous fatigue. The day after the exh. Pa departed on Business to Bath, so I wrote to Goodall enquiring as to the sale of my work. I rec'd no immediate reply & leaving Susan to occupy herself I went to his office in the Strand. His Face was all surprize & he affected not to know why I had presented myself. I asked him directly how many

of the Paintings had sold — When he hesitated I had my answer, &
waiting only to hear it confirmed I left. I walked back in a trance of
mortification, repeating under my breath — Not one! Not one! And
I silently reproved myself for the debacle. My first instinct had been
to decline the scheme, but Vanity got the better of me. I also think
ill of Pa for insisting upon it — of course he meant well & thought
only to use his influence to my advantage, but I would have been
much happier to plough my lonely furrow & maintain the illusion
(at least) that I had ability. Pa could not understand this reluctance.
But there is the difference between us — He has Genius, and paints
because he must. I paint because I have no facility for anything else.

A satiric article in 'The Enquirer' revels in the disgust of those
who attended the exh. last week believing it to be of William
Merrymount's work, not his daughter's — thus now I know for
certain that my work is thought commonplace & derivative. I have
traded obscurity for ridicule.

April [1788]

I might have brooded on my woes had not grievous news overtaken
them. A Silversmith of Regent-street sent his man here yesterday
with an urgent message for Pa. He went off immediately, returning
some hours later with a story as pathetic as it is alarming. It seems
that Molly had visited the shop on Thursday & was noticed behav-
ing oddly — the Manager of the shop engaged her & there followed
an altercation, the burden being that the fellow had discovered
her attempting to 'lift' a bit of Jewellery. I exclaimed in shock as
Pa continued — Molly was seized & under duress owned that she
had absently pocketed a silver brooch but had not meant to steal
it. She was within an ace of being carried off to Bow-street when a
colleague of the Manager observed that Molly was too genteel to
be a common prigger & questioned her. Once it was established
that Wm Merrymount was her Father, a calm was restored & a

messenger dispatch'd to Cavendish-sq. —'Why her husband was not summoned I cannot fathom,' said Pa, though of course he smoothed the ruffled feathers & asked the Silversmith to take into account his daughter's occasional nervous disorders — such thieving was wildly out of Character & he would make all necessary recompense for their trouble. The matter was dropt.

Pa then conducted Molly back to Soho & waited for Mr Lowther. On his appearance they had some converse about Molly — I know not what — & an agreement was made that she must not for the present be allowed to go out unaccompanied. Pa looked weary & vexed on his return. I thought I should attend on Molly but he advised me to wait for a day or two —doubtless she needs rest. Susan still resides here, & I could not help give way as I related the history of poor Molly's Distemper, hitherto concealed from the cousins.

April 17th, 1788

I visited Molly at Rupert-street & was relieved to find her in a quiet & subdued temper. It seems that the delirium of old has recurred & she is now under the care of the Doctor. He has prescribed James's Powder. I asked her about the incident at the Silversmith's & she replied in a broken way that pierced me to the heart — She has no recollection of her larceny & felt deep remorse on hearing the account of her behaviour under accusation. The matter is extraordinary, but I think she speaks truly — 'tis not in her character to be treacherous or dishonest. She has submitted to keep within doors for the present. I gather that Mr L—— has been little at home these last months owing to professional obligations. (I hope that is the reason.) Ma has been fretting over the Business in a way that helps no-one; she is not the least suited to bearing up.

I write this late, the candle guttering, & feel dreary & disturbed as I prepare for bed. I pray God grant us deliverance from these miseries.

April 22nd, 1788

A letter from the office of Goodall — Two of my paintings have
been sold, one of them a small portrait of Ma & Pa, the other a
Landskip. I am astonished & write immediately to ask the name
of the buyer. Goodall in reply said that the buyer wished to remain
anonymous. I conceived then a strong suspicion of who it might
be & felt a renewal of that first disappointment — the purchase
reflecting not upon my worth but on the promptings of sentiment.
In the evening I found Pa in his library & put it to the test — I
said that I would be always grateful to him for the first Lessons in
drawing he had bestowed on me & for his great encouragement
thereafter — likewise that the exh. he had mounted was generous
on his part tho' somewhat premature, since my work was not yet
of a standard to merit a public display. Pa was about to speak when
I came to the point — Hurt though my pride was he should not
have endeavoured to salve the wound by secretly purchasing two of
the paintings. It was kindly meant, I owned, but it served only to
rob me of what remained of my dignity. Pa now looked bemused &
claimed innocence of the charge, asked why he would pay for work
that had been given freely hitherto — Had I not already made gifts
of drawings & paintings to him? So sure was I the purchaser was
Pa & yet — I am mistaken — & baffled.

April 25th, 1788

Still at a loss I took the simple expedient of waiting for the two
Paintings to be collected from the House. When a young man
came to the door this morning with his cart I flew down the stairs
& almost knock'd Sally off her feet to speak to him. He showed
me the Bill of sale made out to one Lord Rothwell, care of Hoares
Bank in Fleet-street. Can it be? This is the man widely rumoured to
be Lizzie's protector — tho' he was not present at the exh. & would

in any event hardly concern himself with such humble trade. Well, perhaps it is to his Taste — I could not say — but it rejoices me to think that it pleased someone's eye well enough to part with money.

June 4th, 1788

I walked to Clerkenwell-close to call on Lizzie, lately returned from her Mother's house at Bristol — she was determined against enduring her Confinement in London. As her Maid admitted me I could hear an infant's cries from the bed-chamber & made haste up the stairs. Lizzie smiled on seeing me — her dark hair fanned out across the pillow like a sea-nymph on a rock — & there at her breast the mewling babe, a boy, his tiny face puckered & pink with distress. He wailed a little more till Lizzie stopt his mouth with her Teat. We drank tea & she gave a fearful account of the Child's emergence — I confess I felt almost sick to hear it. She calls him 'Jo'. She invited me to hold him, & I did so for some minutes — anxious, & fascinated.

Later, while the Child slept, she led me downstairs — she had something she wished to show me. We entered the little parlour & I dare say I gasped in surprize, for hung there on the wall were two Paintings — my own. But how could this be? Lizzie explained that she had long admired both the Portrait & the Landskip — had watched me Paint a little of them — & was desirous to purchase them at the exh. But lacking money she asked her friend Lord R—— to oblige her with a loan & thus bought the pair. I was briefly overcome. That my most debt-harass'd friend should bring further expence upon herself for my sake was too much to bear — I protested that if she had asked I would have handed them to her gratis. — 'What, deprive an artist of her daily Bread? We are Professional players, you & I — payment is our due. Never forget it!' I thanked her, & told her the mortifying story of the exh. These, I said, pointing at the wall, were the only two sold.

'Then I am honoured to be known as the first owner of a Merrymount – The Younger,' she replied.

June 20th, 1788

A fierce rapping at the door heralded a day of confounding alarms. I heard shouts & came down to find Sally remonstrating with a pugnacious fellow wearing a scratch wig & a dirty coat. His voice boomed so loud that it brought Pa from his Painting-room, furious at the interruption. The fellow brandished a sheaf of papers which he claimed to be invoices from a stables in Soho — unpaid, & directing creditors to this address. Pa examined one of these documents & handed it to me. There, at the foot, was Mr Lowther's signature. The stableman desired immediate payment of debts incurred from at least six months ago — which Pa politely declined. An argument broke out, & threatened to become violent when Ma, who never comes to the door, appeared in the hallway & obliged both men to collect themselves. Calmer words were exchanged & soon enough the man was sent on his way.

'So my gadabout son-in-law, not content with neglecting his wife, has taken leave to charge his stabling fees to me. A merry caper, I must say!' Ma pleaded that it must be an oversight of Mr L——'s, but Pa huffed at that — 'old Slyboots' was far too cute. He decided straightaway to pay a visit to Rupert-street & called Newton to bring round the carriage. I asked Pa if I might accompany him so as to be on hand for Molly, who might not yet be apprised of her husband's misdemeanours — he consented. On arriving we found Molly playing at cards, on her own, arranging & rearranging them in patterns indecipherable to me. The distance in her eyes upon greeting us I found perturbing. She said Mr L—— was away from town with the orchestra (I saw Pa shoot his eyebrows at that) but would return on Monday. We enquired as to any trouble her husband might have had with creditors of late — indeed he had, she owned, tho' 'twas 'a temporary inconvenience'. She conducted us to the library where papers lay on a desk & invited us to consult them — we found bills from coal merchants, furniture dealers, Bond Street jewellers, wig-makers, wine importers, silk mercers — & several from the Stables whose representative we had met that morning. Molly acknowl-edged the extravagance but seemed quite unconcerned about the urgency of accounting — Mr L—— had assured her he had matters in hand. 'But in the meantime,' said Pa, 'he sees fit to discharge his debts by referring them to me.' Molly, the mist seeming to clear from her gaze, now remembered Mr L——'s petitioning her to ask her father if he might stand surety for certain expences while his own money was 'tied up' elsewhere. She had forgotten to do so. The gravity of the business was at last evident — a hand suddenly raised to her mouth — & she begged his pardon for the embarrassment they had caused him. I saw her agitation & quickly smothered any hint of accusation against her — but said it behoved her husband to set his affairs in order & that his first point of duty would be to apol-ogise to Pa & remove his name from any further bills, promissory notes &c. 'Let us see how the scoundrel plays now,' muttered Pa.

I could not bear to leave Molly alone in the house so we carried her back to Cavendish-sq. where we had dinner — I urged her to stay for the night but she insisted on returning to Soho.

June 25th, 1788

I caught sight of Mr L—— just before he entered Pa's study. He had been summoned to explain himself, tho' I discerned no expression of remorse in his Face. They conferred for an hour. I gather he 'slunk away' at the end of it. Pa told me later that Mr L——'s finances were in hopeless disarray & that his Bank had refused to extend further credit. Certain business ventures of his had failed & the money he invested was not likely to be recovered. Asked how he expected to keep a wife & a house if this remained so he replied that he intended to give up the Lease at Rupert-street & take lodgings in Kentish Town, some distance from here. It seems that both husband & wife have been wildly extravagant, tho' as Pa sadly remarked, Molly has no better understanding of money than a Child — 'One spendthrift in a marriage is bad enough. Two must be fatal.' The upshot is that Pa will lend him enough to meet their debts on the guarantee that all expences henceforth will be curbed —Carriages, silver, finery, the luxuries to which they became accustomed —all these must cease. Such is the bargain they have struck. I cannot say if Pa has faith in its being kept.

Cavendish-sq, London
October 15th, 1788

Dear Susan — I beg your pardon for my long silence. I had intended to write weeks ago but the house has been in uproar. I must now relate the unfortunate story. In June it became apparent that Molly & her husband were sunk deep in debt — a desperate extravagance the cause. Mr L—— had so mismanaged his affairs that Bailiffs had been at the house & all credit at the Bank stopt. Out of natural kindness (towards his daughter if not his son-in-law) my father paid off their creditors & extended them a loan after Mr L—— offered a solemn oath never to indulge their profligate habits again. Pa was obliged to accept it, having already been petitioned in a scene of great distress by Molly. For a while — several weeks — all appeared steady, the couple removed from Soho & settled at a smaller house in the neighbourhood of Kentish Town. We heard of no further misadventures from that quarter. Mr L—— was away on another tour of the Provinces, while Molly, whose health as you know is fragile, seemed happy enough in her new household. There is a pretty garden she likes to tend, &

for company she keeps a Macaw in the parlour — they talk together the day long. So might we have gone on had not Pa rec'd last week a letter from an old friend of his at Bath, which related the most shocking circumstance — I can hardly bear to tell you of it. This friend, Mr Chalfont, is a lawyer with a considerable acquaintance in the town — & in consequence has become a keeper of many of its secrets. Some weeks ago he was visited by a married Lady from a village a few miles outside Bath. Her circumstances were comfortable — the Lady came from an affluent family & resided with two young children at a manor house. Reports had reached her that her husband, whose profession took him away from Bath a good deal, had most unhappily deceived her — to wit, he had secretly taken another wife & established a home with her in London. Once she had recovered from this disclosure the Lady made it her object to consult a lawyer & seek immediate redress. The name of this double-dealer —as you have guessed by now — is Mr John Lowther. Pa asked Mr Chalfont if there might be any doubt — a mistaken identity could not be discounted? But there was no doubt. We were distraught, of course, not merely in the knowledge of Mr L——'s deception but at the prospect of informing Molly that her husband was a bigamist. 'Very like the scoundrel,' said Pa bitterly, 'to have an excess of everything —including wives.'

Since then Mr Chalfont has been endeavouring to locate Mr L— in the north country. He sent two of his officers on this errand, but on hunting down the orchestra at Hull they discovered their quarry had vanished — we know not where. Now I must resume the story from yesterday when Pa & I made our sorrowing way to Kentish Town. Molly's face, innocent of any suspicion of what we had to impart, was piteous to observe. In the background her beloved Macaw — a creature she names Tybalt — chuntered on. She insisted upon making tea for us, as tho' she meant to delay the grievous blow we came to deliver. I saw Pa's nervous glance at me & so took it upon myself to relate the burden of Mr Chalfont's report. As Molly rec'd the news the colour drain'd from her Face & she fell to the floor in a dead faint. Pa sent for the carriage while I cradled Molly's bleeding head.

We carried her back to Cavendish-sq & put her to bed. This morning the Doctor called & conferred with us about our Molly —He said she will most particularly require rest & quiet to recover. He also prescribed sleeping draughts & a strong opiate to calm her nerves. What is to become of her I dare not guess. The poor dear girl! I had reason, as you know, to think ill of Mr L— in the light of his offence against me, but for Molly's sake I endeavoured to smooth relations between us. I knew him to be careless, vain, self-seeking, improvident, but he had charm withal, & he did love my sister, so I thought. These faults are but a speck on his reputation now —a bigamist, & a villain. To think I once had hopes of marrying him myself! Truly we may never know from what larger calamities fate has saved us.

The hour is late, & my heart is sore. I beg you for the present to keep these tidings secret. They will be known soon enough. Remember Molly in your prayers, dearest coz —never has she been in such need of them.

Remember me too, your fond & affectionate *Laura*

October 21st, 1788

Molly, feeling stronger, rose from her bed yesterday to take breakfast with us. Her strange abstraction is no longer a passing mood, it seems, but a Fixture of personality —the very first enquiry she made on coming down concerned not her errant husband's whereabouts but the Health of her pet. I assured her that during her indisposition I had called at Kentish Town to feed & water Tybalt —or as Pa calls him 'that d——'d bird'. There is still a dullness in Molly's eyes & a slight persistent tremble in her hands, but her spirits seemed livelier. We must at least be grateful for that.

I believe my own nerves have been undone by these troubles, for a dreadful fit of Melancholy seized me today. I was at Clerkenwell taking tea with Lizzie & talking idly (of what I cannot recall) when I felt myself enshrouded by a black Cloud of despond. I fell silent, & when Lizzie asked me if I was unwell I broke of a sudden into convulsions of sobbing. Naturally she assumed it was in consequence of Molly's recent Disaster —I had already related the miserable history — but in truth 'twas something quite other that afflicted me, & only at Lizzie's prompting was I able to express it. The feeling which oppresses me is one of severe loneliness —At home I used to have my paints & chalks for company, but I have not picked up a brush for months. Pa is so busy, Ma too fretful to be of any use. Molly, beloved companion for so many years, seems confin'd within her own mind & talks but little, except to her bird. I have no prospect of Marriage, for I seldom attend parties or dances. I am not beautiful or comely & my years tell against me. After a moment Lizzie said, very kindly, that I must always count upon her as a friend, & I thanked her, tho' even she has less time to spare, what with the Child to occupy her & the likelihood of her touring the Provinces once more. She urged me to resume my Painting, 'for 'tis only by work that women may establish an independence for themselves'. I acknowledged the truth of that, but could not explain to her what a blow to my Esteem was the calamitous showing in April — two Pictures sold, & those to my dearest friend, is not a heartening testament to my Capability. Nor is it a Profession in which one can be secure — as Pa always says, Even a great painter may starve in a Garret if he fails to catch the common Eye.

November 2nd, 1788

Ma now lives more at Kentish Town with Molly than she does at home. She prefers the quiet of a neighbourhood where she may look upon green fields & market gardens. Molly's continuing frailty persuades us that she cannot be left by herself. Pa seems resigned to the arrangement, having failed in his endeavours to have Molly remove to Cavendish-sq. Reports reach us from Mr Chalfont's office that Lowther, now a fugitive from the Law, has fetched up at Brussels, a town said to be notorious for its uncouth & dissolute ways. There seems no prospect at all of his return. Pa naturally deplores his obligation to pay off the creditors, tho' I think he is more relieved to have L—— gone from his sight & unable to wreak further mischief on our family.

November 5th, 1788

Molly & Ma back here at Cavendish-sq & many friends too for an evening to celebrate Lizzie's Birthday. (She owns to me she is forty, tho' claims in the press to be only eight & thirty.) Much jollity ensued when the Musicians asked Pa to join them on his flute —he played a vigorous Reel in honour of Lizzie's Irish blood. Later he persuaded Molly to partner him in a Cotillion. To see her smile again was a joy & recalled gay evenings at Milsom-street, long before we had ever heard of Mr L——. Lizzie looked very beautiful & danced more than anyone — she has the innate skill of a performer, of course, but it is the thing which cannot be taught — Charm, I should say — that sets her apart. At the end of the evening she gathered us again & recited a humorous poem thanking Pa for his 'Merrymounting' — that is, his generosity & friendship. It was now past one in the morning, & 'devilish cold' (as Pa would say), so rather than call the Carriage I asked one of the servants to make up a bed for Lizzie & the Child.

January 26th, 1789

We were pleased to be in a Family Box at Drury-lane for Lizzie's return to the stage this week — She had been in a state of dismal Apprehension, not having set foot in the Theatre for nearly a twelvemonth. She played Lady Restless in Mr Murphy's 'All in the Wrong', which she last did on her Yorkshire tour; this she alternates with the servant-maid Beatrice in Mr Kemble's farce 'The Pannel', adapted I gather from an earlier play — the plot depends on a movable pannel behind which characters are concealed. Her fears prior to her first Performance must have crept up on me, for as she made her Entrance dread stirred in my breast —What if her Touch had indeed deserted her? Idle fears. She commanded the stage with all the assurance of old, indeed 'twas as if the hiatus of months had dissolved & she had never been away from the place. Afterwards in her Dressing-room we were gay & drank toasts to her —all hail, the Queen of Drury-lane.

February 7th, 1789

A curious moment this morning. Pa & I were preparing to walk out to the Green Park as he looked about for his cane — he is recovering from a painful return of the Gout. I supposed he had left it in his bed-chamber & hurried upstairs to search for it. In his Dressing-room I noticed on the floor a pair of spectacles & wondered if Pa had secretly taken to wearing them, tho' they seemed too small & delicate for his Face. When I found the cane & carried it down to him I mentioned the spectacles —Were they his own? Pa said they must have been dropt by a servant —or else the tailor's fellow who called yesterday for his fitting. I was inclined to teaze him for his Vanity but quickly thought better of it. He does not like to be reminded of his advancing years —he is rather like a woman in that regard. But it is surely imperative for one whose living depends upon his eyes to wear them if needs be. When later I returned to the room all trace of them was gone. I asked Sally if any of the servants had mislaid a pair — none of them had.

February 12th, 1789

I woke this morning from a Dream, perturbed & yet enlightened. 'Tis strange how sleep may resolve a conundrum that in waking hours is likely to baffle. I took the Carriage to Clerkenwell & found Lizzie at home. We drank tea while she played with Jo. She must have sensed my strange disposition for she asked me, twice, if I was quite well. I replied that I was, & there followed more inconsequential talk. Then, with seeming lightness I asked if the spectacles she had mislaid had been returned to her. — Yes, she replied, they had. — 'From Cavendish-square, I believe,' I pursued. Now she looked uncertainly at me. — 'I thought I had lost them,' she said. — ''Twas I who found them,' I replied, 'in my father's Dressing-room. Can you account for them being there?' She returned a look of perplexity, then suggested that a servant might have put them there. 'But why would a servant have left them lying on the floor?' She began to speak again, but I was no longer listening. I fancied the accident of my discovery was somewhat theatrical — An enterprising playwright might have used it for a Plot. I thought too of a Play in which she had performed last year, 'The Wonder: A Woman Keeps a Secret'. Aye, what a Secret this woman kept! — the Actress & the Painter conducting a liaison under the noses of his Family. I cursed my wilful blindness — the mysterious absences, the hurried excuses, the signals that only a couple bound in illicit intimacy could have shared. I startled her by interrupting — 'When did you first seduce my father?' She reared back as though I had slapp'd her Face. — 'I! — Seduce him?' Her tone was incredulous, but I would not be diverted. Of course she had seduced him — How else would a man of my father's standing be tempted into such gross infamy?

48

Why else would he risk his honour & the happiness of his Family unless undone by the wiles of a dissembling whore? I spoke the word, & as a black Rage gripped me I gave way to much worse — words that had never been in my mouth before rose up like bile. I was lost to Shame. She might have thrown me out of her house, but she only sat there, pale as ashes, as I ranted on. The Child, hitherto sitting mute on a rug, began to wail — probably he sensed his mother's unhappiness. I left the house, hardly knowing what I was about or where I should go.

February 14th, 1789

Pa asked to speak with me privately. I allowed him to enter my room but I would not look at his Face. His tone was chastened — but what did I care for that? He wanted to tell me how profoundly sorry he was — that he never intended to cause harm or humiliation — 'Tho' you have done both,' I replied. Under my questioning he confessed that the affair had started some three years ago. Three years! I asked why he had allowed himself to succumb to her wiles & he hesitated.

'My dear, I cannot accuse Lizzie of any such cunning. I swear upon the little honour I have left in your esteem she is not to blame. I know you have had unfriendly words with her but I beg you —please don't be harsh towards her.' In that moment I had a fearful presentiment of what lay ahead. If I could not trust the people dearest to me in the world then what could trust ever mean? I was frightened by the asperity of my feelings towards them both — I think I almost hated my father. I could not listen & wanted him to be gone, but still he defended her — 'Whatever her fault may have been she is your devoted friend withal.' Aye, the one good friend I had — & yet she was pleased to deceive me for years.

When I refused to vouchsafe him a reply he hung his head for a moment — then he implored me not to speak a word of this to Ma. Only now did he think to mention his wife! I felt a renewal of my disgust & coldly asked him to leave my sight. 'I like the Truth & day-light,' he once said. What flummery. I can scarcely write this for the shaking of my hand.

February 18th, 1789

My mother senses something is amiss, for tho' much passes her notice in general, the disagreeable Mood that reigns in the house is not to be ignored. At breakfast I see her anxious darting looks between me & Pa — if he speaks to me I reply with the barest Civility. Today she took me aside — her face a Mask of worry — & asked what the matter was. I would tell her if I could, but I know that in this instance the Truth would be a calamity. She would be utterly undone to hear of her husband's base behaviour, while he would resent me for poisoning the well of their domestic content-ment. So I mollify her with assurances that I am merely out of sorts. Would it were so.

I am endeavouring to determine whether Lizzie (Mrs Vavasor, as I should now say) was intimate with my father when first we met at Norfolk-street. If I had known of the Secret then would I have rejected her? Very likely, I dare say — & thus sacrificed one of the great friendships of my life. Probably she had no thought of the Family she was betraying when my father took up with her — but once we became close did it trouble her?

February 19th, 1789

A letter this morning from Mrs V——

'My dear Laura — I have been in the greatest distress thinking of that terrible scene between us a week ago. I would have given the World and everything I love in it not to have seen you so full of rage against me. Your accusations were as scalding irons on my skin. I acknowledge that your passionate ill-feeling is justified, for I deceived you, if not in the commission of a lie then certainly in the omission of a truth. All I can tell you is that I did so most unwillingly. Please pardon the freedom with which I offer the following defence —I know that you would rather not hear it, but my conscience demands that I make it.

I met your father at a desperate period of my life. I had made my debut at Covent Garden & had struggled at first, having but recently recovered from an accident in childbed. I was low in spirits — not a helpful disposition in which to face a new audience. The boos of the crowd would ring madly in my ears. I might have fled back to Bristol, perhaps given up Acting entirely, had not I been rescued by the accident of your father's commission to paint me. I discovered that he was so very unlike the common run of men I had known hitherto, and through his charm and amiability we soon became close friends. His confidence in me, his frequent assurances that I was worthy of the crowd's esteem, were a comfort for which I could never be grateful enough. Friendship ought to have been our bourne, but circumstances conspired whereby a deeper connection became (as I thought then) unavoidable. Now I see that I should have resisted it more steadfastly and spared us our present woes. I did not, and I am sorry for it.

The situation became the more vexed once I had made your acquaintance. I had known of a Miss Merrymount, of course, but I did not expect her to be such an amiable person, still less one who would become a dear and valued friend. I was quite sensible of the treacherous position into which I had strayed. That you had bestowed upon me your Trust — may I say your Love? — so freely and generously while I was entangled in this damaging intimacy caused me untold anguish. There were times when I almost gave way and confessed it to you, but I had given your father my word that no whisper of it would reach your ears. What was I to do? You will say, with justice, that I ought to have withdrawn, and indeed on several occasions I made an end to the affair. But the bonds between us were not so easily loosened and your father —most persuasive of men —was not of a mind to be shaken off. That would suggest I was helpless — a plaything of another. I was not. The blame was mine —was ours.

I know how deeply you have been wounded, and were I able to I would take upon myself your burden of suffering. I would not dare to presume on your forgiveness. But I will continue to hope for it, and pray for it — because I long to be your Friend once more.

God bless you and keep you, my dear girl.

Lizzie Vavasor.'

February [1789]

I have these last three days kept to my room. I have not eaten, for all appetite has deserted me & I write this from my pillow, too weak to rise. I feel that I am ill, tho' I know not what to call the ailment. Enobarbus in Shakespeare died of a broken heart, having deserted Antony, & at times I do feel my heart so sorely afflicted that it might burst in my chest. Merely to think of her makes me drop my head in a faint, moaning the while. She has done me wrong — grievous wrong — & it would rejoice me to see her suffer for it. But how can I wish ill upon her whom I lately counted my dearest Friend? O God, grant me the fortitude to endure this torment. I have striven all my life to be tender, to be merciful, & thus to honour You, our Creator. But a tender heart will bring us to grief, for what defence may it offer against those who would do us harm? Better to be proud & strong & unyielding. For only such a heart can bear the sorrows of this life.

March 15th, 1789

The Ides. I only remembered the omen afterwards. I had thought to reply to her Letter & several times endeavoured to write, but my courage failed me. The words would not come. Ma has been uncommonly sympathetic, a great reversal in our relations —it has been my lot to solace her in her many grievances, imagined or otherwise. She has always favoured Molly, the more susceptible of us two, & the more like her. I suppose I in turn was Pa's pet — much good it has done me.

I had wondered as to the likelihood of his breaking off their Connection, & now 'tis evident no such rupture has occurred. It must have been Pa's design to remove himself & Ma from the house this morning, so that I should have sole run of the place. A maidservant answered the knock & came to the Drawing room to say Mrs V—— was at the door wishing to speak to me. I hesitated, torn between the greater insult I might deliver — either to hurl execrations or to refuse to see her. I told the girl I was not receiving visitors. She left & moments later I heard Mrs V—— calling my name from the hall, importuning me. When I presented myself she looked at me beseechingly & asked most earnestly if we might confer in private. I replied that I had nothing to say to her. 'Did you not read my letter?' she asked, & there followed an argument between us. All the while I thought, 'This woman is a vicious double-dealer' —& the next instant, 'If we were to part now I should miss her terribly.' I might have weakened but instead I determined to make my heart a stone to her entreaties. Nothing she said could pierce the flint fortress I had raised. The servant girl had been cowering in the background while we bandied words. Now I spoke to her —'This woman,' I said, 'is a player & a jilt. She is not to be admitted to this house again.'

When I glanced at Mrs V—— I expected her to look startled or angry at the offending shot I had just fired. But she only looked forlorn, & I swallowed down my Shame as she turned & walked out of the house.

[The second section of Laura Merrymount's journal ends here]

May, 1808

Another letter this morning from Mr Cuthbertson at Leicester. He asks whether I have rec'd the first volume of his Lives of the Painters dispatched some weeks ago. I ought to have written to thank him but in truth I have not yet cut the book's pages. Beneath his politeness I sense an impatience to be getting on with his next — 'I hesitate to importune a lady for her time, but I am ever mindful of the urgency to set down those many vital details pertaining to our subject which living memory can still supply.' Does he fear I am about to die? I suppose I must write to him, being a keeper of certain 'vital details', tho' the prospect wearies me. He is not the first biographer to beat a path to our door & I feel sure he will not be the last.

May 12th, 1808

Yet the attention has the appeal of novelty at least. *Pace* the hurry of Mr Cuthbertson but time passes slowly here in our little backwater of Kentish Town, & callers are few. What business could anyone have with two old spinster-sisters? Molly never repines, Tybalt the Macaw providing all the diversion she requires.

The pair of them remain inseparable from the old days. He looks shabbier now, tho' more vociferous than ever. 'D—— your eyes!' is a favourite imprecation.

Where he comes by such language I cannot fathom.

We have shared this house at College Lane for eleven years. When Ma died in '97 there was nobody apart from a servant girl to look after Molly, so I gave up the lease on Cavendish-sq. & moved here. There are advantages in being out of London — the air is wholesome, & the water I am told is cleaner. But I do miss company. Molly is what I have heard described as 'touched' — not altogether mad but not in full command of her senses. She is prey still to the distempering fits, but sweetly affectionate — & content, I think. I brought with me the piano forte, which she sometimes plays on in the evening. The harp that Pa gave her for a wedding present we sold, for it was unwieldy, & very seldom used. Aside from the biographers, our only regular visitor is my dear cousin Susan, who now lives with her husband at Putney after many years in Sussex. On occasion we return the visit, not so often of late since Molly becomes agitated if too long away from Home. Her sole concern is Tybalt, tho' what harm he should come to I hardly know — he is generally occupied with preening his feathers or chewing upon the wooden pipe Molly carved for him. (She made it after he once got out of his cage & nearly destroyed one of the Dining chairs.) I have just heard a nightingale utter a few strains outside this window. A sweet contrast to our own feathered friend!

May 20th, 1808

This morning a soft mild rain. After breakfast the sky cleared & we walked up Highgate-hill, the fields all glowing green from the shower. Molly singing an air to herself, rather lovely — I wanted to ask her what it was but I knew if I did she would fall silent. She collects nuts & berries in a little pouch to take back to Tybalt. I wonder what he thinks of his Mistress —if indeed he has any thoughts at all. One thing I have never observed in him is an overflow of Gratitude.

May 25th, 1808

A letter from a Picture-dealer in Bath. He is well-versed in the market of Pa's paintings, he writes, & wishes to know if there are any we should be prepared to sell — will pay a very good price. He has a partickular interest in the painting 'The Merrymount Sisters at Night', which he recalls was 'once greatly acclaimed'. I reply to tell him it still is & unfortunately not for Sale, at any price.

Such enquiries that come are nearly always about that Picture. It was exhibited ten years ago at the Royal Academy & created quite a Commotion — it seemed all London was surprized to discover the Painter of Lords & Ladies was no mere phizmonger but an artist endowed with great tenderness of feeling. We always knew him to be so — the Public was simply catching up.

June, 1808

It appears I have agreed to Mr Cuthbertson's visiting us at Home — he writes to say he will be coming to Kentish Town on Wednesday. I have no memory of my agreeing to such a visit, and of course it is too late to renege on the invitation. I really ought to cut the pages of his first volume so as to give the impression of having looked at it. I have forewarned Molly of his visit, tho' for all she cares it might as well be the Czar of Russia come to pay his respects. Her comprehension isn't altogether defective, however, for I later overheard her informing Tybalt that 'a gentleman named Cuthbert' would be calling upon us soon.

I hear her downstairs just returned from her walk, no doubt with an armful of wildflowers. I have rec'd complaints from a woman who saw her taking bluebells from her garden. I was obliged to make her an apology & explain Molly's confusion —that garden not so long ago was an open field. The neighbourhood is changing, & speculators compete for a stake in what recently was meadowland.

June 15th, 1808

Mr Cuthbertson called today, as promised. For some reason I had expected him to be fat — & a great deal older — but indeed he is lean & no more than five & thirty. He is well-mannered, with a watchful eye — I had a keen sense of being appraised. His

Cloaths were somewhat travel-stain'd, for he had taken the early coach from Leicester. His voice bore the provincial sound of that place & at first I was apt to mishear him. For example 'there' pronounced like 'fear', instead of like 'fair'. Also 'once' pronounced 'woonss', instead of 'wunss'. But I soon got the measure of him. We drank tea & he explained to me his undertaking — he intends to treat of Pa's life in a series of essays, viz. his Landskips, Portraits, Life at Bath &c, to which end he should be most grateful for any material pertaining to same. Would I grant him permission to read Mr Merrymount's Correspondence, for example? I did not want to make promises & spoke vaguely of certain Letters of his I believed we had kept. At that he inclined his head, as if he were expecting me to scurry off in search of them immediately. I told him that they were held in safety at our Bank — which may indeed be the truth. He repeated his profession of Gratitude & hoped that I might oblige him the next time he visited. Thus already he presumed there would be a next time. I asked him for how long he envisaged working on his Biography. He could not be certain, he replied, though to judge by his Life of Mr Joshua Reynolds it was likely to be three years or more. His next question I had anticipated — Would I be kind enough to show him the famous 'Merrymount Sisters at Night'? I conducted him to the Dining room where it hangs above the chimney-piece. He stared at it for some moments in silence, then said that the first time he saw the Picture, at the Academy, he burst into tears. I hardly knew what to say — perhaps I felt more kindly disposed towards him after that.

Before he left I introduced Mr Cuthbertson to Molly. He was startled upon hearing from the parlour a voice crying 'Naughty man!' Tybalt had already made up his mind.

June 26th, 1808

In the weeks since I resumed this Journal I have found myself taking up chalks again to draw — I thought I had lost the habit entirely. I am inclined to wonder what might have been had I pursued the living Pa so signally hoped for me. 'Tis nothing to me now, but perhaps I was too easily disheartened twenty years ago.

The exhibition of my Pictures he mounted was untimely, for I had not yet the Confidence that might have enabled me to overcome setbacks —in that instance my failure to sell a single painting. Then there was the obstacle that all children of artists must face — the likelihood of invidious comparison to the parent. I knew that I should never surpass my father in accomplishment, nor was it my Ambition. I hoped simply to achieve something for my own sake, tho' I suppose that unlikely as long as my name was Merrymount.

July 2nd, 1808

To cousin Susan's house at Putney, alone, for Molly did not wish to come. She has no love of strangers' company. Susan & her husband Mr Parminter entertain on a handsome scale, sixteen at table, roasted duck & plenty of claret to drink with it. Much talk of the War & the Iberian Peninsula, about which I knew almost nothing. I must have been very quiet, for the gentleman seated next to me fairly jumped when at last I joined the Conversation, which had turned to the Theatre. They were talking of Mr Sheridan, & I happened to mention that my father had painted him, twice. That I was the daughter of Wm Merrymount provoked very keen interest around the table, & I own that I felt glad to know that Pa's name was still reverenced, even in the distant purlieu of Putney. I answered a great many questions about him —one of the Guests had visited his tomb at Kew Green —until Susan cut in to say, 'Laura is also an accomplished Painter, did you know?' None of them did, of course, & I could have wished that she had refrained from mention of it. Following one or two polite questions about the 'Family tradition', the subject was dropt. I think Susan was rather embarrassed, tho' when she sought me out later I assured her that I took no offence —I am used to indifference.

July 5th, 1808

Another visit from Mr Cuthbertson. I had earlier been ferreting in the attic-room to seek out Family correspondence. Most of it has gone to the vault at Hoares, but I did retrieve two large bundles of Pa's letters to me & to Molly from our years at Milsom-street — I laughed to see the small Drawings he would include, of animals, or Faces, or of himself in attitudes of comical absurdity. When I showed them to Mr C—— I supposed he would laugh too, but he began reading them devouringly & asked for permission to copy them. He wished to know about Pa's youth & the house at Lavenham, in Suffolk, but I could not provide much beyond the dates of his birth, the names of his parents, his three brothers & four sisters, the Family's attendance at a Dissenters' Chapel. I did not mention his Father's bankruptcy —perhaps it will be found out. When I showed him some Drawings Pa had done as a boy Mr C—— fell on them eagerly. But when he asked me as to his Character as a young man I was at a loss. How would I know, beyond the few scraps of Family lore handed down to us?

July 16th, 1808

A letter from Christie's regarding the 'sale' of Wm Merrymount's painting of his daughters. They wish to send a representative to value the Picture & to discuss the possibility of conducting the Auction. Somebody has been making mischief — I wonder if it is Mr Cuthbertson, being the most recent visitor here. I wrote in reply to the gentleman that he should spare his representative the trouble — that I could not account for the rumour regarding 'Molly & the Captain' which was not for sale, nor would be at any future date. I begged him to inform his colleagues likewise.

I begin to find these petitions tiresome. Perhaps they imagine that two genteel country ladies could have no proper understanding of the treasure in their possession. I should like it to be known that at least one of them does.

August 1st, 1808

Mr C—— here again. He presses me for details of Pa's friends, despite my assurances that I have forgotten most of them. On & on he goes, asking & waiting & scratching away with his pen. He very seldom smiles. I remark on his tenacious character to which he replies, 'Madam, 'tis my vocation. As Falstaff says to the Prince, "'Tis no sin for a man to labour in his vocation."' I do not remind him that the 'vocation' to which Falstaff refers is thieving.

I have an impression that he knows a great deal more about Pa's life than I do. When he mentions his friendship with a certain Miss—— or Mrs—— he appears to assume that I am acquainted with the lady in question. But usually I am not, & must own that I have never heard of her. 'Your father was a very gregarious man,' he says, which of course is well-known, & yet I hear in his voice an ambiguity, a hint that Pa's behaviour in company was not beyond reproach. I am minded to ask him exactly what he means to say, but weariness prevents me.

Prudence also —I have an apprehension that he may tell me what I should prefer not to know.

August 14th, 1808

I had a queer premonition of the subject Mr C—— intended to broach today. We were talking of Pa's love of the Theatre, his friendship with Sheridan &c, when he paused a moment, as though of a sudden recalling a name he had forgot to mention. —'Your father was a great friend of Mrs Vavasor, I understand?' Yes he was, I replied. — 'So you also met the Lady, I dare say?' I did, several times.

'But you did not know her well?' No, I said, waiting for Mr C—— to make bold with the question he really wished to ask. I maintained a perfect front of indifference. 'Were you ever aware — pray, forgive this impudence — were you aware of an intimacy between them?' 'Between my father & Mrs V——?' Do not protest too much, I told myself. Be cold, proud, unflinching. 'No. I never heard anything of the sort.' Mr C—— looked very embarrassed, begged my pardon again & the matter was dropt.

What I did not tell him was that on Pa's death I made sure to burn all her Letters to him — I recall they made quite a blaze. Of course, I cannot vouch for what has become of his Letters to her.

September 12th, 1808

I was returning from Green-street with purchases of charcoals, porte-crayons &c when I happened to pass a young man whose Face I thought familiar. He returned my glance tho' showed no sign of recognition. I was confounded, for I felt sure that I had seen him before. Later at a window upstairs I caught sight of him again strolling about the street. Once he stopt to fix his gaze upon our house & I quickly withdrew from my station. I fear that he may be a house-breaker with designs on a certain Picture in our possession. I know that Kentish Town was once infamous for footpads & brigands — travellers ventured alone through the place at their peril. I have told Molly to be on her guard — she in turn has warned Tybalt, apparently mistaking him for a watchdog.

September 21st, 1808

George the gardener came to the door this morning to ask if I had heard of the great Fire at Covent Garden — the whole theatre burnt down! I went off to buy a Newspaper to read its report. The building was discovered to be on fire after midnight on the 19th & so engulphing were the flames that before five o'clock in the morning nothing remained but a heap of smouldering ruins. Nor was this the only calamity — as part of the building collapsed it brought down fiery death upon a crowd standing below. The remains of fourteen unfortunate souls were afterwards dug out & sixteen others, injured & mangled terribly, were carried off to the Hospital. The conflagration spread to some of the neighbouring houses which also burnt down.

The tragic event has preoccupied me all day. I thought sadly of those many evenings passed there with the Family, the dozens of Plays & Comedies we saw under its roof — the scene of so much laughter & delight, gone! I could not help but repine at its loss.

September 23rd, 1808

Morbid curiosity drove me to visit the ruins at Covent Garden. Huge crowds were gathered at the Piazza eager to behold the melancholy spectacle —the stink of melted lead & charred timbers & bitter black smoke almost unbearable. Also accounted among the losses is the organ bequeathed to the Theatre by Handel along with many of his papers & manuscripts. All the scenery, the costumes, the Theatre library consumed in the flames. I overheard a fellow talk of the alleged cause — a fiery spark from a gun discharged during the performance of 'Pizarro' had probably lodged in a crevice of the scenery & smouldered there unnoticed. I stood for many minutes among the jostling crowd unable to tear my gaze away. All those memories, all that human endeavour, up in smoke.

As I walked back north I thought of her & the many performances in which we had delighted. It was in Covent Garden when first we met, I think. Strange to remember her again so soon after Mr C——'s prying inquisition. On occasion I have seen her name on a Playbill & wondered what changes have befallen her in twenty years. Perhaps she has wondered the same of me.

October 3rd, 1808

The young man I had seen skulking about weeks ago is back on his watch. I thought he had disappeared. I no longer believe he means to rob us, however — no thief worth his tools would make such a poor job of being inconspicuous.

Today we passed close to one another & I glimpsed his Face, which is rather interesting — bright-eyed, hollow-cheeked, handsome almost. I sense that he wishes to make my acquaintance but something constrains him.

October 6th, 1808

I decided to have done with our cat-&-mouse games & surprized him on the street. I addressed him directly —said I had marked him loitering hereabouts & would he care to tell me his business? He was a little taken aback, but he smiled & bowed —'Madam, I beg your pardon — Do I have the honour of addressing Miss Merrymount?' I replied that he did, & he introduced himself as Mr Edmund Rothwell. I recognised the name of old, & asked if he were kin of a certain Lord Rothwell. — 'My cousin,' he replied. Indeed, it was under the auspices of that gentleman that he became devotedly interested in the work of William Merrymount, the Painter. I felt a sudden dismay — Are you a biographer perhaps? I enquired. He shook his head, No. He sought only the privilege of discussing a Great Man with the person who had known him best. He spoke with such an earnest expression in his Face that my heart softened & I said that should he come to the house tomorrow afternoon I would be pleased to receive him —I gave him the address & we bid one another good-day.

I have asked George to be on hand tomorrow in case young Mr Rothwell proves a glozing villain, tho' in truth I fear no ill of him.

October 7th, 1808

Mr Rothwell came at the appointed hour & we drank tea. The young man instantly recommended himself to Molly by paying respectful addresses to Tybalt, who was quiet for once. He became very fond of Macaws, he said, ever since they kept one on board his first ship. (I could see he had been much Abroad from his swarthy complexion.) The story came out that he had joined the Navy at the age of eleven as a midshipman —served under Collingwood in the *Triumph* when it joined the Channel Fleet & sailed to the Mediterranean. He saw battle against the French & Spanish & was later raised to the rank of Captain. Molly & I listened to this with astonishment — He seemed too young to have led such a life. He laughed & said he was already Twenty, 'tho' one year at Sea is equal to five on Land'. He had wearied of the Navy & got out of it a year ago, thanks to his Uncle. Did he regret spending his entire Youth at Sea? No, he said — his only regret was to have been ill in the Autumn of 1805 & missed Trafalgar.

Afterwards we took him over the house to inspect the Paintings, many of which he knew by repute. 'I never thought I should be so fortunate as to see them in a private house,' he said. When we went into the Dining room the first thing he said was, 'Ah, "Molly & the Captain", I believe.' — Again I was much astonished.

How came he to know the Family name for it, I asked? —'From my cousin,' he replied, 'who was such an admirer that he once bought a Merrymount, tho' I never saw it.' Then I recalled that Lord R—— had indeed bought a Merrymount — by me, not by Pa. But I chose not to enlighten him. He asked how I came by the nickname of Captain & I told him that as a girl I was thought to be fond of Dominion. At that he did something very charming —he gave me a Navy salute, 'from one Captain to another'.

October 18th, 1808

A warning today of the necessity to be vigilant. I was away on errands in the forenoon & returned to find Molly in the Library gaily conferring with two sly-eyed strangers. She said, 'Dear, these gentlemen have called to borrow some Paintings of ours —here, they have drawn up a Contract.' Without addressing them I briefly scrutinised this 'Contract', its Mast-head declaring it to come from the Offices of a Livery Company (a sham) in London. The burden — they were commissioned to carry off six Merrymount Paintings 'on loan'. Only poor Molly could have been taken in by such a dismal ruse. I advised this pair of sharps in no polite terms to get out of the house, with admonitions that were I to see them again I would summon the local constable. They left with barely a murmur of protest.

Then I sat down with Molly & explained to her that we should beware of admitting people into the house, however much like 'gentlemen' they appeared. She listened very solemnly, like a child, & promised never to conduct business with strangers on her own. *Gentlemen my A—se*, as Pa would have said.

October 31st, 1808

Mr R—— called this morning with a gift of jellied fruits for us, &
a small bag of nuts for Tybalt. He calls here once or twice a week,
which is a pleasure to us — Molly in partickular delights in his
company. But I own it somewhat mysterious that he should concern
himself with two Old Maids. Is it that we rouse his sympathy? He is
natural born, he says — his Father abandoned the Family when he
was an infant, while his mother I think is dead, or else disappeared.
His cousin, the Baronet, was his earliest patron, instructing him in
Painting, Music & Theatre — of this last he now intends to make
a career, as Stage manager. He has lately made the acquaintance of
Mr Sheridan, tho' after what troubles have befallen him one might
think it wise to avoid his example.

He likes to hear stories of Pa, of his early years & his appren-
ticeship in Lavenham. He was desirous of knowing more about
the biography that Mr Cuthbertson is writing. I told him that we
expected another visit from that gentleman next week — perhaps
he would care to come & meet the Great Authority in person? Mr
R—— accepted my invitation with alacrity, indeed when he left
the house a few minutes later he was whistling like a schoolboy.
'Tis a strange thing by what insignificant favours we can make
another happy!

November 2nd, 1808

The leaves fall fast — Nature has nothing to show more melancholy. The light in late afternoon was greenish & lowering, so I
stopt at the window before leaving the house — now it bore an
aspect of dire foreboding. Minutes later there followed a flash &
a crack of thunder that shook the house. A pause for breath, then
rain came roaring down the street. I blessed my luck in keeping
within doors.

November 10th, 1808

We were drinking tea with Mr R—— Edmund as I should call him — when Mr Cuthbertson arrived. I introduced them & noted that the younger man displayed more warmth in his overtures than the older. But then I am minded to think charm is Edmund's ruling Quality — there is about him something naturally open-hearted & genial that sets a company at ease.

We talked generally of the Biography. Mr C—— presented a report on his progress thus far & recited some short passages as an example of his Stile & Method. He then drew his hands together, his voice dropt nearly to a whisper — 'twas time, he said, to enlarge upon the melancholy circumstances of his subject's last days & hours. He had forewarned me of this in his Letter, & I had composed myself accordingly. I had not kept a Journal in that year — 1795, tho' I was able to recall the weeks preceding his Death as if 'twere yesterday. Pa had been troubled for perhaps a year by an inflammation in his Neck, but the doctors could find nothing in it but a swell'd gland —they proposed to disperse it by the regular application of a seaweed poultice. Lately it had become very painful & he could find no position upon his pillow to allow of getting rest in Bed. — 'Did he discuss the affliction with you privately?' Mr C—— asked. A little, I said, tho' I sensed he was unwilling to alarm me. I believe he knew it was a Cancer.

In the May of that year he drew up a Will & signed it. During the Summer he made plans to visit Suffolk & make a farewell to the Family remaining there, but he found himself too weak to travel. Two of his Sisters & a younger Brother (a Naval man) came to Cavendish-square in August. I think they were greatly shocked by his Decline & the unsightly swelling. A sad succession of old Friends visited that same month (here Mr C—— pressed me for Names) but once September came he was no longer able to receive callers. On the 18th, a Sunday, Molly, Ma & I had been at Church in the forenoon. We returned home to find the Doctor at his bed-side —Sally had taken fright at Pa's ragged Breathing & run out to fetch him — & so began the dreadful vigil. That Face, piteous sight, was thin & drawn & pale as candlewax. For hours he lay, his eyes closed, drawing breath as tho' he were being strangled. I listened to Molly & my mother whimpering at the other side of the bed. 'Twas as though some invisible Force squatted upon his chest, slowly pressing the Life out of him. The pity of it. I wished it were over & yet I could not stand to think of him Gone from the world. At four o'clock in the afternoon the breathing slowed again — & stopt. For a long moment we sat there, stunned & lost. I think we said a prayer, I hardly know what. Then Ma smoothed his brow, snipped a lock from his hair. (I have it still in an envelope.)

As I recounted this scene all I heard was the scratch of Mr C——'s pen as he made his Notes, dry & impassive. Molly I saw was red-eyed. Edmund, head bowed on his chest, seemed preoccupied. When he at last raised it I saw his eyes were moist, though he was in command of himself. He went to sit by Molly & held her hand. I told Mr C—— that our talk was finished for the day & tho' he looked surprized he bid us good-day & left the house. Afterwards we talked quietly with Edmund, who owned that he had not thought to weep for the death of a man unknown to him.

November 16th, 1808

Tybalt has taken to mimicking a recent outburst of mine — 'Get out! Get out!' he shrieks, recalling my heated words with the two Picture-hunters. Even Molly is hard-press'd to keep him civil.

After the biographer's last visit I dragged out an old travelling trunk in which were stored all manner of Family memorabilia — invitation cards, Theatre tickets, Prayer books, tattered fans, music sheets, playbills (from Covent Garden), old puzzles we played at as girls, opera glasses &c. Also a scroll, fastened by a ribbon, that disclosed a number of sketches of mine from many years ago. I sat gazing at them for a long time. Two in partickular I had hidden away, unwilling to contemplate them, were of Pa on his Deathbed, eyes closed, lips slightly open as tho' he might speak. I recall how sternly I had enjoined myself to draw him — This poor Face will never be looked upon again, I thought, by you or by anybody, at least in this world. It is the last opportunity to capture what is about to disappear for ever.

When the others were gone from the Room I brushed the tears from my eyes, took out my charcoals & applied myself to the task. They are a pair — one from the side of the bed, one from the foot. I had his Lesson to guide me — 'Tis not the artist's business to invent, only to tell the Truth. So I emptied myself of any inclination to Prettify & bid my hand faithfully record those Contours of his Face & brow & poor swell'd neck, as I believe he would have wish'd. The Truth, or as near to it as I could reach. They are signed & dated 18th Sept. 1795. I think they are the Best drawings I have ever done.

November 27th, 1808

A letter from Mr Goodall, Pa's erstwhile agent. Many years since we have met, as he acknowledges, & of course he only writes now to seek a Favour. Under the aegis of the Royal Academy he means to assemble an exhibition of Great Artists from the last century & to this end begs me to consider releasing several of Pa's best-loved Paintings to his Care. I have a natural reluctance to let a single one of them out of my sight, but I deem it wrong to refuse the Academy. We are the keepers of the Flame, not its hoarders. Posterity must be served.

December 4th, 1808

Mr Goodall called upon us today. He is not much changed in the twelve years since I saw him last — grown fatter, I suppose, with jowls, but his busy darting eyes & his smooth manner were very familiar. Molly squinted at him — 'Were you not a friend of our pa's?' she asked. 'No, his Agent,' I cut in, to Mr G——'s surprize. I conducted him over the house to inspect the Paintings. When we came before 'Molly & the Captain' he nodded & said, 'I had hoped to buy this from your father many years ago.' I remember it well — & can be only grateful that Pa declined his offers. He enquired as to whether the Paintings were insured — 'Of course they are,' I replied, tho' when I supplied him with the details he was aghast & warned me that they were 'grossly under-valued'. He was also astonished that we had no security against house-breakers — no guard dog, for example. We have a cook & a maidservant who live in the house, I told him. —'Tybalt is an excellent Night-watch,' said Molly, who had just then entered.

Before he left Mr G—— begged my permission to send 'a Reputable man' to value them. I suppose he regards us as incapable Dotards.

December 9th, 1808

I had been most curious to see Edmund's lodgings near Russell-square — yesterday evening came the opportunity. He was nervous of inviting us to dine, he said, for the house at Guilford-street is small & lacking in amenities. We came in the Carriage, Molly beside herself with excitement — we know so little of London now-adays — & were most graciously rec'd by our young Friend. I had supposed there might be a company there, but indeed we were the only guests — a very cozy arrangement. I had been anxious about the vittles (Edmund's word from his Navy days) for of course he cannot accommodate a Cook. Instead he had a dinner of mutton & roasted potatoes carried up from the neighbouring Tavern, with ale for himself & wine for us. Before we sat down Edmund raised a Toast to our brave troops in Spain & to the routing of Buonaparte & his generals. He said the London streets had been crawling with Militia these past weeks in preparation for the campaign.

Edmund had his own News to impart — Mr Sheridan at Drury-lane has recruited him as assistant Manager of his Theatre. He says he is astonished to have secured the position so quickly, but I dare say his enthusiasm & energy would recommend him to such as Mr S——. He will begin there in the New Year. I tell him that we have not visited the Theatre in many years — we are too old to venture into the crowds of Covent Garden. 'Oh but you must,' he cried. 'You will be my Guests!' He does not know how many plays we have attended there — all those nights, all those suppers in her company.

'Twas a merry evening. We had sillabubs made with port wine to finish. We encouraged Edmund to tell us of his life as a Tar, & how he was first inspired to enlist in '98 by the wild celebrations attending Nelson's triumph at the Nile. At the end of the evening he sang a nautical song, of which I recall these lines —

Put the Bumpers about & be gay
To hear how our Doxies will smile
Here's to Nelson for ever Huzza
And King George on the Banks of the Nile

December 15th, 1808

When Edmund called today I asked him if he would care to join us for Christmas Day — we would be only a small Party, our cousin Susan & her husband, & Mr Truefitt, an elderly neighbour. It might be rather dull company for a young man but I assured him how greatly it would please us if he came. Alas, he is already under

an obligation — his mother is to visit from Scotland next week &
he will be much occupied as her host. (She has no other children.)
I understand there is trouble betwixt them, for whenever I have
enquired about her his answers are short & somewhat brusque.
He once described her as 'feckless', & in the next instant seemed
to regret it — he is keenly sensible of his Duty to her as her only
child. Whatever her faults may be she must be credited for raising
so amiable a son.

I told him that his mother would be most welcome here, but with
a pained expression he again declined.

December 24th, 1808

Molly & I made our usual Christmas visits to the Parish poor. They
are suffering more grievously on account of the War & the conse-
quent food shortages. We brought them oatcakes & broth from
the kitchen, while Molly handed out gingerbread in linen bags she
had stitched herself. The humble gratitude with which these pau-
pers — children among them — receive any gift of food provokes
a desperate pity in me.

January 6th, 1809

Edmund called to pay us compliments of the New Year – the first
time we have seen him in almost three weeks. We drank tea & he
talked of his new employer — we knew Mr Sheridan a little during
our time at Cavendish-sq. Being often occupied with business at
Parliament he delegates much responsibility to his Manager who
in turn keeps Edmund 'hard at it'. The new season features two
plays — 'The Gamesters' & 'Better Late than Never', which I
recall from years ago. Also a Shakespeare, 'The Winter's Tale'. Mrs
Siddons —the indefatigable — is to appear in all of them. When
I told Edmund that Mrs S—— is but a year or two younger than I

am he looked greatly astonished — I cannot say if the Compliment was to her or to me.

As he was taking his Coat to leave, a tiny silver snuff-box fell out of his pocket. I picked it up to admire — a Christmas gift from his mother — & noticed on its lid a dainty engrav'd 'J'. He smiled & said that his mother's pet name for him has always been 'Jo' — Joseph Edmund Rothwell.

January 7th, 1809

It cannot be — the coincidence is too freakish — I would know if 'twere true. Moreover she is said to reside now in Ireland, not Edinburgh. But the dates — the dates argue in its favour. Twenty years of age! Oh I am harrow'd by awful presentiments of Doom. It cannot be.

January 16th, 1809

No word from Edmund in ten days. Is he become wise to my suspicions? — 'Tis unlike him to be silent for so long. I was so distracted that I had forgot Mr Goodall was appointed to come this day regarding the Academy exhibition. I dare say he was surprized to be greeted by my blank expression. 'Miss Merrymount — I am come for the Paintings we talked of last month?' He had brought his assistants to help with the packing & removal — they set to work as I stood there in a Daze. I had agreed to the loan of six Paintings — the full-length portrait of Sheridan, the half-length of Lord Garvey, two Landskips from Bath, a Self-portrait from 1760, & 'Molly & the Captain'. This last required some persuasion on Mr G——'s part, & I acceded with reluctance.

January 24th, 1809

Lou, our maid, who has a cousin fighting in the Peninsula, reports dire news — The French, having taken Madrid, drove Sir John Moore's army in a retreat north.

When they reached Corunna last week they found the fleet dispatched to carry them home had been held back by adverse winds. In the desperate rearguard battle that followed, Moore was killed. Lou's cousin, thanks be to God, escaped with a wound.

I decided of a sudden to take the Coach into town. When I arrived at Drury-lane I asked if Mr Rothwell was indoors. The man there said he had gone off on business with Mr Sheridan but would return in the afternoon. I could not go home without speaking to him, so I went to a Tea-room in the Piazza to wait. I read the newspapers on the disaster at Corunna. Moore's bravery in the action is much praised. His dying words I noted down — 'I hope the people of England will be satisfied. I hope my Country will do me justice.' But the life of the Town here went on, the bustle of the market people & the cries of the street-sellers continued as tho' Sir John Moore might never have lived, let alone died for them.

I tramped around, stopping at our old house in Norfolk-street that I had not seen in years. It seemed not so very different. I could not help recall it was on those steps I first happened to meet her. What memories.— At about four o'clock I returned to Drury-lane & went within. Edmund was, of course, surprised to see me — perhaps my wearied aspect alarmed him, for he immediately asked if Molly had been taken ill. —No, she is very well, I assured him. I thought my heart would burst with all that roil'd within but I commanded myself & asked if we might talk privately. He conducted me to his Office & we drank tea. I was in a great agitation & at first felt my throat too choked-up to speak. Eventually I asked him if he had played us false. — How so? he said. By withholding the truth of your origin, I said. Can you deny that your Mother is Elizabeth

Vavasor? He went very pale at that — 'My dear Lady, I would not wish to deny it. But knowing the sad history of your connection with my Mother I believed it prudent to conceal the fact. Please do not think ill of me for it. I wanted only to have your Friendship.' I asked him if his mother had encouraged him to seek a rapprochement — He denied it. He said he had already made our acquaintance before he decided to tell her. Once apprised of it she was angry that he had 'gone behind her back' — but then she wanted to know about us, for twenty years have passed since relations were sundered.

In truth, I wonder now whether I already knew Edmund's secret. There were clues enough to prompt my suspicion, yet I think I was most unwilling to have it confirmed. I was deceived by him, but also by myself.

January 30th, 1809

This morning Molly asks me, 'Why does Edmund not come?' I reply that he is much occupied by his new appointment at Drury-lane. Ignoring this she says, 'Have we given him some offence perhaps?' I tried to assure her that we have not, but she looks so confused & dismayed by his absence that it cuts me to the marrow. Tybalt, sensing the vibrations of discontent, cries, 'Gorn! Gorn!'

I wanted only to have your Friendship. 'Tis a plea I cannot easily forget. We have met many admirers of our father, but only one of them was so devoted as to befriend us, his forgotten daughters. If I were to reject him on account of his mother the loss should be so much the keener for us than for him. Pride is the cross on which I am tormented, just as it was twenty years ago.

February 8th, 1809

A letter from Goodall at the Royal Academy. He thanks me again for the loan of the six & invites us to the great opening next month.

He adds that there is much public interest over 'The Merrymount Sisters at Night' — a favourite of the Nation, he calls it. I know it only as a favourite of Pa's.

February 25th, 1809

I was on Little Green-street when Miss Hawkes stopt & asked me if I had heard of the fire at Covent Garden. I was puzzled, thinking there could not be another one so soon after the last. She said the Drury-lane Theatre was burnt down in the night — saw it from her upper window, so enormous was the conflagration. I thought instantly of Edmund & conceived a terror that he had been caught in the building. Without telling Molly, I took the Coach that very hour to London & hurried through the streets —I could see the curls of greasy black smoke rise over the roof-tops as I approached. Just as last year when Covent Garden went up in flames, a huge Crowd had gathered before the spectacle — by now I was frantic with alarm, fearing the worst. I asked one stout Gentleman if he knew of any victims but he only shook his head. I walked about for an hour, hoping to meet with someone I might know — in vain. At a loss I bent my steps to his lodgings at Guilford-street where the landlord told me Mr R— had been gone since the early hours, roused from his bed. That at least gave me hope. I begged his leave to wait in Edmund's rooms, which he granted.

I fretted away the hours, imagining every sort of horror. At about six I heard the door open & Edmund came in, his face & hands streaked black with smuts, his Cloaths filthy, like some poor devil emerging from a coal mine. But even in his fatigue he looked surprized. I could not help but clutch him to me, grateful that his Life had been spared. He had arrived at the Theatre when it was already an Inferno, he said, & tho' they managed to save a few things all the Costumes & props were lost — Garrick's clock amongst them.

Sheridan is ruined. The insurance will not cover even half of the losses. The place had been standing for only fifteen years — We still called it the 'new' Drury-lane. Edmund said Sheridan's behaviour on the occasion was extraordinary. When they fetched him from the House of Commons he came at a dawdle. While his colleagues fought the flames he went instead to the Piazza Coffee House. Twice Edmund went there intending to rouse him to action, but Sheridan would not be moved —'May not a man be allowed to drink a glass by his own fireside?' Such nonchalance! It must be cold comfort in the midst of this dire Calamity.

March 14th, 1809

To the Royal Academy for the exh. of the Master Painters of the Last Century. To my great astonishment Molly asked if she might accompany me. 'Tis the first time in years she has ventured out on such an occasion, prompted not by the Grandeur of the invitation I think but by Edmund's promise of attendance.

Nobody is happier than she about his reappearance at College Lane — he behaves towards her with partickular kindness. I was indeed glad to have him as our gallant, for he prevented us from being trampled underfoot by the Crowds. It delighted me to watch them gape at Pa's Paintings, not the least of them 'Molly & the Captain' — I do not suppose above one in ten present this evening knew that the two girls pictured there moved amongst them. Mr Goodall greeted us with notable warmth, as well he might —without our loan to him the exhibition would have lacked its Principal attraction. I thought of Pa & how much he would have enjoyed himself, not for being Honoured —tho' he liked the acclaim well enough — but for the enlivening roar of a Party. His passion was for Painting but his appetite was for Company.

April 1809

Tybalt has been ailing. His feathers have a dull untidy look, like a pauper's cape caught in a hedge. He was old when Molly first took him in —Age has begun its slow withering. I can hardly bear the sight as she tries to tempt him with a morsel & he turns his head away. When she is gone I stare at the bird & wonder, not for the first time, what thoughts plague his brain. Does he know how beloved he is to his Mistress? Or does he chafe in resentment of the Cage she made his home?

April 11th, 1809

Edmund, without employment after the Drury-lane fire, is desirous of a new position at a Theatre. Fortunately he does not seem to lack for funds, perhaps saved from his Naval days —or does his mother keep him solvent? Sheridan is casting about for new backers but nobody has come forward. Nor has he a new play to stir the Public —his creative fire has not been kindl'd in some while.

Edmund feels a natural compassion for his old employer, tho' he has not the means to rescue him.

April 29th, 1809

Poor Molly, harrowed by Tybalt's decline, today begged our Doctor to attend the bird. He kindly obliged her, tho' of course 'tis as clear to him as to me that what ails the creature is not disease but Age — for which there is no Cure.

May 8th, 1809

Edmund came this afternoon with news that greatly dismayed us. It seems there was yesterday evening a robbery at the Royal

Academy — two of the night-watchmen overpowered before they could raise the alarm. The thieves created a Diversion by setting a fire in one room while they made for the Main gallery, & once arrived tore a number of Paintings from the walls. Amongst them, alas! — two of Pa's, the Self-portrait & (I knew it almost before the words were out of his mouth) 'Molly & the Captain'. I felt an odd calm, as if I had prepared myself for it — the Painting has had so charmed a Life hitherto that 'twas only a matter of time before Disaster struck. The insurance had been secured — Goodall saw to that — but no amount of money can recompense this.

May 10th, 1809

A day of utter wretchedness. The reality of the Loss was borne home & I cursed my own part in it —I ought never to have succumbed to Goodall's persuasion and allowed the Painting out of the house. It mortifies me to recall Pa's steady refusal to sell the thing, and his determination that 'Molly & the Captain' be his Legacy to us. What a poor return I have made on that trust.

Goodall came to the house bearing apologies but no comfort. It seems the Theft at the Academy was carefully planned — a notorious crew of house-breakers are said to be involved, which begs the question of why their 'notoriety' did not alert the watchmen in the first place. I hear talk of the thieves' ingenuity as though it were something to admire — perhaps it is. Goodall promised me the Authorities were doing all in their power to recover the Paintings, tho' I deduced from his tone that there is little hope of that.

May 20th, 1809

Misery upon misery. I was still in my Bed when I heard a shriek from downstairs & hurriedly descended to find Molly weeping, abjectly, at the bird lying dead on the floor of its cage. Poor Tybalt. He had been her Companion for so long.

Edmund happened to call & met Molly's grief with affecting expressions of sympathy — if anyone could comfort her in this despond it is he. After we drank tea he suggested to her that Tybalt be buried in the garden — on her agreeing he took it upon himself to conduct a brief exequies over the spot. I do not suppose he held the Macaw in any great regard, but he knew that Molly had & so behaved throughout with irreproachable solemnity. I bless him for it.

May 23rd, 1809

Nil desperandum! as Pa used to say. Goodall sent a message here this morning with news I hardly dared hope for. Yesterday there was discovered in the yard of a Tavern at Borough a sack of discarded oddments. The innkeeper, or his wife, on investigating found a number of canvases, some scratched & damaged tho' none, thank Heaven, beyond repair. One of them had heard of the Robbery two weeks ago & informed the authorities (I believe a Reward had been offered for the recovery). A man sent from the Academy to verify the contents reported back that one of the Pictures was our own 'Molly & the Captain'. How it came to be abandoned there nobody knows — perhaps the thieves had left their booty intending to retrieve it at a later date. In any event, this is news to rejoice us, tho' poor Molly cannot raise a smile at present.

May 25th, 1809

Edmund accompanied me to the Academy to examine our Picture. The damage was negligible, light scratches & some shredding where they had cut the canvas from the frame — I was thankful, for I had feared much worse. Goodall advised me to let the Gallery carry out repairs, to which I agreed. The question of how to protect it in the future must then be addressed.

A letter comes from the biographer Mr Cuthbertson, whose long Silence encouraged me to hope his enquiries were at an end. He writes seeking my permission to examine Pa's Will. I replied that it remained in the care of Hoares Bank, where he is welcome to apply — I appended a covering letter to that effect. What a doughty digger he has been.

June 1st, 1809

Molly shuffles listlessly around the house, or else sits blank-faced in the same chair in the parlour for hours. I am so worried by her that I asked the Doctor to visit. He told me that bereavement can be as severe, as damaging, as an illness — & the only cure for it is Time. He knew already of her fragile state & agreed that she might be given a Measure of something to ease the pain. He recommended Laudanum. So I administered a tincture this evening, at which she seemed to settle. I also proposed the idea of acquiring a new pet for her but this was rebuffed — like a child she insisted she wanted only Tybalt. Her loyalty is at once touching & rather tiresome.

June 9th, 1809

I was in the garden planting pots of cucumber when Lou came out bearing a letter — from Mr Cuthbertson to say he had news of a perplexing Nature & would I permit him to call directly? I sent back word that he should. I fretted the day long as to what he could mean — the urgency of his tone made me half-sick with nerves. At about five I heard a knock at the door & Lou inviting him within. I felt a strong foreboding as I greeted him but knew that whatever should come must be borne. Mr C—— had visited Hoares, he said, and was enabled by my letter of Permission to study Pa's Will. On Ma's death in '97 his Estate was entailed upon us, with certain annuities paid to our retainers & the bequest of particular paintings to his first Gallery in Suffolk &c. At this he paused — Did I know of a Codicil to the Will? When I owned I did not he said, 'I thought as much. I believe your father wanted it a secret. You see, there are two other legatees he specified in it — I know you are acquainted with Mrs Vavasor and her son, Mr Edmund Rothwell. It seems that your father had an intimate connection with Mrs V—— for many years and wished to make them both secure on his death.'

Both? I asked — But what claim has Edmund upon my father? Mr C—— looked at me gravely & said, 'A claim of kinship. He is your father's son.' I suppose my mouth gaped open, like a goldfish. But his name is Rothwell, I replied — the father abandoned his mother when Edmund was an infant. — 'I cannot vouch for the story told of his origins,' said he, consulting his notes, 'but the facts of the case are indisputable — Joseph Edmund Rothwell was born to Mrs Elizabeth Vavasor at Bristol on May the first, 1788. William Merrymount acknowledges his paternity in the Codicil — the rest follows as described.' I said, Did Edmund know of this? Mr C—— nodded. We talked for some minutes more, I hardly know of what.

When he took his leave he mumbled in half-apology for being 'the bearer of unwelcome revelations'. I sat in the library, dead still, for a long time.

June 11th, 1809

Edmund. The shock of it has dazed me like a knock to the Head — Pa's son, our half-brother. I have been endeavouring to recall the days of twenty years ago when Lizzie — Mrs V—— — resided in Clerkenwell with the infant. There had been doubt regarding the child's sire — she had been living with a man named Royce, or

Boyce, tho' the rumour held that Lord Rothwell was her lover at the time — yet heard no squeak of suspicion that it was Pa. She was an expert dissembler — what else, her being an Actress? — but Pa's Mask of innocence was just as skilfully worn. How many times did I see him in the company of Mother & child & yet he paid them no more than the affection due of a Friend. Was it Shame, or Expedience, that drove him to those extremes of deception?

I think him cruel. It grieves me to write that, but 'tis true. Cruel — not merely to have deceived his wife & daughters in the first place, but to compound the offence by keeping concealed a natural child. He should have known it would one day come to light. Now it has owing to a biographer a shade more curious than the rest — & one unwittingly enabled by me.

June 14th, 1809

In very low spirits I wrote to Susan asking her to visit — Upon arriving she looked so dismayed at my Appearance that I all but broke down & confess'd the matter straightaway. I think she was as shocked as I to hear about Edmund & the Codicil to the Will — that the great Wm Merrymount should have kept such a secret. Yet in Susan's quiet, measured voice I found a sweet relief, & even the faintest stirrings of hope — 'By and by this should be a happy event. Your affection for Edmund was always strong, and his for you — how much the stronger will it be now he is revealed as your own flesh & blood?' I saw the good sense in this, but brooded still.

My mood had cleared during the Afternoon, tho' I wondered where Molly had been all this time. I went up to her room & found her asleep —waking her gently I said that cousin Susan was here & would like to see her before she left. Molly mumbled something & turned over in her bed. I asked her again to come down, and this time I heard a more distinct 'No'. Returning downstairs I told Susan

of Molly's depress'd spirits since the loss of Tybalt —that our Doctor
had prescribed for her a tincture of Laudanum. Susan asked to see
the bottle (her brother is a Doctor) & looked at me gravely — 'Don't
let her have too much.'

June 16th, 1809

I was taken with a Notion that might drag Molly from her pit of
despond. I informed her that Edmund would be calling at the
House in the afternoon with news of a remarkable Nature. 'Can you
guess what it is?' I asked her. Molly looked across at me, dull-eyed,
shook her head. 'But you would like to see him, wouldn't you?' This
at least she conceded with a half-smile. She liked the youth from
the start, which inclines me to wonder if the truth of our blood —
to which I was blind — became an unacknowledged bond between
them. Who could have dreamed such an odd story? Shakespeare,
perhaps. Or God.

For the occasion I managed to get her into a clean dress (she
is careless about her linen these days) & picked flowers from the
garden so as to make the parlour gay. When Edmund arrived I
had a sense of partaking in a one-act Drama, tho' I was the only
Player who had the lines & knew the Argument. Edmund arrived
bearing a little box of apricot tarts, which we ate with our tea. He
told us about his new position at the Haymarket — the place ranks
below Sheridan's but the security is much superior. We discussed
too the Pictures & how repairs were progressing at the Academy.
I had waited for my moment — now came the thrust. I turned to
Molly — 'Dearest, you recall I told you Edmund had some news to
impart —Should you like to hear it?' She smiled eagerly, Yes! So in
expectation I looked to Edmund, whose countenance was disconcerted — 'News?' he said.

'Indeed,' I said, '& very significant at that.' He paused, his smile
gone crooked, wary. 'I beg your pardon —I fear I am not . . . ' — He

stuttered into silence. — 'Well, Molly, (I continued) since Edmund seems at a loss I suppose I must tell you the news instead. You recall the biographer, Mr Cuthbertson? He has been finding out all kinds of things about Pa for his book, and his most recent discovery is very surprising indeed. You see, he consulted Pa's Will & found a document that revealed Pa to have a son! (My gaze was fixed on Molly, tho' I could feel Edmund's agitation next to me.) Now, what would you say were I to tell you (pause) that this son is none other than Edmund?!' Molly, with the pitiful expression that indicates the heart's willingness baulked by the mind's deficiency, looked from me to him as she tried to unpick this conundrum — 'Edmund,' she began — & slowly the light of deduction dawned in her eyes — 'You mean Edmund is ... our brother?' 'Yes. That is exactly what I mean.' — At which Molly rose to her feet and shuffled towards him, holding out her arms. What else could he do but accept her embrace? Mine own eyes brimmed as he sobbed and buried his head against her shoulder.

June 17th, 1809

We talked for many hours, Edmund & I. Whatever deception was played on us I told him the outcome of our father's wrongdoing is a joyous one —for we are united, blood to blood. Now too I discern little flashes of Pa in his brow, in the light of his grey eyes & in his quick wit. 'Twas his own determination to know us that drove him — his mother had warned him not to pursue the Connection, having promised Pa that the fact of his existence should never reach our ears. But when he made our acquaintance on his return to England there was little she could do. She has been working in Ireland & Scotland most of these years — London sickened her, he says. I cannot fathom the strangeness of it all — or the Great good luck of it!

June 20th, 1809

I took Molly out for a walk, thinking to put some colour into her pasty cheeks. She showed herself willing, tho' she is grown a little stout & breathless. We walked about the Heath, foxgloves everywhere, & elder bushes filled with blossom. Sun dodging in and out of long banks of cloud. Children were playing with a kite — Molly watched them intently. (I think she wished herself amongst them.) I asked her if she had been thinking about Edmund —She nodded. 'I often hoped that we might have a Brother,' she said vaguely. 'I do wish he had made himself known to us earlier.' I agreed, tho' I said it was fortunate in the end that he had made himself known to us at all. Then she said, 'Do you suppose he might wish to come & live with us?' I laughed & replied that Edmund being a young man would rather live in London than with two old Maids out in Kentish Town. Molly nodded, said yes, that was probably true. She looked a little sad.

July 1st, 1809

Our Pictures are returned from the Academy, all in their Frames apart from 'Molly & the Captain', which I instructed them to leave alone. It has a burnish'd look after its adventure in larcenous company — the colours in it seem to flare more richly than before. Pa taught me how to stretch a canvas, so I may finish the job myself. I have conceived a scheme to make it safe from thieves & swindlers. But I am uncertain as to whether I can bear to do it.

July 3rd, 1809

I dispense the Laudanum to Molly by my own hand, but I have a suspicion she has been taking nips of it behind my back. I have warned her against this & yet each time I check the bottle the level seems to have dropt. I keep in mind Susan's warning — an excess of it carries mortal danger.

Edmund came in the afternoon — he has agreed to sit for me. A long time since I attempted to draw a Face, & my fingers were stiff as I held the chalk. But by the by I seemed to make a little Progress, felt life come back into my hands. I should have pursued my Talent more rigorously had I not before me the lowering shadow of Genius — my own Father. That anxiety never diminished. I was proud that Pa was the finest Face painter in England — his success bestowed a comfortable life upon us, perhaps too comfortable. I wonder at the Painter I might have been had I been absolutely obliged to make my own Bread.

At the end of the afternoon I showed Edmund what I had done — 'This is very fine!' he exclaimed earnestly. Yes — just fine enough, I replied, to show how poor the handling. 'You will never be satisfied,' he said, 'because you will always set yourself against his example.' But by who else's should I judge myself?

July 6th, 1809

Prodigious rain last night. The garden looked drown'd. The young shoots of our peach-trees have been pinched off by the cold — in July!

I spent the afternoon in a rearrangement of the Pictures. Where once hung 'Molly & the Captain' in the Dining room I have placed the portrait of Pa (my own) in its stead. I had an unexpected opportunity to gauge the Effect when Mr Goodall called on a matter of business. I watched him look about the room & pause in puzzlement at the unfamiliar Picture — 'This was not here before, I think?' I confirmed it, & explained that I was embarked upon a re-hanging. He seemed surprized that I should have put 'Molly & the Captain' in the parlour, a modest setting for such a famous painting. Possibly he thinks me a half-crazed old woman.

July 12th, 1809

My heart is sore — racked for my poor sister. I ought to have been more vigilant, but she was sly & got the better of me. This is what happened. I had admonished her again for taking secret nips of the Laudanum — indeed I was driven to hide the bottle lest serious mischief befell her. Yesterday afternoon I had been out with George to make purchases, forgetting that Lou had taken the afternoon off. I would not usually leave her alone. As we approached the house I saw through the window of the little parlour where she often rests a flash of something — a flame? Hurrying in I confronted the horrific sight of Molly asleep & on fire — I think she must have left a candle burning near that had caught at her sleeve. I shrieked her name & she woke. The dressing-gown she wore was ablaze, the flames dancing up her arms. George, with great presence of mind, tore down a curtain from the window & quickly beat at the flames before enshrouding her. He carried her to the kitchen where we doused her in water, tho' I could see where the fire had already roasted her hands & face. Her cries of agony were terrible to hear. I was overcome, so George went to fetch the Doctor with all haste. He dressed the burns, which were very severe — the best he could do was to dull her pain with an Opiate. This was her undoing in the first place — she must have taken another large dose & fallen asleep, so deeply that not even her own Cloaths on fire had roused her. The parlour walls are blackened, some paintings and furniture damaged.

I write this now at her bedside where she sleeps. The Doctor did not appear hopeful of her surviving the night, such are her injuries. Poor Molly — I have failed her, when I meant only to save her.

July 13th, 1809

The sight of her poor face mummified in bandages rends my soul. This morning she opened her eyes but did not seem to recognise me.

The Doctor came to examine her, took her pulse — 'Very faint,' he said with a shake of his head. He administered another dose of the Laudanum, so at least she is not suffering. I sent for Edmund, who came in the afternoon. As I watched him sitting there, in tears, the fact of our connection struck me anew — here was my brother grieving over my sister. I was desolate in spirit, but I was not alone.

July 14th, 1809

Our vigil at the bedside continued through the night. In the morning she stirred once, briefly, & I spoke to her. I wanted to touch her hands, her face, but held back lest I hurt that blistered skin. At just before one o'clock in the afternoon a piteous rattling noise bubbled up in her throat, & then she was quiet — 'She is gone,' said Edmund, & we held each other & wept. I said a prayer, & bent to kiss her forehead. O my Molly — my poor dear sister. I fear the life she had was a troubled one, a martyr to mental infirmities. Perhaps I loved her the more because of it. She made a dreadful marriage & was abandoned, tho' in the event that might have been a mercy. I know that Tybalt made her happy in later years — as happy as she could ever be.

July 20th, 1809

The vicar of St Anne's on Kew Green was surprised, I think, to see so few mourners — perhaps he imagined the daughter of Wm Merrymount would command as large an acquaintance as her famous father had. We made a sad little procession to the churchyard. Susan & her husband came. Molly was buried in the plot next to Ma & Pa. I had been so distracted by the occasion that I did not notice the veiled Lady standing a little distance behind us in the Church — or else I did notice & thought nothing of her. When the priest had finished the exequies & the gravediggers began on their labours I felt Edmund steer me away with great gentleness, muttering something about an old Friend. Suddenly before me stood the Lady. In the moment before she pulled back her mourning veil I knew who she was. How many times had I imagined this encounter in the twenty years since we had parted? I had once thought that if ever I met her in the street I would ignore her — cut her dead — but today such churlish feelings were gone. I felt no animus at all. She seemed barely changed — a little gaunter in the features, a shadowing around the eyes. Still beautiful. One word came spontaneously to my lips — 'Lizzie,' I said, & held out my hands to hers.

August 15th, 1809

She calls here twice or thrice a week, sometimes with Edmund. She has been telling me of her life in the hiatus of twenty years — working in Edinburgh, in Dublin, & for several years in France. Such are the vicissitudes of her Profession she has known penury — debts have chased her long distances. She is solvent again, tho' her renown has dwindled. (I think Edmund has rescued her from the worst.) 'Here I am returned to London, hoping that someone will give me work.'— She sounded cheerful. She told me she will be fifty-eight in November, but I believe she passed that age some years ago. Today I talked to her honestly about my own life, which in the years since Pa died has been in eclipse. Once his Star was out Molly & I might as well have disappeared along with him. 'And yet your time is not done,' she replied. 'You have people who love & cherish you. Have you not a duty to them to live?' I know she meant this kindly, tho' on melancholy days I feel my life to be almost an irrelevance — an obscure little drawing scorched at the edges by another's blaze of renown. Lizzie smiled & quoted some lines from 'The Tempest' — 'We are such stuff as dreams are made on, and our little life is rounded with a sleep.' She once played Prospero.

I have pondered those words since. Such a little life, a narrow wedge with Eternity stretching fore & aft. Only now do I see that mine has been bless'd — the great good fortune of a Family that loved me & the joy of them that I love still.

August 27th, 1809

Today I finished the portrait of Edmund. Is it good? I hardly know. But 'tis the best of which I am capable. I will surprize him with it when he comes tomorrow. Of its title I am not yet certain — 'Mr Joseph Edmund Rothwell' strikes too formal a note. 'Edmund, brother of the Artist' seems too familiar. Perhaps I will let him decide. I hope he will admire it.

[The third and final section of Laura Merrymount's journal ends here]

Kensington
Gardens

I

In the distance the trees were brooding and opaque, a clotted band of grey-green against the purplish sky. The late glow of the sun had silvered the leaves towards the tops. Beyond lay parkland about the size of a cricket pitch. The evening light, dimming, had reduced the grass to an even shade, though earlier in the day patches of it showed a slight weathering, the colour of demerara sugar. Paul would remember that for later when he was back at home. He liked the Gardens at this time of year, still with the nip of spring at night to keep the late promenaders away. The dark unpeopled avenues that loomed around him lent the place an enchantment, as if this was his own secret garden where he could paint for as long as he liked, alone.

He stared at the picture propped before him; with the light shrinking fast he knew that anything he tried beyond a dab would probably have to be corrected tomorrow. The canvas was small, the size of a newspaper folded in half, but quite large for him, who tended to paint on cigar-box lids, tiny wood panels, the backs of furniture trade cards. He took off his spectacles to clean. As he polished the lenses he stared out again at the trees, now massy, indistinct, greenish-black. It was the effect he so often worked to produce in his painting, the way shapes could swoon into a seeming blur, the solid thing that trembled on the verge of abstraction. He returned his spectacles to his nose and the sharp outlines jumped back at him.

He began to pack up his things, the brushes and palette into his battered old case, the canvas secured to prevent its smudging. Somewhere distant he heard a church bell ring the hour: eight o'clock. He folded up his canvas stool and tucked it under his arm, did the same with the easel. Setting his felt hat on his head he turned up his coat collar and set off. The pathways leading out of the park were forbiddingly shadowed, and the covering line of trees gave ruffians opportunity to pounce. But Paul liked the shadows, and he considered himself insignificant as prey. The stool and the easel were encumbrances that would slow his journey home. But when he reached the road he decided not to take a cab. He enjoyed the meditative time walking allowed.

Queen's Gate, bustling during the day, was quiet at this hour, only a pair of horsemen trotting by. He often wished he could ride. It looked such a joy – and the time he might save. He recalled donkey rides at Herne Bay on a family holiday, he must have been four or five, and even then his father had held him so anxiously he had barely touched the animal's flanks. But then he couldn't run, either, or swim, or climb. A limited childhood. And yet the fates had not been wholly unkind; he had a keen eye and a steady hand for drawing. Talent had come to him as mysteriously as disability. There was nothing in his ancestry to suggest he might distinguish himself as a painter.

He had just turned into Onslow Gardens when a figure emerging from a side road stopped and hailed him.

'Stransom!'

Paul looked up, startled. Before him stood a rosy-cheeked fellow whose raffish check suit seemed to glow from the dark. Richard Melhuish was also a painter, somewhat better known than Paul, and bore the twinkling, cultivated air of a man about town.

'Fancy running into you.' Melhuish grinned. 'Are you on your way home?'

'Indeed I am.'

'My dear fellow,' he said, the grin suddenly a frown, 'you look like a beast of burden with that lot. Here, let me take something ...'

It was quickly agreed they would accompany one another the rest of the way. Paul felt grateful as his friend relieved him of his easel and folding stool; now he just had hold of his picture, the old case and his stick.

He sensed that Melhuish was rather a brisk walker and might not take to his snailing pace, but if so he didn't seem to mind. He had just returned from a painting tour of Normandy – Dieppe, Berneval-sur-Mer, Étretat – where he had got through a deal of work: 'Strong stuff in there, damned strong, though I say it myself.' Paul smiled secretly, for Melhuish was one who invariably did say it himself. 'The light on that coast is remarkable,' he continued. 'And the weather. Some days it changes so fast you have to keep your wits about you. But it forced me to work more quickly. You know that sensation of the paint sort of skipping over the canvas? Makes everything look wonderfully free and offhand.' He sighed a little, and said in a more reflective tone, 'Yes, give me a canvas, fresh air and a beautiful girl ... and you may keep the canvas and the fresh air.'

Paul laughed, and heard a gratified snigger in return. After further enlarging on the pleasures of France, Melhuish at last turned to his companion.

'And what about you? I keep seeing your little things here and there.'

'Oh, steady as she goes,' Paul said vaguely, and realised that if he didn't offer something else the talk would instantly revert to the Life of Melhuish. 'As a matter of fact, I have business in France myself. A gallery in Paris has written to ask if they might represent me. You know the Colbert?'

'The Colbert?! Good Lord, you are coming up in the world.' Melhuish, only three years older, condescended to Paul as though it might have been thirty. Self-absorption occasionally made him

97

deaf to his own rudeness. He added, 'Though why a gallery that has the pick of the French should want to import stuff from this country I've no idea.'

Paul deduced from this remark that the Colbert had not yet sought out Monsieur Melhuish as an artist.

They had reached Chelsea and the labyrinthine dark off the King's Road. By now the lamplighters were out, and gauzy yellow lollipops glimmered though the murk. The door of a corner pub swung open and noise burst forth – almost at once it shut and the street fell quiet again. Melhuish was telling him about the rooms he had just rented at Angel; restlessness caused him to change studios frequently, or else to keep two or three at once – like mistresses, thought Paul.

'It overlooks the canal,' Melhuish explained, 'with an attic view right across the city. You must call in. We'll have an evening at the Collins's.'

Paul, who loved music halls, readily agreed. The conversation had moved on again by the time they reached St Leonard's Terrace, and, coming to a halt, Paul said, 'I really can't thank you enough, Richard.'

Melhuish swung his gaze up at the house. 'I'd forgotten you live here. Funny little neighbourhood, this ...'

'Would you care to come in?' Paul asked.

Melhuish consulted his pocket-watch and pulled a face. 'Thanks, but I'd better be off. An evening at Lady Standish's. I don't suppose you know her?'

Paul admitted he did not. He opened the iron front gate, and after divesting themselves of their various burdens the two men shook hands, and parted. He could hear Melhuish whistling to himself down the street.

In the hall he scented roasting meat, and realised he was hungry. He took off his hat and coat, left his things in the vestibule and began his descent of the narrow stairs down to the kitchen. This also took its time. Mrs Gent, the cook, hearing his entrance, looked around in surprise.

'I thought you must be dining out!'

'Evening, Mrs Gent, sorry I'm late. Maggie, please forgive.'

This latter apology was directed to a woman in a black pinafore dress, her russet hair tied up. Beneath a clever pale forehead her brown eyes were alert, like twin sentries. This was his sister, who was clearing the dinner table. She said, with only mild irritation, 'Where on earth have you been?'

'Just in the park. I lost track of time.'

'Well, you'd better sit down,' said Mrs Gent. 'I'll warm a plate for you.'

He was soon making light work of mutton and potatoes. Maggie brought over a glass of beer and sat down opposite. While he ate he told her about his day's work.

'I don't like the idea of you walking though the park at night,' she said.

'Oh, it's fine,' he replied. 'No thief would consider me worth the trouble, and I never carry anything of value – not even a watch.'

Maggie returned an arch look. 'That much we can tell.'

He studied her over the rim of his glass: he could see motes of chalk dust in her hair, and the small frown line at the centre of her brow was grooved deeper this evening. She looked fatigued. 'How was school?'

'Oh . . . dreary,' she said, and fell silent. He could not tell whether she might turn snappish.

'I bumped into Richard Melhuish this evening,' he said brightly, hoping to lift her spirits.

'What did he have to say for himself?'

'Well, he's been working in Normandy and brought back many wonderful paintings. He's also learning to play golf and turns out to be quite wonderful at that, too.'

Maggie laughed, to his relief – Melhuish's vast self-regard was a comic subject between them. He added, 'He referred to my pictures as "your little things".'

She made a hissing noise like air escaping a balloon. 'I don't know how you put up with him.'

Paul gave an indulgent smile. 'I think the world would be a duller place without Richard. He gives us such sport! And, by the way, he helped me home with my things.'

'He's a conceited so-and-so.'

'Funny, that's the word our old tutor would use about him – *that conceited jackanapes!* I think Richard was rather put out when I told him about the Colbert Galleries.'

She returned a satisfied nod. Maggie taught at the St Pancras Collegiate in Camden. The place was ruled by Miss Dowie, a formidable lady who tended to treat her staff as imperiously as she did their pupils. Paul could usually tell from Maggie's brow whether she had suffered that day with the headmistress. He had no doubt that being in the latter's employ required some forbearance; but he guessed that his sister's prickliness would not make her an easy colleague either.

They talked on for another half-hour before Maggie decided to turn in for the night. Upstairs in her room she stood at the window, gazing out over the back garden and the line of slate-roofed houses enclosing it. Emma, their maid, had set a little fire in the grate. She felt some of the day's frustration smoothed out, like wrinkles under an iron. Paul's equable temper was a balm to her nerves. With a sigh she drew the curtains and began to get ready for bed.

Her discontent was born of both character and unfortunate circumstances. As a seventeen-year-old Maggie had been a student of great diligence and promise, such that her school invited her to sit the entrance examination for Girton. The prospect of Cambridge thrilled her, and she needed no extra incentive to study hard. The same year, by a cruel stroke of timing, their widowed mother fell seriously ill with heart trouble, and the responsibility of looking after her devolved on Maggie, since Paul was incapable and their older sister Ada was married and living down in Surrey. She postponed her application and stayed at home to nurse her mother, who lived another four years – just long enough to crush what remained of Maggie's faltering confidence. Despite encouragement, she could not rekindle her ambition, and the dream of Cambridge withered away. Now twenty-eight, she chafed at her lot, an unmarried woman stuck with a job she disliked and the impression of an interesting future behind her.

In the morning she found Paul in the hallway, preparing to venture out. She had got used to the sight of his small ungainly person loaded up like a packhorse; today, for some reason, it pierced her.

'If you wait for a moment I'll walk with you.'

Paul looked at her. 'I'm not going your way.'

'It's all right. I have the morning off.'

She put on her coat, then unburdened him of the easel and the folding stool, just as Melhuish had the night before. In the time between their mother's death and her starting at St Pancras Collegiate, Maggie had companioned Paul each morning to whichever spot he happened to be working. His favourites had varied between Battersea Reach, Cheyne Walk and Albert Bridge. Only in the last year had he found himself drawn to Kensington Gardens, to the near exclusion of all the others. One day she had asked him, 'Why choose this place out of anywhere in London?'

Paul had thought for a moment and said, 'I'm not sure I did choose it. I think it chose me.'

The late April morning was crisp, and giant placid clouds bumped behind one another in a slow queue. As they proceeded through the streets, Maggie braced herself. She had at first pretended not to notice public reaction to Paul. His crooked back and peculiar dragging walk, like a lead weight concealed within his left boot, were effects of the scoliosis he had from childhood. His appearance excited laughter and cries from passers-by. More often people simply stared, curious, or appalled. One day she snapped and confronted a couple of youths who had begun capering in front of them, making ape noises. After they had run off laughing Paul turned to her and said quietly, 'Don't trouble yourself, Maggs. I believe they only do it to hide their embarrassment.' So Maggie boiled away in silent fury at the cat-calls and jeers. Her being a good three inches taller than Paul had led to dismal confusion. Once they were on an omnibus together when she, daydreaming, looked around in sudden alarm at the vacated space next to her. She called out Paul's name, and a man sitting opposite leaned over and pointed out of the window: 'Your son just stepped off the 'bus, madam.'

Today they made it to the park without incident. Paul had stopped at the spot he had occupied the day before and was laying out his brushes and pigments. He looked up at the sky.

'Will it stay fair?'

'I think so,' she said. 'What will you do for luncheon?'

'Oh, I'll just smoke a pipe. If I get really hungry there's a horrible eating-house up at Notting Hill Gate.'

Maggie clicked her tongue. 'How stupid of me. I should have asked Mrs Gent to make you a sandwich from that mutton.'

Paul smiled. 'Let's have it cold instead this evening.'

She gave him a kiss and walked off, glancing back every so often at his small, crouched figure. What a blessing his work was to him – to them all. And it might never have been. When Paul was born the doctors judged from his tiny frame and weak lungs that he would not live long. That he survived made him precious to Maggie and Ada. Once the curvature of his spine was diagnosed they were afraid that he would never walk, but again he proved them wrong, albeit with braces and crutches. Excluded from games and outdoor jollities, he found diversion in drawing. Outings to Chatham Docks, where their father worked as a shipping agent, introduced him to the life of the river: it became one of his abiding subjects. James Stransom's business prospered and in 1869, when Maggie was eight and Paul five, he moved the family to Chelsea, where the Embankment was under construction and fresh opportunities abounded. Their next-door neighbour at St Leonard's Terrace was a sweet old lady who had grown up there and told them stories of Chelsea when it was a tumbledown village of inns and churches and unpaved roads. At night they could hear carousing from the pleasure gardens at Cremorne and watched the fireworks burst across the sky.

Tragedy sailed out of nowhere in the autumn of 1875 when their father was struck down with pneumonia and died within six weeks. The family were provided for but the shock of his loss reverberated. He had been beloved, especially by Maggie, and for a while it seemed a light had gone out among them. Paul, to whom his father had been companion and protector (nobody would have dared jeer at his boy), retreated within himself; for a time he was afraid to leave the house. But life went hurrying on. Ada married a city stockbroker who took her to live in Haslemere. Paul's accomplishments won him a place at the Slade. Maggie drew the short straw, and remained at home with their mother.

Emerging from Hyde Park she took an omnibus to Tottenham Court Road. From there she made her way to a little auction house in Bloomsbury that she knew, and began wandering in vague search of something for Paul, whose birthday was coming up. One of the rooms was hung with paintings and drawings to be sold the following week. She idly inspected the tags of one or two landscapes; it was modest stuff, dusty old oils probably bought in a job lot from a house clearance. Maggie guessed that nobody had cast an interested eye upon them in years – decades. She was about to leave when her eye caught on something a distinct cut above the rest. Hung on its own in a heavy old frame was a Regency-era portrait of a young man, handsome, in a burgundy velvet frock coat, his smiling eyes seeming to engage directly with the viewer. He was standing in front of a fireplace, above which could be discerned on the wall another portrait of two girls: sisters, perhaps. The canvas was dulled with age and needed cleaning, and the gilding of its frame was chipped; but the charm of it reached out to her. There seemed a kind of conspiracy of affection between the sitter and the painter, she couldn't explain it exactly. The label on it read:

Portrait of a Young Man, circa 1800–1820
School of William Merrymount

That was all. Her absorption in it was such that she nearly jumped when a voice sounded at her ear.

'Miss Stransom?'

She turned to find a tall, saturnine figure at her shoulder. His receding hair was combed back from his forehead in two dark wings.

'Mr Talmash, how d'you do?' She knew him vaguely through Paul. He owned a gallery in South Kensington. 'I was just looking at this ... charming fellow.'

Talmash narrowed his eyes at the painting. He checked the label. 'No estimate on it.'

'Then may I rely on your expertise and ask how much you'd pay for it?'

He smiled, and glanced at it again. 'I'd give five guineas.'

'Is that all?'

'And sell it for twenty,' he said, with a little smirk.

She gave a short laugh. He hailed one of the auction-room assistants and, following a brief exchange, turned back to Maggie. 'The estimate is twenty-five guineas.'

Maggie pulled a wistful expression. 'Much more than I'd anticipated.'

Talmash nodded. 'Yes, considering it's only "school of".' But now he was studying the picture more closely. 'I wonder ... It has the look of a Merrymount, doesn't it? A clever student of his, no doubt. Or else some fellow who knew how to copy him.'

She sensed his interest gathering, and quickly feigned indifference. 'I don't suppose it's worth anything like that. One could buy something quite *significant* for twenty-five guineas.'

Talmash's expression had wavered. 'I dare say . . .'

Had she done enough to put him off? Maggie, a familiar among Paul's crowd, was known to have 'a good eye' and had picked up bargains in sales rooms before now. It would be irksome to spot an unregarded treasure only to have it pinched from under one's nose.

'Are you going to the Club this Friday?' she asked, determined on distracting him.

'Hmm? Oh, I expect so. I've forgotten – whereabouts this week?'

'I believe it's at Mr Brigstock's.'

Talmash nodded, and then they were both silent, as if waiting for the other to leave so that *Portrait of a Young Man* could be scrutinised alone. Long moments passed, and Maggie was the first to crack.

'Well then,' she said, glancing her last at the painting, 'perhaps I'll see you on Friday.'

He returned a bow, and she moved off, thoroughly dissatisfied. The Club to which she had made diversionary reference was the Beaux Arts, a sociable grouping of artists, dealers and camp-followers who met on Friday evenings, the venue switching weekly from one clubman's lodgings to another's. She had asked Talmash whether he was going. But was she? Her attendance was entirely at Paul's discretion; nobody else brought a sister, or a wife. Women were tolerated as an ornament amongst the heavily male crowd. Some Fridays they met at St Leonard's Terrace, where her presence was justified, otherwise Paul hesitated to involve her: he feared she would not much enjoy 'a lot of bearded bores'. In fact, she found the company congenial, and the gossip first-rate.

On her way out of the auction rooms she took note of the forth-coming sale day. It might be worth dropping in to bid, even at twenty-five guineas the estimate. The devil take Talmash!

*

On Friday, just after six, she heard Paul let himself in. Moments later he put his head around the door of the sitting-room.

'Evening, dear. Are you coming tonight?'

'If you don't mind the company,' she said, looking up from her book.

'It'll probably be a dull affair,' he replied in needless warning.

'Mrs Gent has left us a game pie for supper. Shall we have beer with it?'

Once they had eaten they took a fly from the King's Road north to Regent's Park. Halfway up Albany Street they were admitted to a house where lights shone from the upper floors. As they ascended, the competing strains of men's voices drifted down the stairs. On the landing they were greeted by their host, Denton Brigstock, a suave, bewhiskered man in his mid-twenties who Maggie always imagined to be Irish, though in fact his accent was smartened-up cockney.

'Miss Stransom, you are very welcome. I hope you won't find the company here too rowdy . . . '

She laughed at his teasing. 'If you could see the girls I teach you'd know what "rowdy" is.'

He returned an amused nod, then pointed across the landing: through an open door they could see men gathered around a table. 'They're playing whist in there, if you fancy,' he said, but then steered them both into the room from which he had just emerged. The lamps had been turned low. A mutterish throng of young men stood or lounged about, the fug from their pipes and cigars almost solid in the air. The dark coats most of them favoured were here and there brightened by the bohemian touch of a brocade waistcoat or a loose-collared shirt. One fellow wore a velvet fez, with pince-nez and a clay pipe protruding from the side of his mouth. *If only he knew what a fool he looks*, she thought.

Paul had been immediately seized upon by two of his confreres, so Brigstock conducted Maggie to the makeshift bar he had set up against the wall.

'This lot are drinking porter,' said Brigstock, with an airy gesture, 'but there's hock if you prefer.'

She did prefer, and they stood together leaning against the chimney-piece. He stared at her candidly, as was his custom.

'You know, I always thought Rossetti would have loved to paint you. Your pale skin and green eyes were just his thing.'

'He lived near us. Paul met him once. I think he was far from well.'

Brigstock nodded sadly. 'He had terrible depressions, poor man. Chloral and drink finished him. But enough of this gloom!' He clinked his glass against hers. 'How's life in Chelsea? I gather Paul's not much seen at the Embankment any more.'

'No. He's at Kensington Gardens the whole time.'

'Painting the trees . . .'

'It's what he loves. They're selling, too. Did you know that the Colbert has taken him on?'

'Have they, by Jove?! Good for him. Of course, he'd never tell me that himself. Altogether too modest, your brother.'

'And yourself – hard at it?'

'Just had a couple of weeks in Dieppe, painting away.'

'That's funny, Paul ran into Melhuish the other evening – *he'd* just been in Normandy too.'

Brigstock rolled his eyes. 'Yes, I saw him there, and a few others. It's too bad when one sneaks off to France only to fetch up among the very people one left London to avoid.'

'I should like to go to France myself one day,' said Maggie suddenly.

'You mean to say you never have?' He looked faintly appalled.

'I always meant to, but circumstances got in the way. Paul and I have talked about going . . . I think he's a little nervous of the idea.'

'But if he's being shown in Paris now would be the time to go!'

She looked at him. 'He isn't gregarious like you, Mr Brigstock. Or as self-assured. There was a time when he hardly went out at all – I surely don't need to explain why.'

'If London doesn't daunt him I don't see why Paris should. He gets about all right, doesn't he?'

'It's not just that. People on the street ... they can be horribly cruel. Paul pretends not to notice, but I know he does, and it affects him. He would hardly be human if it didn't.'

Brigstock made a rueful expression. 'I wouldn't like to claim that the public over there is more delicate, but you should try to persuade him. He would love Paris. And so would you.'

He took her glass and went off to recharge it. In his absence Maggie felt herself under the casual scrutiny of several pairs of eyes, being the only woman in the room. On first hearing of the Club she had imagined a gathering of young artists earnestly discussing their work: a salon of the high-minded. Experience had corrected this assumption. The Friday-night congregants talked of many things – women, politics, horses, gambling – though of art itself they seldom did, except in reference to the money they were making (or being cheated of). Drinking and smoking were the sacred pursuits. Occasional spats would flare up among them and be gossiped about for weeks; rival cliques of artists would be disdained as talentless frauds. Maggie enjoyed the tittle-tattle, and belonging herself to a profession infamous for talking shop she quickly ceased to be surprised by the pettiness of it all.

She inclined her gaze towards the large spotted mirror above the fireplace, where a stuffed puffin stared sightless beneath a glassed dome. She watched a figure in the mirror's reflection detach himself from the crowd and approach her. It was Edgar Talmash. He greeted her with a bow.

'I was hoping you'd be here. Since we met I've been working up a little theory about that picture—'

He was at that moment interrupted by the reappearance of Brigstock, bearing drinks.

'Talmash,' he said, looking from him to her, as though something might be afoot between them.

'I was just telling Miss Stransom about a painting we both admired at the Holborn auction rooms.'

Brigstock's eyes sharpened with interest.

'Portrait of a young man,' Talmash continued, 'painted around the early years of this century. It's listed as "school of Merrymount", which made me wonder, so I went to the London Library and did a bit of digging. There's extant correspondence which indicates that Merrymount wasn't the only artist in the family. His elder daughter also produced some work, including two sketches of her father on his deathbed. Whatever else she may have done is lost. This portrait, though, it's of a different quality from most of Merrymount's imitators. I have a notion it might be by the daughter.'

'Based on what?' said Brigstock. 'A couple of sketches wouldn't tell you that.'

'Indeed, no,' replied Talmash. 'I'm basing it on a clue within the picture. You recall, Miss Stransom, the young man stands in front of a large portrait?'

'Yes – of two young girls,' said Maggie.

'Exactly. A portrait which I believe is "The Merrymount Sisters at Night", one of William Merrymount's most admired pictures – destroyed, alas, in a fire. This miniature reproduction may be the only visual evidence we have of it.' Talmash paused, held up a finger. 'But there's more. You see, "The Merrymount Sisters at Night" was exhibited very rarely in public – once at the Royal Academy during the 1790s. Otherwise it hung always at the artist's house in Cavendish Square. Despite many offers, Merrymount refused to sell it. Which means—'

'That the portrait of the young man was probably painted at Merrymount's house,' said Brigstock.

'Quite so. And who else would have had reason, or access, to paint there but a member of the household?'

'What happened to the daughter?' Maggie asked.

'Oh, a life of obscurity. She looked after her mad sister for years. The latter died in the same house fire that destroyed Merrymount's painting.'

'How terribly sad,' she murmured.

Talmash nodded. 'Yes ... one of the great lost masterpieces, they say.'

Maggie looked at him: he had misunderstood.

'What's the estimate on this thing?' Brigstock asked.

'Twenty-five guineas,' said Talmash, widening his eyes. 'I thought that was rather high on first viewing. But if my little theory is correct it has been grossly undervalued.'

'D'you suppose anyone else suspects?'

The dealer's expression was sly. 'We shall find out next week.'

At a quarter past midnight Paul and Maggie were ready to leave. The other guests, and the card-players, showed no sign of flagging. Brigstock, who had flitted around Maggie most of the evening, accompanied them to the front door and then went on to the street to hail a cab.

'I've been trying to persuade your sister to make the trip to Paris,' he said as he helped Paul into the hansom. 'Might you not enjoy the fuss?'

'Perhaps,' said Paul. Maggie could tell from his tone that he meant *No*.

'Thanks for a splendid evening, Dab.'

'My pleasure,' he replied, looking at Maggie as she settled into the cab. 'I wish you good luck at the auction rooms.'

'I fear Mr Talmash will be a tenacious rival,' she replied.

'What *is it* about this painting?'

She gave a little shrug. 'Oh ... it's hard to define. This young man's face has such a speaking look – as though you were in the room listening to him. And the painter renders it in such a fond and intimate way. But of course I have no expertise in that line ...'

Brigstock's smile was curious, and lingering. 'You make me want to see the thing for myself. Goodnight!'

He closed the car door and waved to her through the window. As the cab rattled through the midnight streets they were quiet, until Maggie abruptly said, 'Why d'you call him "Dab"? Brigstock, I mean.'

'Oh. His initials – D.A.B. Quite appropriate for a painter.'

She smiled into the dark. Her next question was more thoughtful. 'Is he an eligible sort of man, d'you think?'

'Brigstock? Well, he's got family money on top of his earnings. And his charm would certainly recommend him.'

Something unspoken lingered between them, and a minute or two passed before Paul said, 'I'm awfully fond of Dab, as you know . . . but he isn't the sort of fellow you'd be happy to see squiring your sister about town.'

'Why on earth not?'

Paul's silence felt uneasy. 'I don't know,' he said presently. 'I'm not sure he's quite a gentleman.'

Maggie was about to laugh, then checked herself. It was so unlike anything Paul would usually say that she suspected something else behind it. In deference to him she dropped the subject, and they talked of other things until the cab arrived at St Leonard's Terrace.

II

The following week Paul was back in the park. He had finished 'Late April, Kensington Gardens' and had moved on to a different spot in sight of the pond. He had stretched and primed the canvas, seven inches by five, slightly larger than a postcard: his favourite size. To his right was a little patch of grass jewelled with cowslips and bluebells; to his left a row of elms that looked very promising. The air this morning was soft, pollenish, with a faint breeze ruffling the branches; he could almost imagine they were waving at him. Very distantly he heard the whirr of wheels and the busy metal tick of hoof beats from Bayswater Road. All else was calm.

For most of his life he had drawn and painted in the open. When he began at the Slade he had to change the habit of years and adapt himself to work in a studio; but he quickly learned that the atmosphere of interiors was not for him. He needed the trees, the streets, the river, in front of him. He required the variable effects of light and temperature to get the paint moving. Within four walls he felt himself at a sensory disadvantage, like trying to read a book in the dark. During the period of his most extreme agoraphobia he found that, confined at home, he couldn't work at all. In the end it was the imperative to paint that lured him outside again. There he could express not just what he saw but what he felt – how to paint the warmth of the sun, the soughing of the wind in the trees, the elegiac mood at the end of summer.

In his early youth he studied Constable, minutely. He looked at individual brushstrokes, wondering how pigment had conveyed those temperamental Suffolk skies. He wanted to discover his trick of painting a sky so bloated with rain that, as Fuseli said, one wished for an umbrella when standing before it. But it was another painter still living, and nearby, whose work struck Paul with the force of a revelation. He was sixteen when he first set eyes on *Nocturne* by Whistler. He had often stared upon the Thames at night, but this painting made him doubt if he had ever really *seen* it before. Here was the river turned to gloaming and fog, a mysterious blue-green blur on which floated two ghostly forms that might have been vessels – might have been mirages in the dusk. It was a vision of the material world fading into the last moment between light and darkness. Paul, mesmerised, felt as though he had been spoken to: *This is the way you should paint.* The task was not to ape nature, but to pay nature its dramatic due. And this was how, in the weight of the brushstroke across the canvas – the brushstroke that was more beautiful than the scene itself.

He heard the church clock strike eleven, when he would usually stop for a pipe or else exercise his legs for five minutes. But this morning he worked on, partly encouraged by the new brush he was trying out from Barnard's, his supplier. Its bristles were superfine and of a firmness that no detail felt beyond his touch. He was so absorbed that he didn't heed the footfall of company until it was right behind him. Paul felt the shadow halt, heard a throat being cleared, but gave no sign of noticing. The chief hazard of painting *en plein air*, aside from an untimely squall, was a passer-by seeking diversion. Some paused for only a few moments before walking on; some lingered, ready to engage with the painter if only he would acknowledge them. But Paul never did, unless they directly addressed him: even then he wouldn't turn around, only offer the polite minimum and keep his eyes fixed on the canvas, or the middle distance. Most just wanted to look. Saturdays and Sundays in the park during fine weather would guarantee the crowds, and he kept away. One could never be certain of uninterrupted solitude.

'Fine mornin' for it.' The voice was a man's, middle-aged, London.

Paul gave the smallest tilt of his head in agreement. He kept himself very still, hoping that this attitude of concentration would discourage further comment. It often did. He watched a fat magpie stalking about, and waited.

'You always paints so small?'

Without turning he said, 'I do. I find the canvas cannot be larger than enables me to see around it.'

He sensed the man parsing this reply, as if it might contain a riddle. 'Mind my asking,' came the voice again, 'you makes a living from this?'

Oh hell, he thought. This one was a moocher, with time on his hands. Slowly, he did turn to his interlocutor. 'More or less.'

The man facing him was short, dark, about sixty, dressed in a brown shooting-jacket and checked britches. His boots were very worn, and the jacket was fastened by one button at the front, all the others missing. At his side lay a violin case. He had taken off his hat and was picking at its band. Of all the street folk he encountered it was the musicians who most enjoyed a chat. Paul took out his pipe and began to fill it. He felt the man watching him, and after a moment he reached into his breast pocket for his cigars.

'Would you care for a smoke?'

The man's eyes lit up. 'Very 'andsome of you, sir!' He took one and hid it behind his ear. Paul nodded at the violin case.

'You've been playing this morning?'

'I 'ave, sir, just down at H'oxford Circus. Not much business there, I'm afraid.'

He looked downcast, and Paul asked him if he might play something now. The man looked bemused, but then stooped and took out his violin. He stuffed a dirty-looking kerchief against his collar as a chinrest. With a brief moment to set himself he proceeded with 'O God, Our Help in Ages Past', followed by 'For All the Saints'. There was a plangent tone to his playing Paul rather liked.

'You were brought up in the Church?' he asked, when the man had finished.

'No, indeed, sir. Hymns are just them I plays when I can't get a farthing for me troubles.'

The hint was too plain for Paul to ignore. 'Hard times,' he said gently, which the man of course took as an invitation to tell his life story. He had been born near Canterbury and raised among a family of musicians who toured Kent playing at fairs and pier shows. He had come to London in his twenties to try his fortune and found work in pit orchestras – the music halls were always in need of players, he said, and he made a good living there. Then he got into trouble with drink and began missing appointments. The orchestra work dried up so he joined a street band and played at concerts, processions, public gatherings. Most of these musicians were untrained and only played by ear – 'but they was better than a lot of the h'educated players – and I've known both, sir'. His story became more desultory as he recalled the times he had spent in public houses and penny gaffs, 'when things went very bad for me'. He was reduced to distress for some years and moved around the casual wards, 'on the spike', until a friend came to his rescue and took him into his lodgings. Since then he had pounded the pavements on his own, at the mercy of the elements, 'like yusself, sir'.

His tale was ended. He gave Paul a meaning look. 'P'raps you'd care to hear somethin' else. Do you 'ave a favourite ho-verchewer?'

Paul cocked his head thoughtfully. 'Well ... I'd prefer something from the halls, to be honest. I suppose you know the songs of George Leybourne?'

'Of course! Matter of fact, I met Mr Leybourne, God rest his soul. Did you know 'e used to ride about in a carriage-an'-four?'

'I heard that,' said Paul.

'Died poor, though,' the man said quietly. With a misty-eyed look he tucked the fiddle under his chin again and bowed a few notes. The song was a dream about everyday people acting against type – an honest jockey, a cheerful postman, a policeman who 'came when he was wanted' – which the man performed with a mechanical gusto. Paul thought how queer the scene must have looked to someone passing by: a ragged musician in the middle of the park playing to an audience of one. When it was over he cried 'Bravo!' and searched in his pocket for a coin. He was relieved to find half a crown, and the man accepted it with a little bow, adding, 'I didn't 'spect a gennleman like yusself to arsk for somethin' from the 'alls.'

Paul replied, with a disowning smile, 'I'm just a Kentish man like you.'

The man's eyes lit up once more – 'Just fancy sir being from Chatham!' – and there followed more fond reminiscences of their old county. Paul nodded along, willing him to take his leave but too kind to deny him a respite from his loneliness. Eventually the man said, with a sigh, that he ought to be moving on. He put away his instrument in its case, thanked Paul for the coin and said, 'Goodbye to you, sir, and lots of luck.'

Paul held up his hand in farewell and watched the man amble away into the distance. He hummed the tune of the Leybourne as he returned to his picture, mixing the pigment viridian – his principal green – with cobalt and cerulean blue, bone black, red earth, yellow ochre and lead white. The challenge was in finding the exact shade he needed, for the green of the grass was slightly different depending on the angle of the light; and it was wholly different from the bark of the tree, from the arsenical green of the park railings, from the olive-green bushes over yonder. He took from his bag a little tin in which he kept a runny pigment called 'sauce'; it was an invention he had learned from Whistler, essentially a compound of turpentine, copal and linseed oil which he applied to the paint as a tone-enhancer. Sauce had to be used sparingly, otherwise it would drip down the canvas and off the edges. Worse, if you weren't quite careful with it the canvas would dry in a patchy way that looked amateurish. He had destroyed whole paintings for just that fault.

With his palette knife he dipped into the mixture and began spreading it, lightly, like syrup on a slice of bread. Then he used a fine brush to even it. When he was satisfied with the consistency he laid the picture flat on his stool. He would have to wait maybe an hour for it to dry.

He stretched, put on his coat and headed for the Bayswater Road. He had come to trust that his things would be safe in his absence. Only once had he returned from a wander to find a scene of disarray, his paints strewn about the grass, the canvas trampled on, the easel and stool tossed into the Round Pond – the mischief of wanton boys, no doubt. Maggie was more angry about it than he was.

Emerging on to the road he turned west, past the baked-potato stall he sometimes ate at ('Penny a tater – all 'ot!') and into the bustle of Notting Hill. Hansoms and broughams wheeled by, then an omnibus. The clatter of hooves was brusque, impatient: no lull in London, not any more. Hauling himself along the pavement with his cane, he drew glances here and there. You saw crippled soldiers on the street all the time, but they excited pathos and respect. A short crippled man in a slouch hat and frock coat was an object of curiosity, puzzlement, sly ridicule. At school he had fought with boys who persisted in mocking him – they always seemed surprised when he launched himself at them, fists flailing.

Time had knocked the edges off his indignation. Now, aged twenty-five, he affected a kind of innocent gentility before the pointing and the sniggering; if he perceived some youth behind him aping his ungainly movement, he might stop and gesture extravagantly to his imitator as though to say – *My affliction is light in comparison with your own, please, have the right of way.* But he could still be astonished by 'ordinary' behaviour. Once, passing in front of a mother and young child, he overheard the latter say, 'Mama, what is wrong with that man?' The mother, without softening her voice in any way, replied, 'Oh, he's just a poor cripple, dear.'

He entered the less filthy of the two dining rooms facing one another on Notting Hill Gate and seated himself in a booth. He ordered a chop with potatoes and green beans and drank a glass of pale ale with it. A steady thrum of chatter reverberated around the wood-panelled room. At the next booth he eavesdropped on a conversation between two women. The louder of them was recounting some recent and infuriating misdemeanour.

He idled a little, just for the pleasure of his neighbours' prattle.

'Oh, it's a proper how-d'ye-do. Just like her Ladyship – looks one way and rows the other.'

'She's got a nerve ...'

He finally dragged himself away. Retracing his steps back to the park, he thought again of the Colbert and the possibility of a trip to Paris. Brigstock had been quite serious about it. He knew Maggie would like to go. But shyness, physical self-consciousness, were persistent obstacles. He did not want to imagine the startled – quickly corrected – looks of the Parisian *beau monde* on presenting himself. He was satisfied being known through his work; he had no desire to be feted in person.

Back in the park the afternoon light had taken on a mellow, faintly rosy tint. He filled his pipe again and stood examining the canvas he had left to dry: it had come up well, no mottling, no blotching. He was about to sit down when through a break in the trees he saw two blurred figures. In fact there were three, all in white dresses, standing perfectly still. One was a lady, the other two children, spaced slightly apart. Paul squinted, took a step forward: they were too far away to make out clearly, yet he had the unnerving sense that all three of them were staring directly at him. He blinked, and of a sudden cried, '*Ouch!*' A fiery black cinder had leapt unnoticed from his pipe and was burning on his wrist. He shook it off, and saw a tiny purple blemish on the flesh.

He refocused his gaze. The three figures were no longer looking towards him – if they ever were – but appeared to be playing a game of catch. It was a mother, or else a governess, with her two small girls. They inhabited the very spot he had been painting. He stared hard at them, lost in thought. Minutes passed as his eye switched from the three figures to the picture he had finished. Or thought he had finished. Figures were a rarity in his paintings. He liked unpeopled scenes – a riverbank, a clearing among trees, an avenue at dusk. When he did include them they were distantly outlined, perhaps a pair of strollers, or a nursemaid pushing a perambulator. The unexpected appearance of this trio felt like a prompt he should not ignore. He squeezed out a dab of lead white and began to thin it with linseed oil until it was nearly translucent. But the white was still too stark, white as a new tooth, so he mixed in a little ochre to soften it. Then he picked up his fine-bristled brush and began.

Maggie had meant to get to the auction rooms in good time but the massed wheel traffic on Euston Road had put paid to that. She arrived to find the front rows of cane-backed chairs all occupied and even the spaces further back filling up quickly. She seated herself next to an aisle and, removing her gloves, began to flick through the catalogue of the day's sale. There it was, *Portrait of a Young Man, circa 1800–1820*. She cast a furtive eye around the assembled; most of them were men, some in clusters of three or four, their faces shuttered like card-players'.

The man sitting next to her was also studying the catalogue and marking certain lots with a pencil cross.

They were beginning to settle when someone leaned down to her shoulder: it was Talmash, wearing a dark suit and a plump silk neck-tie speared with a pin. *He has come dressed for it*, thought Maggie. He tipped his hat to her.

'I thought I might see you here.'

'Mr Talmash. It seems rather busier than usual.'

He looked around, nodded. 'Let's hope we haven't all come for the same thing.'

'Shall we wish one another good luck?'

'I would count it generous if you did,' he said, implying that he was not going to return the compliment.

The auctioneer at that moment called the room to order, and Talmash with a twitch of his brow took leave of her. She watched him claim a seat towards the front. The sale was soon underway, the lots coming and going at a smart bat. Occasionally there would be a longer contest between bidders, a polite back-and-forth across the room till one of them surrendered. Maggie herself bid for a small oil of an Oxfordshire landscape – a birthday present for Paul – and to her surprise got it almost without challenge for three guineas. The man next to her bent his head to say quietly, 'You have a bargain,' and she smiled. It gave her heart for the larger quarry ahead. She fidgeted helplessly through the next hour, willing the picture to come round, but the brisk business of earlier had slowed: men got up to stretch their legs, wandered off, came back. She kept her eye on Talmash, who remained in his seat throughout. So long as he didn't move, she wouldn't either.

On and on it went, the auctioneer's inquisitive sweep of the room, the silent back-and-forth, the final call, the hammer. She began to recite to herself one of the dreary long speeches in *Richard II* in an effort to pass the purgatory of waiting. It must have worked, because suddenly on the easel came *Portrait of a Young Man*, looking lustrous; it had perhaps been cleaned since she first saw it. She felt her heartbeat quicken as the bidding began. Talmash led it, as expected, and for a while she matched him as the bid went from twenty-five guineas to thirty-five. At forty she paused; she had promised herself that this would be her limit.

'Would the lady care to . . . ?' She nodded, and the numbers continued to ascend. At forty-six she hesitated again. Talmash had deep pockets, and would continue bidding indefinitely. She shook her head at the auctioneer, feeling a mixture of deflation and relief.

But there was a surprise in store. The painting was about to go under the hammer when out of nowhere a new bidder came in. Maggie raised her head to get a closer look – the man was seated on the other side of the room – but she had no idea who he was. Talmash had turned in his seat too, and fairly glowered at this rival who had sneaked up on the rails. The bidding quickly climbed to fifty-two, fifty-four, and then, as if tiring of these gradual increments, the mysterious interloper called, 'Eighty.' There came an audible intake of breath in the room: here at last was a jolt of drama to enliven the proceedings. Talmash, evidently wrong-footed, had paused to consider. Some of the congregants were eagerly searching their catalogues to check whether *Portrait of a Young Man* was indeed the overlooked star of the sale.

'The bid is with the gentleman over there,' said the auctioneer, and turned an enquiring look at Talmash. 'Sir, would you care to go to ninety?' With a tight lift of his chin, sir indicated he would. Maggie wondered then if Talmash's secret theory of the picture's provenance was a secret no longer. She was amused to note the contrast between the two bidders: Talmash fidgeted with uncertainty and irritation, while his opponent radiated a calm bordering on indifference. He had all the time in the world. He even glanced at his nails. Meanwhile the bidding accelerated, one hundred guineas, one hundred and fifty, one hundred and eighty. When it stood at two hundred the room seemed to hold its breath as Talmash looked down, looked up – and with the greatest reluctance shook his head.

'Sold to the gentleman at two hundred guineas,' called the auctioneer, looking rather pleased. The lot had gone for eight times its estimate.

The hum of the auction resumed. Maggie watched Talmash get

up to leave and followed him out of the room. She caught up with him in the foyer, and he turned when she called his name.

'Miss Stransom,' he said in a low voice. His expression was clouded.

'I'm sorry about ... I didn't imagine anyone else bidding for it.'

'Nor I. But one can never be certain of anything in an auction room.'

'Do you know who he was?'

Talmash shook his head. 'Maybe someone from outside London – or even outside the country. Though he didn't look foreign.'

Maggie felt again the little pang. 'I feel rather sad when a painting like that is sold, because one knows one is never likely to see it again.'

'The way of the world,' he replied airily. 'I suppose the fellow must know what a catch he's got. It might do very well on the market.'

She realised that they were talking at cross-purposes: she was lamenting the loss of something beautiful, he the loss of something profitable. But then he said, in a changed tone, 'It was quite something, wasn't it?'

It seemed he did have a feeling for it after all. She nodded, and they said good bye.

III

O n certain Sundays at St Leonard's Terrace Paul's friends from the Slade would gather at the house for what was known as a 'pipe and beer night'. This evening had brought a couple of painters – Towne and Hackett – who shared nearby rooms on Oakley Street, and a friend of theirs named Philip Evenlode who was possibly a writer, or a teacher, Maggie wasn't sure. This fellow rather fascinated her. He was about thirty-five, clean-shaven and lean with skin as pale as a martyr, dressed in a neat but worn frock coat and boots that looked in terminal disrepair. His dark hair was spiked and quilled in the untamed manner of a vagrant's. In fact, she would have been alarmed by Evenlode's appearance but for his lonely brown eyes and the appeal in them for understanding. He had called two or three times before, and on each occasion Maggie had been struck by the contrast of poverty and graciousness.

This evening he had arrived late and brought a gift, which he shyly handed over to Maggie in the hallway. She looked inside the paper bag as she led him into the living room.

'Walnuts,' she said, bemused. 'Thank you, Mr Evenlode.'

Towne, already settled on the sofa opposite Paul, rolled his eyes. 'Good heavens, Phil, if you're going to ingratiate yourself you should really bring your host something *nice* – like a bottle of sherry.'

Maggie privately agreed with this, though Towne, a large, bluff, bearded man, had scarcely earned the right to rebuke his friend, having brought nothing himself. Evenlode blushed and said to Maggie, 'I'm sorry,' which embarrassed her in turn into muttering something about liking walnuts particularly.

She went down to the kitchen and put them in a bowl, then carried them up with nutcrackers and two large bottles of pale ale. She filled their glasses and took a seat between Evenlode and Hackett, an intense, dark-complexioned man about Paul's age who used his hands expressively when he spoke. He was talking at present about Carlyle, who had been a near neighbour when he first came to Chelsea.

'I used to pass him quite often on his walks, glowering away. I always meant to introduce myself to him but found I was ... intimidated.'

Towne laughed and said, 'You wouldn't have understood a word he said anyway. That accent of his was denser than fog – *Ye ken wha' I'm sayin', ya Sassenach?*'

Paul recalled something he had been told by a friend who knew Carlyle. 'I gather he disliked painting – said it was all worthless apart from portraiture. And he only made that an exception after Whistler painted him.'

'Did you know he was also against the use of chloroform in surgical operations? He reckoned that pain was a "natural" accompaniment to the procedure.'

'The more I hear about "the Sage of Chelsea" the more I am inclined to think him a fool,' drawled Towne.

'But surely he was the great historian of our age?' said Maggie, feeling that some defence was necessary.

'So they say. But if his views on art and medicine are anything to judge by I should approach his work very cautiously.'

'I shall bear that in mind when our history class moves on to the French Revolution,' she replied.

Thick blue clouds of smoke now hung in the room; Paul and his friends all favoured long clay pipes on which they puffed away contentedly. Only Evenlode did not partake. Maggie offered him one of her cigarettes, which he accepted gratefully. Having lit it he said to her, 'How goes the teaching, Miss Stransom? Is your head-mistress still the *Gorgon* of legend?'

She returned a quick nod, pleased that he had remembered her disobliging sobriquet from weeks ago. 'Only I find Miss Dowie rather more a reality than legend these days.'

Evenlode smiled, and tilted his head thoughtfully. 'Ah, a *realistic* monster. One might perhaps call her a Gorgon-Zola.'

Maggie and Paul both laughed, but Towne groaned theatrically at his friend's pun. 'Really, Phil, most unworthy of you.'

'I disagree,' said Maggie, twinkling. 'I think it captures the lady perfectly. To answer your other question, I'm trying to interest the girls in Shakespeare at present.'

'What are you studying?'

'At the moment, *Richard II*.'

Evenlode pulled a comical face. 'I fear that would be a challenge even to the mature reader. Perhaps you could try something that might ... stir the blood.'

'Oh, like *Macbeth*?'

'I was thinking along more romantic lines – *Romeo and Juliet*, perhaps?'

Hackett, overhearing, said, 'Phil here used to tread the boards, Miss Stransom, did you know?'

'No, I didn't,' said Maggie, staring at him. He had such a secretive air about him that she could easily believe it.

His gaze dropped to the floor as he said, 'I was with a small rep company for a few years. My career was quite undistinguished.'

'But you did Shakespeare, I dare say?' she asked, intrigued now.

'Oh yes. We did a *Hamlet* once that came to London.'

Paul said, 'I see you as Horatio, Phil. Or maybe Laertes?'

Evenlode smiled shyly. 'You will find this hard to believe, but I – well, I played the Prince himself.'

This disclosure surprised even Towne, who harrumphed indignantly. 'You never told us that. Hamlet, indeed! Though come to think of it, you do look rather like a student.'

'The production received little notice, apart from the lady who played Ophelia – you recall Susan Liddell?'

'Of course. She was rather well known in her day,' said Maggie. 'Susan Liddell as Ophelia . . . I wonder what happened to her?'

'*Drowned, drowned*, alas,' said Towne facetiously.

'I think Mrs Liddell just disappeared,' said Evenlode, adding quietly, 'It's a devilish hard business to live by.' There was a personal implication here that was impossible to ignore, though when Maggie made to pursue the matter a warning look from Paul silenced her.

'Talking of drowned,' said Hackett, 'I happened to be on the Embankment last week when they dragged out that poor woman from the river.'

'I read the report,' said Paul. 'There was some doubt as to whether . . .'

'Suicide? It was. Column about it in the *Illustrated News* – she had sewn a number of stones into her coat. D'you know, I don't think I'll ever forget the sight of her dreadful whey face as she came out of the water . . .' Hackett shuddered, and Maggie patted his hand in sympathy.

'Why always the river?' Towne said, shaking his head. 'I mean to say, if I was going to end it all I'd do it in my own home, with a quick draught of Prussic acid or a pistol to my head.'

'You presume too much,' murmured Maggie. 'If she was an unfortunate, as seems likely, she may not have had a home.'

Evenlode nodded at that. '*The bleak wind of March made her tremble and shiver/ But not the dark arch or the black flowing river/ Mad to life's history, glad to death's mystery, Swift to be hurl'd/ Anywhere, anywhere, out of the world.*'

They were all silent for a moment as the words sank in. Maggie was impressed, not just by the spontaneity of Evenlode's brief recital but by the feeling in his voice. She knew the Hood poem from schooldays – everyone did – but it seemed she had never properly felt the tug of those lines before, or the strange rhythm they made. The moment was interrupted by a knock at the door and Emma the maid entered carrying a platter of sandwiches and cold cuts.

Towne gave an appreciative sigh. Maggie always made sure there was supper ready when these three came; she imagined that for at least one of them it was the only decent meal he could depend on all week. She watched him out of the corner of her eye. Evenlode ate quickly, furtively, like a squirrel, as if he feared that the dainties in front of him might be suddenly snatched away.

By silent agreement the subject of the drowned woman was dropped. Instead the talk alighted on the matter of sales and galleries. It was known to some in their circle that Paul had been taken up by the Colbert, though he hesitated to mention it himself this evening lest it cause awkwardness among the company. Towne, he knew, struggled to be generous about others' work while the public remained indifferent to his own. Hackett, a more easygoing character, would be pleased for Paul's success, but his tendency to ask about the precise details of fees and commissions would most likely infuriate Towne and bore the others. It was better to keep mum about the whole business.

Towne was holding forth about a recent exhibition of portraits at the Grosvenor. 'One can't help noticing how very conventional this country's portrait painters are. There is technical accomplishment in abundance, and no doubt the ladies and gentlemen whose likenesses they capture are flattered to see themselves on display. But oh, how stiffly they are posed, and how dreary they all look. Not a speck of animation in 'em!'

Other well-known names of the genre were offered around, which Towne dismissed one by one. It was a kind of parlour game among them, to name an artist who might be spared the rod of his schoolmasterly disdain. Hackett at one point seemed to have found such an exception.

'Come come, Towne, I heard you praise that fellow Sargent the other day as a "superior society painter" – I remember it distinctly.'

'He's done a few satisfactory things,' he replied airily, 'but scarcely of the first order. And of course he's burdened with the temperamental flaw of all Americans.'

'What's that?'

'Vulgarity.'

Maggie gave a half-laugh. 'You are a hard man to please, Mr Towne. Is there any portrait painter in, say, the last hundred years you would approve?'

Towne nibbled at an olive, considering. 'If we are to go that far back I'd say Reynolds, for one. Romney also. Oh, and Merrymount I think we can call a master. They belong to the last great age of British painting.'

'To Merrymount I would heartily assent,' she replied. 'As a matter of fact, he and his family have been on my mind of late.'

'Oh?'

She told him about happening upon the portrait of the young man at Holborn, and about Edgar Talmash's speculations on its provenance.

Paul said, 'Maggie was so keen she competed for it with Talmash when it came to auction. Tell him how much it went for, Maggs.'

She did so.

'Good Lord,' Towne exclaimed, his interest plainly piqued. 'Even if it was by the daughter that's an extraordinary sum. And Talmash paid it?'

'No, to his chagrin. He got into a bidding contest with someone – another dealer, I supposed – and in the end he backed down.'

Towne was stroking his beard pensively. 'I have a friend who's quite the authority on Merrymount. I imagine this little conundrum might be just up his street. You've no idea who bought it?'

Maggie shook her head. 'And I don't suppose we ever will.'

*

The company broke up just before eleven o'clock. Hackett and Towne went off together, shortly followed by Philip Evenlode, who had grown quieter as the evening drew on. When Maggie was seeing him out he lingered in the hallway a moment, apparently struck anew by his surroundings.

'Is something the matter?' she asked him.

'Oh no. I was just thinking what a lovely house this is. It seems to me so ... cheerful.'

Maggie laughed, covering her surprise. If that was the impression created it was Paul's influence, not hers. 'Whereabouts do you live, Mr Evenlode?'

'Just off the Tottenham Court Road.'

'So you'll get an omnibus?'

'No, I'll be walking.'

'But it's rather late, isn't it?'

'It's no trouble. And I like to walk.' He flashed a quick smile. 'Thank you so much for your hospitality, Miss Stransom. I always enjoy seeing – being here.' He put on his hat (worn, like everything else) and made a bow before walking smartly down the path and into the night.

On returning to the living room she began clearing up the dishes. Paul, who had lit another pipe, said, 'Don't bother with that now. Emma will clear it in the morning. You go to bed.'

As she was dousing candles on the chimney-piece she mused aloud: 'Mr Evenlode's a peculiar creature, isn't he?'

'Hmm. That hair of his ...'

'Do you think he cuts it himself?'

'I don't suppose he can afford a barber's.'

'His clothes are so ... I was half-afraid that coat of his would fall apart as he put it on just now. Is he terribly poor?'

'I fear so. He does some tutoring in the evening. Makes a pittance from occasional pieces in the reviews.'

'He spoke that bit from "The Bridge of Sighs" so nicely.'

'Yes, you can tell he was an actor once. The voice has music in it. I should like to have seen him as Hamlet – or anyone else, come to that.'

Maggie paused, remembering it, and an idea abruptly sparked in her head. 'I wonder if Mr Evenlode might be persuaded to exercise his talent for recital at the school?'

'How so?' Paul asked.

'Well, I was telling you how little enthusiasm the girls have for Shakespeare. Perhaps they might respond differently if a professional player were declaiming the verse. He could be the very man to bring it alive for them.'

Paul looked at her. 'His appearance might be alarming to the girls.'

Maggie shrugged. 'I'm sure he could be made to look perfectly respectable if it were necessary.'

His expression remained dubious. 'Even if your headmistress agrees, Philip may not care to perform for schoolchildren. You know how proud actors can be.'

'But he's not an actor any more. And I could arrange remuneration. He looks like he might be grateful for a few shillings. He couldn't even afford to take the omnibus home.'

Even as she spoke she felt the prospect going cold. Evenlode might be embarrassed by the request; she didn't know him well enough to tell. 'It was an idle thought,' she said after a moment, offhandedly, before bidding her brother goodnight.

And yet when she awoke next morning the brightness of her idea sprang back undiminished. She could see no harm in petitioning Evenlode, who in all likelihood would be pleased to help. She was also faintly thrilled by her own initiative. Instead of spooning out the required measures of Shakespeare, like medicine, she had hit upon an alternative method of engagement, and one she felt sure that Miss Dowie – no stick-in-the-mud, whatever her other faults – would approve. Before she could persuade herself against it she went to her bureau and wrote him a brief letter, setting out her plan. She didn't butter it with blandishments. But she did admit that it was his feeling quotation of the Hood which had inspired the idea. From her shelf she took down a volume of verse and turned to the poem. When she came to the lines

> *In she plunged boldly—*
> *No matter how coldly*
> *The rough river ran—*
> *Over the brink of it,*
> *Picture it – think of it,*
> *Dissolute Man!*
> *Lave in it, drink of it,*
> *Then, if you can!*
> *Take her up tenderly,*
> *Lift her with care;*
> *Fashion'd so slenderly,*
> *Young, and so fair!*

she had a sharp memory of first reading it as a schoolgirl and her eyes brimming with tears as she saw, almost heard, the doomed woman being lifted from the river. *Take her up tenderly* ... The poet wrote as if he had witnessed the mournful sight himself. Perhaps he had. She went up to Paul's painting-room, where she found him gathering his materials together for the day.

'Do you know this?' she asked, handing him the volume open at the page.

He put on his spectacles and read for a few moments. 'From years ago, yes.'

'I've written to Mr Evenlode, in any case. He can always refuse.'

'He might not,' Paul conceded.

'Do you have his address?'

'No, but I can get it from Towne if you like.'

After he had left the house Maggie went back to the bureau and wrote a letter to Ada at Haslemere; with summer approaching it was time to arrange her sister's annual visit to St Leonard's Terrace with her children, Maggie's beloved young nieces Isobel and Gwen. There had been a suggestion this year – unprecedented – of Ada's husband Bernard joining the party, but it now seemed that work would prevent him. Maggie privately rejoiced at this: Bernard was pleasant, and dreary, and would always get in the way of the free-flowing talk that made the family fortnight so convivial. She also hated the name Bernard.

She posted the letter on the King's Road, where she caught an omnibus in the direction of Camden. Her first two appointments of the morning were with older classes – the poetry of Tennyson and Matthew Arnold, followed by the Wars of the Roses, which was more of a challenge. Whenever the girls asked a question on which she was hazy she would often divert them with a saving extract from Shakespeare's *Henry* plays. As long as she had them to quote from she felt confident, and the class didn't seem to mind their history lesson being enlivened by poetry.

At lunchtime she sat under the large sycamore in the staff garden, sharing her sandwiches with Lucy Gray, a garrulous and good-hearted colleague a few years older than Maggie. She was the only teacher there who had become a friend. Lucy lived in one of the genteel pockets of Highbury with her parents and her three younger sisters. Their father had been an army surgeon in India and had brought back the family ten years ago, possibly in the hope of settling his daughters in matrimony. So far none of them had obliged him.

Maggie was discussing her plan to invite Evenlode to the Shakespeare class. 'He used to be on the stage and has this won-derful melodic voice.'

'What does he do now?'

'Paul said he does a little teaching.' She paused before adding, 'He's awfully nice.'

'Oh ... and handsome?'

'Not really,' Maggie replied, with a little wince. 'He's odd-looking. His clothes have seen better days. He's not ... well off.'

Lucy sighed. 'Pity. I'd prefer money *and* looks, but would accept one or the other. Having neither – well, I'm sorry.' It was as if she were establishing a particular principle the world should know about her availability.

Maggie smiled. 'I don't imagine Mr Evenlode has ever considered the possibility of marriage. He can barely keep himself alive, let alone a wife.'

Marriage made a frequent topic between them. Lucy was forthright in calculating a man's eligibility, and once she twigged that this amused her friend she exaggerated her pragmatism for effect. Maggie was more circumspect in weighing the odds. The obligation of looking after her mother and Paul had narrowed her acquaintanceship along with her horizons. When she was twenty-one she had confessed to her diary, 'I think no man will ever ask for my hand in marriage'. She had written it lightly, in the hope of contradiction. But seven years later no man had.

The sandwiches finished, Maggie had a quick look over her shoulder before taking out a cigarette and lighting it. Lucy's expression was frozen with alarm.

'Maggie!' she hissed. 'If Dowie catches you with that you're for it.'

Maggie took a nonchalant drag and exhaled. 'There's no one about. And besides, I'm rather weary of her reprimands: she should understand we're her employees, not her pupils.'

Lucy raised her eyebrows, unaccustomed to this bold talk. 'On your head ...'

Maggie took out the packet again and offered it to her. Lucy reared back as though it were a tarantula, and Maggie laughed.

Above them the leaves shivered, stirred by a breeze. It had been a warm May so far.

'Talking of theatre,' Lucy continued, 'we went to the new Garrick last Friday.'

'What did you see?'

'Oh, a Pinero. *The Profligate*. Rather good, as a matter of fact. About a woman who marries without knowing her husband's disreputable past. Father didn't care for it – no surprise there – but Mother and the girls were much taken with it. You should go.'

She would ask Paul, perhaps, though he was less keen on the theatre these days. He and his friends preferred the rowdiness of the music hall. She had gone with him a few times, to the Bedford, the Oxford, the Old Mo on Drury Lane, and while she could see their attraction as places of 'atmosphere', she found the entertainment trivial. She didn't mind coarseness, but she despised silliness. She recalled a conversation about it with Brigstock, who was a devotee of the halls and often took his sketchbook there. He said that there was no better place to study the character of the London people. But then Brigstock had queer ideas about all sorts of things.

From somewhere inside the school building a bell came sharp and clear, calling them back to business. Maggie squashed the tip of her cigarette and placed it in the packet; no point in leaving evidence. She and Lucy ambled back into the hall, parting amid the bustle of girls on the staircase.

Outside the heavy oak door of Miss Dowie's study she paused a moment to neaten herself. On her knock a voice within said 'Enter'. The college headmistress was a short, stout woman who by force of personality gave the impression of towering over people considerably taller than her. She had an owlish aspect not unlike that of the Queen, whose dark funereal dress and white silk cap she also favoured. Maggie, having started out rather terrified in her presence, had learned that the best way of dealing with such a martinet was to show no fear; in certain cases strength only respected strength.

'Miss Stransom, you wished to see me?' She invited Maggie to take a seat.

'Thank you, yes – I should like to make a proposal regarding the fifth-year Shakespeare class.' She outlined her plan, enthusing over Philip Evenlode's achievements as a repertory actor, slightly vaguer on his current status as a 'tutor'. Miss Dowie listened, her rapid blink and pursed mouth giving no indication as to whether she approved the idea or not. Maggie's voice slowly tailed away into silence, and she waited.

'We have received guest speakers at the college, before your time I believe – Sir Henry Masters, the archaeologist, and Mr Geoffrey Unwin, the famous engineer, were the most recent. Their lectures were most edifying, and our students greatly enjoyed their respective discourses.' *Archaeology and engineering*, thought Maggie, *I can just imagine* ... 'We have had representatives from the arts, too,' Miss Dowie continued, 'though never from the theatrical profession. I am not certain the governors of the school would acknowledge it as quite respectable.'

'Oh, I don't think that Mr Evenlode is the sort to frighten the horses. Or even the governors.'

Miss Dowie's gaze sharpened at this pertness. Maggie held her breath, and the moment passed. 'Well, if Shakespeare's poetry can be enhanced by public recital so much the better. Perhaps you could ask this gentleman when it might suit him to visit us.'

Aware that an exceptional favour had been bestowed, Maggie thanked her with particular warmth and was rising to leave when the headmistress said, 'One moment, Miss Stransom. Pray be seated.' Her voice was of a sudden more admonitory. 'As I'm sure you are aware, I hold that the conduct of my staff should be beyond reproach. The students look to us not merely for education but for moral example. Should they happen to witness a teacher of mine *smoking in public*, that example would be most grievously undermined. I would have no scruple in dismissing the offender without notice.' Her eyes flashed with queenly displeasure. 'Do I make myself understood?'

Maggie, her fighting talk of earlier forgotten, boiled with shame. She confirmed to Miss Dowie that her message had been understood perfectly.

IV

Paul had felt unsteady from the laudanum, but the walk to Kensington Gardens cleared his head. He had been taking tiny doses of it to ease the shooting pains in his back, an occasional evil of his spinal condition. The late May morning had brought a freshening breeze, and feathery clouds shimmered in cavalcades across the horizon. In the park he had placed canvas and stool about a hundred yards from his latest study, a conspiratorial huddle of lime trees; he hunkered there like a woodland creature beneath a vast and gloomy oak. It was a vantage that made him all but invisible to passing promenaders.

The mother and her daughters had appeared earlier than usual this morning. He had seen them most days, their figures had become familiar to him, though he was always too distant to make out their faces. They were dressed, as ever, in white or cream summer dresses, the mother sometimes carrying a parasol, the girls playing a game of catch. Today there was a man with them – the father, he presumed – straight-backed like his wife, and bespectacled. Perhaps it had been his idea to bring a cricket bat and ball: he chose a sapling as a target to bowl at, while the girls took turns to bat. The mother stood some yards behind, the responsible wicketkeeper. Their shouts and chatter sometimes reached Paul's ears, and he would gaze at them for a while before returning to his canvas.

It was getting on for midday. His latest preoccupation was a nightshade-green pigment he had happened upon by accident; he was trying it out as a background when a sudden flurry of footsteps and giggles broke in on his solitude. A young man and his lady had ducked from the main path to canoodle in the shade of the oak tree, her laughing objections mingling with his low-voiced advances. They were both quite unaware of Paul's presence mere yards away, so thoroughly was he camouflaged. It was embarrassing, of course, for it placed him in the invidious role of eavesdropper, and however reluctant he might be to listen he couldn't help catching the back-and-forth of the couple's sweet nothings. He realised he ought to have coughed or something to warn them that they were not alone, but the moment had passed.

As they continued spooning, Paul idly wondered at the chasm between love scenes familiar from the stage or from a novel, and the love scene presently playing out in earshot. The former, of course, were the stuff of artifice, a writer's contrivance, and thank heaven for it, he thought, because if this real-life scene were to be set down *verbatim* no playgoer, no reader, could endure it. The excruciating triviality of the couple's flirtatious chatter could not have been of interest to anyone but themselves, and from the man's increasing impatience it seemed even he was slightly tiring of it. And yet their complete delight in one another's company seemed undeniable: it *was* a love scene, however banal, and Paul felt a prickling melancholy that he had never been a recipient of such intimacies himself.

The talk had come abruptly to a halt. The woman's voice had dropped to an undertone, advising her companion: they had a listener. He heard the man click his tongue in irritation and mutter something, then a shuffling of feet as they moved off. Paul felt a flash of shame, though he knew himself blameless. Their laughter in the distance was carefree, touched with scorn.

Paul, staring out at the trees, took off his spectacles to clean. He would be twenty-six tomorrow. Twenty-six years was a long time to live, he thought, without a woman's love. Most days he didn't think about it, he was too preoccupied with his work. He didn't have time for romance, even if such a thing were to offer, which it never had. But then he would without warning be ambushed by an ache of longing, triggered by a glove rolled off a woman's wrist, or a dark tendril of hair against a pale neck. The things you wanted – needed – you could choose to ignore or not. What you couldn't do was hide from them.

And what of Maggie? He could not think of his own deprivation without also lamenting hers. She was outwardly more passionate, certainly more gregarious than he. She enjoyed the company of men and yet seemed, like so many of her age and sex, unwanted, ignored, surplus to requirements. He had resigned himself to being alone on account of his impediment, but Maggie was an able-bodied, attractive woman who would make someone a true companion if only ... if only she hadn't been tethered during her marriageable years to the care of their mother, and then to the care of him. Fate had been unkind to her, but didn't he bear some responsibility himself? He ought to have put a friend of his in her path, encouraged a courtship ... only most of his friends were unworldly, feckless or mad. The few who had money weren't to be trusted, and the ones without would never be able to afford a wife, a child, a home. His thoughts turned to Evenlode, dear old Phil – there wasn't a gentler fellow in London. Maggie had taken a shine to him, but it was plain she recognised him as a hopeless case.

Ada would be coming to stay with her children at the end of next month. The sight of Maggie swooning and fussing over their nieces slightly discomfited him, for there could be no more obvious reminder of the family she hankered after. She appeared to be lit from within whenever they were in company together. He wondered if Ada too felt the poignancy of this; he suspected not. His older sister's affable unchanging serenity seemed to exclude awareness of the lives going on around her.

He had put his spectacles back on. Some subtle shift in the landscape had occurred since he had been daydreaming, and at first he could not identify what it was. But it came to him now. The couple and their cricket-playing daughters were nowhere to be seen. He had the unaccountable feeling that they hadn't gone so much as vanished.

At breakfast the next morning Emma, having set down their toast and eggs, shyly presented Paul with a parcel wrapped in brown paper. He untied the string to find a sampler, framed under glass, of a house – their house – with *St Leonard's Terrace SW* and Emma's initials stitched beneath.

Paul lifted his gaze from it to the girl, her round face slowly crimsoning with pride and embarrassment. 'Good Lord, Emma, what a lovely thing! Your own handiwork, I see.'

'Yes, sir,' she replied, nodding at Maggie across the table. 'And miss got it framed for me. I mean – for you.'

'Well, I'm very, very pleased to have it.'

Emma smiled. 'Happy birthday, sir.' She followed with a quick curtsey and left the room. Maggie watched him examining it. She could see that he was touched.

'Nice to be popular, isn't it?' she said, buttering her toast.

'She's a sweet girl. I feel ... honoured.'

'You should!' Maggie laughed. 'She's never given *me* anything.'

Paul rose from the table and propped the sampler on the mantelpiece. He stared at it for some moments.

Maggie gave way to a snort of reproach. 'It strikes me you're more taken with that than you are with my present.' She had already given him the small oil of Oxfordshire she bought at auction.

Paul shook his head, turning to her. 'No. This thing of Emma's is charming. But that painting is exquisite.'

She pulled a face, warily appeased. When he came back to the table she poured him a fresh cup of tea.

'How's your back today?' she asked.

'A little better, thanks. I took another dose before bed last night.'

Maggie frowned at him. 'You must be careful, dear.'

'I take no more than the doctor has prescribed, Maggs. Though I must confess, the dreams I had last night were more fantastical than ever.'

'You know how dangerous opiates can be.'

He raised a hand, half-acknowledging, half-dismissing her concern. He noticed she had not asked him about the dreams, which he understood. They were of no particular interest to him, so it would be perverse to describe them to somebody else. Although now he came to think of it, there *was* one from last night that had lingered on the edge of his consciousness. He had been passing along a wooded path overlooking a river, somewhere unfamiliar, and happened to see a young woman, dressed in white, at the water's edge. He was walking on when of a sudden he heard cries of distress below. He ran back to see the same woman now up to her neck in the river and shrieking for help. The path on which he stood was far too steep for him to scramble down. Frantic, he looked about for a point of access, but could find none. The woman, meanwhile, had caught sight of him and was desperately calling for him to rescue her. *You there!* she cried. *You there!* Of its ending he had no memory.

They were still at the table ten minutes later when they heard the letter box clack and the postman's footsteps recede down the path. Maggie went into the hall, and returned with a letter for each of them. Hers was from Ada, confirming the dates of their fortnight up in Chelsea ('. . . As I mentioned, Bernard is very sorry not to join us'). Maggie permitted herself a mean little laugh.

Paul looked up. 'I've a letter from Brigstock.'

'Extraordinary handwriting he has – like a woman's.'

'Seems he'd like to invite us for tea.'

'Us?'

'"Please do ask your sister to come along, if she is amenable."'

'Does he say why?'

He skimmed the single page across the table. '*Voilà tout.*'

Maggie read the letter through. 'Well, it's friendly of him.'

'Perhaps he has a new stuffed bird he wants to show us. Remember that puffin on his chimney-piece that night?'

She did remember. Then she considered Brigstock in her mind's eye, tall, languid, an expression of intelligent curiosity perched on the brink of amusement. He had made no secret of liking her.

'Tell him I'd be delighted,' she said, with a nonchalant air.

He dreamed again of the woman in white, and the river. To Paul, who couldn't swim, water always carried a ripple of danger. The woman was about his own age, dark-haired, pretty. Sometimes when he heard her call it sounded like a cry for help; at others it was a greeting. *You there!* This time he followed her into the water, which came up to his knees, then his waist. She was calling him on, insisting he should take another step while he quailed at the rising line of the water, now up to his chest. Something in her voice reassured him that it was safe, that he could keep going, at which moment she disappeared.

The appointed day of Brigstock's invitation came around, a Saturday in the middle of June. The afternoon weather was close, and the pavements dusty. They walked to the Underground at Sloane Square, where began their journey north to the artist's studio. From King's Cross station they passed through streets of tenements and rough ale-houses Maggie hardly knew, though they were not far from the school. The air of dereliction made her wonder why a man of means would care to set up shop here. It was very different from Brigstock's home in Regent's Park. When she mentioned this Paul laughed.

'For a certain kind of painter only outcast London will do.'

They found the address, a gaunt house in Somers Town, and were admitted by a landlady. Brigstock greeted them on the stairs and led them up three flights to a back room that was perhaps formerly a workshop. He was dressed in an open-collared shirt with waistcoat and pale trousers. His feet were bare. Canvases lay stacked in casual disorder, and a large hessian back-cloth had been hung across the far wall. A bulky H-frame easel dominated the room. The sash windows had been thrown open, offering a view on to the railway. A train happened to be rattling by at that minute.

Maggie, standing at the window, said, 'Does the noise bother you?'

'On the contrary,' Brigstock replied, 'I rather like it. Whenever one passes it gives me a jolt and I think, *I must get on!*'

He went off to a little camp stove in the corner where he made them tea. He and Paul chatted about the Grosvenor exhibition while Maggie made a slow circuit of the room, pausing at this or that picture. She stopped to examine a half-finished portrait of an aristocratic young pair, and wondered how far Brigstock's rumoured family money had spared him the necessity of patronage. It was quite hard to place him on the social ladder, so ambiguously did he present himself.

'Seen anything you like?' he said, approaching her now. She only nodded, and looked at him enquiringly.

'You're perhaps wondering why I've invited you,' he said, with a smile. 'If you'll give me one moment . . .'

He went to the heavy easel and turned it about, then left the room, returning with a squarish object wrapped in a loose cloth. Dispensing with that he positioned the picture on the frame, and turned it back around to display to his guests. In the moment before Maggie saw it she realised what it would be – what it could only be – but still couldn't help a startled 'oh' as she faced it. It was the portrait of the young man she had last seen being sold from under the nose of Edgar Talmash at the auction rooms. Paul, though seeing it for the first time, knew its significance immediately.

'I thought – Maggie told me – it had gone to an unknown buyer.'

'The fellow I sent to bid is an agent of mine,' said Brigstock. 'I didn't want to be there in person in case Talmash thought I was trying to get his back up, as the saying goes.'

Paul smiled. 'You must have enjoyed it all the same.'

'I confess I did!' he laughed. 'But having the thing was my principal motive. Poor old Talmash just happened to be in the way.'

'But when we spoke about it at your house you hadn't seen it,' Maggie said, finding her voice at last.

'Indeed. Such was my curiosity I went to Holborn the next day for a look.'

Maggie gazed at the *Young Man* again. Her delight in the picture was only somewhat impaired by a touch of possessiveness. She had entertained a fancy, however brief, of owning it herself. But two hundred guineas ... It cast its owner's private means in an interesting new light. And to think of it being kept here! It was probably worth more than the house in which they were standing.

Paul's thoughts had been running along the same lines, for he now said, 'Do you consider what you paid for it fair?'

Brigstock tilted his head. 'That's deuced hard to say. The picture enchanted me, and fortunately I was in a position to bid for it. Whether I've paid above the odds is for others to judge. But there isn't another like it in the world.'

'Talmash will get to hear of it, of course.'

'Just between us, his feelings don't really concern me. He wanted it only to sell elsewhere.'

The three of them stood before it, lost in contemplation. *It has a spell*, thought Paul – Maggie was right. Does it matter in the end who painted it?

'I wonder ...' Maggie began. 'I wonder if that young fellow had any inkling his portrait would one day be sought after. His clothes don't suggest he was well-to-do. And yet he bears himself with such confidence. That gleam in his eye.'

'Yes, he's quite a jolly dog, isn't he?' said Brigstock. 'When I first clapped eyes on him I thought he might be an actor.'

He took out a case of small cigars and offered it to Paul, before lighting one himself. They talked of other things for a while. Brigstock said he was planning to run down to Eastbourne for a week's painting. He liked to go walking and dine on oysters at one of the big hotels on the front. 'Last year I got the fright of my life there. I was taking a dip in the sea when I came face to face with – what do you suppose? A seal. Big whiskered thing, looming right out of the brine at me!'

Paul laughed. 'Imagine how terrified *it* was. You're rather a big whiskered thing yourself.'

'And you were probably trespassing on its home,' Maggie added.

'In any event, it barged right past me and I lost my stroke. Went under for a moment and swallowed a huge mouthful of sea-water. Ugh!'

He made another pot of tea as the trains sounded below. A cat crept along the window ledge and paused, seeming to listen to their conversation before it lost interest and sloped off. The early-evening sun came slanting through the windows and laid stripes across the Turkey carpet. As they were about to leave Maggie could not resist another look at *Portrait of a Young Man*.

'Where will you hang it – not here?' she asked.

Brigstock looked at her, slightly startled. 'Why not here?'

'I was thinking ... about the neighbourhood,' she said, trying not to sound genteel.

'I agree it's not Chelsea,' he said with a laugh, 'but paintings aren't the sort of thing the criminal classes trade in.'

'All the same, Dab,' said Paul, 'word gets around. There'll always be some cracksman on the lookout.'

'I'll have it insured, of course. Maybe put a new lock on the door.' His expression had become pensive, as if the safeguarding of his new acquisition had only just occurred to him. 'Or I might take it to Albany Street and hang it in the card room. Give the card-players something to stare at.'

On their way back to the railway station Paul and Maggie discussed the painting, and Brigstock, and money. It was Paul's view that their friend enjoyed his possession of the *Portrait* more than he admired the thing itself. He deduced this from the way Maggie's question as to where he might hang it had disconcerted him. For some it was enough merely to own a thing.

'Oh, I don't know,' she said. 'I think Brigstock has the soul to appreciate it.'

'At least we'll have the pleasure of seeing it again. He's a good fellow, Dab. And he likes *you* an awful lot.'

Maggie wondered if this judgement had been revised since that strange remark he had made about Brigstock not being 'a gentleman'. It was true that he treated her with something more than common friendliness; her boldly expressed opinions seemed to delight him.

She said, 'I enjoyed his story about the seal. It was like something from *Punch*, only much funnier.'

'Hmm, I've heard quite a lot of his stories before, but that one was new. By the way, what would you say to a week on the coast? All his talk about promenades and oysters has put me in the mood.'

She smiled, and on the train back to Chelsea they talked about where they might like to go.

The park was dressed in its finest summer attire, and the elms, which had looked tentative and wary in the spring, now opened out gloriously like a peacock showing its feathers. Their leaves were rich and glossy, and the sound they made within the vaulted green cathedral was sibilant, almost urgent, with meaning. What were they insinuating? Paul listened, sensing there was a particular message for him.

For the last few days he had not seen the mother and her daughters. The father he had seen but the once, playing cricket. Paul wandered around Kensington Gardens hoping to spot them. Of course they may have left London for the summer, or had simply chosen a different park to visit – not everyone was as loyal to the place as he. But an intuition told him otherwise: they had not come because they could not. Something had prevented them, and whenever he happened to ponder their disappearance a melancholy weighed on him. But following an absence of three weeks or more, he caught sight of them – or rather, of her, for she was without the girls. Dressed as ever in white, she was walking on the outer perimeter close to the Palace. Her head was bowed. He left his canvas on the stool and made for the path himself. The crowds were out – it was the middle of a sultry afternoon – and as he quickened his pace he began to pant. At one moment he was close enough to call out to her, but what on earth would he say?

The distance between them lengthened. His dragging gait was not equal to the pursuit, and sweat was beading his forehead. He stopped, and her figure was lost among the other promenaders. He returned to his spot and sat down, but he didn't pick up a brush or look at his canvas; for a long time he simply stared out at the trees, thinking. A connection had taken root in his mind between the mother who visited the park and the woman whose watery fate had in some muddled way become his responsibility. It didn't make sense (dreams seldom did) but it persisted, and it disquieted him.

V

Maggie stepped off the 'bus halfway up Tottenham Court Road and turned westwards into the maze of streets. It was the morning she had arranged to introduce Philip Evenlode at the College. Only after securing his agreement to attend did she give way to anxieties about her guest. She had not seen him since the Sunday evening at St Leonard's Terrace, and her memory of his eccentric appearance returned to trouble her. The pale, starved face and the threadbare clothes could not help but excite pity; the wild, stand-up hair was more likely to provoke derision. What had she been thinking of, subjecting the poor man to the scrutiny of daughters of the professional classes, who had known only convention and respectability?

On reaching Cleveland Street she found the number of the lodging-house where he resided, a grimy terrace with clouded windows, though no worse than any of its neighbours. Paul had it from Towne that Evenlode occupied a single room at the back of the building. Maggie knocked and waited, trying to compose herself on the step. Moments later the door swung open and Evenlode stood there with a hopeful smile.

'Miss Stransom,' he said with a little bow, and closed the door behind him. Evidently Maggie was not to be granted a glimpse of his lodgings. 'Since we are in good time I thought we might stop for breakfast on the way?'

Maggie allowed him to lead on. His aspect was changed since they'd last met; his apparel was old but less dowdy, and she noticed just before he donned his hat that the spiked hair had been plastered down close to his head. This small attempt at grooming touched her. As they passed up the street she noticed that the forbidding edifice on the right was a workhouse, and wondered if Evenlode's sense of irony had inclined him to take rooms so close. The morning was bright and warm. As they crossed the Euston Road he seemed to her more at ease than he had been at their house, throwing out light-hearted remarks about his own schooldays and enquiring as to Maggie's association with the College.

'Did you always want to be a teacher?' he asked.

'Heavens, no. I had an idea that – oh, well, it doesn't matter.'

'No, please tell me. I gather you had a place at Cambridge . . .'

'I was unable to take it. I suppose my original fancy was to study art and then compile a great tome like Vasari's.' She laughed at the thought.

Evenlode looked at her seriously. 'That strikes me as a noble ambition. We all should have one.'

'And you, Mr Evenlode?'

He looked down, gave a helpless half-laugh. 'I fear the limit of my ambition is to keep body and soul together.'

Maggie, aware of the need to step cautiously, said after a moment, 'Given your early success, did you not wish to pursue the acting life?'

His expression crinkled with regret. 'I wanted to. Alas, I . . . could not.'

His reluctance to say more only piqued her curiosity. What misfortune had disrupted his career? They were walking past Euston railway station when he stopped and said, 'Ah, there's the fellow.' He indicated a coffee-stall, where a handful of workmen were at present grouped. Hot potatoes and saveloys were chalked up on the bill of fare. Steam wafted from its counter. This was not the sort of breakfast Maggie had anticipated, but on seeing how his enthusiasm rose at the sight she made no comment.

They both had coffee, and Evenlode ate a slice of bread and butter with the same furtive alacrity she had observed in him at the house. She had an awful intuition that this would be his only sustenance for the rest of the day, and she encouraged him to have another slice, which after a momentary hesitation he did. As they sipped their coffee she briefly went over her plan for the Shakespeare class. Would he mind if Miss Dowie were present for his recital?

'Not at all! I'm most eager to meet the lady. I only hope she will live up to the mythological grandeur of your description.'

His tone was humorous, and Maggie worried now that he might twit the headmistress for the sake of pleasing her. 'Oh, she's really not so terrible as I've . . . She will regard your visit as a great favour.'

He had finished eating. They were ready to leave when he saw Maggie taking out her purse to pay.

'Ah, Miss Stransom, you must allow me—'

She held up an admonitory hand. 'I have dragged you out for the morning, so I must at least be allowed to pay for our breakfast.'

He looked rather unhappy at this. 'But if I'd known I should never have taken another piece of bread . . .'

She waved this off and handed over the coins to the stall-holder. 'There!' she said, turning to her companion with a smile and a flourish. They continued on their way up Seymour Street. His pathetic air of gratitude for the breakfast reminded her again that even small expenditures were a drain on him. *How dreadful it is to be poor*, she thought.

Inside the College she led him towards the Headmistress's office. The girls swarmed about them along the corridors and on the stairs, passing an occasional glance at the stranger. Young men were not a common sight in these precincts unless they were janitors or delivery boys. Evenlode showed no consciousness of being out of place;

when she turned a reassuring look on him he acknowledged it with a bemused smile.

'Not your usual element, of course,' Miss Dowie said to him on shaking hands, 'but I trust you will find our students an attentive audience.'

As she spoke Maggie observed the headmistress conduct a hawkish inventory of their guest. Her matriarchal sense of propriety never seemed to flag: to her an ill-sewn button would be considered improper, and an unstarched collar deviant. But perhaps his being a member of the acting profession would excuse him.

'I count it an honour to be received here, Miss Dowie. Thank you for the invitation.' It was charmingly said, and Maggie breathed a secret sigh of relief. Evenlode's garb might be found wanting, but his manners never would.

Miss Dowie took the compliment in the same way she took obeisance – as a due, to be quickly ignored. 'Miss Stransom tells me of your distinguished career on the stage' – only Maggie heard the tiny choked laugh at the back of Evenlode's throat – 'though for myself I seldom find the time to visit the theatre. You are engaged with a company, I suppose?'

'Not at present,' he replied. 'I have recently taken time away to finish writing a new history of Roman comedy, with particular reference to the plays of Terence and Plautus.'

Miss Dowie blinked at that. 'I see. I had no idea you were ... a Latinist.' She sounded, despite herself, impressed. 'You have Greek as well?'

With a modest inclination of his head he confirmed this. It transpired that he had also acted in several productions of Aristophanes, including *The Wasps* and *The Frogs*, 'in the original, of course'. Miss Dowie's eyes actually widened at that; here was accomplishment. She consulted her watch.

'Well, we should delay no longer. The students must have the advantage of your erudition, Mr Evenlode. Miss Stransom, will you take our guest to the hall? The girls are already assembled there, I believe.'

On their way down to the hall Maggie confessed that *she* hadn't known he was a classical scholar, either. 'Are you really writing a book about Roman comedy?'

He laughed pleasantly. 'Of course I'm not. I just wanted to see the look on her face.'

Maggie giggled. 'But you have Latin?'

'Not much, beyond *veni vidi vici*. And *caveat emptor*.'

'You took a risk there. Dowie can quote Latin till the cows come home.' He laughed again, and she added, 'The funny thing is, I really believed you!'

He smiled mischievously, shaking his head. 'You did? Then perhaps I'm a better actor than I know.'

In the assembly hall a chatter of anticipation fell silent as they entered. On the dais a lectern stood with a volume of collected Shakespeare opened at the ready. The girls, seated in rows, had brought their own copies, though Maggie had been careful to present the occasion as an entertainment rather than a lesson. She felt quite proud as she introduced Evenlode to them, imagining their surprise that *Miss Stransom* should count this bohemian among her acquaintance. She proceeded to describe his early career on the stage and enumerated the various roles he had played, including his 'acclaimed' Hamlet in London. He stood next to her, listening to this glowing overture as if it pertained to someone else entirely. He seemed almost amused by it. Was this nonchalance, she wondered, or had he actually *forgotten* the achievements of his former life?

On finishing she ceded the lectern to him, and he thanked her. He stood, right arm crooked against his hip, and looked out over his audience. His voice was low and velvety as he began, recalling how, as a boy, he had watched his first Shakespeare play 'in a fog of incomprehension', dazed by the language. It fell upon his ears as a mere flurry of 'words, words, words . . .' Indeed, so overwhelmed was he that after a few scenes he sneaked out of the theatre – 'which was remiss of me, given that I was actually a member of the cast'. There was a second's delay before someone laughed, and then the whole class was laughing. From that moment they were in his hands. Like most things worth knowing, he went on, Shakespeare required a little patience before one might uncover his meaning; he described the experience as entering a vast dark hall and stumbling about, helpless, until someone pointed him to a candle, which he lit. Thereupon he began to glimpse in its dim illumination the true wonders of the room, with its magnificent frescoes and beautiful stained-glass windows. He looked up and saw its vaulted ceiling spangled with gold leaf; he looked down and saw the intricate tes- sellated floor on which he stood. And as he stalked around the hall he found other candles, and the tenebrous place that had at first baffled him was now ablaze with light.

'And there followed the marvellous realisation that this was but one room of many! I found a door that led off to other rooms, to tragedy, history, comedy, got up in quite different styles and man- ners. Here was a palace of inexhaustible varieties, a Great Exhibition of the mind, waiting only for my discovery.' At that, Evenlode paused. 'And there, my young friends, is the glory of Shakespeare. As I discovered – and as you will too, I hope – Shakespeare allows us to imagine more fully, and in doing so enables us to live more feelingly.'

Without bothering to consult the text he then recited a sonnet, adding a short explanation before reeling off another, and another. He delivered them so fluently and nimbly that Maggie herself was sometimes at a loss to distinguish the verse from the reciter's poetical interpretations. They had hardly caught their breath when he gave them a suite of speeches, beginning with the 'seven ages of man' from *As You Like It*, followed by Claudio's 'death is a fearful thing' from *Measure for Measure*. He modulated his voice with each selection. When it came to Polonius's counsel to Laertes he slyly impersonated a fussy old man, and for Enobarbus's eulogy of the queen in *Antony and Cleopatra* he roughened his tone to military knock-about. The evident pleasure he took in his recital seemed to cast a spell on the girls, their uptilted faces as absorbed as any theatre audience. When he delivered his last, Maggie stood up and led the applause. Forty-five minutes had passed in a blur. She was preparing to thank Evenlode when Miss Dowie, who had been standing at the far wall, still as a statue in its niche, stepped forward.

'Mr Evenlode, I know it is the custom following a performance of great virtuosity for the audience to demand an "encore". Would it be trespassing on your time to oblige us now?'

Evenlode returned a graceful bow. 'I shall in all my best obey you, madam.' He turned away for a moment, considering, then said, 'Very well. For this finale I will require the assistance of another. Miss Stransom, would you be so kind?'

Maggie, caught unawares, began to demur when Miss Dowie interposed, 'Of course. Miss Stransom, if you please ...' She was not to be given a choice in the matter.

She rose from her seat and stepped on to the dais. Evenlode, smiling at her sudden discomfiture, produced from his pocket an old edition of *Twelfth Night*, which he handed to her, open at the scene of the first meeting between Olivia and Viola, disguised here as the Duke's amorous proxy. Maggie, aware of her inferior skills as a player, nevertheless responded to Evenlode's mischievous bantering, and once she relaxed she found herself almost enjoying her moment in the limelight. When Evenlode, as Viola, addressed her loftily

I see what you are; you are too proud

she wondered if he had chosen the scene specifically with her in mind, but soon dismissed the fancy – the man barely knew her. She had to suppress a laugh when, on being asked about his 'parentage' he followed the line 'Above my fortunes, yet my state is well' with an ironic lift of his brow only she could have seen.

When the scene was done Evenlode took a formal step back

and extended his arm in tribute to Maggie. 'Bravo to you, Miss Stransom!' His gallantry triggered another volley of clapping from the girls. Even Miss Dowie, the presiding Gorgon, seemed to smile.

She took her guest to the staffroom for a recuperative cup of tea. Exhilarated by the success of the morning, she found herself gabbling – his talk had been *so* enlivening, *so* clever! Evenlode laughed off her compliments, and professed amazement that the students should have received him as they did.

'That kind of audience is a rarity,' he said with a smile.

'You bewitched them,' said Maggie, who now couldn't help herself – she had to know. 'Mr Evenlode, may I ask, why did you give up the stage?'

He looked at her sadly for a moment, then stared off. She was about to make apology for prying when he said, 'For a very dismal reason, though it's the truth. I took fright.' Her look of confusion prompted him to go on. 'The affliction is more common than you'd think. I'd been a professional for about fifteen years in a touring company, quite a decent one – that season we'd had a success with *The Ticket-of-Leave Man*. I must have played in it thirty or forty nights when we got to Canterbury. Do you know the Old Theatre Royal? We were booked there for a week. The first night I hadn't been at my best, muffed a few lines, but thought nothing of it. The second ... I was out there and suddenly my throat felt constricted. I simply couldn't get the words out. When I did I kept drying. The others covered for me, and somehow I managed to stumble to the end. It felt like ... like some malign force had taken up residence in my body, denying me the power of speech.'

The crisis came to a head the following night. 'All I can remember is sitting in the dressing-room gripped by – I don't know what. I began to shake, *actually shake*, about an hour before the curtain went up. The manager came in, eventually they called a doctor. I couldn't stop shaking.'

'Did you go on?'

He shook his head. 'Not a chance! Nothing could have induced me to walk out in front of that audience. Fortunately there was an understudy to hand.'

'What happened then?'

He drew a hand slowly across his brow, shielding his eyes. 'I took a temporary leave. I talked to other actors who had suffered the same. One of them suggested I took two large tots of brandy before going on.' He laughed, but sadly. 'Well, he was right about feeling no nerves. But drunk on stage is as bad as tongue-tied. The lines won't come.'

Maggie felt the pathos of his situation. 'Might a doctor have helped you?'

'I consulted a doctor – two of them, in fact. They tried their best. But stage fright is a mystery no doctor I know could unravel.'

'But you must have tried to . . .'

'Go on again? Several times. And on each occasion I was a hopeless, stuttering wreck. It's hard to understand unless one has trod the boards. What once had come quite naturally was of a sudden the most terrifying ordeal you could imagine. It had the quality of a nightmare. When I was at school I was regularly picked on by a master. Hickling was his name. A brute! It didn't really matter what I'd done, he would always find some excuse to beat me. Well . . . one of the recurring visions that harrowed me was the idea of the audience as a single monstrous being, waiting out there in the stalls. Its form was Hickling.'

'But as you said – a thing of nightmares, not something real.'

'You regard it as irrational, I understand. It *is* irrational. We are prey to fears that have no grounding in reality. But they torment us none the less.'

'And you have not acted since?'

'Alas, no. I miss the life, the companionship. I could bewail my fate, but others have borne greater misfortune than I.'

Another bell was ringing. She would soon be required elsewhere. Evenlode saw her glance at the clock on the wall and took up his hat.

'I must allow you to get back to your charges,' he said, rising. 'Thank you for your hospitality, Miss Stransom.'

They shook hands at the entrance and she watched him cross the schoolyard. He cut a waifish figure as he walked. The story of his aborted career had affected her. To lose one's livelihood was bad enough; to have lost it in such traumatic circumstances must be grievous indeed. It would have pleased her to be of help. But what could she do, beyond being a friend to him?

VI

The vigils Paul had been keeping at the park had yielded nothing. The woman and her daughters had not returned. He had taken to carrying a dainty pair of opera glasses on his outings, not trusting his weak eyesight, and every time a female clad in white came into view he discreetly held the glasses to his eyes. He now felt almost certain that she wasn't coming back.

She had not altogether vanished, however, for she continued to haunt his sleeping hours. There, she either stood alone at the edge of a lake, or else was in the water, in difficulty, when she would directly appeal to him, *You there!* On his attempting to save her the dream would dissolve, leaving him in a mood of bewildered futility.

Making his way out of the Gardens one evening he happened to pass one of the park attendants preparing to lock up. Paul was on nodding terms with the man, and now saw his moment to formalise their acquaintance. He hailed him, and the man, recognising him for a regular, lifted his chin in acknowledgement. He was fortyish, swarthy, dressed in a corporation jacket and peaked cap. They fell into conversation about painting, until Paul forced himself to broach the subject uppermost in his mind. He rarely painted people, he explained, though in the last few months he had made an exception – there was a lady, in white, who often came to the park with her young daughters. Had the fellow seen her, perhaps?

'I sees a fair few people most days, sir …' The man smiled uncertainly.

'This family – well, you might have remembered them sometimes playing cricket.'

At that his brow contracted. 'Can't say's I've noticed 'em. But it gets busy here in the summer, like …'

Paul nodded – of course, he quite understood – and seeing the man's confusion he tried to explain. 'I had been painting them, on and off, and meant to make myself known to them. Then they – well, vanished! And I wondered if something … had befallen them.' He made a quick grimace, as if admitting the oddity of this line of thought.

The park-keeper looked at him for a moment. 'Strange sort of fancy, sir, if you don't mind my saying.'

Again Paul nodded, slightly embarrassed. 'I beg your pardon. I dare say I spend too much time alone!'

The man, taking it in good part, said that it was more than likely the lady and her two daughters had simply chosen to visit a different park. 'Though personally I've seen 'em all and I don't believe there's a finer one than this in London.'

'On that we can agree,' Paul said with a laugh that released them both from further intimacy. 'Goodnight to you.'

'Goodnight, sir,' the man said, holding the gate open for him to pass through.

A few evenings later Paul alighted from the 'bus at Islington Green. Crowds swarmed about the streets, on the scout for entertainment. It wasn't a part of town he knew well, but there was the music hall, lit like a jack-o'-lantern, and there the pub that adjoined it, the Lansdowne. The latter was a rowdy sort of place, mirrors on the wall, sawdust on the floor and a close, prickly atmosphere of bonhomie tinged with menace. Ale was carried to the tables in jugs.

'Stransom!'

The voice came from the end of the bar. Richard Melhuish stood there in check suit, high collar, flashy pin and watch-chain over his waistcoat, a cigar clamped in his teeth. Paul sidled through the press to greet him.

He smiled at Melhuish's rakish attire. 'You look like a masher out on the stroll.' They drank half-and-halfs in thick pewter tankards while Melhuish yarned about the evening's bill; it seemed he knew one of the performers. 'I first saw her at the Star in Bermondsey – Miss Rose Daubeny.'

'I don't know the Star,' Paul admitted.

'Oh, I've had some rorty old times down there. One of the toughest halls you've ever seen, but heavens, they know how to enjoy themselves.'

Eagerly surveying the crush of bodies at the bar, Melhuish laughed. 'Look at that snout-nosed blackguard,' he said, a little too loudly in Paul's view: his voice carried uncomfortably, and the 'blackguard' stood close enough to hear.

Melhuish had come by an item of gossip from the art market which he considered of 'toothsome interest'.

'I had it from Edgar Talmash the other day. Told me about a painting he'd bid on at auction – an obscure thing, unsigned, went for two hundred guineas! Talmash didn't know the buyer, so he asked around. Turns out it was none other than Denton Brigstock!'

'Yes, I know.'

'You know – how?'

'As a matter of fact, I saw it at his place, a few weeks ago.'

'*Did* you?' Melhuish reared back in surprise. 'It's a devilish lot of money ... What's the fuss about?'

Paul stared into his beer. 'Well, the main question is one of provenance. Talmash believed it might be the work of Merrymount's daughter, although to my eye it could have been by the man himself. Brigstock admits he probably paid over the odds, but it doesn't bother him.'

'I never knew he was such a man of means,' said Melhuish wonderingly. 'Of course if it *is* a Merrymount he's got himself a bargain. Who's the sitter?'

'Also unknown. A handsome fellow, possibly from the theatre. Towne wants to have a friend of his examine it. So far nobody seems to have a clue.'

Melhuish consulted his pocket-watch and exclaimed. 'Well, drink up, my boy! Mustn't be late for Rosie's turn.'

They edged their way out of the heaving mass of the pub and entered the foyer, walls plastered with playbills. The place was as thronged as the Lansdowne, though its clientele were more socially varied. Gents in opera cloaks rubbed shoulders with mashers and their sweethearts, rough-looking types skulked about the bar while dandified swells sat in the pit ogling the girls. The mingled smell of cigar smoke, greasepaint and peeled oranges was one Paul had never encountered anywhere outside the halls.

At the pay box Melhuish said, 'Fourpence in the gallery or a shilling in the pit?' Paul chose the gallery – he always preferred the shadows – and they ascended the stairs. The front benches were already occupied by those who had paid 'early doors', but Melhuish found them a spot round the side of a fluted column. Opposite them rapt and glimmering faces peered through the rails, waiting for the next round of entertainers. The fish-tail gas jets flickered in their cages of wire. It was a pictorial scene Paul sometimes wished he could paint – the plaster cupids, the curving balconies, the gilded cornices, the flames of the footlights – but he knew it was not his métier; that he could not do it so well as others did.

Brigstock, for instance.

The bell rang as they were taking their seats. A stocky Master of Ceremonies in bold checks and billycock hat strode on to the stage to announce the second half of the evening. There would be serio-comic singers and jugglers and dancers and comedians, 'a veritable *cornucopia* of first-class h'artistes'. Most pleasing to the audience were the sentimental ballads of cheeky costers and mournful milkmen, relating how some terrible stroke of fate had undone them. Following one lachrymose performance ('The Lost Daughter'), Melhuish remarked in a sly undertone, 'Not a dry seat in the house after that, I'll wager.' Yet if the singer hit a wrong note, or outstayed his welcome, the mood could turn and whistles and jeers would rain down. Like the pub next door it housed a volatile crowd, and Paul sensed it would take courage to face them.

As the MC struck his gavel and announced the star turn of the evening, Melhuish gave Paul a nudge. The shouts and screams of laughter suddenly died away. 'Lediz 'n' gennumen, a hand if you please for the "Muse of the Halls" 'erself – Miss Rose Daubeny!' The orchestra struck up its jaunty overture and on to the stage strolled a young guardsman, with buttons flashing on his tunic and a scarlet stripe down his black britches. It quickly became apparent that he was a *she*, very cleverly got up.

'Evenin' all,' she said with a smile. 'Sorry I'm late, I got blocked in the Strand.' A ripple of laughter greeted that, and she proceeded with some roguish patter about her recent escapades 'down the 'Dilly'. When she came to sing, the audience seemed to let out a collective sigh, so warm and sweet was her voice. Then she went back into character as the fly young soldier on the prowl.

The effect was confounding. In the shimmer of the footlights you could see the soft cheeks and carmined lips were clearly a woman's, yet in the perfection of her swagger and the light tenor of her talk she could easily have passed for a slightly effeminate young man. Paul was transfixed. Miss Daubeny's absolute command of the stage seemed to hypnotise the spectators, loud and hot as they were. Her last number, 'Bloomsbury Square', which she dedicated to 'my dear departed pal George Leybourne', concerned the rescue of a lady who finds herself unable to pay an irate cabman. The rescuer not only pays the fare but lends her money for a dress –

Bloomsbury Square! Bloomsbury Square!
Seldom I'd met with a darling so fair
Lovely brown hair! Right down to there!
And the angel she hung out in Bloomsbury Square!

– only to discover that the 'angel' is actually a swindler and her fine address a fake. The applause at her final bow was thunderous. The crowd begged for an encore. Paul very much hoped she would oblige them, but it soon transpired she was done for the night as the next act came on.

He turned to Melhuish. 'Well, that was . . .'

'I know. Quite a stunner, ain't she?' He searched Paul's face for a moment, and laughed. 'Well, since you're so beguiled p'raps we should pay the blooming Rose our respects.'

They watched the remainder of the bill, though they seemed to Paul distinctly second-rate after Miss Daubeny's turn. He fidgeted in his seat – the hall had become unbearably close – and hoped that an interval might come soon. He had taken a tot of laudanum before leaving the house and could feel his limbs growing heavier by the minute.

'Are you all right, dear boy?' Melhuish was staring at him in concern.

Paul admitted he was feeling queer, at which his companion suggested they should take the air. He led Paul out of the gallery and down the stairs, shouldering him through the crowds in the foyer. Outside, the night was warm but a faint breeze brought some relief, and he found his legs again. A brougham had just pulled up and decanted a party of revellers on to the pavement; they swept into the hall's entrance on a wave of shouts and laughter.

Melhuish had lit a cigarette while he waited for 'the patient' to collect himself. Once satisfied, he showed Paul down a narrow cobbled alley between the pub and the hall. Shadowy figures skulked about, and a reek of stale beer and urine pinched the air.

A single lamp at the end of the alley illumined an old door, on which Melhuish gave a peremptory rap with his cane. His knock was answered by a youth who, after a muttered converse, admitted them. Inside they walked down an unlit passageway ('Careful here!') and up clanging iron stairs, thence down another, brighter corridor, where they encountered a couple of the 'h'artistes' they had seen on stage, now on their way off home. Denuded of costume and make-up they looked rather shrunken.

They had passed a row of identical doors when, at the very last one, Melhuish stopped abruptly, turned and winked at Paul. He tapped twice – Paul now saw a small handwritten card in the slot, *Miss Rose Daubeny* – and pushed it open. For some reason he had expected others to be in the room, another performer, or a manager, or a well-wisher, but in fact there was nobody. Nobody but the woman herself, 'the Muse of the Halls', seated at a small table in front of a looking-glass.

'My dear,' cried Melhuish, 'pardon this liberty – only I was most eager to congratulate you, *and* to introduce a friend of mine.'

Miss Daubeny rose from her chair and, smiling, extended her hand, first to Melhuish, then to Paul, with a tiny dip of her head.

'Mr Stransom. How d'ye do?' Her gaze was so frank and direct that Paul could not hold it for long. Her eyes were of a remarkable olive green, in a heart-shaped face. 'Mind if I take off this paint while we talk?'

She gestured to a little sofa, which Paul sat upon. Melhuish, more forward, slouched against the table next to her. 'Shall we order drinks?' he said.

'I asked them to send up a bottle of hock but it looks like they forgot,' she replied, eyeing Paul in the glass. She began to smear her face with cream, and then applied a cloth. Beneath the grease and powder her skin came up very white. Up close she was older than Paul had first judged, possibly thirty, or more.

'My young friend here took a "turn" of his own just now. I think the excitement got to him.'

'But you're recovered?' she said, with concern.

Paul waved away the question. 'I was much taken by your performance, Miss Daubeny.'

'Ah, call me Rose, dear. My, that was a lively house tonight. All that stampin' and shoutin' – like a Christmas panto!'

Her voice, whose cockney inflections she had exaggerated on stage, had a country burr to it, though Paul didn't know from where. He found it difficult to drag his gaze from her.

'So Richard tells me you're a painter like him?' she said.

'Not really like me,' Melhuish interposed. 'Stransom is a master of miniatures – tiny little paintings of trees in parks. My work is more, ah, panoramic.'

Paul, beaten to a reply, offered a quick hapless expression to Rose, who smiled at him in a kind of sympathy. Richard, grasping the conversational reins, was hurrying on about his forthcoming show in St James's, the fruits of his spring sojourn on the Normandy coast. He was in no doubt as to its quality. Rose, listening distractedly as she removed the last vestiges of her stage-paint, was evidently as used to his blithe self-regard as Paul.

'Well, you must send me an invitation, dear,' she said kindly, once Melhuish had paused for breath. The hair she had tied up and hidden beneath her guardsman's cap was now let down (*Right down to there!*) in a dark swag of soft reddish-brown. She had nipped behind her Chinese screen to divest herself of the uniform, reappearing in a summery dress with pearl buttons all down the front. While Paul admired the transformation, he sensed something lost – a lightness, an impudence – on the shedding of her disguise. They talked on for a while, the promised hock from downstairs having arrived, until Rose glanced at her watch.

'I'll have to turn in for the night, gents. I'm pooped.'

They escorted her through the dusty stage door and the cobbled alley by which they'd come. Outside the Collins's tight clusters of people loitered about, smoking, talking; one or two of them nodded at Rose as she passed. Paul assumed that they would hail a cab for her, but in fact she made a beeline for a brougham waiting opposite. Richard was heading back to his studio in Noel Street.

'Where d'you live, Mr Stransom?' she asked.

'Oh, Chelsea. Just off the King's Road.'

She looked at him. 'Then let me give you a lift home.' Paul began to demur, feeling the offer had been made out of pity, but she brushed off his objections. It was late, they were going the same way, it would be silly not to. So with a quick goodnight to Melhuish, who didn't conceal his surprise, Paul climbed in after her and the driver, with a muttered *hee-up*, moved the horses on.

As the carriage made its way along Upper Street towards the Angel, nocturnal London was still in a roar, pouring out of the pubs and swarming along the pavements. The traffic thinned once they turned up Pentonville Road, and the wheels beneath them turned more quickly. For a while Rose hardly spoke, seeming to collect herself from her exertions on the stage, and Paul kept a respectful silence at her side. After a while, though, her animation returned, and she turned an interested look upon him.

'So how d'you know Richard?'

'We met at the Slade a few years ago. He was already becoming quite successful.'

'He's certainly got a lot to say for himself.'

Paul laughed. 'Richard believes that people take you at your own estimation, and so far he's been proven right.'

She considered this. 'But you're not like that,' she said after a moment. 'At least you don't seem to be.'

'I haven't his self-assurance, it's true.'

He hadn't meant the remark to sound poignant, but he sensed a minute hesitation in her response. 'D'you mind my askin' – were you lamed in an accident?'

'No, it's a condition I've had since I was a boy. A curvature of the spine.'

She nodded, and said quietly, 'Is that why you were indisposed back there?'

'Er, not exactly. It's ... something else.'

'Oh dear ...' He sensed her face still angled towards him, alight with curiosity.

'I hardly know how to ... For some time I've had *dreams*, or rather the same dream that recurs in different ways.'

'That so?'

'It started when – about two months ago – I saw a lady and her two young daughters at play in Kensington Gardens. I don't know why they intrigued me, they just did. They would visit the park perhaps two or three times a week. I never talked to them, they were always in the distance, and in any case what would I have said? Around this time the dreams began – a woman in a river, apparently drowning, calling to me to save her ...'

'Oh my,' said Rose. 'And did you – save her?'

'I don't know. Whenever I went to her aid the image of her would dissolve, and I'd wake in a panic. As though I'd failed her.'

'This woman – do you know her?'

Paul shook his head. 'And yet, for reasons I can't fathom, the woman in the dream is linked in my mind with the lady in the park, with the daughters.'

'Who are all fine as can be and safe as 'ouses,' said Rose, as if settling the matter.

'But that's just it. They've gone. I haven't seen them in weeks. And the dream persists. I feel that she, or they, are in danger, but what can I do?'

A silence fell between them, and all that could be heard was the clatter of the carriage wheels and the horses. They were heading down Great Portland Street, the passing glimmer of street lamps briefly whitening their faces in the dark of the carriage. It struck Paul as odd that he should confide to a stranger something he hadn't told another soul. Perhaps it was *because* she was a stranger that he felt able to.

Rose spoke up again. 'We're most of us distressed by dreams from time to time. I remember when my ma died, years ago, she would appear to me in my sleep, just as real to me as you are now. It was ever so strange. At first I found it a kind of comfort.'

'A comfort?' said Paul.

'Yeah. Like she was watchin' over me or something. I was fourteen at the time. But later it just felt sad ...'cos she was always saying goodbye.'

'I'm sorry. I know what it is to lose a parent one loves. You're not from London, I think?'

'Oh no. From Norfolk, I am. Yarmouth. When I first came down here I lived at Hoxton, then Islington. That's how they all know me there!'

'And now you live very fine and large,' Paul said, gesturing at the carriage in which they sat.

In the dark he could hear her grinning. 'This old bruffam ain't mine. It b'longs to my manager, he just sends it for me. But moving up west, that's all right. I like livin' by the park.'

They had crossed Marble Arch and were rolling down the Bayswater Road. About halfway down the brougham slowly pulled up outside a large mansion block, screened by trees. Rose spoke instructions to the driver, having ascertained Paul's address. 'And Arthur,' she added, 'make sure to take him to his door.'

But she didn't immediately get out of the carriage. Her expression had become intent as she said, 'What you were saying, about the lady you believed to be in danger. I know someone you might consult, someone who's in touch with ...'

'Consult? What d'you mean?'

'Well, she's a palmist. I've been to her, and so have friends of mine. She's rather queer, of course, but she's not very often wrong. If you like I could send you her address.'

'By palmist, you mean a fortune teller?'

Rose leaned back slightly. 'I can see you're doubtful. Some reckon it's mumbo-jumbo. I don't. You have a think about it.' She extended her hand, which Paul took, and she climbed out of the carriage. On the pavement she turned back, waved, and disappeared into the shadows. The driver touched his whip to the horses, and the coach rattled on again.

They were rebuilding the bridge at Battersea. Paul had watched as the new design began to take shape, the arches with their cast-iron girders slowly and massively slotted into place while the river flowed on beneath, unimpressed. The construction workers looked as insignificant as ants on a stone step.

He had been sketching here for a few days, having made a conscious break from Kensington Gardens. He thought that if he took time away from the place it might help. And to some degree it had, for his nights were less troubled by visitations, and he slept better than he had in months. The trouble was, his work suffered for it. He would sketch the new bridge, the traffic on the Thames, the factories and wharves and warehouses on the south side, the comings and goings of folk on the foreshore: boatmen, mudlarkers, scavengers, children at play. But none of it held much savour for him, and he filled his sketchbook mechanically. He saw nothing he wanted to paint.

When he returned to the park a week or so later he felt at home again. June had melted into July, and the grass, pounded by the sun, looked parched and bald in places. The elms stood to attention, apparently listening to the soft flutter of their own leaves. The crowds were approaching their midsummer peak, and he occasionally wandered amongst them on the off chance of seeing her – in vain.

Packing up his things one evening he was approached, to his surprise, by the park-keeper he had spoken to some weeks before. At first Paul assumed it to be mere friendliness on the man's part, and they stood chatting as the shadows around them began to lengthen.

It was a slight change in his tone which indicated that the man's purpose wasn't entirely social.

'I recalls you arskin' me, sir, about a lady who sometimes came here with her two daughters, and your, um, worry as to what became of 'em . . . '

'Indeed. And I can't explain it any better now.'

He nodded, thoughtful. 'Well, it must have been botherin' me 'cos I 'appens to mention it to old Nate, who worked here once, and he told me a story which I thought might interest you . . . '

'Oh?'

'Nate remembers a lady who used to frequent the park with her two young daughters – said as they always dressed in white – pretty, like . . . ' He paused, and Paul sensed what was coming next. 'Well, it's a brief story, an' a tragic one, sir, for one day she and her two girls were out in a boat on the Serpentine. Somehow or other they got into difficulties. I gather one of the girls fell into the water and the mother went in after, trying to save her. The girl *was* saved. The mother drowned.'

A sombre pause stood between them.

'Surely this would have been in the papers,' Paul said.

'Oh, indeed it was, all over them. I believe there was an inquiry.'

'But I – I didn't read *anything* about it.'

Paul would not forget the meaning look that seized the man's face. 'Well, no sir, you wouldn't have. This happened twenty-odd years ago.'

VII

29 St Leonard's Terrace, SW
July 7th, 1889

Dear Miss Daubeny,

It was a pleasure to meet you at Islington the other week.

I beg your pardon in writing on so brief an acquaintance, but you will perhaps remember what we spoke of just before we parted that evening. I would not presume on your time, only you happened to recommend a certain lady who reads palms. May I trouble you to supply her address? I would be in your debt.

Believe me, very respectfully yours,

Paul Stransom

The sky was purplish by the time they emerged from the theatre. On Charing Cross Road hansoms were trotting by in search of fares. Maggie breathed in the night air gratefully.

'*Heavens* it was stuffy in there,' she said, producing her fan.

'Do you refer to the temperature or what we've just seen on stage?' asked Paul.

At his side Ada, their sister, gave a demurring sort of laugh. 'Oh really, it wasn't as bad as all that! In the end I felt rather moved.'

Maggie turned on her a disbelieving look. 'Moved?! You mean when she says to him, "Let us from this moment begin the new life you spoke of"?'

She said this in a fluting tremulous voice that mimicked the unfortunate actress's all too well. Paul chuckled. It seemed Maggie had detested the play as sincerely as he had – Pinero's *The Profligate*, which had opened the new Garrick Theatre back in April. They discussed this unsatisfactory entertainment as they sauntered through Covent Garden on the way to supper. It had been chosen as a treat for Ada, just arrived that afternoon with her daughters. They were to stay for a fortnight, though from the amount of luggage unloaded from the fly Paul wondered if they'd decided to see out the month.

'D'you know, I felt almost ashamed to be watching such twaddle,' said Maggie, warming to her theme. 'The whole argument of the thing is absurd. A young lady marries a man who *apparently* has a disreputable past. The young chit he may have dallied with – *apparently* – follows him from London to Florence, alerting the new wife to her husband's alleged infamy. In the meantime, the wife's brother falls in love with the chit! The contrivance was so . . . *feeble*.'

Paul nodded his agreement. 'Indeed. Though not half so feeble as the characters themselves. The schoolgirl-wife seemed absolutely unacquainted with real life. The wronged girl was a wet lettuce. As for that prig of a lawyer, I wished him to the devil every time he opened his mouth.'

'I think you're both very harsh,' said Ada mildly. 'I don't go to the theatre expecting "real life"—'

'A sound principle,' Maggie cut in. 'So what do you expect?'

'Well, I suppose, a sort of romantic . . . diversion. Reality isn't the attraction of theatre. It may even be a disadvantage.'

'Mr Pinero would seem to agree with you,' Paul remarked.

Ada gave a characteristic shrug, as if the subject was really of no consequence. Maggie noted the gesture. It was somehow of a piece with her bland good looks and matronly attire. There was something about Ada's unwillingness to look too deeply into things that quietly amused her. At one time it had infuriated her. When their mother had fallen ill years ago it had simply been assumed that Maggie would be the one to nurse her. Yet the responsibility might easily have fallen otherwise.

By now they had arrived at Rules on Maiden Lane, where the doorman tipped his hat and ushered them within. Paul liked the place for its low lighting – there was no chance of being stared at. The sealing-wax green of the leather banquette almost glowed in the discreet gloom.

While they were considering the menus, Paul mused aloud, 'What you were saying about theatre may be true, Ada. It does have more in common with romance than realism. But doesn't it require both? I was in the park a while ago and overheard a couple talking the most egregious rot to one another. One couldn't have put their dialogue in a play because an audience would have been bored to tears. But I didn't doubt the pair of them were in love.'

'So what do you mean?'

'I mean that the playwright must steer a course between truthfulness to life and a duty to art. Pinero fails on both counts. No wife could be so naive about her husband's failings, and no man would be so cowed by his wife's virtue.'

'About the husband I would agree,' said Maggie, 'but you're wrong about the wife. Some women are kept in such meek subjection that naivety is their natural state. And most men are cynical enough to believe they can get away with their bad behaviour.'

A tinkling laugh escaped Ada. 'When I think of how Isobel and Gwen pleaded to come this evening! I must say I'm very glad they aren't listening to you two.'

'True, they've had a narrow escape,' said Paul. 'Tonight's experience might have put them off the theatre for ever.'

They had the soup, then Maggie and Ada had pink-frilled cutlets and Paul the beefsteak. The candlelight and the wine lent their faces a merry look as they talked of the fortnight ahead. Ada was easygoing about arrangements, though she knew the girls were keen to go boating and to visit Mme Tussauds.

'Didn't they do that last year?' Paul asked.

Ada nodded. 'And then talked of nothing else for weeks.'

Maggie looked at Paul. 'Shall we invite your friends round on Sunday evening? Ada might enjoy their company.'

Paul pulled an uncertain face. 'Towne and Hackett, you mean ...?'

'Yes, though I was thinking more of Mr Evenlode.' She told Ada about his Shakespeare recital at the school, and of his struggle with stage fright.

'Poor man. Did he go back?'

'No. I don't think he ever will.'

'I'm surprised Phil talked to you about it, Maggs. He was always most reluctant.'

Maggie wondered if that reflected on her greater sympathy as a confidante. Men weren't good at confessing amongst themselves.

They were finishing their coffee when a party of diners passed by their table. One of them stopped abruptly, and hovered. Paul looked up to find Edgar Talmash's aquiline gaze upon him. They greeted one another.

'Maggie you know, of course,' Paul said, 'and this is my other sister, Ada.'

Talmash bowed, and they exchanged a few pleasantries. He then addressed himself to Maggie. 'A report came my way recently which I believe might interest you, Miss Stransom.'

'Oh, really?'

'It concerns *Portrait of a Young Man*. I gather a certain Merrymount scholar asked to make a proper examination of it. Brigstock agreed to let the fellow have a look.' He paused, waiting to see what effect his story might be having.

Maggie, to oblige him, said, 'And what was the verdict?'

Talmash's expression was Delphic. 'According to this authority – some fellow at the Academy – the painting *isn't* by the daughter, as first thought. He says it's a late work by the man himself.'

'Merrymount?' Paul said.

The dealer nodded. 'I'm told the man has very persuasive evidence,' said Talmash. 'If he's right then Brigstock has got himself a bargain – the bargain of the century!'

Presently he bade them good-evening, and to Ada's eager enquiries Maggie supplied a brief history of the elusive painting. It seemed strange to her that she might inadvertently have spotted an Old Master. She laughed suddenly.

'Do you know, when I was bidding against Talmash for the portrait I had a sort of rush of blood. I had somehow convinced myself *I must have it.* It was silly, of course, to think I could go beyond forty guineas. But I believed Paul would lend me the money if necessary,' she added.

Ada looked from her to Paul. 'And would you have – lent her it?'

He puffed his cheeks. 'Two hundred guineas?' He gave an extravagant shrug that seemed to say 'of course'. But on consideration it might just as easily have meant, 'Are you quite mad?'

Over breakfast the next morning Paul and his eleven-year-old niece Isobel had their heads close together over a word game while the others discussed plans for the day. Maggie's school had finished for the summer, so she was able to accompany Ada and the girls wherever they fancied.

'I'd like to go on an omnibus,' said Gwen, two years younger than her sister.

'Whereabouts would you like to go?' Maggie asked.

'I don't know,' she replied, smearing her toast with marmalade. 'Anywhere, really, so long as we can sit on top.'

'It's being on the 'bus that matters,' Ada explained. 'She'd ride around all day if she could.'

Maggie suggested a trip to Kew Gardens, or the Tower of London, or the Crystal Palace. This last destination won Gwen's immediate approval, possibly because it contained the words *Crystal* and *Palace*.

'You're dead!' cried Isobel at Paul from the other end of the table.

'What on earth are you playing over there?' asked Maggie.

'Hangman,' said Paul, holding up the paper with a stick figure hanging from a gibbet. 'We're doing cathedrals of England and it seems I'm first to the gallows. He squinted at his uncompleted clue.

S – – S – – R Y

'I'm sorry, Izzy, I've still no idea what cathedral that is.'

The girl sighed at his ignorance, took the paper from him and carefully filled in the blanks.

S O L S B U R Y

'Ah,' he said. His niece's expression was triumphant.

'I think you may have been hanged innocent, dear,' said Maggie quietly.

'Rather a morbid sort of game, this,' remarked Ada.

Paul went off to fetch his things from the painting-room. On descending to the hall he found them still preparing for their excursion. Izzy and Gwen were in front of the mirror admiring their straw boaters while Maggie fixed each hat with a flower in its band. Ada was helping Emma to pack the picnic basket. He doubted the iced buns would look quite so appetising by the time they reached the Crystal Palace. They had just checked the barometer: it was going to be a hot one. Paul sidled to the front door and shouted a cheery farewell that was lost amid their own frenzy of departure.

He walked through the shimmering streets as the heat of the morning lay in wait. Spirits in the house were giddily high since Ada and the girls arrived, and would take a few days to calm down.

Jollity was the dominant key of the family fortnight. Yet Paul felt an atmosphere looming between Maggie and their older sister: if actual hostility between them was rare, faint notes of antagonism would twang on the air. They were very different women, his sisters. He was close to Maggie, though he feared her hot-blooded temper and sardonic tongue. Ada, on the other hand, was demure, and passive. Paul wondered if her unnoticing serenity was an affectation or not; either way, he recognised its potential to provoke Maggie. He felt uncomfortably on his guard.

He decided to think of something else – of Isobel's triumphant satisfaction at breakfast. Solsbury! She had looked very like Maggie at that moment. No wonder she adored the girls. They had more of her spirit than their mother's.

By the time he reached the park he was pouring with sweat and the fire in his spine was incandescent. He had lately been weaning himself off the laudanum as the pains abated, but this morning they had renewed their assault. Sitting down was no good. But he found some relief in lying down, feeling the warmth of the grass beneath him. Yes, that was better, so long as he could keep perfectly still. The oak tree under which he lay gave generous shade, and tiny spangles of sunlight peeped here and there through its lattice of branches. He found a tune in his ear, and hummed it softly as the leaves shivered on high.

He came to with a start. A dark shadow loomed over him, blotting out the light, and for a moment he was afraid.

'Oh, I am sorry, I've woken you,' came a voice – a woman's.

Paul struggled upright, disoriented. He found his spectacles and put them on. It took him a few seconds to recognise the person standing over him as Rose Daubeny. She wore a plum-coloured silk pinafore dress. The shade that she cast came from the fringed parasol she was carrying.

'I beg your pardon, I lay down to relieve my back and must have ... dropped off,' said Paul, now on his feet.

She was looking at him half in apology, half in amusement. *One feels at a disadvantage when caught dozing*, thought Paul, brushing himself down. In the daylight Rose's eyes seemed more vividly green than he remembered.

'Er, what are you doing here?' he asked.

'Well, you told me you often worked around these parts, so I took a little stroll – and here you are.'

'Did you receive my letter?'

'Eventually! My manager put it with the bundle of post from admirers, so I didn't chance to read it for about a week. I'm awful sorry ...'

'Don't think of it,' said Paul, waving away the apology.

She was peering interestedly at the work propped on its short easel. 'My, it's ... You did say you painted small!'

He gave a helpless shrug. 'Please, sit down,' he said, gesturing at his canvas stool. She did so, and he once again lowered himself to the grass. She picked up an ancient little tin, and with her eyes asked permission to open it.

'What's this?' she asked.

'Charcoal dust. I mix it into the paint when I'm trying to catch the smog.'

'Secrets of the trade, eh?' She replaced the lid; then produced a dainty silver cigarette case. 'Care for a smoke?'

He took one – Turkish, stubby – and they both lit up. She had been doing two shows a night since May and longed for a break but Sam – her manager – was keeping her at it. 'He says I've no business takin' time off, I needs to be out there performing else the audiences will just forget about me.'

'How could they forget the Muse of the Halls?'

'Very easily, according to him. "You ain't the only pretty face out there, dear," he says ... I can't do this much longer. I'll have to take a holiday else the voice'll end up cracked.' At which she took a long drag on her cigarette. 'That's the other thing – he doesn't like me smoking, neither. Says it's "unladylike" to be seen in public with a cigarette.'

'Does he make many such objections?'

She cocked an eyebrow. 'He never objects to the money I earn him ...' In a swift, thoughtless movement she picked a fleck of Turkish tobacco from her lip. *I should remember that little gesture*, thought Paul. Then she picked up a brush from his box and examined it.

'It must be wonderful,' she said, after a moment, 'to sit here all day and just paint. *I paints and paints – hears no complaints – and sells before I'm dry ...*'

'What's that?' Paul asked, half-smiling.

'Oh, just some ditty doing the rounds. You wouldn't believe the junk I keep up here!' she said, tapping her temple with her finger.

'How d'you remember all of those songs?'

'Dunno. It just comes natural. My ma used to sing to us kids all the time, so I s'pose it was in the family.'

'We have our older sister and her daughters staying with us at the moment. They were preparing for a trip to the Crystal Palace when I left them this morning. My older niece has been teaching me a game called Hangman.' He explained to her how it was played, and she listened with an eager open smile.

'That girl sounds like she's got all her buttons on,' said Rose. A silence intervened for a moment, and she said, 'You arsked about the lady, the palm reader. Are you still ... suffering?'

'Not as severely,' he replied. 'Though there is something else I must relate.' He told her the story of the park-keeper and his disclosure of the Serpentine boating accident. 'The details matched almost exactly – a mother and her two daughters, who had been noticed in the Gardens playing at cricket, games of catch. I believed the mystery was solved – until he mentioned the date.'

Rose stared hard. 'Twenty years ago?'

'Twenty-three, in fact. I went to the library to consult newspapers from the time. It was in the London press, the report of a young mother's death by drowning. The summer of eighteen sixty-six.'

'What d'you think it means?'

'I don't know. The lady and the two girls I saw here were as real to me as you are now. But I never spoke to them; I didn't come closer than twenty yards. So could it be I saw—'

'Ghosts?'

Paul looked at her. 'I'm not inclined to credit the supernatural . . .'

'What happened to the daughters? Isn't it likely they'd still be alive?'

'Even if they are what good would it do? I don't imagine they'd welcome a stranger who claims to have seen them and their dead mother in his dreams. In any case, I want to know why that dream persists.'

'That's why you need to see Mrs Searle,' said Rose. 'If there's anyone can explain it, she can.' She withdrew from her sleeve a small square of paper, folded twice. Paul briefly glanced at the address and thanked her.

'She's perfectly respectable,' she said, seeming to read his doubt.

'Of course. In any case, I believe I'm at the point where I feel bound to try anything.'

Presently Rose got to her feet. Paul did likewise, and they faced one another. 'I'd better be off. I'm glad I managed to find you.'

'So am I,' said Paul.

She thrust out her hand, which he took. 'I do wish you luck.' She walked away in the direction of Bayswater Road. More than once Paul turned round to watch her figure recede until she and her parasol were lost in the green folds of the park.

VIII

It was the moment Lucy Gray spotted Philip Evenlode that
Maggie sensed the evening about to slide away from her.

Her original plan was to have Paul's friends from the Slade
over for a supper party. Then she thought of inviting Lucy and
several other teachers at St Pancras who might enjoy the gathering and offer Ada some relief from the all-male company. So
instead of a formal dinner she laid out a buffet that guests could
pick from – ham and cold roast fowl, small pork pies, oysters,
a salad, bowls of Spanish olives and almonds, a cheese board.
For pudding Mrs Gent had prepared pistachio ices and a gooseberry fool. Izzy and Gwen had been allowed to stay up late for
the occasion.

It had also been part of Maggie's scheme to introduce Lucy, her
companion in spinsterhood, to a suitable bachelor friend of Paul's.
Towne she dismissed as too morose, but she saw possibility in
Hackett, who at least knew how to dress properly, and perhaps in
Mr Arrowsmith, another artist, rather short and gauche but friendly
withal. By nine o'clock the living room and even the parlour were
thronged, and Maggie felt pleased to see Ada being charmed by
their more metropolitan friends.

A few minutes later she noticed Philip Evenlode arrive, and made
a beeline for him. His clothes, as worn as ever, had a poignant air

of grooming, like an old rug that had just been beaten. She greeted him warmly, put a glass of wine in his hand. She was on her way to the kitchen when Lucy waylaid her.

'You didn't mention that you'd invited Mr Evenlode,' she said, watching him over Maggie's shoulder.

'Didn't I?'

'I must congratulate him on that wonderful recital he gave us.'

'Well—'

'He's actually rather dashing, isn't he?' she said, still appraising him.

'I want you to meet that fellow over there, Mr Hackett. I think you'd rather like him.'

She went to consult with Mrs Gent about the ices and the pudding. On returning to the living room ten minutes later she found Lucy in animated conversation – with Philip. Well, she thought, he has such nice manners that he's able to talk to anyone. She stalked around the room, topping up people's glasses, until she came to Paul, and bent to whisper in his ear.

'I think we ought to put Lucy and Mr Hackett together, don't you?'

Paul looked around to see how the two were presently occupied. 'They both seem content. I'd leave it for the moment.'

Irritated, she moved on. She got talking to their neighbour, Mr Roberson, a land agent whose knowledge of local properties would ordinarily have interested her, but this evening she could barely digest a word. Once she had excused herself she found Mr Hackett at last and steered him towards the end of the room where Lucy was still hogging Philip's company. To interrupt them would be awkward, but she did so anyway.

'Lucy, this is Mr Hackett, the gentleman I was telling you about ...'

Philip made room for Hackett to slide himself into their space, though Lucy made no effort to include him. Maggie loitered there for some minutes. Lucy, scented and coiffed for the occasion, was enjoying her moment and hurried on in her usual garrulous way, while Philip seemed happy to listen. Hackett, thrust cold into their midst, perhaps wondered why his hostess had forced him to play the gooseberry. Eventually he withdrew, as did Maggie, chagrined at her failure to separate them.

The party rambled on. A chorus of coos greeted Mrs Gent's pistachio ices. Paul, sensing thunderclouds over Maggie, decided to get the music started and asked Isobel to do her party piece. The girl responded by tearing over to the piano and giving the assembled a smudged rendering of a Chopin prelude. The kindly applause that followed she took as encouragement to play another, even looser than the first, at which Ada – perhaps thinking of Mr Bennet – suggested in a whisper that others might like to 'have a go'. While the rest dithered, Lucy grasped Philip by the arm and, laughing, jostled him to the side of the piano. She herself took the stool and inspected the sheet music on the stand. Plucking out *Selections from Esmeralda* by Goring Thomas, she and Philip had a short muttered exchange before she composed herself, and began. It was an aria, 'O Vision Entrancing', sloppily played by her and magnificently sung by him.

Maggie watched in a trance of near-horror. How it had come about that Lucy Gray, her unfancied colleague at school, not only had her hooks into Philip but now took leave to be his accompanist?

> *O vision entrancing, full lovely and light*
> *My heart at thy dancing grows faint with delight*

When they were finished the applause came with cheers and cries of 'encore!' Philip, smiling, gave a little bow and looked ready to move away, but Lucy immediately launched into 'Charlie Is My Darling', and so he remained to sing that as well. Their example induced others to shed inhibitions and perform, and soon the piano was ranged around with guests as merry as Christmas carollers. When Lucy and Philip were called upon for yet another song, Maggie retreated to the kitchen. A more insufferable occasion she could not recall.

The following morning Maggie came down uncharacteristically late for breakfast. Paul noted on her forehead a warning frown line. Isobel and Gwen also seemed to sense an atmosphere as their aunt sat down in silence and poured herself a cup of tea. They stared at her briefly and kept their voices low. Only Ada failed to detect anything amiss.

'Well, *what* a jolly evening that was!' she began brightly. 'And Mrs Gent surpassed herself with the spread.'

'She did indeed,' said Paul.

Maggie, silent, scraped butter over a slice of toast. Ada burbled on oblivious, praising the food again and recalling which guests she had particularly liked. Paul's heart sank when she mused, 'Though I do wish I'd talked to that odd-looking man who sang—'

'Philip,' Paul supplied quickly.

'A lot of people wanted to meet him,' said Maggie quietly.

Paul said, 'Maggie, I didn't get a moment to tell you – Towne buttonholed me last night with news about Brigstock's picture. This is the portrait we were talking of the other day,' he added for Ada's benefit. 'Another scholar has backed up the man from the Academy – says it's a genuine Merrymount ...'

Maggie glanced at him, and said, 'Interesting.' She could not have put less feeling into the word.

'But only think what it must mean to Brigstock,' Paul persisted. 'What'll he do with it?'

'I should advise him to have his insurance increased,' she replied, expressionless.

She continued her breakfast without another word, until even

Ada noticed her taciturnity, breaking off a monologue to ask, 'Is everything all right, dear? You're awfully quiet.'

Maggie assured her she was quite well. From the corner of his eye Paul spotted Emma hovering uncertainly in the doorway; having sniffed the air, like a mouse, she decided to withdraw. She knew her mistress's moods, perhaps better than anyone. When Ada and the girls had gone off to ready themselves for the day, Paul, proceeding with the caution of a skater on a frozen pond, said, 'I'm not sure you enjoyed yourself last night.'

She stared at him for a moment. 'Why do you say that?'

'Did you?'

'I could have enjoyed it more if Miss Gray hadn't chosen to monopolise your friend's company.'

'Just the party spirit, I suppose ...'

'I think it bad manners to press someone into a corner and deny anyone else the chance to talk to him.'

Paul said, forbearingly, 'They delighted everyone with their music.'

Maggie gave a little groan of disgust. 'I hope never to hear that song played again. "O Vision Entrancing", indeed! Did you notice the simpering look she kept giving him?'

'I imagine Phil was rather charmed. He isn't used to such attention.'

She scowled at that. 'She oughtn't to have encouraged him. I told her he was on his beam ends.'

'What's that got to do with it?'

'Everything, in this case. You know as well as I do Mr Evenlode can't afford to get married. It was wrong of her to mislead him—'

'Married? Maggie, she barely flirted with him. Where is the harm? I don't suppose either of them has marriage in mind.'

Now her eyes blazed. '*She* does! I'd told her there would be an eligible young man present but she ignores Mr Hackett very rudely and throws herself at Mr Evenlode ...'

Paul shook his head. 'I think you're making too much of this.

All I could see last night was people enjoying themselves, with the music and drink and Mrs Gent's food. It was entirely convivial. You mustn't find fault where none exists.'

Maggie made no reply. She felt she had already said too much. Paul also sat silent, wondering if the storm had blown itself out. In the back of his mind a conjecture had half-formed about the true cause of Maggie's resentment, one he would later dismiss as far-fetched, and possibly absurd. But he did believe she was too much at home, and that it behoved him to expand her horizons. He must make good on that promise of a holiday on the south coast. Sea air and long walks would set her right. Though even as he settled on this he knew that his sister's unhappiness required a cure above and beyond a mere change of scenery.

The address was a house halfway up Wimpole Street. A landlady answered Paul's knock and asked if Mrs Searle was expecting him. On replying in the affirmative he was led up the staircase to rooms on the second floor. When Rose had told him about the palmist – or 'chiromantic', as she was listed in the services directory – he had imagined her as a dark-skinned lady swathed in a shawl, with dramatic earrings and perhaps a veil across her face. He had further pictured a room adorned with exotic hangings and scented with perfumes of the Orient, an impression immediately dispelled as he entered a gloomy living room whose dominant feature was a large wilted aspidistra on the table by the window. The only scent he could identify was a faint one of cats. The strange aqueous green of the wallpaper and the heavy mahogany furniture made him feel as if he had entered the hold of a sunken galleon. Through the half-drawn curtains seeped a grey afternoon light. Sounds from the street below were muffled.

He was still unable to explain to himself why he was there.

The servant girl who answered the door asked him to wait while her mistress prepared for their interview. It was immoderately humid. On entering the room Mrs Searle proved to be neither foreign nor flamboyant; she was neat-figured and whey-faced, attired in a black bustle dress with a ruffle collar. A jet necklace hung dully at her throat. She was perhaps a few years off forty, again confounding him – he had expected her to be a matronly fifty or sixty. She was decidedly no kin of Madame Blavatsky.

'Mr Stransom, how d'you do?' she said, extending a dry slim hand. She pointed him to facing armchairs in front of the fireplace. A small cherrywood table stood between them. He felt her watching him as he limped across the room. The girl had brought in a jug of cold lemonade, draped in a muslin lid weighted with green and white beads. Mrs Searle sat down opposite him and poured each of them a glass. Up close Paul flinched at the piercing candour of her blue eyes.

She asked him how he had heard of her business, and on mentioning Rose she smiled wanly and nodded. 'Ah yes, Miss Daubeny and I have had some profitable meetings. She is still at the halls?'

'Yes. And carrying all before her,' he replied.

She blinked slowly. 'You are a professional man, Mr Stransom?'

Paul told her that he was a painter. Her eyes gleamed at that, and she handed him a piece of paper and a pen. She asked him to sign his name. For a moment he imagined she wanted his autograph. But when he put aside the pen she ignored the signature and took the hand – his right – which had written it. 'Your working hand,' she explained, 'where your energies and ambitions are invested.'

She kept hold of it, as though she might be taking his pulse. After a few moments of concentrated scrutiny she explained to him the different lines traversing his palm: the life line, the fate line, the heart line, and two others that he promptly forgot. She asked him to relax, so that she might more easily 'read' these lines and the narrative inscribed therein. But her blue gaze, meeting his eyes, still disconcerted him, and her voice, though intended to be soothing, had an edge to it. He felt unpleasantly warm.

'I sense that you are not at ease,' she said suddenly.

Paul wondered if she meant in general or at that very minute, in the stuffy room. He answered to both: 'That is true.'

'Why is that?'

Now he would have to pick one or the other. 'I am – I have been – disturbed. In my sleep. For some while.' He thought to keep it vague so as to put the onus of interpretation upon her – it was why he had sought her out, after all. She was looking at his hand again.

'I see a change coming in your life. But in some way you are resisting it.' Paul nodded uncertainly. Wasn't he always resisting change?

'You are to travel . . . perhaps not far. There is water. You are at sea.'

Not a bad guess, Paul thought, given that he and Maggie had just agreed on tripping down to the coast.

'There are three strangers in your house at present?'

'Not strangers. Family.'

In a lower voice Mrs Searle said, 'There is a woman. A lady. You have a strong connection to her, I think.'

'Yes.'

She paused, and looked at him with a frown. 'This lady . . . she has betrayed you?'

Who is she talking about? he wondered. 'I'm not sure—'

'No, a moment,' she interrupted, as though she had misheard her own message. 'She *will* betray you. Whatever trust you put in her, she is going to break it.'

'How? Who?'

She gave no sign of having heard. 'The arrow of time does not invariably point forwards. The past still inhabits the present. There are patterns in life that answer to patterns in the beyond, warning us . . .'

Now he felt alarm. 'What – am I in danger?'

Instead of a reply a long silence ensued. Mrs Searle, eyes half-closed, seemed to be nearly asleep. He could almost have believed it mischief on her part – a way of prolonging the suspense. The light in the room had thinned and cast the pale oval of her face in a kind of relief. Paul didn't make a sound lest he break the mood of tremulous divination. Then her eyes snapped open again and he was caught in the glitter of her gaze.

'Do you know your Shakespeare, Mr Stransom? "If it be now, 'tis not to come; if it be not come, it will be now; if it be not now, yet it will come: the readiness is all." Hamlet to Horatio. One may hazard upon the future, but one cannot alter it. Whatever is coming will come.'

Paul stared back at her. 'Then what use to me that you read the future?'

'Only this – that you are prepared for it.'

'Please, speak plainly. Is the danger close to me?'

A beat, and she said, 'Yes.'

He sat back in the chair for a moment. Shadows were now crowding at the edge of the room; her face had lost definition in the failing light.

'One more question, if I may. Should I defy augury?'

He discerned a half-smile crease her mouth. 'You may try. A man's life is his own – make of it what you will.'

She spoke a little longer in her oblique riddling style. Fragments of good sense he grasped at like a shipwreck to floating spars. At length she rose and went to open the sash window, as if she had only just noticed the stifling temperature. She then sat at her desk and spent some minutes writing. It was so quiet he could hear the nib of her pen across the paper. Paul supposed she was making notes on their interview, setting it down while it was still fresh in the memory. On finishing she rolled a blotter over it and brought a folded note over to him; with her eyes she indicated that he should open it. Inside he read, in her exquisite flowing hand, a bill for ten pounds. He smiled at her. The consultation was over.

*

As he made his way west through Marylebone Paul reviewed the hour just passed. She was a discomfiting figure, not at all as he'd envisaged. Seers, clairvoyants – whatever one might call them – were supposed to be outlandish creatures, with a touch of the fraud. If Mrs Searle had been so it would have made it easier for him to dismiss her. But she had delivered her presentiments in a perfectly even and self-possessed manner, one that had compelled his attention. She had spoken of a lady with whom he had a connection, someone who was going to betray him. But who? The only women he regarded as close were Maggie and Ada, neither of whom he would ever suspect of plotting against him. There were women who had modelled for him, but none of them he knew very well.

The only other woman who had been on his mind of late was the mother he had seen in the park. He had to face the possibility that she had been a figment. He recalled Mrs Searle's line about patterns corresponding to one another in life and 'in the beyond'. If the mother and her two daughters in Kensington Gardens were indeed phantoms then what did it matter? They were dead and gone. Unless – as Mrs Searle had explained, the arrow of time travelled either way – they had appeared to him as a warning of what was to come. A mother and two young daughters ... *Oh my God*, he exclaimed aloud – Ada, and the girls. How could he have been so obtuse? The palm reader had asked him about three 'strangers' staying in his house, and he had corrected her. But the pattern – the numerical pattern – was right there. Was this the sign from beyond, that his sister and nieces were in danger?

He felt his pace quicken along the pavement. He was putting it together in his head. The Kensington Gardens trio, the mother and daughters he had observed – had painted – were messengers from the netherworld, come to warn him of disaster. And now another horror was borne in on these sudden conjectures. Hadn't Ada said that they were to go boating, and wasn't it planned for this very day? He felt himself breaking out in a sweat as he stumped through Portman Square. He was muttering to himself. Why hadn't he connected Ada's arrival with the white-clad figures in the park?

He managed to flag down a cab and climbed in. The afternoon was almost done, so if Ada and the girls had gone boating he was too late anyway. *Take her up tenderly, / Lift her with care . . .* The tragic lines came back to him. Oh God, let them not drown. The halting progress of the hackney through the streets caused him twenty minutes of anguish. He again asked the God in whom he didn't believe to have mercy.

On reaching the house he paid off the cabman and hurried in. He immediately yelled for his sisters at a volume that brought Emma out of the parlour. She looked at him in alarm.

'Where are they?' he cried.

'I believe the missis is in her room—'

Without waiting to listen to the rest he dragged himself up the staircase, calling out for Ada. She met him on the turn, her expression not much less alarmed than Emma's.

'What's the matter?'

He stared up at her. 'I was worried that you ... Where are the girls?'

'Maggie took them to Tussauds while I went off to Derry and Toms. Why, what has happened?'

Paul felt himself flood with relief. Not boating after all! 'Nothing. Nothing has happened. I had a momentary panic that you were – well, it doesn't matter. I'm just glad that you're safe.'

Ada looked at him curiously. 'Safe? Why shouldn't I be? Honestly, dear, you gave me such a fright!'

Not half so bad as the one I gave myself, he thought. 'Forgive me, I didn't mean ... Did you buy anything?'

Ada, not one to enquire too closely into things, took the change of subject in her stride. 'Oh, some linen, gloves, a few little things for the girls, you know.'

About twenty minutes later he heard the front door open and the voices of Maggie, Izzy and Gwen floated up. He went down to greet them. The girls were full of stories about Tussauds and their dreadful delight at the Chamber of Horrors (an extra sixpence for admission). They also described for Paul's benefit the effigies of Shakespeare, Wellington and Dickens as though they had met them personally. Then Aunt Maggie had treated them to ices on the way home.

'It was such a lovely day that we walked back through the park,' Maggie said.

Paul, thinking ahead, waited for the girls to move out of earshot before saying, 'Do the girls still hope to go on the Serpentine?'

Maggie, with a shrug, said, 'I imagine so. Why?'

This had to be the moment, he knew, and he could only tell Maggie. He had decided to relate a modified version of his dream, making no mention of the spectral figures in the Gardens, or of his recent visit to Mrs Searle. Put together it would sound too bizarre for words. But he made it sound frightening enough for her to take it seriously.

'How awful,' said Maggie, when he had finished. 'So all three of them ...?'

'Drowned. Which is why I'm in an absolute terror of you and the girls coming to grief.'

'But that was just a dream. You don't really imagine anything like that could happen to us?'

'I don't know. I realise how dotty it sounds, but I'd feel much happier if you *didn't* go boating.'

'Oh, Paul, you don't expect us to—'

'Maggie. Please. Will you not indulge me, just this once?'

'But what will I tell Izzy and Gwen? And Ada, come to that – she's as much a child as either of them.'

'Tell them there's been a string of fatal accidents on the lake, and it's generally considered to be unsafe.'

'If it's so important why don't *you* tell them?'

'Because they'd take no notice of me. You've got the authority – they'd believe you, I know they would.'

She fixed her eyes upon him, not altogether pleased. He held her gaze, and slowly she began to shake her head. 'They're not going to like it ...'

It was assent, and he returned a grateful look.

IX

A few days later the Stransoms were finishing breakfast when
Ada, at the window, observed there to be a man hanging about
on the street. 'I saw him only half an hour ago, skulking up and
down.' That her sister had noticed anything beyond the length of
her own nose prompted Maggie to rise and join her at the window.
She gave a start on recognising him.

'Why, it's Mr Brigstock,' she said, turning to Paul, who looked
up from the morning paper.

'Are you sure?'

'Come and look for yourself,' she replied. Putting on his spectacles he strained his gaze at the figure patrolling the pavement: there
could be no doubt it was his friend.

After a moment, Maggie said, 'I'd better go and find out what
he's doing there.'

'Tell him there's still coffee and toast if he'd like to join us,' Paul
called after her.

By the time Maggie came down the path and on to the street
Brigstock had gone – but no, there he was, leaning against the railings across the road. She crossed over and approached.

'Mr Brigstock – how d'you do?'

'Miss Stransom. Good morning.' He lifted his hat.

'What are you doing here? I presume you've come to see Paul—'

'As a matter of fact, no.' He gave an awkward little laugh. 'I was actually hoping to see you.'

'Me?' This came as a surprise, but she covered it. 'Well, please come in.'

He declined, but said he'd be most obliged if she'd spare him ten minutes or so, on a walk. She saw no reason to refuse. 'I'll just fetch my bonnet and I'll be with you in a moment.'

When she returned Brigstock inclined his head and with a sweep of his arm they proceeded through Tedworth Square. The morning was a bright one, with the sun high on a ragged divan of clouds. He spoke to her pleasantly, though haltingly. She thought she knew what he wanted to talk about.

After a brief silence she said, 'I gather the *Portrait of a Young Man* has been the talk of the galleries.'

He made a sly face. 'The Ashmolean and the Academy seem convinced it's a late Merrymount. But questions of provenance aren't so quickly settled – the scholars must all have their say.'

'But what a coup if it *is* one of his,' she said encouragingly.

'I feel unable to take any credit. *You* were the one who first spotted it, after all. I just happened to have the ready money.'

They were now halfway down Tite Street. As they passed a tall and gloomy-looking red-brick house Brigstock said, 'You know who lives there, don't you?'

She smiled. 'Of course. Though I count myself rather unfortunate. In all the time he's lived here I've never once caught sight of him. Paul, on the other hand, sees him quite often, out walking with his wife.'

'Ah, the heiress. Constance.'

'You know them?'

'A little. We were introduced one evening at the Café Royal. You won't be surprised to hear he was very entertaining.'

Maggie gave a little sigh. 'Perhaps I should simply wait in the street on the chance I might see him.' Her tone was jesting, and he laughed, embarrassed.

'Why didn't you knock at our door just then?'

Brigstock shot a glance at her. 'Well ... your house, charming as it is, didn't quite suit my purpose for the conversation I wished to have.'

They had reached the Embankment, at a distance halfway between the Chelsea and Albert Bridges. Brigstock directed their steps towards the latter, claiming it to be the prettier of the two. An intuition had stolen upon Maggie that he might have an offer of work in mind, either one of his own devising or else a position that had become vacant in the art business. He had spoken admiringly of her eye for a painting – and she would readily accept a job that would take her away from teaching.

Brigstock had stepped slightly ahead of her on to the bridge. He paused at the parapet, staring out over the river and its sluggish flow. In the morning light it was a greyish green; by evening it would have shifted from blue to black. Maggie leaned herself against the parapet, arms folded, next to him. He had now fallen silent.

'You seem in a strange mood, I wonder if—'

'Miss Stransom,' he said, talking over her, 'I invited you out this morning with one intention in mind. That is, to ask you, most humbly, to be my wife.'

She stared at him. The colour seemed to have drained from his face, possibly out of fright at the extraordinary proposal he had just made. For a few shocked moments she could only half-gasp in response.

'I'm – I don't know what to say ...'

'You must be aware of my deep admiration. When I sent that invitation to inspect the portrait, it was your brother I wrote to. But it was *you* I wanted to see.'

'Admiration, yes,' she said, composing herself, 'but I had no inkling of ... You don't even know me.'

'I know you well enough to believe you are the finest woman

I've met. Do you remember that night you came to Albany Street and we talked with Talmash about the portrait at the auction rooms? You spoke about it with such brightness in your eyes, such delicate understanding, I felt bewitched. It was as if you had handed a precious secret to me. You know I went to see the painting the next day, and everything you'd said about it was true. From that moment I was determined to have it, so that one day I might ... well, that I might present it to you on the day we are wed.'

'You bought it ... for me?'

He nodded. 'For us. It will remind me of the instant I realised that I needed you. That my happiness depends on you. Please don't let me hope in vain.'

He reached out to take her hand, and she didn't resist. 'I don't know what to say,' she almost wailed.

'Say yes! That is all. Maggie – may I call you Maggie? I flatter myself that I could make you as happy as you will make me.'

His expression, more often given to savouring some drollery, was in deadly earnest. Could she? Dare she? She gazed down at the tide below, swaying steadily onwards. In a woman's life there could be no more significant moment than this, an offer of marriage. But she needed to consider the odds, to weigh up the chances, knowing that once she had accepted him she would be cast upon unknown waters, with no firm idea of how to stay afloat.

Presently she said, 'Mr Brigstock, please understand ... I am very touched by what you have said. And I realise, truly, what an honour it is you do me. But I cannot answer you immediately.'

'Why not?'

'Because I need time. I cannot do justice to your offer without first giving it proper consideration.'

She watched his face as it fell. It was clearly not the answer he was hoping for. 'I understand it has come as a surprise,' he said slowly, 'but I thought you might receive my proposal more ... warmly.'

She clasped at his hand. 'I do feel warmly – I do. But you must allow me to think on it.'

After some moments he said, in a hurt voice, 'Do you not trust me?'

'Yes, I do. But I don't know if I trust myself. If I go plunging in without a care I may live to regret it – we both may.'

He turned again to face the river. Neither of them spoke for a while. She wanted to say something encouraging, but she dared not mislead him.

'A good thing I did not come into the house, you see,' he said. 'Your family would have wondered at my long face.'

'Mr Brigstock, I have suffered disappointments in my life. It has made me cautious, I'm sorry. Will you grant me a week to decide?'

He looked at her. 'A week ... and then you will give me an answer?'

She nodded. It was the best she could do for him. At last he smiled at her, but ruefully. He put his hat back on, bowed briefly and walked away.

She made her way back slowly to St Leonard's Terrace, in a fugue of bewilderment. She noticed nothing of the houses she passed, the traffic on the streets, the people whose eyes caught hers. The encounter had left her shaken. It was true, Brigstock had never made a secret of his regard for her. He liked her company and took her opinions seriously. But she had not for a moment imagined his feelings might compel him to ask for her hand. It seemed wholly out of character. His public persona had been cultivated to suggest a carefree man about town. He was the sort who gambled and travelled and lived to please himself. Marriage didn't appear to fit with that life. He was also young, perhaps six-and-twenty, younger than she: he still had, in the phrase, wild oats to sow.

And yet he had made his proposal in such a heartfelt way. His unwonted nervousness beforehand had given the clue, and his disappointment at her indecision confirmed it. She could tell he had anticipated her acceptance. And why shouldn't he have? He had all the eligibility – wealth, talent, a name, and charm to boot. As for herself, she was surely too old to be considered a catch, and in terms of accomplishment she had little to boast about. Teaching at a young ladies' college was hardly the acme of success. She had some money from her father's will, but nothing that would make up a dowry.

So she had to suppose that he had been attracted on the strength of her character alone. The thought made her blush with pleasure, and in the next moment she scolded herself for vanity. He must be mad to want her!

Her brain was still teeming with speculations when she let herself in at home. She stood irresolute in the hallway for a few moments, trying to collect herself. She could hear the girls downstairs helping Mrs Gent to make a pudding for dinner. In the living room she found Paul and Ada, both evidently waiting for her return. She felt an uncommon thrill at what she was about to spring on them.

'So?' said Paul.

'So what?' she asked. She moved into the room and plumped herself down on the couch.

He rolled his eyes at that. 'What did Brigstock want?'

'You'll never guess . . . '

'Then please tell us,' said Ada, who couldn't endure suspense.

Maggie briefly examined her nails. 'He asked me,' she said, 'to be his wife.'

For a moment neither of them said anything. Then Ada managed to half-shriek 'What?' and looked to Paul for assistance.

'Marry you?' he said in a stunned whisper.

'Yes, and I see it comes as as great a surprise to you as it has to me,' Maggie replied evenly.

Then Ada made all haste to cross the room and fling herself upon Maggie's neck. 'Darling! That's the most wonderful news!'

Paul, slower to absorb the shock, said, 'Maggs, I'm scarcely ... well, it *is* wonderful.'

Maggie detached herself from her sister's embrace. She knew this would be the awkward part of the conversation. 'I should say that I haven't accepted him.'

'You haven't – but why?'

'Because I've yet to make up my mind. His proposal caught me unawares, and I need time to think it over.'

'But you do *like* him?' Ada said, still hopeful.

'What little I know of him, yes. He's clever, and amusing—'

'And very well off, by the sound of it.'

'Yes, that too,' said Maggie, her tone more distant.

'You know that he's always been fond of you,' Paul said. 'And he's a decent fellow, Dab.'

Maggie looked at him. 'You didn't always think so. I recall not long ago your remarking that Mr Brigstock wasn't quite a gentleman, and that you didn't much like the idea of him "squiring your sister".'

'Did I?' Paul looked surprised.

'Your very words. Perhaps you know something about him that I don't – in which case you should probably tell me. It could save us a lot of trouble.'

Paul, rummaging in his memory, did now recall some offhand remark he had made to her, but it wasn't seriously intended, and he'd probably been a little drunk at the time. 'Well, I never meant to set you against him,' he said weakly.

Maggie kept her silence for a moment. Then she said, 'He's agreed to give me a week to decide. So may I ask you to spare me any further discussion of it until then.'

Ada looked beseechingly to Paul, who merely shrugged. At that point they heard voices outside and Isobel and Gwen came lolloping into the room, ready for another day's entertainment. So the matrimonial stunner was for the present dropped. Ada had to take the girls to the West End to 'look at the shops', while Maggie was going to have a day of study. She accompanied Paul as far as Sydney Street, neither of them making further reference to the matter. Then she bent her steps in the direction of Chelsea Public Library on Manresa Road. She intended to make a start on preparing her Shakespeare classes for next term – *The Tempest* was first of the set texts – and on arriving found a quiet corner to settle. Her desk was soon stacked with critical tomes from whose pages rose the mingled scents of dust and disuse.

For nearly an hour she managed to devote herself to Caliban and Prospero, the cloud-capped towers and the gorgeous palaces and the stuff that dreams are made on. It somehow soothed her to live inside the rhythm of the verse. But as the tick of the library clock dripped on and the light changed through the windows, she felt the events of the morning worm their way back inside her head, disrupting her concentration. To have received an offer of marriage! And from no mean quarter, either. If she was unconvinced of Brigstock's suitability she could not doubt his sincerity in making it; his earnest looks and his expression of dismay when she asked for time were no fakery. Nor could he have told a more affecting story than that of his determined pursuit of the Merrymount portrait. That he had bought it, however quixotically, with her in mind was flattering enough – that he intended it now as a wedding gift almost dizzied her. A painting that was found, and lost, and found again. To think she might be mistress of a house in which it was displayed ...

The text of the play was open before her, and her eye fell upon

> *Our revels now are ended. These our actors,*
> *As I foretold you, were all spirits, and*
> *Are melted into air, into thin air*

They were lines she had last heard spoken by Philip Evenlode, during his recital at the school. She had barely spoken to him when he was at the house last week, thanks to Lucy Gray having taken him hostage. Not that Maggie could ever have hoped ... it was useless even to entertain ... he would never have conceived ... These half-formed thoughts flashed across her brain, as quick and dazzling as fireworks, and as melancholy in their sudden fading. But those hours they had talked at the school, his anguished account of stage fright, the humble chivalry of his manner ... Had she not caught a spark of interest in his gaze? There was *something* in it. She tried to imagine herself telling him that she was to marry Denton Brigstock, and what his reaction might be. He was too gentlemanly to do other than congratulate her. But would she detect in his face – or in that lovely voice of his – a wistfulness?

In the end it came down to money. Men like Brigstock could afford to be married and men like Evenlode could not. It wasn't a matter of deserving, but of financial capability. *Needy men the needful need* ... Philip did not seem the type of man to rail against fate. And yet to think of him eking out a life in hired lodgings, with solitude his lot and a woman's love his impossible dream!

On returning home late in the afternoon Maggie sensed an odd febrile atmosphere in the house, as though some occasion were in the offing. A birthday, perhaps – or a wedding. Upstairs in her room she changed for the evening, and wondered what Paul and Ada had been saying about her. She had begged them for a moratorium on the subject, and at dinner was relieved to find it observed. The conversation revolved mainly around the day's outing, through the Green Park and thence to Parliament Square and Westminster Abbey. They had last visited the place during the Queen's Jubilee two years ago.

Mrs Gent served them roast duck, followed by the lemon sponge which the girls, her proud assistants in the kitchen, were allowed to carry into the dining room with the cream and wafers.

'After the Abbey we took a 'bus to the Strand,' said Ada, 'and Gwen announced to us her latest ambition.'

They all looked in her direction.

'I want to drive the horses on an omnibus,' the girl replied, eyes alight.

'They won't let a girl do that,' her older sister said flatly.

'Well, you never know,' said Paul. 'If Gwen shows herself to be an excellent driver ...'

Maggie said to Isobel, 'And you, Izzy, what do you propose to be?'

The girl tipped her head on one side. 'I haven't decided – but I know what I *don't* want to be.'

'Oh, what's that?'

She pursed her lips primly: 'A member of the public.'

Maggie looked from Ada to Paul. 'Heaven forbid.'

After dinner Paul was dragooned into several rounds of Hangman while Ada and Maggie went off to read in the living room. Maggie sensed her sister pretending to be involved with her magazine while covertly observing her. She was beside herself with the news of the proposal. But Maggie did not look up from the novel she was reading and no amount of sniffing and sighing from across the room would distract her.

Once the girls had been packed off to bed Paul joined them in the living room. He too felt agitated, though he was better at hiding it than Ada. He showed Maggie the invitation to Richard Melhuish's private view next week, a selection of the Normandy paintings 'which he thinks so highly of', Maggie noted sardonically. Paul, smiling, wandered over to the fireplace where he paused and clasped his hands behind his back. It was a vaguely patriarchal posture that didn't suit him. After a moment he said, 'I'm going to have a glass of sherry. Would either of you ... ?'

This in itself was unusual in a house that favoured beer and hock. Ada declined, but Maggie said, 'Yes, why not?'

He unstoppered the decanter and poured them each a glass. Maggie took hers and sipped. Still she sensed an awkwardness in the room, like the moment in church when the congregation is supposed to respond but doesn't know the liturgy. She saw Paul shoot a helpless look at Ada, who gave a little twitch as she cleared her throat.

'Darling,' she began, 'Paul and I have been in high feather about your, er – *news* this afternoon ...'

Maggie looked to her lap and began smoothing out invisible creases on her dress. 'I see.'

'And – and we couldn't help wonder where your own thoughts might be tending. At present. Is there anything perhaps you'd like ... to talk about?'

'No, not really.'

She thought that terseness might thwart any further discussion, but Ada was not so easily put off.

'It's just that we're so very eager that you give Mr Brigstock's proposal serious consideration—'

'Do you imagine I would give it anything less?' Maggie said sharply.

'No, of course not, it's only that ...' Ada, at a loss, turned to her brother for assistance. Paul knew better than to press Maggie like this, but now that Ada had got the ball rolling he felt beholden to add his voice.

'Maggs, please don't blame us for being excited. Whatever I might have said about him previously, Brigstock is a good fellow with much to recommend him – he has talent, a reputation, he's prosperous, well-to-do even ...'

'I'm aware of his eligibility. I also happen to like him personally. But it doesn't follow that I want to be bound to him for life.'

'But what objection can you possibly make against him?' Ada asked.

'I have nothing against him. But you must allow me to entertain a doubt! This is the first offer of marriage that has ever been made to me – am I to seize on it without so much as a second thought?'

She looked at them both, and a suspicion began to form as to what had really been worrying them.

Paul said, in a gentle tone, 'You're our dear sister, Maggs, and naturally we would support you in whatever you decide. But only think of it. Brigstock would provide you with a home, with security, perhaps in time – I don't know – a family. It would be hard to bear if you dismissed such an opportunity out of . . . mere wilfulness.'

'Wilfulness? That makes me sound like a petulant schoolgirl. I can only tell you that Mr Brigstock has given me a week's leave, which I hope will be long enough to make up my mind. There's nothing else to say.'

Her tone was steady, and the pause that followed seemed to indicate that the matter was concluded. But Ada, with a half-groan, broke out again.

'But if you should refuse him, dear—'

'Then what?' Maggie cut in. It was as she suspected. 'You mean to imply that this might be the only offer I'm ever likely to receive.'

Paul heard the danger in her hardening tone. 'That isn't what we mean,' he protested, though the quick glance at Ada spoke otherwise. Maggie was alive to it and felt a righteous fury bolt through her blood. She rose to her feet.

'But *it is*. You both fear I'm to become an old maid, wear dark-green bombazine and an old bonnet, no doubt arranging flowers and doing good work around the parish. Only now your conscience can be eased, and my dreary fate averted if I simply marry the first man who asks me. Then you can thank God for Brigstock coming to the rescue!'

Ada turned to Paul in dismay, but received no answering look. 'What – whatever do you mean, "your conscience"? Are we to blame for something?'

Maggie threw out a scornful laugh. 'I might have known you'd play innocent. But *you* know what I'm talking about, don't you?'

Her gaze had fallen on Paul, who felt himself shrink from the accusation even as he understood its justice. Her grievance, on the back stove for years, was coming nicely to the boil at last. He didn't speak: his silence was admission enough. Ada, bristling now, said, 'May I hear of what I'm accused?'

'You still claim not to know?' said Maggie, shaking her head. 'Very well. When mother fell ill, why did you assume that her care should be my responsibility?'

Ada blinked rapidly. 'Because there was no one else, dear. Izzy had just been born, we lived miles away – Surrey! What was to be done?'

'She could have lived with you. You have servants, and a cook, just as we do. But your refusal forced me to give up a place at university, the one thing I had worked for – longed for. Do you even now understand the sacrifice I had to make?'

'Mother wouldn't have liked to move. Her home was here.'

'That's very convenient for you to say. But she could have moved. If you had made her welcome she *would* have moved. Instead, I spent the best part of four years as her nursemaid. Four years up in smoke. And not once – *not once* – did you even thank me, because that would have reminded you of your own selfishness.'

She felt herself shaking with rage. Tears that had sprung to her eyes she brushed away; she wanted to howl, to scream at her sister's willed ignorance. She felt the empty sherry glass still in her hand, and as her eyes stung with salt she hurled it with force at the fireplace. It shattered exultantly against the grate.

Paul, closest to it, jumped in fright. 'Maggie, for God's sake!'

The sudden crash stunned them into silence. Directly above them a floorboard creaked; the girls had heard it too. Without another word Maggie swept out of the room. Paul and Ada stared at one another, immobile. Then Ada moved towards the door, muttering about a dustpan and brush, but he stayed her, cocking an ear. Outside they could hear Maggie in the hallway. A moment later the front door slammed, and footsteps retreated down the garden path.

X

It was fortunate that only two more days remained of the family visit. In the shocked aftermath, Ada talked of leaving with the girls first thing in the morning, thus avoiding the risk of any further unpleasantness over breakfast, but Paul persuaded her to stay. Maggie would no doubt feel chastened after her outburst, and to leave prematurely would open up a serious rift. Ada, who didn't much relish changing her travel plans anyway, agreed it would be best to see out their stay. Something of her sister's heat must have scorched her, though, for as she was going to bed she asked Paul in a nervous whisper: 'Do you think ... am I to blame – about mother?'

His reply was measured. 'I don't know. Probably we both are. Neither of us did much to help her.'

'Yes, but that wasn't our—'

'It's late, dear,' he cut in. 'We can talk in the morning, if you like.'

He knew his sister: by next morning Ada would be less inclined to ponder the question of blame. She might even have forgotten about it.

When Maggie, last to arrive, sat down to breakfast a brittle politeness held sway. No mention was made of the previous evening, at least not by anyone who had been in the room. Gwen, with a nine-year-old's mixture of innocence and knowingness, said musingly, 'I heard such a loud smash last night. Did something get broken?'

'Just a little accident with a glass, dear,' Ada said shortly.

'Whose fault was it?' the girl pursued.

'Mine, I'm afraid,' said Maggie, who, contrary to Paul's forecast, didn't seem at all chastened. 'I was doing a little party trick I know, trying to balance the glass on my forehead.'

Gwen frowned, and said quietly to her mother, 'Is that really a trick Aunt Maggie can do?'

Nonplussed, Ada replied that she had 'no idea'.

Maggie, however, was in an expansive mood. 'You don't believe me? Very well, would you like a demonstration?' At which she picked up her egg in its cup and to the astonishment of all leaned her head back at a ninety-degree angle. Then, with a balletic movement of her arm she balanced the egg-cup on her brow, and folded her arms.

'Good Lord,' said Paul, while the girls cooed their delight and clapped.

Maggie unfolded her arms and coolly removed the cup from its resting-place. Upright again, she smiled at Gwen. 'Last night I tried it with a sherry glass, which *wasn't* so successful.'

For the remainder of breakfast Paul watched her chatting away happily with the girls. She even played Hangman with them. Ada had silently excused herself in the meantime, perhaps wary of renewed accusation from her sister. But Paul sensed that Maggie had drawn a veil over the unhappy history of their mother's care. She had said her piece, memorably, and lanced the boil of a long-standing resentment. Whether it had given her satisfaction he was unable to tell. In his experience nothing contented his younger sister for very long.

He was back in his painting-room later that morning when a knock came at the door and Maggie entered. He felt an involuntary tension in his shoulders, though it seemed she was still in good cheer.

'You're late going out today,' she remarked.

He held up a tin of the runny pigment he was mixing. 'Preparing the sauce.'

As he returned to his chore she wandered around the room, stopping at this or that canvas. Paul could tell from her very step that she had something on her mind, and to help her along he tried an amiable overture: 'The girls were very impressed by your trick at breakfast. As a matter of fact, so was I.'

She smiled distantly. She went to the window and lingered there for a moment, composing herself. The only sound in the room was his knife-blade against the tin. Presently she said, 'May I ask you a serious question?'

'Of course,' he replied, not without a small foreboding.

'Is it better to marry for love, or to marry for security?'

He drew in his chin, surprised. 'Well ... I dare say one should marry for both, if possible.'

She returned a slightly impatient nod. 'Yes, but if it came down to it, which would you choose?'

He saw the searching gleam in her eye and knew he must answer honestly. 'I suppose I would say – for love.'

'Why?'

He hesitated for a moment. 'When one marries for security one is merely making a deal. But to marry for love one is making a commitment.'

This time her nod was slow, and thoughtful. She said nothing, but the expression on her face was touched with gratitude. He continued turning the knife in his tin of sauce, until curiosity prompted him to say, 'May I ask you a question in return?'

'You may,' she replied.

'Do you hesitate over Brigstock because of your feelings ... for someone else?'

She stared at him, then looked away. 'I don't know. Perhaps. That's something I must determine in the next seven days.' Seeing that he was keen to pursue the matter she became brisk. She had promised to take Isobel and Gwen to – she couldn't remember where – but she ought to get herself ready. She grazed Paul's cheek with her lips and hurried out of the room.

Paul spent the rest of the day in a maddening maze of conjecture as to whom his sister was 'perhaps' counting upon. And he drew nothing but blanks. In the course of their social life Maggie would meet various fellows of his own circle, at the Friday nights of the Club or the pipe-and-beer evenings at home, but none of them had paid her court. The only individual in whom she had shown particular interest was Evenlode, and he was a nonstarter. Where else might she have met someone? She attended their local church, of course, but that was hardly a trysting-place. The staff at her school were all women. Indeed, her horizons were so narrow the pity of it struck him with renewed force: he had not realised how lonely she was.

Ada and the girls completed their stay without further incident, and Paul waved them off at the door in a muddle of relief and regret. He would miss his nieces, for their playfulness and their bracing effect on the mood of the house. Towards Ada he remained affectionate, though he saw too well the provocations her character would always hold for Maggie. Following the confrontation they had behaved towards one another with a clipped civility. He wondered if it would be forgotten by Christmas.

There had been one other notable change: his nights were no longer harrowed by dreams. He marked this strange development from around the time he had visited the Sybil in Wimpole Street, though whether that was coincidence or not he couldn't say. A cloud had lifted, and he now considered the fee she had charged money well spent. At Kensington Gardens, too, he felt more at ease, reconciled to the disappearance of the lady and her children. He felt it almost as a certainty that he would not encounter them again. Sometimes he imagined they were spirits, melted into air; then he would look at the two canvases in which he had figured them, amid the shadows of the elms. They still looked real to him.

In the week following he was kept busy with gallery business, and had no time to assess Maggie's mood as her deadline drew near. Brigstock would have her answer on Friday. A more congenial diversion was Richard Melhuish's private view at Duke Street, where he hoped to encounter Rose Daubeny. He had been tempted to return to the Collins's, and then decided against it – shyness, and a reluctance to be seen 'stage-dooring'. Paul had asked Maggie if she cared to accompany him to Duke Street, but after a moment's thought she declined, and he suspected the reason: Brigstock was likely to be present.

So he went there alone, edging through the scrimmage, nodding at this or that acquaintance. He could tell that Towne was present merely from the boom of his voice, and of course Hackett and the rest of the Chelsea mob had come out, along with various cronies from the Beaux Arts. One could count on a decent crowd with Melhuish. The paintings, as so often at a private view, were a sideshow amidst the roar of the gossiping throng. Paul, ever the solitary, preferred to sidle around the room contemplating his friend's work, most of it painted in Paris and Normandy. He admired the way the bold brushwork caught something of its creator, of his outward-facing personality. The gaiety of the café paintings was so different from his own quiet exercises in light and mood. He felt no envy of Melhuish's success, for he knew that he himself could only paint as he must. Style to him was a compulsion, not a choice.

He was lost in thought when he felt a light touch on his sleeve. Edgar Talmash had ghosted to his side, as discreetly as an undertaker. Paul found his presence vaguely unsettling – civil enough, but quite devoid of warmth.

'How do you like these?' Paul asked him with a glance at the wall.

'There's merit there,' Talmash replied in his spiritless tone. 'A little, um, *unbuttoned* for my taste.'

Paul could believe it: Talmash would always be suspicious of exuberance. They talked on while they surveyed the room.

'What's the latest on the Merrymount portrait? Last time we met you said there had been developments.'

'The debate continues,' replied the dealer. 'It's one of the most vexing attributions I've come across. The father or the daughter?'

Paul nodded. 'I suppose in the end it doesn't really matter – it's a beautiful portrait, whoever painted it.'

Talmash retracted his chin sharply. 'I couldn't be so cavalier about the provenance. To those in the business of buying and selling it matters very much whose hand it's by.'

Paul, seeking relief from this diet of dryness, spotted a tousle-haired creature hovering uncertainly and with a lift of his chin welcomed him over. Philip Evenlode, stepping forward, looked shy as Paul introduced him to Talmash. The latter surveyed the interloper with the slightly affronted air of a dowager pressed into company with a match-seller.

'We were just discussing the Merrymount portrait, Phil. You recall the story?'

'Ah yes. We talked about it together. Your sister, I think, had a particular interest in it.'

Paul nodded. 'Along with Talmash here. They both bid on it.'

Talmash, ignoring Evenlode, said, 'If Brigstock is going to sell he ought to do it now. Have you seen him lately?'

'As a matter of fact, he called round last week.' Paul checked himself: he didn't want to share confidences with Talmash. And now there would be no danger of doing so, for the latter, without ceremony, slid away. Evenlode had perhaps felt the discourtesy but was too polite to make complaint. He merely stared after the retreating figure, nodded and turned his smile on Paul.

'What a crowd! And your sister – she's here?'

'I'm afraid not. She's, um, indisposed.'

'*Oh ...*'

Paul instantly regretted his white lie. 'Well, she isn't really. But she has rather a lot on her mind.'

His friend's brow darkened with concern, though he was too well-mannered to pry. Paul felt that he could be trusted with the secret.

'She's, well – *entre nous* – Brigstock has asked her to marry him.'

Evenlode's expression froze, briefly, before he managed to shape a reply. 'And – she has accepted him?'

'Not yet. She wanted time to consider. They meet on Friday.'

'Friday. I see.' Paul discerned his inward struggle to digest the news.

Something unspoken shimmered between them, and he continued, 'Dab's a good fellow, as I keep telling her. But she'll make up her own mind.'

'In his favour, d'you think?'

Paul gave a helpless shrug. It was the question he had been ceaselessly turning over for days. He had never known suspense like it: Pinero might usefully study it when making his next drama. He looked about the room for sign of Brigstock. Perhaps he had stayed away for the same reason as Maggie.

'I'd better be off, old fellow,' Evenlode said abruptly. 'Please would you pass on my regards to your – to Miss Stransom.'

'Of course, Phil.'

The two shook hands, and Paul moved on. He had walked another circle of the room when he happened to pass the exit to the foyer, where he saw Philip Evenlode standing alone. His head was bowed in an attitude of deep rumination – a brown study, as they called it. People passed in front of him, and he remained stock still. An aura of pure loneliness glimmered around him.

Evenlode just then woke from his reverie. Still unnoticing, he put on his hat, turned on his heel and disappeared into the night.

And there, in a starburst of intuitive clarity, Paul had it – it was Evenlode whom Maggie held a torch for. The certainty of it came together all at once: the Shakespeare recital, her fury at Lucy's monopolising him at the party, her odd question about marrying for love or security.

He had been slow to divine it, but the truth it undoubtedly was.

'Will you not even wish me a "good evening", then?'

Paul started at the voice – a woman's – and turned to find Rose Daubeny, her expression caught between amusement and offence.

'I'm so sorry—'

'I've been standing here for ... I've not seen someone look so faraway since my old dad used to study the racing form!'

Paul stuttered out, 'I'd just been spying on a friend of mine who ... well, it doesn't matter. How are you?'

'Not so bad,' she beamed, and looked around the room. 'You know a lot of these people?'

He nodded. 'Richard's a popular fellow in our world.'

She smiled, appraising him in a candid but friendly way. 'Whenever I'm at Kensington Gardens now I can't look at those trees without thinking of your paintings. Like you've put a spell on the place.'

Paul took the compliment with a chuckle. 'I'm honoured by the association. Those trees are very dear to me.'

'I was wondering how it went with Mrs Searle. Did she tell you anything useful?'

'An interesting lady. As to her prophecies ... they await confirmation.' He had decided to treat the Sibyl's disclosures as a Roman Catholic priest would the secrets of the confessional. But he added, 'One good thing came of our interview – I have not had a single unpleasant dream to disturb me since.'

'There you are!' she cried. 'She's a lucky charm, see.'

Paul wondered if the actual reason behind his dreamless nights was to do with forswearing the tots of laudanum he had been habitually taking. His back pains had receded, and slowly he had got clear of the drug.

'Well then,' Rose continued, consulting her pocket-watch, 'is there anyone to keep you here or will you squire me back to Bayswater?'

'At your service,' he replied, smiling, and offered her his arm as they headed towards the exit.

Maggie, having instructed herself not to dwell every minute on the dilemma, was nevertheless consumed by it. She turned it over in her heart, seeking the answer. One reason she had responded so furiously to her sister's apprehension was a needling anxiety that she might be correct. What if this were indeed the only proposal of marriage she ever received? She went to bed on Wednesday night hoping that the next morning would bring a decision, and that she would rise in full consciousness of what must be done. She in fact awoke during the irresolute hour between five and six o'clock, the light outside grey – and found herself still in doubt.

When Paul had reported to her that Brigstock hadn't shown his face at Melhuish's event she'd interpreted it as a sign: he was just as reluctant to chance a meeting before Friday.

'You were home late last night,' she remarked.

'I accompanied Miss Daubeny – Rose – back to Bayswater. We ended up talking past midnight.'

'Oh. Are you that friendly?'

'We always seem to have a good deal to say to one another.'

Maggie saw reflected in Paul's eyes the significance of the next twenty-four hours, but neither found the words to meet the moment. Just before he left the house he thought of telling her about running into Philip Evenlode at Duke Street, and Talmash's rudeness to him. It would have been a way of testing the ground, but again the old reticence held him in check. They had been the closest of strangers to one another.

She pondered the scene of Brigstock's proposal, wondering if his ardour still endured or if the interval of a week had induced second thoughts. She felt she wouldn't have blamed him if he *had* gone cold on the idea, for it would at least lighten her load of responsibility. In truth, she was so flattered by his offer of marriage that a strong instinct prompted her to accept it. Brigstock surely knew plenty of women, and might have asked any one of them to marry him in the assurance of a favourable reply. That he had asked her, whose social orbit had been vanishingly narrow, was a compliment.

A rendezvous had to be made, and on receiving his note asking her to name one she had decided it must be on neutral ground. Kensington Gardens was the obvious choice, but then she was conscious of it as Paul's place of work, and didn't want to ask her brother to stay away. Brigstock lived close to Regent's Park, so she wrote back suggesting they meet there at midday. On Friday morning she woke in a mood of decisive clarity. She had made up her mind – she would accept Mr Brigstock after all. He was charming, had good looks, and seemed to her a gentle and decent man; that he was also well-to-do could not be denied. She would be financially secure, probably for the rest of her life, which, if not being quite the all-consuming priority to her that it seemed to Ada, was nevertheless a motivation. And, reluctant as she was to admit it, her sister's fear of the missed opportunity did weigh with her. The chance of such an offer might never come again.

She caught the omnibus from Chelsea. The air was warm as she ascended to the upper deck, though the mouse-grey clouds massing in the west glowered. London raced on around her as the 'bus jolted northwards. Distractedly she pulled at a loose thread on one of her glove-buttons, managing only to unravel it further. Now it looked merely untidy, hanging there, and she plucked it away, leaving a little knot. Damn!

She alighted at Oxford Circus and bent her steps up Portland

Place. The walk would allow her to compose herself, though it would mean arriving late for their appointment. Well, he had waited a week already; another ten minutes would be no imposition. A bell rang the hour from somewhere on Marylebone Road as she entered the park and headed along the tree-shadowed Broad Walk. Some minutes later she caught sight of him, waiting at the water fountain. He was handsomely turned out, cane in hand, wearing a navy frock coat and grey trousers. His beard looked freshly trimmed. On seeing her he raised his hat. Her heart began to quick-march.

'Miss Stransom,' he said with a faint smile.

They fell into step. Brigstock began talking of inconsequential things, occasionally turning his gaze on her. She made short replies, her voice sounding strange in her ears. The purpose of their meeting brooded in the space between them. A few light spots of rain dotted the pavement, answering to the earlier warning of the clouds. Her eye caught on a blackbird as it settled on the overhanging branch of a tree; she watched it preening itself for a moment. Then it looked busily about, and in a fluttering instant vanished again. She thought then of the stuffed bird under glass on Brigstock's mantelpiece.

Following a brief silence he said, 'You asked for a week to consider my offer to you. May I now expect an answer?'

She paused. The certainty she had felt some minutes earlier had dissolved. Some new instinct had taken over and was pushing against the decision she had made. 'I am sorry to have kept you waiting. And I am sorrier still that I must decline your proposal.'

He gave a little start. 'I see. Will you tell me why?'

'Please understand, I feel the honour of it deeply. No man has ever proposed marriage to me before—'

'I find that hard to believe.'

'It is the truth, all the same. Your words came as a shock to me, and a pleasure. I know in what high esteem you are held—'

He waved that off with an impatient hand. 'If it was a pleasure, why do you refuse me?'

There's the rub, she thought. 'My principal reason is that we are nearly strangers to one another. However attractive seems the prospect, I cannot commit myself to a lifetime with a man I barely know.'

Brigstock shook his head. 'But we are friends, surely? And marriage will enable us to become something more than that. Do you suppose every man and woman know each other thoroughly before they ... plight their troth?' The archaic phrase brought a half-smile to his face. But not to hers.

'I believe some foreknowledge of the person one chooses to wed is vital. Indeed, it seems to me one's responsibility. Marriage is always in part a gamble, but I imagine one stands a better chance of success if a real acquaintance precedes the commitment.'

His expression was grave as he listened. For some moments they continued in silence, the only sound the soft tap of his cane. At length he said, 'Your doubts about me, then, might be resolved by the simple expedient of ... time?'

'I was speaking more generally about marriage,' she replied. 'A couple might avoid many pitfalls of a life together if they took the precaution of trying to understand one another first.'

'Forewarned is forearmed ...' At that moment the spots of rain came down quicker, and he looked up at the sky. 'Talking of which, I might have been better prepared had I brought an umbrella instead of this thing.' He swished his stick in annoyance. 'Here, come ...'

He guided her to shelter beneath the dense foliage of an oak tree. As they waited there the rain grew heavier, and people hurried past, hunching beneath coats and umbrellas. She sensed him trying to retrieve the thread of their interrupted talk.

'Maggie, I take your misgivings seriously. What if – what if we were to set an engagement for, say, six months hence. Or a year?'

She heard something defenceless in his tone, and it stabbed her with pity. 'You would be prepared to wait a year?'

'If I thought you would eventually assent, then yes.'

She saw that she had opened the door a crack, and it disturbed her. 'Such an arrangement wouldn't be fair to you,' she said gently.

'Why not? You would have more time, and I would have your pledge.'

'But it isn't a pledge. Even a year might not change my mind.'

He stared at her, his frown deepening. The rain in the trees sounded a percussive melancholy. 'So you don't foresee a time when you might . . . love me?'

The pain of that word, only spoken now, rasped on her soul. 'I don't know. I honestly don't know. But I have too much respect for you to make a promise I mightn't be able to keep.'

'Is there anything I can say to change your mind?'

She turned her face to his. 'I'm sorry.'

'Perhaps not as sorry as I am,' he said quietly. 'I had a notion that you might hesitate, and then would come round. My error. To be rejected is hard. But to be rejected when there is no other attachment to prevent you—' He abruptly realised his presumption and said, in a different tone, 'Unless I have been under a misapprehension?'

She shook her head. 'There is no one else. It would have been impudent of me to delay if there had been.' It was the truth, but in a distant avenue of her consciousness an unresolved figure lingered, and she felt, against all reason, that she must keep him in view. Oh, the yearning of this little life!

Around them the trees dripped steadily. Brigstock gave out a sad sigh. 'A blow to my hopes *and* to my pride. You are given a choice between me and nothing – and you prefer nothing.'

In a sudden onrush of tenderness she clasped his hand. 'Please, *please* don't feel bitterly towards me. I have nothing but admiration and friendship for you, and it would grieve me if this caused an estrangement between us.'

His gaze searched her face, and then dropped. 'I don't feel bitterness. People are disappointed in love all the time. But I must tell you that you have dealt me a blow – a severe blow. I feel something has died in me.' He held her hand for some moments, then looked out at the dismal curtain of rain sweeping across the drive. 'Well, the weather answers my mood,' he muttered, then turned to her. 'Goodbye, Miss Stransom.' He tipped his hat to her, and walked away.

XI

'Here's what Bradshaw has to say about it ...' Maggie, the handbook open on her lap, read aloud: '"A favourite and recommended resort ... The shore is not abrupt, and the water almost always limpid, and of that beautiful sea-green hue so inviting to bathers. The constant surging of the waves, first breaking against the reefs, and next dashing over the sloping shingle, is not unwelcome music at midnight to the ears of all who sleep in the vicinity of the shore."'

'I like a little music at midnight,' remarked Paul, seated opposite her in the thrumming carriage. Their train was bound for Hastings. Having boarded at Charing Cross an hour ago, no one but the ticket collector had disturbed them since. As the somnolent meadows and orchards slid past their window Paul felt an unburdening in his limbs the like of which he hadn't known in many months. He had timed their trip to the coast for the week after Maggie's fateful Friday, reasoning that they would both profit from a break, whatever her decision might be.

She had returned from Regent's Park soaked through and somewhat bedraggled. On arriving home she went straight to her room and gave way to an hour or two of wretched contemplation. The memory of Brigstock's beseeching expression, and his lonely figure as he walked away, forced tears to her eyes. For a long while she lay very still, her face pressed to the pillow. Yet she could also admit that her tears came not merely of regret but of relief. So anxious had been the week preceding, and so exhausting her vacillation, that simply to have faced the music had a cleansing effect upon her. She could breathe again. When Maggie came down to dinner that evening Paul marked the distress in her raw-rimmed eyes, but beyond informing him that she had refused Brigstock the matter was not touched upon: it was understood she would supply an account of what had happened when she was ready.

"'Delicate persons,'" Maggie continued reading, "'who desire to avoid exposure to the north-east winds, may pass the cold season here with advantage. Owing to the close manner in which this place is hemmed in on the sea by steep and high cliffs, it has an atmosphere more completely marine than almost any other part of this coast ... '"

By way of reply Paul took out his long-stemmed clay pipe, filled the bowl from his pouch and lit it, drawing deeply. As Maggie went on, he only half-attended her recitation of the town's delights. His mind was still absorbed in picturing 'the Muse of the Halls' – Rose, by any other name – after their meeting at Duke Street. On arriving at her mansion block she had invited him in for a nightcap – there was no landlady to negotiate, nor was Rose the sort to fret over Mrs Grundy – and so the evening had magically extended over whisky and soda. Her apartment, overlooking the Bayswater Road, was expensively furnished and carelessly maintained. Velvet plush sofas, brocade curtains and vast gilt mirrors impressed a worldly glamour upon the mood, though the full ashtrays and smeared plates and burn-holes in the cushions indicated that Rose was no domestic stickler.

She was, however, an excellent hostess, not only topping up his drink but rustling up a fillet of fish for a late supper: 'I've got an arrangement with a feller who keeps a stall across the road,' she explained.

Once they had eaten he nodded towards the gleaming black grand – did she play?

'I never learned prop'ly,' she said. 'But I can remember enough to get by.'

'Play something now,' he said, and when she gave a demurring laugh he added, 'Please?'

For a while her hands fluttered along the keys, beginning a tune and then abandoning it, but of a sudden she smiled and said, 'A friend of mine wrote this daft song – I quoted a bit to you the other day, remember? It's called "Starvin' in a Garret", about a painter, like you. I mean, not *exactly* like you . . . ' She set herself, and began.

Paul watched her as she played. The song unfolded over several verses a comical tale of artistic pretension and failure. The 'h'artist' believes himself to be a Rembrandt of the London commercial class, able to turn his hand to all genres and styles – he would indeed be the toast of the 'Royal H'academy' if only he could persuade them to recognise his talent.

> *Do your portrait – why, of course!*
> *Paint your wife, or that old horse*
> *Yet times for me is tough, I don't know why*
> *I'm starvin' in a garret*
> *All I've 'ad to eat's a carrot*
> *But you'll want to buy my pictures when I die*

Rose, concluding on a pert note of drollery, turned on the stool in clear expectation of applause. But her face fell as she saw Paul's unsmiling expression.

'What's the matter?' she asked in alarm.

'You ask me that after holding up my profession to mockery?' he said coldly.

She stared at him, open-mouthed. 'But Paul, honestly – I didn't *mean* anything by it. It's just a silly bit of fun . . . '

He might have continued with this show of affront if his smirk hadn't given him away – and he collapsed into laughter.

Now *she* looked outraged. 'Oooh, you're wicked, aren't you?'

'Sorry,' he said, doubled up. 'I couldn't resist. The look on your face was wonderful to behold.'

She shook her head, then a tiny smile creased the edges of her mouth. 'You devil! I thought you'd really got the hump . . .'

The sound of a train's hoot broke in on his reverie. Maggie was staring at him. 'What's that smile for?'

'Oh, nothing,' he replied. 'I was just recalling a little mischief I played the other night. On Rose Daubeny.'

She smiled, hoping he would say more. Mention of her name seemed to conjure an animation in his features she saw at no other time, and she wondered if the lady held him in the same high regard. But nothing else followed.

At Warrior Square they emerged from the station to the sound of gulls cawing and screeching at one another. The moist air carried a tang of brine and fish – the scent of holidays. They took a fly with their luggage to their hotel, the Sussex, on the front. Once installed, Maggie felt in need of a lie-down, so Paul went out for a walk alone. Though he had visited the south coast during his childhood, he had never been to Hastings. He was lightly prejudiced against the place, or against its reputation, bracketing it with Brighton – which he did know – as an enclave of fashionable idiocy. Drab covens of black-clad matrons occupied the esplanade and the 'sloping shingle', and the tea-rooms fronting the Parade were thronged with foolish faces.

But once among its cobbled lanes and arboreal squares the town showed a quite different face, stately yet modest, and oddly serene. The parts of it dating from the previous century – fishermen's cottages, bow-windowed shops, tiny taverns – recalled their old Chelsea neighbourhood before it vanished beneath the building of the Embankment. The light, too, was a painter's gift, soft, nacreous, with a blush of violet in its upper regions. He came to a park where he bought an ice from an Italian vendor, and ate it while strolling the perimeter. It was not a rival to the beauty or grandeur of Kensington Gardens, and being a Saturday in August its greenery was overrun by promenaders and picnickers. But he saw possibilities here, perhaps if the crowds thinned out during the week. He had packed paper and charcoal, along with a small box of oils – yes, this might be the place ...

Seated on a bench, he was idly surveying the scene when, at the corner of his eye, something, some*one*, shimmered into view. He started in fright. He knew from the white dress, from the very sway of her shoulders, that it was her. She was walking, at a pace neither hurried nor leisurely, along one of the radial paths that led towards the park entrance. Suddenly he was on his feet and gravitating in her direction. Fear lent a spurt to his steps, though of course his gait was draggy and uneven. He could sense people watching him, an ungainly little man stumping along, but he didn't care – he had to confront her, ask her why she was – *who* she was. After vanishing from his sight for weeks, months, he had assumed her gone for good, but there she was, only forty yards away, thirty ... Should he call out, address her? *Stay, illusion!* He was closing on her, but she was nearly at the entrance where a good deal of human traffic was about – the ice-cream stall with its queue, a juggler and his little audience, people taking a constitutional on this late summer's day.

The sight of her was now obscured by the tall hedges. Soon after Paul reached the entrance, breathing heavily, and looked left and right down the avenue. Nothing. The woman had, true to form, vanished into the ether. He blinked a few times, as if he might dismiss an hallucination from his eyes. But he knew what he had seen.

He made his way back to the hotel just as the afternoon light was shrinking. The rattle of bathing machines being hauled up the shingle marked the day's end. Maggie answered his knock at her bedroom door. She was restored after her nap and fancied a stroll before dinner, so they made an agreement to meet downstairs in half an hour. Paul returned to his room, where he sat before his window, smoking, and thinking. Outside his window the gulls kept up their loutish racket. At the appointed hour he went down to the foyer, where he found Maggie waiting in her stout boots. In wordless companionship they began walking east along the esplanade. Just before the pier they descended the stone boundary to the beach. On the shingle they watched the sun stage its melancholy descent. 'Where did you go on your walk?' Maggie said presently.

'Hmm? Oh, to the Old Town. I found a nice little park. I had a smoke and . . .'

She looked at him, waiting. After a period of silence he said, musingly, 'Have you ever seen a ghost, Maggs?'

'I don't believe so. Why?'

'Oh . . . I think I'm being haunted.'

She gave a snuffling laugh. 'You're not serious . . .'

But when he didn't reply she became grave, and asked him what on earth did he mean. And so, haltingly but not reluctantly, he told her the story of his summer in Kensington Gardens, the first sight of the mother and her daughters playing cricket; the reappearance of the mother in his dreams, always in white, the sense of foreboding around water – and the park-keeper who had told him of the drowning accident in the Serpentine.

'Twenty years ago?!'

'More than. That's when I turned to the metaphysical world for an explanation . . . I even consulted a palmist.'

'Oh Paul!' Her tone was sceptical, but he merely shrugged.

'Well, by this point a fortune teller didn't seem such a bad idea. D'you remember that day I was very agitated about Ada and the girls taking a boat trip? I'd just seen the lady – the palmist – and was afraid the accident might be reprised. I know it sounds outlandish, but you must understand, this lady in white – she's not going to leave me alone, Maggs. She's *here*.'

There was an edge of consternation in his voice, and she now saw the meaning behind his hollow-eyed looks. Gently, she said, 'Are you still taking those draughts of laudanum?'

He stared at her a moment. 'Not any more. I knew I'd been ... well, I haven't touched the stuff in weeks.'

Maggie lifted her hand to his arm. 'There must be a *rational* explanation, surely? We both of us know there's no such thing as – the lady you saw today – it must be you're mistaken, dear.'

'Believe me, I've been over it, countless times. I know it's the same woman, I know it without a shadow of a doubt. She will not leave me be.'

They fell to watching the breakers roll in and foam across the shore, seething, withdrawing. The sea's cobalt surface of earlier had dulled to a grey, and beneath it stirred a restlessness. Presently, Maggie said, 'What, then? What does she want from you?'

Paul slowly shook his head. 'Deuced if I know. The lady in Wimpole Street told me I was in danger, but it can't be from my apparition, I think, because she flees at the sight of me.'

'What sort of danger?'

'I don't know. All she said was – it was near.'

Maggie stared at him. 'Why didn't you tell me this?'

He gave a shrug. 'I didn't want to alarm you. And I'm still not sure that it mightn't be a lot of bosh.'

'Exactly. Palmists, clairvoyants – they're most of them frauds, you know.'

'Mrs Searle came highly recommended ...'

'By your Miss Daubeny, I suppose. What next – table-rappers?'

He laughed, and blushed. His sister's shrewdness often came with a little spike of acid. He saw no use in further talk of auguries, and amiably slipped his arm through hers.

'Shall we have dinner? All this sea air has made me ravenous.'

She returned a willing look, and they walked on.

When he repaired to his room that evening, his senses pleasantly blurred from the wine they'd drunk, he had a strong apprehension of a restless night ahead. He never much cared for a hotel bed. He supposed a dream, or indeed a flurry of dreams, was inevitable. In fact, he slept quite soundly, waking only once on hearing a long continuous murmur; this was followed by a rhythmical sort of wheezing, like a giant taking deep stertorous breaths. After some moments, lying there, he realised it was the sound of the tides, heaving back and forth. *Break, break, break* ... He got out of bed, pulled up the sash window and stared out into the dark. Even at this height, and a wide parade separating them, he could feel the salt spume on his face.

After Paul went off the next morning with his loose-leaf paper and paints, Maggie lingered over her tea in the hotel lounge. There was something she felt she must do, if only to set her mind at rest. The story of his haunting had perturbed her, and as a rational being caused her to wonder: could the balance of his mind be in peril? Nothing else in his behaviour indicated trouble. He was always steady in temper. If he had shown any difficulty in getting down to work she might have been concerned, but painting was the thing Paul never shirked from or neglected – it was his true companion. Nevertheless, she had to reassure herself.

Upstairs in her room she waited until she heard the chamber-maid on her rounds. She stepped out and called her – Would it be possible to check in her brother's bedroom along the corridor? She had mislaid her fan the night before and thought she might have dropped it there. The maid saw no objection, and unlocked his door for her to enter. Maggie thanked her, but the girl remained outside, hovering, so she knew she had to be quick. On the chest of drawers a few small items were austerely arranged: a razor and soap, a small bottle of cologne, a hairbrush. She opened his travelling bag and went through its contents – clothes, in the main, spare collars, shirt-studs, a cigar case. She undid a buttoned side-pocket and felt a bottle inside, fearing the worst. But on inspection it proved to be a bottle of turps, not laudanum. She made a cursory sweep of the room, just in case he had secreted it elsewhere. There was nothing. Even if he had brought the drug with him, he would not have seen the need to hide it – for why would anyone go snooping in his bedchamber? She thanked the maid and returned to her room.

She felt relieved. But she remained somewhat puzzled that he should have told Miss Daubeny of his supernatural visitation before telling her. Why confide in a stranger rather than his own sister? A stranger, moreover, who believed in consulting fortune tellers. To Maggie the idea smacked of charlatanism: time was when Paul would have thought so too. Either despair had driven him to consult a palmist or else he had become enthralled to his cockney song-bird – 'the Muse of the Halls', if you please! Perhaps Miss Daubeny regarded Paul as a soft touch and had encouraged him to patronise the woman. She'd heard that 'professional' clairvoyants charged extravagant fees, and there were always people gullible enough to pay. It wasn't impossible that the two women were in cahoots.

She stopped herself. The speculation was mean, and unwarranted. Nor was it pertinent to Paul's anxiety: *he* believed he had seen this woman, in Kensington Gardens, and here. And he did so in full possession of his senses.

They had been at Hastings for three days when a letter came for Paul. It was of no great length, and he read it while standing in the hotel lobby. Maggie, on further study of the Bradshaw, had already left that morning to visit the castle ruins overlooking the town. He decided to set out after her. The sun, hoisted high, was stronger today, and the ascent to the castle from Wellington Square was more arduous than he'd anticipated. By the time the ancient walls and bastions were close he felt quite breathless and had to pause; sweat poured down his brow and stung his eyes. He rested on a bench by the steps while sightseers filed up and down the winding path. At one point a short, vigorous-looking old lady stopped to ask if he was quite well, and he thanked her, with assurances of his health. He was touched, and rather embarrassed: she was perhaps forty years his senior.

On reaching the summit of the ruins he strolled among the other visitors, families with children done up in sailor suits, boatered gents and their sweethearts, boisterous youths whose careless volume cut the air as harshly as the seagulls. From this lofty vantage he could see, to the west, Beachy Head, Eastbourne and Bexhill. Down below the sea glistened, immense, indifferent. It would be quite something to paint at this height, he thought, although he quailed at taking on that hill again. He spent a while looking about for Maggie, in vain. He supposed she had already exhausted the sights and was on her way back down. He wandered towards the edge of the promontory, away from the crowds, and finding a secluded spot he lowered himself on to the grass. He took out his pipe and pouch and soon had the bowl aglow.

'Paul? What are you doing here?'

He looked around, shielding his eyes against the sun. Maggie stood there, hands on hips.

'I came hoping to find you,' he said as she went to join him. 'This view ... I feel I should tell Richard Melhuish not to bother with Normandy. Everything he needs is here.'

'Yes, except that Étretat sounds more prestigious than Hastings. And a French name will put an extra ten guineas on the price.'

Paul laughed. 'You ought to be a dealer – give Talmash a run for his money.'

'So what *are* you doing here?'

'I had a letter this morning – from Towne, of all people. Emma forwarded it.'

He produced it from his pocket.

She looked at him. 'You're not going to tell me he's made his fortune?'

'Sadly, no. He has other news. The verdict has been delivered on *Portrait of a Young Man*. It's not a Merrymount, according to the experts. "Not sufficiently splendid to be from the Master's hand," says Towne, "and much too fine to be from his daughter's." They think it's the work of someone in his circle, or else a brilliant imitator.'

'I wonder how Mr Brigstock took the news.'

'Philosophically, according to Towne. He didn't know the picture's provenance when he bought it, so the imbroglio that followed was, strictly speaking, irrelevant. Tantalising, all the same – who wouldn't wish to stumble on a lost masterpiece?'

Maggie was sitting with her arms loosely clasped around her knees. 'He bought it for me, you know. Brigstock. That morning he asked . . . he said he wanted to present it to me on our wedding day.'

'Oh, Maggs . . .' he said, shaking his head. Then: 'Were you tempted?'

She smiled sadly. 'I was touched. The romance of it. I *do* admire him,' she added, looking at Paul.

'But not enough . . .'

She paused again. 'Something else he said – that his happiness depended on me. Perhaps he believed it, but something in me recoiled. You can't allow your happiness to depend on another person.'

'It doesn't seem an unreasonable hope when you propose to someone.'

'But it's too great a burden on the other. Can't you see that?'

Paul made an ambiguous expression. 'I must take your word for it,' he replied softly.

Maggie heard the feeling beneath his tone, and her heart dropped a curtsey. 'I can hardly claim great experience of the subject. I am only trying to tell you why I couldn't accept him.'

He nodded. 'I understand – really. But I also see it from Brigstock's point of view. I know better than most what sort of woman he has lost.'

She smiled, and put her hand in his. 'I hope he won't take against me.'

'He'll recover, in time. He's a stout fellow, and he's generous.' Another silence intervened before he said, 'When I asked you, a few days ago, whether there was someone else . . . is it Philip Evenlode?'

She gave a sharp blink. 'How – how did you know?'

'I didn't. I guessed.' He told her of the night he had met Philip at the private view and had mentioned Brigstock's proposal. 'I saw him just before he left the gallery. He had the air of a man in profound despair.'

Maggie's eyes were downturned, seemingly drawn to her laced boots, or the parched grass. Perhaps Philip Evenlode did return her feelings, after all, but what good could it do? In worldly terms he was quite impractical. He would no sooner think of asking a woman to marry him than he would apply to the Queen for a loan. He had every grace and charm – and talent, if only he could use it. What he didn't have was a farthing to his name.

Paul was waiting for her to say more, but she felt herself weary of confession. Perhaps there was nothing more to be said. She rose to her feet and brushed herself down.

'Shall we go back?'

Their seaside sojourn was proving a tonic. The honest talk about Brigstock and marriage had not only cleared the air but had renewed the amity of feeling between them. The days were spent in their own pursuits, Paul going off to paint, Maggie out walking or taking one of the coach excursions to nearby sights. In the evening they dined together and afterwards read or played whist in the lounge. One afternoon she decided to have a dip in the sea, and found it so exhilarating that she did the same the next day. The warmth of the sun and the pensive swell of the water were calming, and smoothed away the anxieties of the past few weeks. She even found time to write a breezy postcard to Haslemere, all the ill-feeling of that night apparently forgotten. Paul had spared her the trouble of communicating the Brigstock news to Ada.

It was agreed they should spend their last full day, the Saturday, together. They lunched on whelks from a stall on the esplanade, then took a turn around the park that Paul had visited on the first day. It was hot, hotter than it had been all week; on the sea, tiny boats lost their definition beneath the hazing sunlight. The gulls wheeled overhead, screaming blue murder at one another. Maggie wanted another swim, and while she prepared herself in a bathing machine Paul found a spot in the shade close by. With a pipe clenched between his teeth he took out his small palette and a stiff-backed display card whose text he had scraped away to a *tabula rasa*: he would paint his own postcard. He aimed to catch the wobbling aquamarine of the sea in mid-afternoon, the bounce of the light on the water, the emerald distances.

On the pebbly strand a man was hauling one of the striped bathing machines into the water. Minutes later Paul saw Maggie lolling amid the swell, perfectly at ease: she was the only one of the family who had learned to swim. Now she was striking further out, and her head had turned towards the shore. She had spotted him, and he met her wave with his own. Beyond her, miles beyond, a steamer inched across the horizon before dipping out of sight.

He mixed the paint slowly. It was hot there, even in the shade, and the lazy slap of the waves sounded a siren call to him. He loosened his collar. To spend a week on the coast and not even get your feet wet – it was unnatural. He laid aside his palette. Pulling off his boots and stockings he rolled up his trouser legs and tiptoed over the shingle to the water. The tide lapped voluptuously around his ankles. Shielding his eyes with his hand he looked around him: a few promenaders with parasols, some bathers, children horsing around. He felt himself almost invisible. He began wading along the shallows, hands in his pockets, feet in the churning sand beneath.

He sensed her before he saw her. What else would have made him look up at that instant to see the girl in white, dress rippling in the thin breeze? Her stride was steady, purposeful, as she entered the sea fully clothed, fifty yards up the strand. He recognised it instantly as the motion of one intending never to come back. Nobody else appeared to have noticed her. Paul dashed the pipe from his mouth and quickened his pace, but, as in a dream, he felt himself flounder, baulked by the resisting tide and his old incapacity. She was up to her waist when he called out, *Here! I'm here!* They were the first words he had ever addressed to her, and he felt a shock as she stopped and turned, looking in his direction. Her face, partly obscured by the curtain of dark hair, was young – he thought he could see freckles – but her eyes, flickering, fearful, were those of a woman who had seen too much, or lost too much.

'Stay,' he called to her. 'Please – don't go any further.' He couldn't be sure, but he thought she half-smiled, as if moved by this desperate plea. Sweetly, tentatively, she raised her arm in farewell, and drifted on into the waves.

He too was up to his waist; and the sea which moments before had tilted serenely back and forth now bared its teeth, hissed and bucked and tore him down in its undertow. As he sank he took a mouthful of the brine and came up again, gagging. The shock of its ambush winded him, and he scrambled for a foothold that was no longer there. Down he went, helpless against its tug, feeling the wild spasm of panic as he plunged. When he burst to the surface again he managed to fill his chest with air, and flung out a cry for help. But who was there to catch it?

Lungs exhausted by his frantic flailing, he felt the resistance to oblivion leaking away. He was going down, down, lost in the fathoms, down into that cavernous gloom where no one and nothing would cradle his cold head. *We perished, each alone* ... Where was she now, the woman he had meant to save? Lost, like him, her tendrils of dark hair streaming like seaweed as she sank ... *But I beneath a rougher sea, and whelmed in deeper gulfs than he.* But no, his summoning her to mind had stirred her to action, it seemed, for hands – a woman's hands – had laid hold of him, were forcibly dragging him back from the dark. Brightness again. The sound of ragged breathing loud in his ear. His own feeble clawing at the air. He had been thrust back into the daylight, his exhausted limbs hauled backwards through the gulf, snatched words of reassurance the last thing he heard before passing out.

The next thing he knew his chest was being pummelled, his agonised lungs snatching, gulping for purchase. Maggie's face loomed anxious over him, wet from the sea, her hair dripping. Next to her was a stocky, stubbled fellow – a local fisherman, as he later learned – almost squatting on him as his hands pressed out a rhythm. Paul suffered a violent shudder, and leaning sideways he groaned and vomited seawater. Around him he sensed a little crowd watching. Someone said distantly, 'Thought he was a goner.'

The fisherman pumping his chest heard that, and shook his head. 'Not today,' he said quietly. 'The sea only takes you when it's ready.'

XII

Paul was taken to the new hospital at White Rock, though this was by no means an end to his troubles, or to his sister's anguish. The congenital weakness in his lungs had been exacerbated by his near-drowning, and he succumbed to a virulent bout of pneumonia. For some days he haunted the shadowline. Alone in the hotel, Maggie fretted herself to distraction; nothing – long walks, library books, cigarettes – brought her relief. Each morning she set foot in the ward she braced herself, awaiting the doctor's sorrowful shake of the head, or worse, finding the bed she had visited the previous evening empty of its occupant. It recalled those long days of her childhood when dread over Paul's infirmity harrowed them all, and the house was permanent host to a doctor. Death was the neighbour that kept threatening to call.

Now, on the evening when his chances narrowed almost to vanishing, Maggie thought of sending a telegram to Ada to make haste from Surrey. She ought probably to have done so before, but a pale superstition stayed her hand: if she didn't write, then there was no cause for alarm. She was also mindful of the dire possibility of Ada's arriving there just as Paul's body was being wheeled off to the mortuary. It proved a fortunate hesitation, because the next morning an improvement was noted in the patient. In the afternoon he took a little broth, the first sustenance he had managed, and by the evening he was sitting up, his voice rising to a whisper.

His first enquiry was to one of the nurses: what had become of the young woman he had tried to save that day? Had she drowned? The nurse looked puzzled. As far as she knew there was no one drowned; the lady who had saved him, his sister, had been at his side these last three days. When Maggie came into the room he felt the tender shock of her appearance – bruised eyes, her face drawn, an air of oppressed fatigue. His fault, he knew. But she brightened on seeing him there, propped on the pillows, and a single tear raced down her cheek. She clasped his hand, and they gazed at one another for some moments.

'So as well as everything else,' he began, 'it seems I owe you my life.'

She smiled. 'You had a lucky escape.'

'I've had a rather confusing account of it from the nurse. Can you explain?'

'Only if you tell me what made you plunge into the water like that.'

'To save her, of course – the woman.'

She stared at him. 'What woman?'

'You mean, you didn't . . . ? The woman I saw in the park, the one I told you about, in a white dress.'

Maggie shook her head. 'There was no woman, Paul. There was nobody near you. That's why I couldn't understand . . .'

A silence fell between them. 'Maggs, I swear to you, she was right there – I even looked into her eyes.'

'I believe you. But she wasn't real. And she nearly caused you to drown.'

'But why . . . ? What am I to her?'

Her gaze mixed pity with incomprehension. It wasn't a question she could answer.

'Mrs Searle spoke the truth after all,' Paul continued. 'She said I was in danger, did she not?'

Maggie pulled a face. 'Let us say her wild conjecture happened to hit the mark.'

'*There are more things in heaven and earth, Horatio* ... I count my blessings, Maggs. And you're the best of them.'

She sidestepped the compliment by smoothing out the counterpane and plumping his pillow. 'We must get you back on your feet.'

'That might be days. I fear it'll be tedious for you.'

'You needn't worry about me.'

'I think we could do with some company.'

'I was going to ask Ada ...'

Paul closed his eyes, as if slightly pained. 'Please don't. Or not yet. I want someone cheery, someone who'll beguile the time.' He paused, and smiled. 'In fact, I know the very man – Philip Evenlode.'

She drew in her chin. The idea alarmed her, and pleased her. 'I'm not sure he'll ... D'you suppose he'd like to come?'

'"Like" has nothing to do with it. He'll come once he hears I've been at death's door. Would you write?'

'You want *me* to?'

'Well, I'm hardly in a fit state to do it myself.'

She looked at him uncertainly. 'If that's what you want ... I'll write to him this evening.'

He shook his head. 'Write this afternoon, he'll get it first thing tomorrow.'

She walked back to the hotel, rehearsing what she might say in her letter to Mr Evenlode. He *would* come, of course, out of regard for them both. Wouldn't he consider it odd, all the same? There was also the question of where he should stay. The Sussex was not exorbitant in its prices, but they were nevertheless vastly beyond Philip's means. It was quite possible he had never roomed at a decent hotel in his life.

She wrote first to Ada, careful to keep the matter vague lest she panicked her sister into coming immediately. Paul had been in an accident, she wrote, but he was recovering and would soon be 'up and about'. Then she wrote a less guarded letter to Philip, explaining what had happened, and found herself confessing the anguish of the days since.

> ... Of course I shouldn't like you to feel under any obligation, for you may have other engagements to honour. But if you were able to come down I know how much it would please Paul. I hardly need add that it would also be a great kindness to me.

She wondered how deeply that last sentence would weigh with him. Alone at dinner in the hotel she fretted over the imposition she had laid on a man she barely knew. How would *she* regard an acquaintance importuning her out of the blue to visit her brother in hospital? The more she considered it the more presumptuous her request appeared.

There was little chance to brood. The next morning a telegram arrived for her at the hotel: Philip would be arriving from Charing Cross later that day. In the meantime, she had resolved the problem of his accommodation through the simple expedient of putting him in Paul's room at the hotel.

They were seated beneath a spreading sycamore in the hospital garden that afternoon when Maggie spotted a slight, tousle-haired figure approaching down the lawn. She hurried to him, feeling a skip in her chest.

Philip clasped her hands with great warmth.

'How kind of you to come,' she said, leading him over.

Paul, swathed in valetudinarian blankets, beamed up at his friend. 'It does my heart good to see you, Phil.'

'My dear fellow, I came as quickly as I could. When I read of your ... I feel relieved just to set eyes on you.'

His arrival had an enlivening effect on brother and sister. For the first time since they had carried him into hospital that day, Maggie could see an end to her wretchedness. They talked in the shade of the tree for an hour, until the nurse insisted that her patient must rest. They said their farewells for the evening, with promises to return the following afternoon. Paul was on his way to the ward when he stopped at a first-floor window overlooking the front. He was just in time to catch sight of them walking slowly westwards along the esplanade, Maggie with her face canted towards Philip, who carried himself with the deferential forward tilt of a willing listener.

Paul nodded to himself: he had made a start in repaying his debt to her.

Before dinner they walked towards the cliffs as the evening light took on tints of rose and amber. Gaslights on the pier winked through the descending dark. They made their way up to Fairlight Glen, a sylvan hideaway overlooking the town, and rested on a wooden bench. Such was the drama of the last few days that their talk never felt likely to flag: she enjoyed his exclamations of horror and relief as the story of Paul's brush with death came out. She tried to downplay her own part in the account but Philip would have none of her self-effacement.

'Good heavens, saving your own brother's life by your pluck – it should have been a story in the newspapers!'

For all the companionable sympathy between them there remained a sense that one subject in particular was being avoided. Maggie, aware of Philip's natural delicacy, broached it by a round-about means.

'We had a letter from Mr Towne about the *Portrait of a Young Man*. The weighing of the evidence is over. It's probably not a Merrymount after all.'

'Yes, there was talk of it at the Beaux Arts. Is Brigstock disappointed?'

Maggie shrugged. 'I wouldn't know. I haven't talked to him about it.'

Philip looked bemused at this. 'Ah ... I'm sorry, I thought you were – from what your brother told me – he had hopes of marrying you.'

'Yes, he did,' she said evenly. 'But I'm afraid I turned him down.'

A silence held as Philip digested this. 'Turned him down?'

'You seem surprised.'

'I confess I am ... Brigstock's a fine fellow. And most eligible.'

'I went through no little trouble before I made up my mind.'

Philip, blinking rapidly, was still coming to terms with this astonishment. 'May I ask why – why you rejected him?'

'A number of reasons – I won't burden you with them.'

He nodded, and Maggie only wished she had the courage to tell him the principal reason. She turned to find him looking at her.

'I too have news ... though it hardly ranks in significance to your own.'

'Oh?'

'Well, an old friend of mine has written to me, from Sydney. He moved there to set up a boys' school a few years ago. He knows of my interest in poetry and Shakespeare and so on, and it seems a position has come up for an English teacher – he thinks I might be able to do something on the theatrical side, too, if all goes well. It's not badly paid and looks to be—'

'In Australia?' Maggie said suddenly, swallowing hard.

Some dismay in her voice seemed to throw Philip, who paused for a moment. 'It's a perfectly respectable place, the school,' he said, and added, with a little laugh, 'and it's not as though I'll be going out in shackles! We stopped sending them convict ships some years ago.'

His humorous reassurance was lost on her. All she had taken in was his intention to go to Australia. Australia! She tried to sound composed even as she felt a spiralling, fluttering panic in her chest.

'And you mean to go?'

He smiled, and shrugged. 'I think so. It's a fresh start. Maybe just the thing I need – after all, I haven't made a great success of things in London.'

'But you – you have friends here. Friends who care about you … who'll miss you.'

He pulled a face, half-accepting the compliment. 'I dare say I'll miss them as much. But … my friend seemed very hopeful I could make a living there.'

Maggie nodded, and seemed to be listening as Philip went on about his plan. But all she could think of was the near-certainty that once he had gone he would never be coming back. She grew quieter as they walked back along the front. It was unbearable to hear him sound almost cheerful about the prospect of departure. When they reached the hotel she pleaded fatigue, and asked if he would mind taking his supper alone. Philip gently expressed concern, but she brushed off his suggestion of calling a doctor. He plainly had no idea as to the real cause of her indisposition.

In her room she lay awake, her mind in seething tumult. The waves outside, breaking and withdrawing, seemed to measure out the span of time she had left with him. It had somehow seemed possible to her that she and Philip might one day … Was not that the hope which had emboldened her to reject Brigstock? She knew it was, and yet that fragile little flame of hers he had just unknowingly doused. He was leaving. Leaving, bound for the other side of the earth, without an inkling of the true tenderness of regard in which she held him. Or else he knew and despaired of it, the lifelong solitary, the hopeless case. *You will go away*, she thought, *and I will be left alone to bear the weight, to ponder all the things we will never know. All that we could have had, could have shared, could have been to one another …*

Outside, the sea heaved back and forth, relentless, implacable. This, the sea that would carry him away.

The next morning she rose early and wrote a brief note, which she pushed under the door of Philip's bedroom. Then she went out for a long walk around the town, returning at the hour she had asked to meet him. The sun was out, though a freshening breeze had got up to cool the air. She stood at the top of a stairwell on the promenade, directly opposite the hotel, and waved to him as he emerged. His cry of 'Good morning!' was both genial and unsuspecting; so far her morning had been one of restless preoccupation.

They descended to the beach and strolled for a while over the shingle. Maggie had rehearsed something to say while she stalked through the town, but the words still came haltingly.

'I confess, your news last night gave me rather a shock,' she began. 'I didn't know you were preparing to quit the country.'

'I had little idea of it myself until a few weeks ago,' he replied. 'My friend's invitation came as a bolt from the blue. But once I'd got over the surprise I realised there was much to recommend it.'

'Australia, though ... To forsake all that you know and love.' The tentative note she sounded on this last word would have melted a stone.

'My friends, of course ... but I have no family left, aside from a few distant cousins.' It was regret, but she heard nothing else in his voice.

'I know of one friend who would grieve your going – quite particularly.'

As she said this, she kept her gaze downturned. She couldn't bring herself to make an open appeal; pride played its part, as always, and fear, too. She waited for him to speak for what seemed an eternity. And just when she felt her hope shrinking away he said quietly, 'I can only say the loss on my side will be felt just as keenly.'

Feeling flooded her eyes. She reached for his hand. 'Then let me beg you not to go. If you care anything at all for me, I ask you, most humbly, please don't go.'

He put his hand over hers. 'But my dear Miss Stransom, I cannot be what you ... You must *marry*, if not to Brigstock then to someone else—'

'I don't want someone else, Philip – may I call you Philip? The only man's love I want ... is yours.'

He stared at her. 'Do you – really?'

'Yes! But do you return it? I feel that you do.'

'Of *course* I do,' he cried, and crushed her hand to his lips. 'You are the finest woman I know. If fate had allowed I would fall to my knees and beg you to marry me. But you see what a wretch I am.'

'No. You are the opposite of a wretch. You are noble and sweet—'

'And most confoundedly poor. Too poor to seek a wife!'

'What concern is that when I have enough for us both?' She touched his face with her hand, confident now. 'You are rich in all the things that matter, like kindness, and gentleness. And poetry! D'you know it was your voice I first fell in love with? That evening you recited "The Bridge of Sighs". *Take her up tenderly, / Lift her with care ...*'

He beamed at her, still shaking his head. 'And if I asked you – to marry?'

'Then I would say yes! But only if you agree not to go to Australia.'

He laughed. 'How could I go now?'

'Will you promise to write to your friend at the school and tell him that you must decline his offer?'

His smile was assent enough. 'I hardly know what I've done to deserve you. When did you first conceive the idea we might ... ?'

'I think it was the occasion of our little party. You spent the entire evening in the company of my colleague.'

He frowned in recall. 'Ah ... the young lady I accompanied at the piano.'

'Mm. "O Vision Entrancing" – a song I cordially loathe. I thought you'd taken a fancy to her, and I was wretched!'

He laughed, shaking his head. 'I liked her well enough. But there was only one vision entrancing me that evening.'

Her gaze on him softened. 'Philip. You cannot know the turmoil I endured these last few hours when I thought you were going away. Will you *please* write to your friend in Sydney? I mean, without delay.'

'This very day, I promise,' he said. 'In the meantime, give me a kiss and say – you will love me always.'

Maggie smiled, and obliged him very willingly on both counts.

Paul received their news that day with a glad heart. It seemed that his idea of inviting Philip to stay with them had been a timely one. Another few weeks and his plan to sail to Australia might have been irreversible. He had never thought to see the day Philip got married, but it pleased him very well that his own sister had made it possible.

Maggie kept their engagement private for two reasons; the first, to allow them both the opportunity (vital, in her eyes) to gain a better understanding of one another; the second, which she admitted only to herself, to spare the feelings of the man who had previously asked for her hand. Her respect and affection for Brigstock were such that she wanted to soften the sting of any humiliation he might feel on hearing the news. She would write to him, but no reply would come.

Let lapse the ensuing twelve months, and come to a late afternoon in September, 1890, one of those days when summer and autumn seem to lie in each other's arms, like lovers. Leaves were falling, they carpeted the pavement in crisp gold and green, but the sun turned a mellow face on the London streets. For Maggie, on her way home from the West End, it was a day of surprises. She had her first on turning up Tite Street, unpeopled at this quiet hour aside from a man stepping towards her, silver-topped cane in hand. His figure was thickset, almost burly, his gait heavy yet with a daintiness, like a circus elephant's. As he drew near she recognised him, though they had never met, and she quickly absorbed what he was wearing – a fine, slightly crumpled dark suit, silk tie, waistcoat, set off by the greenish carnation at his buttonhole. Perhaps in recognition of their being the only ones on the street he smiled (without showing his teeth) and raised his hat. She responded with a dip of her head, and a blush. Without a word they were past each other, though she couldn't help glancing backwards. *He won't remember me*, she thought, *but I'll remember him*.

After letting herself in at St Leonard's Terrace she put her head around the dining-room door. Emma had already laid the table for dinner. She found Paul and Philip smoking in the living room.

'I've seen him, at last,' she announced.

'Seen who?' asked Philip, sitting up.

'Our famous neighbour! We just passed one another on Tite Street.'

'Ah. And was he "larger than life"?'

'Well, he certainly had large pink jowls. Like an overripe fruit. But he raised his hat to me very charmingly.'

'And on his own?' said Paul. 'He's not usually seen these days without his band of apostles.'

Philip said to her, 'There's a parcel for you, by the way. It's in the hall.'

She must have walked right past it. On her way out she said, 'Who's coming to dinner tonight? I noticed the table's laid for four.'

'Rose. She has a night off. I hope you don't mind?'

'No, of course not.' It amused Maggie that both men deferred to her as if she were the household empress.

The parcel was large, squarish, trussed up with string. Emma, on being consulted, said that it had been delivered by a messenger boy. The label read 'Mrs. M. Evenlode, St Leonard's Terrace, SW'. She was still getting used to the name. With a pair of kitchen scissors she cut through its protective layers of cardboard and old newspaper, and as they fell away she realised with a shock what it was. A letter had been pinned to the reverse of the painting, and she opened it.

As you will remember, I bought this picture with a particular recipient in mind, so it has been hanging rather accusingly in my studio ever since. Because I can no longer look at it without a twinge of conscience (or a shadow of regret) I hope you will now accept it as a belated wedding gift. It comes with my most respectful regards to you and your husband. Please don't think of returning it, for I always considered the thing to be yours.

Denton Brigstock

PS By the time you read this I will be on my travels south – Menton for a few weeks, then across the border to San Remo. I shall send my poste restante address in due course.

She stared at the young man, whose face had first beguiled her. How she wished she knew his name – his people. What place he came from. What he had done with his life. He appeared to be enjoying her warm confusion of feelings. What were they? Astonishment, gratitude, guilt, a rising elation. But mostly it was disbelief, that Brigstock should possess such generosity of spirit! She picked it up, mesmerised by the young man's fineness of feature, though now her eyes were rather too blurred to focus.

When Philip saw Maggie in the doorway he started in alarm. 'My dear, what on earth ... ?' He was at her side as the tears ran helplessly down her face. She shook her head, unable for a moment to speak. But on the other side of the room Paul had spotted the painting she held at her side, and he understood.

The Flowers
of Romance

1

It is a morning in late March. Nell, in the garden, is on her hands and knees poking around with a trowel. She keeps hearing a noise from high in the laburnum, a delicate tap-tap-tap, repeating, like the vibration of a tiny drill. She gets to her feet and peers upwards. A silence, and as she steps around to get a different angle she spots it – a woodpecker, black and white with a raffish red-orange crest. She watches and listens, till it starts up again, tap-tap-tap, prospecting for insects. It has been here before. *I must get my camera*, she thinks, and takes a backward step towards the house. But this time her movement is noticed by the bird, and in the blink of an eye it's off, darting through the treetops.

She sighs, and returns to what she's been planting: gladioli, agapanthus, lilies. Her mother used to employ a gardener here, and together they kept the place in a blaze of colour. Decades later Nell has let it slide, and now guiltily intends to revive it. She loves herbaceous borders, but painting rather than planting them, and wonders what that says about her. She looks down at her hands, caked with dirt. She is rather taken with the idea of a flower garden, only she's not sure she has the patience. She sometimes peeks over the fence at the neighbour who's in his garden at all hours, furiously raking and seeding and clipping – and it still looks a mess.

Nell is about to go inside and get changed when her eye catches on a flash of white half-buried in the soil she's just been turning over. It looks like a bone of some kind. She kneels, and fishes it out with her finger and thumb: not a bone but a small clay pipe, its stem broken and the bowl with a faint hairline crack. She remembers other bits and pieces that have come to light – a medicine bottle, coins, a rusted apostle spoon – the detritus from previous tenancies of this mid-Victorian house. Like a lost property office that no claimant will ever visit. When she had the upstairs bathroom renovated a few years ago they uncovered an old fireplace, and found inside it a pair of workman's boots. How in God's name had they ended up there? They went on the skip at the time; now she wishes she'd kept them.

She examines the pipe again. Its stem was probably long and curving before it snapped. She knows from somewhere that clay pipes back then were meant to be disposable, you could buy them a dozen at a time. Strange to think of a man (surely it was a man?) here in this stretch of garden a hundred years ago, puffing away in his easy chair, perhaps, laying his pipe aside while he has a nap and then forgetting all about it. A hundred? Maybe more. She has just been reading that the long road she lives on in Kentish Town was established in the 1820s, and this terrace was built on it about twenty years later. She wipes off the dirt from the bowl of the pipe and slips it in the pocket of her smock: a happy bit of history.

In the kitchen she puts the kettle on. The TV people are coming at midday, but she must have a cup of tea before she begins sprucing herself up. And a cigarette – she opens a drawer and takes out her quitter's ten of Player's Navy Cut. From the hallway she hears the thump of another cardboard box being stacked: her lodgers, Sue and Simon, are moving out this week. Nell has always had lodgers. She began taking them in when her first husband left her with two daughters to raise and no money for maintenance. Once her painting took off and the girls moved out there was no longer a need for extra cash, but she found she missed the company and so the top two bedrooms were rented out. One of her lodgers, an Irishman named Roy, briefly became her second husband, and after that she made it a rule not to take in single men.

She has just lit up when Sue sidles into the kitchen. She is about twenty-five, sensibly short-haired and gangly, with an innocent dimple in her cheek. She has taken a few days off work – in the admin department of a North London poly – to pack up their stuff.

'Hello, love. Just making a cuppa, d'you fancy one?'

Sue smiles, shakes her head. 'Aren't the TV people ...?' *Aren't you going to change out of those filthy duds?* is what her look implies.

'Any minute,' says Nell, breezily twiddling her cigarette.

'Sorry, you can't move in that hall for boxes.'

Sue and Simon, her civil servant boyfriend, have been here these last five years. She doesn't really want them to go, but they've bought a little flat in Borough and are off on Friday. Nell fears she might blub when the moment comes. With cigarette and tea in hand she has a look into the hall.

'Have you got a van big enough for all this?'

Sue bites her lip. 'Simon's mate is lending us his VW camper thing, but I'm not sure ...'

'If there's too much you can always borrow my car,' says Nell.

Sue looks at her gratefully – she might take her up on that. They natter on for a while until Nell glances at the kitchen clock and realises she's got ten minutes to make herself presentable.

Hurrying upstairs she has a quick wash in the bathroom, shucks off her gardening gear and wriggles into her second-best pair of jeans and a brown Jaeger cardigan Billie gave her last Christmas. In the mirror she brushes her hair – dark, heavy fringe, filaments of grey – and stares at herself. Her figure isn't bad for sixty-two (she modelled in her younger years) and those cheekbones are forever, though her skin is finely crackled from a lifetime of worry and cigarettes. She strikes one of those pout-over-the-shoulder poses once common in the modelling world, then narrows her eyes. It occurs to her that the cardigan looks a bit mumsy, so she changes it for a long-sleeved T-shirt, gunmetal-blue and flecked with paint like nearly all of her clothes.

They are coming to interview her for *Nationwide*, trusty old-stager of early-evening telly. It is to herald a retrospective of her work, which has been enjoying an upsurge of attention after someone, also on TV, pointed out a painting of hers in one of the reception rooms at Downing Street. The *Camden New Journal* was on to this in a flash, and the coverage began to snowball. Her gallery in Hampstead was overwhelmed by enquiries, and a career that had drifted into the backwaters was being trumpeted in the Sunday supplements and *Harpers & Queen*. It has been gratifying, of course, though somewhat baffling to Nell, who had happily painted in semi-obscurity for decades.

The doorbell goes. Where will they talk? Not in her studio, which she doesn't even think of as a 'studio', just the room where she paints. Too cramped, anyway. The first-floor living room might be best, with its tall sash windows and view on to Fortess Road. She goes down to answer; on the doorstep stands a young bearded man in a lumpy cord jacket and grey trousers. Behind him his camera crew, three of them, wait in readiness.

'Mrs Cantrip? Jolyon Truefitt from the BBC.'

She holds open the door in invitation and they troop in, gazing around them in that unselfconscious way TV people have, as if they're on a visit to a museum, or a zoo.

'Please call me Nell,' she says, and goes off to make them tea while they set up in the front room, Jolyon's choice: he adores the chimney-piece and the chandelier he calls 'retro'. She can hear him in there giving out orders. As the kettle's boiling Jolyon wanders through, hands in pockets.

'Hi. They'll just be a few minutes, then we can get started.' He rakes his gaze around the kitchen, peers through the window into the garden. 'Charming house. Lived here long?'

'Most of my life. My parents bought it, ooh, fifty years ago ...'

'So your husband – your first husband – lived here too?'

'Yeah. We got married, spring of nineteen thirty-nine. I was looking after my dad, who was an invalid, and we were planning to buy a house when the war broke out. Johnny went off to fight in Egypt. He didn't have much money when he got back, I'd just had the girls, so we decided to stay here.'

'Right. And your younger daughter, of course, is Billie Cantrip. Who *everyone* knows. You must be very proud of her.'

Nell smiles. 'I'm proud of both of them. Tash – Natasha – teaches design at Central. She's married with a kid. So I'm a grandmother!' Nell thinks it's better to get that out of the way, like it's no big deal. She watches as Jolyon prowls about the kitchen, examining this and that. At a certain angle he's quite good-looking, she thinks, though he's got rather a hearty backside. Must be public school – that well-fed look. Now he asks if he can see her studio, so she leads him upstairs to the first-floor back. The bare floorboards and the uncurtained window lend a little echo to their voices. He picks up one of the unframed canvases propped against the wall and frowningly considers it, as if he's about to make an offer. It's of parrot tulips in a cream-coloured vase.

'Is this for the retrospective?'

She nods. 'There'll be a whole room of the flower paintings, going right back to the fifties.'

'Does all this publicity make you think, *About time*?'

'What d'you mean?'

'Well, you've been painting for forty years or more. Some might say you've never had your due.'

She gives a shrugging look. 'That didn't really occur to me. Starting out it was pretty tough; I took part-time jobs – cleaner, secretary, a bit of modelling. When my paintings began to sell I felt grateful – amazed, really. After all I'd been through it never seemed possible.'

He listens, then asks another question in a sort of mechanical way. She realises he's trying to warm her up, get her in the mood before the camera starts rolling. She answers as honestly as she can, though she fears she disappoints people as an interviewee. She doesn't care to talk about her painting, even with friends, because her work isn't something she entirely understands. Others can try if they want, but that's not her job.

The ten minutes the crew promised it would take to set up has turned into half an hour, by which point Nell feels she has exhausted her small store of newsworthy anecdotes to tell Jolyon Truefitt. The living room has been impudently rearranged, the big sofa shoved against the wall, the coffee table likewise, the floor now a coiled chaos of leads and cables you have to tiptoe around. In front of the fireplace two armchairs await interviewer and subject while the camera holds its implacable stare. After another wait they begin, and Jolyon, perhaps sensing Nell's unease, gently bowls questions about her life – her adored mother, who died when Nell was seventeen; her father who ran a furniture business in Soho; her first drawings as an eight-year-old when she illustrated the Hans Christian Andersen fairy tales she loved to read; then her struggle against the teachers who tried to 'correct' her left-handedness ('I'm still left-handed, by the way'); her beginning at the Slade; the interruption of the war.

'Was there an artistic side in your family?'

'Not that I know of. My mother was musical – she sang in her dad's pubs. She had a lovely voice. Otherwise ... there were theatre people, the Rothwells, on my dad's side. I had a Great-aunt Alice, who was an actress in the Victorian era. But I don't know much about her ...'

When he broaches the topic of her first marriage she tries not to sound defensive.

'You were very young when you married.'

'Yes, I was nineteen.'

'Johnny Cantrip was quite a famous figure at the Slade, wasn't he?'

'Mm, he was my tutor. Very talented – handsome! I was head over heels in love. Then the war came and Johnny joined up so we didn't have much time together at first ... But our two daughters came along and once Johnny was demobbed we began to ... well, we settled down as a family.'

'Was it hard, as a young mother who was also trying to be a painter?'

'Yes, it was ...' She pauses. She could tell the truth here, that Johnny, damaged by the war, became lost to booze, had several affairs, was dismissed by the Slade – then abandoned her and the girls. Attempts were made to patch things up, with promises on his part to reform, but they came to nothing. He died of liver failure at an Earls Court dosshouse in 1956. She can still taste the bitterness of those years, like copper on her tongue.

Instead, she merely says, 'It was a struggle,' and Jolyon, catching the appeal in her eyes, changes the subject. He's actually a good interviewer, she thinks, coaxing her along, appearing to listen even when she knows he's got his mind on the clock. The only moment that stumps her is when he asks about her 'philosophy' of painting.

'I don't think it's – I'm not sure I have one. I'm a painter, you see, not a philosopher.' Jolyon laughs at that, though she wasn't trying to be funny. 'I see something and I want to paint it.'

'Yes, but a lot of your later work deals in abstraction. Are you "seeing" something then, too?'

'Painting to me is a pattern,' she says haltingly. 'The colour, the form, the texture sort of come together. And if it doesn't then you try it another way. With painting, I don't have an intellectual explanation ... I just paint the things I want to look at.' She thinks that sounds feeble, but Jolyon nods as if it's a perfectly accept-able response.

Afterwards, while the others are packing up, he offers her a cigarette and they stand in the hallway, smoking. In the last hour she's upgraded him from 'quite' to 'very' good-looking. He's got a sweet smile, he's just tall enough, and even his big arse isn't that objectionable. It's his clothes she doesn't much like – sort of drab, unappealing. First thing she'd do is get him down to Kensington Market and shop for some decent clobber. He's smiling at her again. Well, maybe *second* thing she'd do ... No wedding ring on him, she notices.

'D'you mind my asking – how old are you?' she says, squinting at him through the smoke.

Jolyon gives a surprised laugh. 'I'm thirty-eight. Why?'

'Just curious.' She gives him her most sphinx-like smile. If Billie were here now she'd be rolling her eyes and thinking, *Oh Mum*. But Nell can't help it. Her inclination to flirt has not waned with the years. Jolyon responds with a chuckling remark about how he's never met a model or even an ex-model before – and at that moment they are interrupted by a noise overhead. It's Sue, tottering on the half-landing with another giant cardboard box. In an instant Jolyon does the gentlemanly thing, taking the stairs two at a time to relieve her. With a minimum of effort he shoulders the box down to the hall and parks it next to the others.

'Thanks ever so,' says Sue, who has taken no time at all to spot Jolyon as a person of interest. She looks expectantly at Nell for an introduction.

'This is Sue, my lodger,' she says, 'who's just about to leave us.'

Jolyon raises his hand. 'Hi. Jolyon Truefitt. BBC.'

'Did it go well?' Sue asks.

'Like butter off a knife,' he says suavely, and then starts making small talk with Sue about where she's moving to. Oh yuh, he knows Borough, *really* interesting part of the city ... Nell, sidelined, notices how Jolyon sharpens his conversational focus in the presence of this younger woman, indeed his whole demeanour seems to take on definition. The air is bristling with pheromones. *Nature's way*, thinks Nell, who was going to make Jolyon another cup of tea and now decides not to bother.

2

Billie, seated at the Savoy Hotel bar, glances at her watch: she'll give him another couple of minutes and then she's off. The meeting was scheduled for 2 p.m., and it's now half-past. Not that she's grand or anything, but really, as the lead actress she oughtn't to be kept waiting.

'He's a snot-nosed punk,' Penny Rolfe, her agent, has told her on the phone, 'but right now he's hot. His name'll bring the kids in. Do you want me to be there?'

'When we meet? No. Just let me know when and where.' Since then Billie has done research on the snot-nosed punk, otherwise known as Robbie Furlong, pop star. She's read an interview with him in the *NME* from 1980, just after he'd split from The Dead March, the 'jazz-punk' band he fronted. They put him on the cover, too, a skinny youth with a surly pout, peroxide-blond hair and cheeks lightly dusted with acne.

The Dead March are too wild for her, but she has bought his first solo LP, *Chain Lightning*. It's in the window of the Virgin Megastore this week. The sound is a mixture of soul, rock and jazz, and she's rather taken with his sensitive-troubadour warble, a bit early Van Morrison, a bit John Martyn. She had expected the LP cover to feature a moody portrait shot, but instead it's a black-and-white photo of a blurred figure, back to camera, crossing a city street at night. It seems to announce him as a 'serious artist'. Billie has encountered a few male rock stars in her time – berks, mostly, with no regard for appointment-keeping.

In the bar's narrow inlaid mirror she finds her reflection – short, straight nose and wide-set violet eyes that hold a stare unblinkingly. In her twenties her face looked as beautiful as a cartoon. Now, in her late thirties, something wary inhabits its neatly sculpted contours.

She half-turns on her bar stool to survey the room: a couple of suits sharing a bottle of wine, a gaunt youth reading alone in the corner, a floozy vamping an older man at a table near the door. Early-afternoon trade. She looks again at the youth in the corner. It can't be, can it? She climbs off the stool and takes a few paces towards him. He is reading so intently that she's practically leaning over his table before he notices her. He wears a brown suede jacket over a black-and-red checked shirt.

'Er, Robbie?'

The youth looks up, startled. This close he looks about eighteen. He is doe-eyed, like a girl, his dark hair short at the sides and fluffed up on top, with a fringe. The acne, she notices, has cleared up. 'Oh, are you ... ?'

'Billie. Have you been here all this time?'

He nods worriedly. 'Gah, sorry, I wasn't sure what you looked like.' *Loike.*

That's a West Country burr she hears.

'And I thought *you* had blond hair. Is that your natural colour?'

He smiles. 'Yeah. The blond was just ... a mistake.'

'Well, I'm at the bar. Shall we have a drink?'

He draws up a stool next to hers and tosses his paperback on the bar counter. *Gertrude* by Hermann Hesse. Billie orders another vodka and tonic. Robbie asks for a Coke. (He doesn't like the taste of alcohol.) Their agent, Penny, has arranged this meet-and-greet in preparation for a feature film they'll be making in London. It's called *Heaven and Earth*, about a professional dancer who starts to hear 'voices' and believes she's going mad. The voices, it transpires, belong to a pair of angels, good and evil – the former played by Robbie. They have shed their wings, dropped to earth and now compete for control of her destiny. Billie doesn't love the script, but the money they're offering is too good to turn down.

'So . . . your first film part?'

'First *acting* part. Aside from a shepherd in our school nativity play. This film . . . my manager advised me to do it.'

'Penny said you're taking lessons.'

He nods. 'My tutor's not impressed. Nor will you be, I imagine.' She smiles at this self-depreciation. 'Have you done a lot of films?'

She stares at him. 'You really don't have a clue about me, do you?' She ought to be offended, but she's not. 'I've done some film, but mostly TV and theatre.'

'Sorry,' he says again. 'Penny says you're, like, this huge star, and I'm embarrassed 'cos I don't really watch telly.'

Billie shrugs. "Sfine. Anyway, with your LP all over the record shops looks like the huge star is you. I like the cover, by the way.'

He makes a rueful grimace. 'The record company wanted my mug on the front. We had a massive argument about it. In the end I took a cut in the contract just to get my way.'

She can understand the record company's point of view: a face like his would sell. He's pretty, in the androgynous way that's fashionable at the moment. She takes out her packet of Silk Cut and offers him one. He shakes his head.

As she lights up she says, 'Don't drink, you don't smoke. Not very rock 'n' roll. You must have one vice?'

He nods. 'Wanking. And golf.' They both burst out laughing. Billie orders more drinks.

'We'll have to do a read-through, at some point.' When he looks blank, she explains: 'They have to make sure we've got, you know, chemistry.'

'Right.' *Roight.* 'Do you know this feller who plays my oppo?'

He means Maurice Venning, cast as the evil angel. 'Mm, he's a friend. We've done stage work together – he's great.' She decides not to mention that Maurice is also gay, waspish and likely to show Robbie no mercy. They talk on about the film, which will begin shooting in May. Robbie listens attentively, like a polite schoolboy. It becomes clear that his ignorance of the movie industry is fathomless; as well as Billie he's never heard of the director, the screenwriter or any member of the cast. The last film he saw in the cinema, she discovers, was *Grease*, five years ago. She's not even going to start with him on theatre: he's lived in London for four years and hasn't been to a single play. Half-amused by this cultural innocence, Billie asks him how old he is, and is surprised to learn he's twenty-two – he looks, and sounds, much younger.

'So what d'you do with your time?' she says eventually.

His answer is simple. 'Playing music. Or writing it. Or listening to it. It's all I've ever done.'

His father, he explains, was a jazz trumpeter who played the club circuit around Bristol in the '50s and '60s and steered him and his sister Evie towards music from a young age. Robbie could play the piano, the ukulele and the clarinet by the age of fourteen ('not all at the same time') before he switched to the guitar. He joined his first band, a punk outfit called Dogs of War, in 1977. A year or so later he quit to form his own band, The Dead March. They left Bristol for London, made their self-titled debut LP, played *Top of the Pops* and *The Old Grey Whistle Test*. They sold out shows at the Hammersmith Palais, made another LP – and split.

'What happened?' Billie asks.

'Oh . . . personal and musical differences,' he says with heavy irony. 'Well, it was just personal by the end. We couldn't stand each other.'

'Was it about you going solo?'

'Partly.' He stares off into the distance. 'I've got a few more dates left on the tour, then I'm done. The last one's here. D'you know the 100 Club?'

'Of course. Oxford Street. Maybe I'll come and see you.'

She's half-joking but Robbie stares at her eagerly. 'Would you? I can put you on the guest list, if you want to bring a friend.'

'I haven't been to a gig in ages. Do they still call them "gigs"?'

Robbie nods, taking out a pocket diary and pen. He's quite serious about this. She watches as he writes down her name in a tiny cramped hand.

'Billie is with an "i-e",' she says in gentle correction. 'Like Billie Holiday.'

'Gah, stupid . . . ' He carefully amends it.

It's getting on for four o'clock when Robbie says he must go: band rehearsal in an hour. They wander out on to the hotel's circular concourse where a doorman is shepherding guests into a cab. Robbie's paperback pokes out of his jacket pocket like a sixth-former's on his way to class. He puts on a pair of black Ray-Ban Wayfarers. Billie points out that it's not sunny.

'I gotta think of the fans.' He giggles and peers at her over the frames. 'So don't forget, next week, 100 Club. Name on the door.'

'OK, OK.' It's as if he doesn't quite believe she'll show up.

'Which way you goin'? I thought you lived west.'

'I do,' she says, 'only I'm off to my mum's for dinner. Kentish Town.'

They shake hands and she watches him walk off down the Strand, head down, his gazelle legs slightly bandy. He isn't what she expected, but that's all right. She has a feeling they will get on just fine.

Nell is proudly showing her what she's been up to in the garden. She has always grown vegetables there; now she's planted rows and rows of bulbs, they should come up late summer.

'The bloody squirrels are a nuisance, though,' she adds, 'digging them all up.'

'It's dinner to them,' says Billie, absently wandering up the stone path.

'I'll have to buy netting to keep 'em off.' She turns to Billie. 'What's that tune you keep humming?'

'Oh, it's been on my Walkman all week. You know Robbie Furlong, the kid I met this afternoon ...'

'How did it go?'

'Very sweet. Doesn't know much about anything, except for music, and on that he's phenomenal. I mean, jazz, classical, soul, rock – whatever – ask him anything and he'll know it.'

'Robbie Furlong,' says Nell blankly. 'Can't say I've heard of him.'

Billie laughs. 'Like *you're* some pop-picker!'

'I listen to the radio all the time,' she protests. 'I like the one that goes *I was dreamin' when I wrote this, forgive me if I duh–duh–dee.*'

'Prince. Yeah, well, Robbie's nothing like that. I've got the cassette with me; I'll play it for you.'

Back in the kitchen they drink tea and smoke. Nell watches Billie as she carelessly flicks through today's *Guardian*. It strikes her that she often painted her daughters when they were girls but has never done them as grown-ups, when they are far more interesting to look at. Billie's face is heart-shaped; her eyes are fringed by long, dark lashes and she has a pretty mouth with regimentally straight teeth. She doesn't look very like Nell, who has a longer, leaner face and brown eyes; her teeth are more characterful – slightly crooked, and discoloured from years of smoking. Yet Nell can discern in Billie those tiny echoes of resemblance that only a parent sees in a child, fleeting, elusive things she can't put into words though she might be able to catch them in a drawing. Of course, there is another face ghosting there, one that is forgotten to most but inescapable to her. Johnny's.

'More tea?' she asks Billie, who hands her cup across the table. After a pause Nell says, in a different voice, 'How's everything else?'

This generalised question is in fact a plea for disclosure. Billie looks over at her, understanding. She and her husband have been living apart for almost a year. He is Bryn Parish, also an actor: they met on a film set in 1975 and got married the following summer. It hasn't been a happy union.

'He's written to me again,' Billie says, raising her eyebrows. 'Says he wants to come back.'

Nell keeps her expression neutral. 'I see. Have you talked yet?'

The wedding was featured in the papers at the time, Billie in a white trouser-suit with kick flares, the groom in Tommy Nutter pinstripe and a knot in his silk tie as big as a fist. Bryn was coming off the back of his one and only hit movie, so for about six months the press followed them around, snapped them at parties and premieres, waited outside their flat until, to Billie's relief, the caravan moved on elsewhere.

Bryn, however, hadn't exhausted his taste for publicity and his charmingly lopsided grin became well known on TV. With his Welsh basso profundo, good looks and taste for the high life, he styled himself on Richard Burton. Billie had no desire to play his Liz. She didn't mind his attention-seeking. But she did mind when an eagle-eyed paparazzo caught him unawares smooching a young actress in a nightclub. They had a row about it, and then made up. A couple of months later he stayed out all night and was photographed leaving a house in Maida Vale – a different actress this time. The story emerged that it had been going on for a year, and Billie felt a bit of a fool.

'We talked on the phone. We're going to meet next week.'

Billie endures a spasm of shame here: she has already met him twice, for a drink, but can't bear to admit it.

Nell felt resistant to Bryn from the start. She never much cared for the ones who came before him. Billie, sane and sensible in most regards, has one disabling flaw. She picks badly – wasters, cheaters, wrong'uns. One of them, Jeff, whom she lived with for years, turned out to be psychotic: they sectioned him in the end. The problem is that Nell has her own terrible record with men – the first husband who bolted, the second a gambler who stole from her and hit her children. Other boyfriends have come and gone, none of them any great shakes. Nell worries that the flaw is hereditary, at least where Billie is concerned. Tash has managed to break the Cantrip curse and find someone, thank God, who loves and cherishes her (she hopes he'll be coming this evening).

'So you'll let him – move back?' Nell forces herself to ask.

Billie exhales, shaking her head, though it's a gesture of uncertainty, not of denial. Nell knows that people will make their own mistakes, and she must bite her tongue. Maybe he can change – though Johnny never did. Also, Nell feels she has burned her boats. To recall the things she has said about Bryn in front of Billie is embarrassing.

Since they've been talking the time has crept on close to six, and the start of *Nationwide*. The piece about Nell is on tonight's show. The family are coming over to watch, and she's got a lasagne in the oven for later. She and Billie have just settled in front of the TV when the door goes: it's Tash, and her nine-year-old, Gil, with his sky-blue Adidas T-shirt and Jackson Five afro. He gets straight down to it. 'Mum says you're on the telly tonight.'

'That's right! I don't s'pose it will be anything spesh, just me rabbiting on ...'

Tash says, 'Don't put yourself down. Millions of people will be watching tonight.'

Four years older, Tash is not the open, accommodating person that Billie is. Short-haired and long-limbed, she is sternly self-possessed, with a challenging glimmer in her eyes. The resemblance to her late father is more pronounced, though she doesn't smile as much as he did. Nell has always felt rather feather-headed next to her older daughter. In truth, she's a bit frightened of her.

Billie brings from the kitchen a bottle of wine, and a Fanta for Gil. On *Nationwide* the interview with Nell has been trailed, and every segment until then seems strangely irrelevant. The show's cheerful mix of stunt motorcyclists and enterprising pensioners isn't pacy, either. The waiting eventually prompts Gil to murmur, 'When is Nell on?' (Nell's glad that Gil has been trained by his mother to call her by her name, not 'Granny' or 'Grandma'.) Another interminable item winds up, Sue Lawley is back on camera and once the words 'The story of modern British painting' are out of her mouth Billie turns up the volume: here it comes. Images of Nell, images of her paintings, flash across the screen as Jolyon Truefitt's voice delivers a neat precis of her career. The interview, intercut with archival footage of the Slade and 1960s London, passes very quickly; the conversation hardly gets going before it's over. As the closing shot of Nell painting cuts back to the studio, Billie sing-shouts 'You're a star yes-you-are!' and gives Nell a side-on hug.

'You were really good,' says Tash – a rave by her standards. 'Wasn't she, Gil?'

The boy nods vigorously.

Nell, however, can't seem to find her voice. She has barely listened to the interview, and struggled even to watch herself.

'Mum? What's wrong?'

Her eyes are moist. 'I can't get over how *old* I looked.'

This provokes a storm of denial from them that Nell hears but doesn't heed. Seeing herself on screen is actually appalling. That dried-up prune, inconceivably, is her. The face she sees every day in the mirror is not that of a sexy, happy-go-lucky woman after all. She is not simply older; she is old. How she wishes she had refused the BBC. Now she has been undeceived about herself. She gets up from the sofa and, without a word, returns to the kitchen. She pours another glass of wine and takes a slug. It tastes like vinegar.

In the living room Billie and Tash talk in low voices. They know their mother; know her disabling susceptibilities as well as her whip-cord strength. Age has never appeared to dismay her before – she celebrated her sixtieth two years ago without complaint. Because she is self-sufficient and devotes most of her time to painting (and because she is their mother) they have made assumptions about her. One such is that Nell no longer considers herself a sexual being.

'She was upset about Sue and Simon going,' Billie says, *sotto voce*. She can see Gil is trying to earwig. 'They were very fond of each other.'

'Well, she enjoys company.'

'Yeah, but ... this is something else. I think she might be lonely.'

'Lonely? We see her or talk on the phone almost every day.'

'That's not the kind of lonely I mean. You know how she likes to flirt, to have a man interested in her. Possibly ... she misses it.'

'Oh, she's past all that,' Tash says firmly.

Nell was quite a beauty in her day: photographs of her from the '40s and '50s, just seen on the telly, confirm it. She was always admired. People who are used to being noticed aren't easily reconciled to invisibility. Billie doesn't think of her mum as a Norma Desmond-type, but it's hard all the same to know you were the prettiest girl in the room, and never will be again.

They are halfway through dinner when Chris, Tash's husband, arrives with apologies and a bottle of wine. 'Sorry I missed you on the TV, Nell,' he says in his languid reassuring tone.

'You didn't miss anything, love,' Nell replies, helping him to the lasagne. Chris is a youth counsellor who works long and unsociable hours. He and Tash met when they were both involved in the protest against the demolition of Tolmers Square, near Euston, ten years ago. Now they live in Leighton Road, about five minutes' walk from here.

Nell's mood noticeably picks up as Chris asks her about the plans for her show. She loves it when a man pays her attention, even if the man is just her son-in-law. Then they all watch and clap as Gil does a street dance he's learned from *Top of the Pops*, called moonwalking. There's a bit of mime in it, too, which makes them laugh. The *mauvais quart d'heure* of earlier is forgotten. Billie, watching Nell, is relieved, but she is also remembering an occasion from long ago, when she was eleven – the first time she saw her mother in genuine distress. It must have been some weeks after their dad's funeral (she and Tash in floods, the widow dry-eyed) when one night she finds Nell slumped on the living-room sofa, face hidden against her folded arms. At first it seems she might be napping; then she sees her shoulders heave, and she knows. On the Dansette the same song plays, over and over, which is why the scene remains so vivid to Billie. Sarah Vaughan is singing '(I'm Afraid) The Masquerade is Over'.

Johnny had left them for good, years ago, and drifted almost into dereliction. The marriage was defunct. The news of his death that winter of 1956 was a shock, but it wasn't a surprise. Did her mother love him still, or was she only mourning the memory of him? Billie stands there for what seems an age, appalled and moved, until Nell looks up, eyes blurred with tears, and holds out her arms. Billie runs to her. They sit there, nearly in the dark, hugging each other for dear life.

3

Nell is in the painting-room, smoking, while Véronique, her dealer, makes notes on the pictures she intends to take. The retrospective is scheduled for the end of July. Véro is in her late thirties, about Billie's age. Her streaked blonde hair in a severe bob, she wears a mannish white shirt and a modishly cut black leather jacket that emphasises her slim figure. When Nell feels the sleeve she coos, 'Mmm, buttery soft, isnit?'

'Yeah, it's Alaïa,' replies Véro.

'A liar?' repeats Nell, puzzled.

'Azzedine Alaïa – I bought it in Paris.' She goes to Paris to stay with her mother, long divorced from her husband, Véro's dad, who's a luxury car salesman, or possibly an arms dealer. That's where the money comes from, enabling Véro to run a gallery, live in Kensington and dress herself in couture. (That she once spent £400 on a pair of shoes is still a source of wonderment to Nell.)

From the garden on this brisk April morning a faint rhythmical tapping drifts up. Nell steps over to the sash and raises it, her ears pricked.

'It's back!' she cries, turning to Véro. 'My little friend.'

Véro stares at her. 'What little friend?'

'My woodpecker. Come and have a look.'

Rather reluctantly Véro puts down the canvas she's been

examining and moves to the window. They stand watching, listening, for a few moments.

'It's very rare, apparently,' Nell explains, delighted by the soft rat-tat-tat echoing from the tree. 'And look at its gorgeous orange mohican.'

Véro says, 'Fascinating,' and returns to her inventory of the paintings. On the mantelpiece sits the little clay pipe found in the garden the other week. Nell was also going to show her this but decides not to. To Véro it will be just a broken bit of junk. Indeed, she would find most things here quite tatty, including the sixties wallpaper, the exhausted furniture, the chipped paintwork – and probably Nell herself, who is not wearing couture but paint-spattered dungarees and plimsolls. All that interests Véro are the canvases racked against the walls, ready to be converted into hard cash. Some aren't yet framed. Nell would usually have them done by her local man, Horace, whose shop has been in Kentish Town for over eighty years. But Véro prefers a smart place she knows down in Chelsea that will do the job at greater (reassuring) expense.

She is holding up a picture now, sixteen by twenty, her dealer's eyes narrowing. It's a portrait of a man with floppy dark hair, his serious gaze directed away from the painter, refusing to engage. She has not seen it before.

'Who's this?'

'You don't know? It's Johnny. The girls' father.'

Véro is scrutinising the date on the reverse. 'Gosh, nineteen forty-six ... *early*. And rather wonderful, too.'

Nell has such mixed feelings about the picture, and about its sitter, that she finds it almost impossible to judge. Nineteen forty-six was the year before Johnny first bolted. She was still in love with him then. Véro places it squarely on the mantelpiece to have another look. She strikes her professional, folded-arms pose, and says, 'This will give the first room such a focal point.' They have agreed on a rough sequence to the show. The first room, of four, will comprise

Nell's earliest work, from the Slade to the mid-fifties. The second will be her flower paintings: signature work. The third will follow her late break into abstraction during the sixties. The last will take the story up to the present.

Nell says, in an afterthought, 'Darling, would you mind marking that one not for sale?'

'Really? You know it could get—'

'I don't care,' she says evenly. 'I'd rather not let it go.'

Véro stares at her, and shrugs. A few moments later she says, 'By the way, I've been thinking about titles. For the show. How about "A Maverick Eye"?'

Nell isn't keen. The name conjures James Garner in that ancient TV series, which Véro almost certainly won't know. At that moment the telephone rings, relieving her of the obligation to reply. She goes down to the hall to answer.

'Hello. Am I speaking to Nell Cantrip?' says a voice on the line, a woman's, Home Counties posh. 'This is Hilary Polden. I don't suppose you've heard of me.' Nell admits she hasn't. 'I saw you being interviewed on the television last week, and you happened to mention a great-aunt of yours, on the Rothwell side of the family. Well, believe it or not she – Alice Polden, née Rothwell – was my great-aunt, too. Which means you and I are second cousins!'

Nell is taken aback. 'I'm sorry – Hilary, you say? I had no idea. How did you ...?'

'Oh, I just found you in the phone book. I hope you don't mind my ringing you out of the blue like this.'

'No, not at all. Alice ... did you know her?'

'Afraid not, she died some years before I was born. But she was quite famous for a while, on the stage – just like your daughter. In fact, we come from rather an illustrious line. Are you aware of this?'

'Illustrious?'

'Yes, I know! A long story, which I'd be happy to tell you. Would it be possible to meet?'

'Of course,' Nell replies. Hilary lives in Aylesbury, but she often comes down to London to visit her daughter in Clapham. So they work out that she will call at Fortess Road one day next week. Nell wonders if Hilary is a bit strange, because she then delivers a rather giggly, convoluted ramble about their forebears in which certain names keep bobbing up, like answers to a quiz Nell hasn't entered. But it would be intriguing to meet this relative she didn't even know she had. They settle on a time, and ring off.

Nell returns upstairs, dazed. She finds Véro still clacking imperiously about the room, making notes in her Filofax.

'D'you know, I've just had the oddest conversation. Turns out I have a cousin in Aylesbury . . . Hilary, she's called.'

'Really?'

'She saw me on telly last week. When I mentioned this great-aunt, Alice Rothwell, she realised we must be related. She's going to come and see me.'

'Oh!' Véro's tone has changed. 'I hope she's not after your money.'

Nell laughs. 'What money?!'

'I'm serious, darling, I've seen this before. You're going to be much richer by the end of this year, and you may suddenly find you have *lots* of relatives crawling out the woodwork, looking for a handout.'

'Oh, it's nothing like that. She sounds posher than you are.'

Véro purses her mouth at that. 'I'm just saying, be careful. Money has a habit of attracting all sorts of undesirables.'

After further consultation Véro decides her list of paintings is complete. She will send the van around from Kensington tomorrow to collect them. In the meantime, she asks Nell to think of a title, since she doesn't care for any of the ones suggested so far.

'How about "A Painter in Kentish Town"?' says Nell.

Véro wrinkles her slightly pointed nose. 'Not very sexy, is it?'

'But it's true.'

'Mm, that's not the point. We want a title that will, you know, sock it to 'em ... and better be quick about it, darling. We have to get the catalogue to the printers by the end of this month.'

The cork as the waiter pulls it makes that delectable half-sucking, half-popping sound – their second bottle of Chardonnay this evening. Opposite her sits Bryn, her estranged husband, whose idea it was to book this place, Langan's on Stratton Street, where they had their first date. He's got them a good table, too, right by the Hockney. He is wearing a nailhead dark blue suit with a skinny tie (modish rather than raffish) and his dark hair, longer now, obliges him to keep flicking a quiff back from his narrow forehead. He's forty-five, eight years older than Billie, and looks well on it – better than he deserves.

'D'you remember that first time here together?' Bryn, sentimental about the early days, fixes her with his lopsided grin. 'God, I was nervous! When you agreed to have dinner with me I was, like, *You've hit the jackpot, baby!*'

'Were you nervous?' asks Billie. 'I thought you behaved like you always did.'

'How's that?'

'Cock of the walk. I remember those tight disco pants of yours – you strutted around like Barry Gibb.'

He shrugs. 'I'm a woman's man – no time to talk'.

'Actually, you did nothing *but* talk. Typical Welsh. By the time we got to pudding I'd forgotten the sound of my own voice.'

'Oh, that's not fair!' he says, choking off a laugh. 'We tired the moon with our repartee. That's what I thought was so great – you're a woman, but you know how to have a laugh.'

She decides to let that go.

The mood between them – fond, familiar, lightly mocking – is a reverb of how it used to be, in the years before Bryn decided to barge his way into the limelight. Billie likes him in this more reflective manner; she believes it's his real self, and the Burtonian party animal merely a put-on. She doesn't mind him showing off, it comes naturally, but it coarsened him later. He fell in with a younger druggy crowd of actors, and the nights he and Billie used to spend together were given over to new temptations. If she decided to complain at his absences he would dismiss her as a killjoy. He became fast friends with one particular actress named Jenny Daunt, whom he'd met, like his wife, on a film set. Billie didn't believe the rumours about an affair until the morning it was smeared across the front of the *Mail*.

She doesn't want to think about all that now – the public humiliation, the screaming rows, the sudden shock of his moving out – but she keeps probing it, like a loose tooth. He has told her he wants to come back, to start again, and the romance of it appeals. (But there's a pragmatic element, too. She'll be thirty-eight in October and a decision has to be made.) He's persuasive in presenting himself as a reformed character, chastened by their separation. She's teetering on the edge of believing him.

Bryn is loosening an oyster from its shell when she says, 'So what happened, by the way? With Jenny.'

He looks up. 'It didn't work out. I think I annoyed her even more than I did you.'

'That would take some doing. Are you seeing anyone else?'

'Of course not. Why would I be seeing someone when my whole project is getting you back?'

'Well ... it wouldn't be the first time you've run two women at once. I thought I'd better check.'

He stops fiddling with the oyster, puts down the fork. He stares at her. 'Do you really hold me in such disdain? I mean, short of dressing in sackcloth, I don't know what I can do to convince you I'm sorry.'

She hears stress in his voice. 'All right, fine. But you understand why I might be gun-shy? You *hurt me* – remember that.'

Bryn pushes the drooping comma of dark hair back off his

forehead again. It's becoming a tic. He looks troubled. Absently he picks up the wine and refills their glasses. There is a long moment before he speaks.

'D'you remember that time you said to me, "It's always a surprise to see you doing wise or kind-hearted characters when I know deep down what a bastard you are"?'

'Mm. It was after watching you play Sir Robert Morton in *The Winslow Boy*. I was amazed by how convincing you were as a morally upright man. It didn't seem possible that you could pull it off.'

He laughs in spite of himself. 'For some people acting seems to carry a moral implication – they confuse the life of the character with the person who's been paid to play it. It's a common mistake. But I never imagined that *you'd* make it. Are you anything like the people you've played on stage – on telly?'

'Sometimes. But that's not my point. It's the surprise of it I'm talking about. Most people watching you as Morton wouldn't have a clue about who you really are. But I did, and the contrast between you struck me as ... mysterious.'

'But it's just acting!' Bryn rejoins. 'You know that. Somebody else's words from somebody else's mouth. Sounds like you're complaining because you were taken in by my brilliant impersonation of probity.'

'Maybe I am,' says Billie. 'But is it naïve to think that some aspect of a character might be absorbed, a little bit, by the actor playing them?'

'Actors aren't sponges, my darling. It's hard enough for us as it is. We seek attention and they accuse us of being narcissists. We perform, and they tell us we're showing off.'

'*If you prick us, do we not bleed?*'

'All right, I've said my piece,' he replies, holding up his palms in surrender. 'Though may I add, just for the record, that *Winslow Boy* is one of the best things I ever did.'

'I agree. You were brilliant in it.'

'Thank you.'

He leans back in his chair, placated. Their sparring, which might once have turned nasty, is put on hold. The flirtatious warmth of some minutes before is restored, and they move on to the safer topic of work. Bryn is doing Chekhov in Greenwich, lots of prestige, not much money. Billie tells him about *Heaven and Earth*, trying to make it sound less like the feeble hokum she knows it to be.

'I met Robbie Furlong last week.'

'Ooh, the pop star.' Bryn's eyebrows rise enquiringly. 'Is he is as cute as his photographs?'

'No. But he's much nicer than I expected. He's like a sixth-former with his floppy hair and his Herman Hesse paperback.'

'Can he act?'

'Don't know yet. But he's got a great voice. Have you heard any of his stuff?'

Bryn wrinkles his nose. 'How old d'you think I am – twelve?'

'There's more to music than Barclay James Harvest, you know.' It's a joke between them. When Billie first visited Bryn's flat theirs was the record at the front of his stack, and she's never let him forget it. 'Matter of fact, he's playing the 100 Club tonight and my name's on the guest list. You can come with me.'

He makes a demurring expression. 'Not sure it's my scene . . . And I thought we might go on to the Nines after this.'

'Oh, did you?'

'Only if you fancied.'

Billie is aware that a late-night drink might speed things along between them. It is something she ought to refuse. She has set a careful tempo to their meetings – a brief drink or two, a dinner – to keep Bryn on the back foot, make him wait and wonder. Accepting an invitation to the Nines, his club in Mayfair, is more than likely to segue to a night at his place, at which point her finely paced campaign of resistance would disintegrate. Still, they haven't had pudding yet, so there's time to stiffen the sinews and make it clear that she's calling the shots.

They are racing through the second bottle. Bryn is enthusing about her mother's appearance on *Nationwide*.

'You saw it?'

'Of course. You told me she was going to be on.'

'She got a bit depressed about it. D'you think she looked old?'

'Not at all,' he replies instantly. 'She looked fabulous – you can tell her from me.'

'Since she's been on her own she's lost some of her self-confidence. She needs ... well, she likes the security of being with someone, feeling she's admired.'

'Don't we all?' says Bryn archly.

'But it's not the same for you. Men can always pick and choose. For a woman, if you miss your moment that's it. Mum's still attractive, but she knows no one's going to make a play for a sixty-two-year-old. I try to gee her up, so does Tash, but there's nothing much we can do.'

'Can't you find some nice old gent to move in? There must be loads of them out there.'

Billie shakes her head sadly. 'She's had a rotten time with lodgers, you know that. Usually ended in tears. Or in marriage, which was worse. We basically had to tell her not to take in any more single men. For her own good.'

'What was the name of the second husband?'

'Roy. An Irish tinker who nicked from her to pay his gambling debts.'

'Ugh ... forgotten he was Irish. Those Celts ... '

She fixes him with a knowing look. 'Hereditary weakness.'

Her father, though born in London, made much of his Irish roots, always playing John McCormack records at home and slugging Jameson like it was milk. Billie has a childhood memory of sitting with him in an Irish pub in Holloway, odd in itself because he usually left her outside, with the other kids. At one point in the evening he stood up to sing 'How Are Things in Glocca Morra?' in his affable tenor. They all roared at the end, and as he sat down he winked at her. She'd never felt so proud of him.

Bryn is looking down the list of *digestifs*. 'Fancy an Irish coffee? Just kidding. I might have an Armagnac.' He hands the list to her, waits a beat, then says, 'Or we could go on to the club for a nightcap.'

Billie glances at her watch. Nearly ten. She supposes Robbie will have been and gone at the 100 Club by now. He was so keen for her to come along. Well, there'll be other times.

'All right. Just the one.'

Bryn smiles, and signals to the waiter with a flourish of his invisible pen.

4

'She came from a very large family, of course – the youngest of *eight* – so we may have all sorts of lost relatives out there.'

Hilary Polden, Nell's cousin, is seated at the kitchen table at Fortess Road. She is talking about their great-aunt, Alice, whose passing mention by Nell on *Nationwide* the other week has brought them together this morning. Hilary is a bright-eyed, talkative, pudgy woman in a merino roll-neck and elasticated slacks.

Her large unstylish glasses are tinted, and rather age her, though Nell guesses she is a few years older than Hilary. The chocolate digestives she put out with their coffee have been snaffled up, so she empties the rest of the packet on to the plate. Nell has been trying to spot hints of a family likeness in her visitor, so far without success. But Véro's warning that Hilary may be 'on the make' is surely misplaced. For one thing, she is too well informed about the Rothwell family tree to be a fraud; and she shows no sign of wanting anything from Nell, aside from company, and the biscuits.

'But with all respect to Alice, she's not the ancestor of ours who most interests me,' says Hilary, dipping into her wicker shopping-basket and producing a hardback book, its pages frayed and foxed. She holds up its cover, with its watercolour illustration of a domestic scene from the Georgian era.

'Does that mean anything to you?' Hilary asks. When Nell shakes her head she continues, 'I didn't think it would. This was published in, let's see, nineteen sixty, a few years after they discovered this lady's papers in a house clearance somewhere in Wiltshire. They'd been mouldering away in a trunk unopened for decades and would probably have remained so but for a certain Colonel Burlingham. So, he had found among the letters and diaries a connection named Joseph Rothwell.'

'I suppose we're related to him – to Joseph?'

'Yes, but it's more intriguing than that. You see, Laura was the older daughter of William Merrymount, and what she reveals in this journal is rather extraordinary. To give you the short version, you and I are descendants of the great man himself.'

Nell stares at her. 'Really?'

'Yes! It's all in here. William was a bit of a roué, and had a long affair with an actress named Elizabeth Vavasor. She gave birth some time in the seventeen eighties to a boy, Joseph Edmund, but didn't let on who the father was. The name she gave to the child was Rothwell, after one of her friends, but it wasn't until years later that Laura – the daughter – discovered that Joseph Edmund was, in fact, her father's illegitimate son. And that she, therefore, was his half-sister.'

'That must have given her a shock.'

'Of course. It's rather an interesting story, Laura's. She was taught to paint by her father and hoped to be an artist herself. But she never made a success of it. Joseph became great friends with her and her sister when they were living in Kentish Town. Everyone else had forgotten about them. There's one painting Laura did of him, *Portrait of a Young Man*, that became quite famous – she mentions it here, and there's a photograph of it in the plates.'

Nell, beguiled by these revelations, finds herself warming to her cousin. Hilary, she learns, has lived in Aylesbury most of her life, married to Des, director of a pharmaceuticals company. They have a son and a daughter. She has recently retired as secretary to the headmistress of a girls' school, which allows her time to pursue her genealogical interests. Nell feels a twinge of shame at first clapping eyes on Hilary – *Who's this frump?* she thought on the doorstep. That they might have remained strangers but for that reference to old Alice! A slender thread. And what if Hilary hadn't been watching *Nationwide* that evening, or if the BBC editors had decided to cut that part of the interview, as they cut so much else? The biscuits have nearly vanished while they've been talking. Nell asks Hilary if she'd like to stay for lunch, and of course she would. In the meantime, the sun has come out, and they go into the garden while she has a cigarette.

They sit on the ornamental bench, a sturdy iron two-seater, which faces the rear elevations of the neighbouring houses on Fortess Road. Nell has stared at this higgledy-piggledy roofline so often it feels like an old friend. It has changed over the years, adjustments made after the Blitz, extensions added in more prosperous times; there is even a tiny conservatory whose windows offer an inviting view, though Nell has never seen anyone in it. She points out to Hilary her favourite part of this aspect, which is the Victorian brick walls, ordinary London stock at first glance yet multifarious if one cares to study them: mauve, beige, biscuit brown, slate grey, lead, rust, even a mustard yellow. The cumulative effect is that of a mosaic, its patterning accidental, everyday, and somehow ravishing. She sees how its presence has sneaked through the back door of her mind into her painting, this intricate, weathered arrangement of colours.

'You must have been pleased to be on *Nationwide*,' says Hilary. 'Think of all those people watching it – like me! I didn't know of your paintings before then.'

'Not many did,' replies Nell. 'I've been painting for most of my life, but only in the last three or four years has there been any fuss about it.' She talks a little about the retrospective, and how they have unearthed paintings from the 1940s that she had forgotten about.

She is listening out for the woodpecker: no showing today. Back indoors she cooks them an omelette. While they eat, Hilary smooths out the scroll of paper on which she has plotted their family tree. Here are names that Nell recognises from family lore, and others quite unknown to her. At the top of it sits William Merrymount (1730–1795). How odd to think of her connection to him, a painter whose work has been so intrinsic to her mental furnishing she hardly notices it any more.

'So what's our exact relation to him?' she says.

'He's our, let's see, our great-great-great-grandfather.' Hilary looks at her over the top of her glasses.

'There's something quite thrilling about it, isn't there?'

'Of course! Two hundred years after he lived you've become an artist, too. History coming full circle. You even have two daughters, like him.'

Nell smiles. 'I can't wait to tell them. Well, I don't suppose Tash will think it a big deal. But Billie certainly will.'

'I saw Billie at the National about ten years ago, little knowing! She's married, isn't she?'

'Separated. Though he's trying to get back with her again.'

'You don't sound very pleased about it.'

Nell shakes her head. 'The danger of a charming man. The awful thing is, I can't really talk to her about it. I've been married twice myself, you see ... In fact, Bryn – my son-in-law – reminds me of Johnny, always the good-time guy, friend to everyone ... except his wife.' She stops herself, embarrassed, and looks at Hilary. 'Sorry, I shouldn't be telling you this. You hardly even know me.'

'That's all right,' Hilary says gently. 'I'm family, aren't I?'

Nell, touched, leans over and places her hand on top of Hilary's.

*

At the Twickenham Film Studios they have broken for lunch on the set of *Heaven and Earth*. Billie is chowing down egg and chips in the canteen with Maurice Venning, fellow actor and longtime friend. Work always makes her hungry, even though they're only doing a read-through. This morning's might have passed like any other, the cast in mufti seated around a long table, each reading from a script while the director, Vernon Sparks, interposes himself now and again to encourage, advise, keep them 'at it'.

What no one has bargained for is Maurice's outlandish take on one particular scene of high emotion. Cast as the story's evil angel, he has been camping it up in his signature style – lots of ad-libbed asides and extravagant line-readings – which Vernon has so far decided to indulge, despite some eye-rolling from others at the table. Then comes the big moment when his character realises he has been outfoxed. The frustration that has been smouldering within suddenly erupts: 'How in the name of Satan's tits am I to bring chaos and misery to the earthlings when my own kin conspire against me?' The line could be spoken in one breath, and probably should be. Maurice has other ideas. For him, the line must be an event. He first rises to his feet and, pausing only to flex his neck muscles, boxer-style, he picks up his chair (folding, wooden) in both hands, swings it above his head and smashes it against the floor (poured concrete) on the words TITS, does the same on CHAOS and MISERY, then speeds up so that an ear-splitting crack lands successively on the final flurry of words. With exquisite timing the chair shatters into pieces on AGAINST ME?

A stunned silence reigns in the echo. The others sit motionless. Vernon, clearing his throat, quietly says, 'Thank you, Maurice. But I'm afraid you'll have to pay for that chair.'

Across the canteen table Billie watches Maurice placidly spooning tomato soup into his narrow mouth, his bravura tantrum of twenty minutes ago apparently forgotten. His vulpine features and heavy-lidded, saturnine gaze, always on alert before the camera, are now at ease. The clatter and hum of the lunchtime rush make no impression upon him.

'So what was that all about?'

Maurice looks up, expressionless. 'What do you mean?'

'Your wild-man act back there.'

'Man? I was aiming for Bette Davis in *All About Eve*,' he drawls. 'I don't remember her smashing up a chair ...'

He gives a little pout. 'It was the "fire and music" aspect I had in mind.'

'But why? Grandstanding is for the audition. You've already *got* the part.'

He sighs and stares at her. 'Have you ever been so beside yourself with boredom that you would do just about anything to whip up a scene? The torpor in that room was like an old people's home. Drama must have energy, or it's nothing.'

'It's a read-through, Maurice, not a first night.'

'It still wanted waking up. I can't bear to listen to that dreary English drawing-room dialogue, the polite back-and-forth of it. Of course, the script doesn't help.' He lowers his voice. 'Honestly, darling, have you ever encountered such simpering, quarter-witted banality in your life?'

Billie considers. 'I was once in a production of *The Prodigal* a few years ago.'

'The Pinero? Oh, you poor thing. Anyway, my little display will give them something to talk about. Frankly, there's not much else.' He pauses, and in a changed tone says, 'What did you make of the boy wonder?'

'Robbie? I think he was a bit nervous. Kept tripping over words.'

'Sentences. Paragraphs ...'

'It's his first time,' Billie says forgivingly. 'He's still finding his feet.'

'Hmm. It's not his feet that are at issue. Did you notice the way he kept eyeing you?'

'Me?'

Maurice has a knowing look. 'Possibly he was overawed by *your* fire and music.'

Billie laughs. 'I think you're making mischief, dear. Robbie Furlong has an adoring fan club of teenage girls.'

'Yes, but you get sick of veal on the menu every day. Perhaps he craves the taste of something a little more ... mature. *Comprenez?*'

He finishes his tomato soup and dabs the edges of his mouth with a paper napkin, a fastidious gesture that amuses Billie. She can't tell if Maurice is joking or not. She isn't aware of any *tendresse* on Robbie's part; indeed, if anything he seemed rather brusque with her before they sat down this morning. Maurice, meanwhile, has caught sight of someone across the room and lifts his face in greeting. She turns to see Robbie ambling between the tables towards them.

'Talk of ...' croons Maurice.

Tensely holding his tray of food, Robbie asks if it's OK to sit with them. Maurice, with an air of exaggerated amiability, pats the seat next to his in invitation. Robbie's lunch is a meagre assemblage – a bread roll and butter, a wan-looking sausage, and a glass of water. Billie, inspecting it, says, 'Is that all you're having?'

'I'm not that hungry,' he replies.

Maurice frowns at him. 'Come, come. A growing lad like you requires proper sustenance. What about a salad?'

Robbie turns up his nose. He slices the roll, and butters it to make a sausage sandwich. After taking a bite he looks up and says to Maurice, 'That was some performance. You often do that sort of thing?'

He smirks. 'It's not encouraged.'

'You have to understand,' Billie says, 'Maurice is principally an exhibitionist.'

Robbie, chewing, nods earnestly. 'I remember when I smashed up my first guitar on stage. Little club in Bristol, it was.'

'Why is that such a compulsion – with rock stars, I mean?'

'Dunno. 'Cos Pete Townshend showed us the way, I suppose. It's great fun, whirlin' it round your head an' that!'

'How many guitars have you smashed?'

'Oh, not that many. I stopped doing it when our manager told me he wouldn't pay for a new one. It got to the point where I'd spend more time patching up the guitar I'd bust than playing the bloody thing.'

'Very sensible,' says Maurice. 'So ... how are you coping with us?'

Robbie winces slightly. 'I find it a bit tricky ... I've got dyslexia, see, and the words don't always come out the way I intend.'

Maurice glances at Billie, who says, 'Does Vernon know?'

Robbie shakes his head. 'Please don't say anything. My agent told me to keep mum about it – she said they'd fix any dialogue in post-production, or whatever it is.'

That sounds like Penny, thinks Billie – *take the money, sod the work.*

'Don't worry about it,' she says. 'If needs be you and I can run the lines together beforehand. I'll make sure you're up to snuff.'

He returns a look of startled gratitude. 'Would you do that?'

'*Of course* she will, Roberto,' Maurice cuts in, pursing his lips in a mischievous *moue*. 'Billie loves to take a young actor in hand, don't you, dear?'

Robbie, oblivious to the double-entendre, says, 'That'd be so kind of you.'

Maurice looks at his watch. 'Well, I'll leave you to work out your Henry Higgins routine. See you back in there.'

'What can we expect this afternoon?' Billie asks him. 'Setting fire to the curtains? Setting fire to *yourself*?'

He gives a friendly half-snort of laughter before he saunters off.

Robbie, finished eating, glances at Billie from under his brow. He's on the verge of speaking, then stops himself. A moment later he says, 'You didn't fancy it, then?'

Billie looks at him, uncomprehending.

'The 100 Club. Last week. I put your name on the door but you didn't show.'

'Oh God, sorry. I meant to, but . . .'

'But you had something better to do.' The hurt in his voice, like a boy's, is unmistakable. So she didn't imagine his offhandedness before.

'No, I really am sorry. If you must know,' she hardly sees the need to explain herself, but presses on, 'I was out with my ex, well, he's not my ex-husband, but we're separated, and we had quite a long talk about . . . what's happening.'

He nods, warily appeased. 'And what *is* happening?'

Is he slightly backward? She stares at him; she could slap him down, but his manner is so ingenuous there would be no point.

'To be honest, I'm not sure. It's quite complicated.' *We're grown-ups, you see*, she doesn't add. 'Let's meet anyway, you and me, we can read through the script without Vernon breathing down our necks.'

'Tonight?'

Billie laughs, shakes her head. She hasn't heard keenness like that since she was a teenager. 'Can't do tonight. Some time over the weekend?'

Tash calls around and finds her mother in the garden, sketchbook open, a cigarette on the go. It's an early evening in May, quite warm. She bends down to examine what Nell's up to; a pencil-sketch of the rear elevations of Fortress Road, the bricks and windows and drainpipes creating a sequence of geometric patterns, the jagged roofline faintly limned. Nell thinks of it as a test-run for something else, maybe a large painting of the backs, a fresco of brickwork in subtly different shades.

'There's a beer in the fridge,' says Nell, eyes still on her sketch. 'You could get me one while you're at it.' Tash returns to the kitchen, takes out two small bottles of Pilsner and lops off their caps before taking them out.

'Ooh, ta,' says Nell, slugging from the bottle. Cold beer is one of her two favourite drinks. The other is champagne.

Tash sits sideways on the garden bench, drawing her knees up to her chest. She's stopped here on her way to a dinner with friends. (Chris has taken Gil to football practice.) She's wearing an Art Deco collar necklace over a silver-green linen shirt that she made herself, black leggings with ballet pumps. Nell sometimes wonders where Tash and Billie get their style from. She notices other people's clothes, though she's not that fussed about her own. Maybe it was the war that did it – there just wasn't anything nice to wear.

Tash picks at the label on her beer bottle. 'I suppose you heard about the election . . .'

Nell looks round blankly. 'What?'

'God, don't you ever listen to the news?'

She protests she's been out in the garden all day; when she's working she doesn't allow much to interrupt her. Tash says that 'she' – the prime minister – has called an election for June 9th, so it's all hands to the pump from here. (Tash is a longtime member of the Labour Party.) Nell goes back to cross-hatching with her soft pencil.

'I was wondering if you'd help with canvassing,' says Tash.

'Me? Oh darling, I don't think so . . .'

'Look, we need people more than ever. You know it's going to be the most important election since the war? Another five years of her and we're done for.'

Nell has heard this before. She admires Tash's fighting spirit but she's not a political animal like her. 'To be honest, I've got my hands full with this show. Véro's on the phone to me every day, there's that commission from London Transport, I'm behind with everything—'

'It's two nights a week, Mum. And it all makes a difference.'

Well, it probably does, thinks Nell, *and I still don't want to*. She wonders how honest she can be with Tash at this point: there's a risk she might get her head bitten off. She takes a breath, and says,

'I'm not even sure I'm going to vote for them this time. I mean, he's a really *old geezer*.'

'Foot? He's only in his sixties.'

'I just read that he'll be seventy this year. It's no job for a man his age. They need someone with a bit of vigour, someone to rally the youth.'

Tash is shaking her head. 'He's all we've got. Anyway, who else would you vote for? Not the SDP!'

'I might. I've voted Liberal before.'

'Yeah, so you should know by now what a waste it is. Just think about it for a minute – what, to you, are the things this country most needs to fix?'

Nell sighs, waits a beat. 'I dunno. Jobs. Health. Education.'

'Exactly. And I'm telling you, there's only one party that's committed to fixing them.'

'Mmm. You think they know how to?'

Tash rolls her eyes at that and begins to explain, counting on her fingers, as if to a child, how Labour will undo the wrongs of the last four years, stop flogging public assets, get industry moving again ... Nell, half-listening, returns to her bricks, her shading. Her work is the escape, the refuge. If it wasn't for that she wouldn't know what to do with herself.

She doesn't hear Billie arrive but she's pleased to see her, double-pleased, in fact, because it allows her to duck out of Tash's firing-line. They don't even say hello, Billie just kisses the top of her head and leaves her to work. She'll rejoin the argument, soon, she just needs to get this down on paper while she has the light. Michael Foot, though ... She was surprised to learn he was sixty-nine; only seven years older than she is. He's always seemed much older, in the way certain public figures do. Compared with him, why, she's positively youthful, a slip of a thing!

In truth, she's never felt old. She'll be sixty-three in November, but she *feels* about seventeen. She acts it, too, sometimes.

'That book on the kitchen table,' says Billie, calling Nell back to earth. '*The Letters and Journals of Laura Merrymount*. You reading it?'

'I've had a look. It's the one our cousin Hilary brought when she came.'

'Are you sure she's right about us – I mean, being related to Merrymount?'

'Well, she convinced me,' says Nell. 'But we're very faraway cousins, I think.'

Tash says, 'You should tell Gil about this, Mum. He's doing a school project on family trees. What was she like, by the way?'

'Hilary? She's a really nice lady.'

Billie smiles. 'You only ever say "lady" when you mean posh.'

'Do I? She used to be a school secretary – that's not posh. The husband's in pharmaceuticals, her kids are grown up and gone. I think she's at a loose end, nothing to do all day. She could certainly talk – and eat!'

Tash consults her watch, stands, stretches. Time she was on her way; she's got to be in Notting Hill for dinner. When she goes to kiss Nell goodbye she mutters something, half-joking, about 'not letting you vote SDP'. Nell shakes her head, as if to disown the idea. Funny, she thinks; the last person who told her how she should vote was Johnny, just after the war. And back then she did as she was told.

Later, in the kitchen, Billie is riffling through the Laura Merrymount book again. 'Mind if I borrow this?'

'Course,' says Nell, 'but look after it. I've got to return it to Hilary.'

She is washing up at the sink, aware that there's something not being talked about. She's been meaning to ask ever since Billie arrived, but delays for the simple reason that she dreads to hear the answer.

'So . . . how did dinner go the other night? With Bryn.'

Billie looks up, her gaze untroubled. 'Oh, yeah, it was fine. We went to Langan's, Bryn's idea. We hadn't been there in a while.'

Is she being deliberately evasive? Nell may not like what's going on between her and Bryn, but she will not be fobbed off.

'And how's he? Still working his way back to you?' She almost said *worming*.

Billie laughs. 'He's all right. Chastened. He was very nice about you, actually.'

'What?'

'He saw you on *Nationwide* – said you looked "fabulous".'

'No he didn't.'

'Honestly. His very word.'

Nell, who has always operated by instinct, knows at that moment that Billie will take Bryn back – perhaps she already has. She knows it from something in the tone of her daughter's voice, and from the way she has reported that little compliment Bryn paid her, like a peace offering; like an apology. She doesn't care that he called her 'fabulous', it's just another of his smarmy insincerities. But in Billie's choosing to mention it is the awful implication of Bryn's return.

Back at her flat in Kensington Gardens Square Billie is making a cup of tea before bed. She feels a prickle of guilt over not being straight with Nell. That nightcap she had agreed to with Bryn after Langan's was (she knew too well) a dangerous concession to make. They stayed drinking in his club until half-past midnight. Bryn of course asked her back to his place, and she refused; she shrank from the idea of his bachelor lair, where who knows how many women had been up to God knows what beneath his sour sheets. No, not to be endured.

So they went back to her place instead.

5

Billie steps off the tube at Fulham Broadway. It's early after-noon on Saturday, and as soon as she hits Fulham Road she's immersed in shoals of Chelsea fans swarming towards the Bridge: final day of the season. The smell of burgers and frying onions coats the air. She gets clear of the crowds and turns into the wide thor-oughfare of Gunter Grove. He has told her what number he's at, but she checks again in her pocket diary. The first warning of what's to come is the Ford Escort parked outside – on cinder blocks. The house is a tall porticoed Victorian mansion, the stucco veined and crumbling like old cheese, brown streaks of water damage down the walls. The windows are screened with drooping flags and graffitied sheets. THE POP GROUP. CND. NO FUTURE.

She ascends the steps, spattered with pigeon shit, to a porch where a cluster of buzzers flanks the door. She tries them all – dead. She lifts the heavy brass knocker and gives the plate a loud double rap. Through the frosted half-window nothing stirs. She waits a few moments, then goes back down the steps to look for a sign of life. 'Robbie?' she calls up, once, twice. She fills her lungs. 'ROBBIE!' A window is raised on the first floor and a girl pokes her head out.

'I'm looking for Robbie Furlong,' she shouts, and falters, doubt-ing. 'Does he live here?'

The girl disappears for a moment, then her face returns. A flash of something silver through the air lands a couple of yards from Billie: a ring of keys. The window slams shut. Welcome to the neighbourhood. She picks them up, goes to the front door again and uses the Yale to open it. Inside the hall she almost gags on the smell, a compound of old cooking, damp dog, unwashed clothes, stale beer and men's piss. From somewhere upstairs comes the muffled thunk of bass-heavy music. She takes the stairs, uncarpeted, half-dreading what she might find. On the first landing she sees a door ajar and looks in, empty but for a stained mattress. At the front she opens another door and feels the blast of music tear past her; a reek of beer and dope. Two people slumped against a wall, a couple supine on a battered sofa, a girl crouched at the music system. She turns, bleary-eyed. The one who chucked her the keys. Billie raises her voice above the music – 'Is Robbie here?'

With a languid sweep of her arm she points upwards.

More graffiti on the walls as she takes the next flight. Another empty room, and a bathroom of medieval squalor. Voices filter through another door, and she knocks this time. 'Yeah?' She opens it to find Robbie, sitting on the floor in untucked shirt and combat trousers, barefoot, rolling a huge prison spliff. He smiles on seeing her. 'All right?' On the rumpled mattress sits a spiky-haired girl, Spanish-looking, with beautiful forget-me-not eyes.

Billie says, 'Sorry, am I interrupting?'

He shakes his head, 'No, no; come in!' He introduces the girl, Mara – or is it Martha? – then shinnies over on his knees to mutter something in her ear. The girl nods, unconcerned, and slinks out of the room, like a cat.

Playing the host, Robbie wheels over an office swivel chair, the room's single piece of furniture bar the mattress and a chaotic dress-rail of clothes. He invites her to sit, taking the edge of the mattress for himself. Billie hardly knows where to begin. Even in her boots, flowered shirt and linen jacket she feels, under this roof, out of place. *Bourgeois*, as they probably say around here.

'How long have you, er, lived here?' she asks.

'On and off, 'bout a year, I suppose. There's another place I some-times stay, but it's not as friendly.'

She looks at him to see if he's joking. He isn't. 'You don't pay rent for this, do you?'

'Course not! It's a squat – can't you tell?'

'Yeah, it's just, you didn't say . . .' She looks around the room, the floor strewn with magazines, books, lighters, a deck of cards, empty bottles; in the corner, a heap of clothes she takes to be dirty laundry, and, propped against the wall, an acoustic guitar whose gleaming blue finish reminds her of something, or someone. On the far wall patches of damp, like a ghostly atlas. She adopts a careless tone. 'I thought you'd have your own place, you know . . . bought somewhere?'

He pulls a face. 'Ain't had a chance to look.'

'But you've got the money, surely?'

'My manager looks after all that. I get a sort of weekly allowance. Prob'ly for the best – I'd just blow it all.'

On what? she wonders. He resumes construction of the spliff.

'I thought you didn't smoke?' *I'm sounding like his mother,* she thinks.

'Not cigarettes. This is weed – you can buy it round here,' he adds brightly, as if she might care to do some shopping while in the neighbourhood. 'Shall I get you a cup of tea?'

She briefly imagines the state of the kitchen. 'No, I'm fine, thanks.' She opens her shoulder bag and takes out her cigarettes and the script of *Heaven and Earth*. She's offered her services as coach, so they may as well get on with it. 'Ready?'

He scrambles back across the mattress, eager as a puppy, to grab his own dog-eared copy. Settling himself cross-legged, he licks and seals the giant spliff and holds it up enquiringly. 'D'you fancy . . . ?' But one look at her expression and he realises. 'Maybe leave it for now.'

Below them the rolling thunder of the music makes the floor vibrate. She looks at Robbie, who's oblivious. 'All right, let's pick it up from page seventeen,' she says. They start to read, slowly, taking the long duologues between Horatio, Robbie's character, and Billie as Gemma, the dancer. He stumbles, though not as much as he did in the cast read-through, and he responds to her patient spoon-feeding ('Say it like this ... Take it slower ... Put the emphasis here'). She can sense him gaining confidence, his words finding a rhythm as they read on. But still comes the steady bass throb from the room below, like being trapped inside a giant's headache.

'Does that go on all day?'

Robbie looks up, seeming to hear it for the first time. 'I'll tell 'em to turn it down,' he says, getting to his feet.

'No, don't,' she says, staying him. It's not her house, and she won't play the disgruntled square. 'Let's get out of here and do this over a coffee.'

He nods, and goes to rummage in the pile of clothes. He finds one sock, then its pair, and pulls them on. His shoes are black suede Gibsons.

'I'm all set,' he says, standing before her. Billie meantime has been eyeing the blue guitar in the corner, and now realises where she knows it from.

'That guitar – it's like the one Bowie played when he did "Starman" on *Top of the Pops*.'

His face lights up. 'Yes! My Egmond. I had it custom-made, 'cos I'm left-handed. Great, innit?'

'So are you going to play me a tune before we go?'

He doesn't need persuading. He straps on the guitar, and clenching a pick between his teeth quickly fiddles with the tuning. Once satisfied, he says, 'There's this song I've written for the film – did you know? It's for the scene when you go down into the Nite Owl club and find my earthly twin, or whatever he is, doing his set ...'

'And our eyes meet,' she says, with a laugh.

'It's not quite finished yet, but . . . it's called "Black-eyed Boy from Cloudy Fields".' He holds the guitar high on his chest. His eyes take on a faraway look as he starts to strum. The song is short, two verses, a chorus, middle-eight, its lyric about a one-night stand that left the singer – wouldn't you know – sadder but wiser. Robbie gets the ending muddled up and meanders to a halt: 'Gah, I need to fix that.' He gives a little bow as she claps.

'I love it. Very . . . tender,' she says.

'Yeah?' He looks pleased. 'Good. 'Cos you're gonna be hearing it quite a lot in the next few months.'

They are in the hall when Billie realises she needs to pee, and he points her downstairs. With some trepidation she descends (at least there's nobody around) and pushes open the door. It's a dark, dank little closet, the toilet bowl stained with those ancient brown skid marks that look burned into the porcelain – but there *is* a bog-roll, so she braces herself and hovers, tinkling. She's just flushed when she catches a glint of something – a biro? – discarded in the murk below the cistern. She cranes her head closer to inspect and – *Oh Christ* – abruptly pulls back: not a biro but a needle, with a tiny measure of rusty liquid in its barrel. She's out of there in an instant and hurrying back up the stairs.

On her return Robbie says, 'You all right?' and she tries not to look flustered. They leave the house and descend on to Gunter Grove, Billie leading in the direction of King's Road. They are ambling along when he stops of a sudden and grabs her arm, pointing up to a house, as seedy as the one they've just left.

'Know who used to live there?' He holds the reverent gaze of an apostle. 'The Pistols. And their court. Just think, in that building Johnny Rotten and Glen Matlock wrote "Anarchy in the UK", "Pretty Vacant", "God Save the Queen", all those great songs . . . *we mean it, maaaaan*!'

'Maybe they'll put up a blue plaque,' murmurs Billie.

Her light satirical dart flies right over his head. 'I had tickets for Colston Hall, on the *Anarchy* tour – and they bloody cancelled!'

'So you never got to see them?'

He shakes his head sadly. 'I saw Public Image Ltd in Paris couple of years ago, but . . . it wasn't the same. I wanted to see him – John – in his prime.'

'Never mind. One day some kid is going to say, "I saw Robbie Furlong at the 100 Club, when he was in his prime."'

'What?! I ain't reached my prime yet.'

With a wistful parting glance he turns away, and they walk on. King's Road has changed since Billie used to hang out here. The shops are losing their quirkiness, and Chelsea's mixture of village London and '60s razzle-dazzle is also on its way out. She tries to explain this to Robbie, who still regards the road as 'cool' – he doesn't seem to notice the tourist tat or the high-street chain shops. She could argue with him, but she likes his wide-eyed enthusiasm for London, for everything. At a crossing she notices a couple of girls shoot him furtive glances; one of them stops him to say hello and to praise his new record. He thanks her, smiles, and they move on. Billie decides to take him to one of her favourites, the Picasso, a survivor from the road's old days.

They settle at a table; she's got a coffee, he's got a Coke. What she saw back at the squat is bugging her. It doesn't seem likely, but she has to make sure.

'Robbie. Listen. I've got to ask you something, and I need you to be honest, 'cos it's really important.' He looks at her, nonplussed. 'Are you on drugs? I don't mean weed. I mean . . . hard drugs.'

'What? You think I'm a junkie?'

She mentions the used needle she spied in the loo. He grimaces, and admits that a couple of them in the house use 'skag'. She still stares at him.

'Not me. Here, look.' He pulls up the sleeves of his shirt to reveal his pale unpunctured arms. 'You know I'm Mr Clean.'

She nods, relieved. 'Look, I don't want to sound ... You shouldn't be living in a house with junkies. I should know. I once had a boyfriend who was an addict. They'll steal from you.'

'They already have,' he says, with a half-laugh.

'Can't you find somewhere else? Your manager must know people who could put you up somewhere.'

'Not his problem. 'Slong as the money's coming in and I turn up for gigs on time he ain't bothered.' He shrugs. 'It ain't such a bad place. And it's free.'

She tells herself it's none of her business, that he's an adult and can look after himself. And yet there's something about him that touches her, the innocence; he appeals to her protective instincts, like the kid brother she never had. She would offer him a bunk at her flat – there's a spare room – but now that Bryn looks likely to return the timing is wrong. She knows Bryn won't be happy with a good-looking kid like Robbie staring at him over the cornflakes.

Then an idea comes to her, one that could solve two problems at once. But it will require some delicate negotiation on both sides.

'What if,' she begins, 'I could find you a room in a really nice house, for not much money?'

He looks at her uncertainly. 'Not sure I'm ready for a move at the moment.'

'So you're telling me you'd prefer a smelly old squat to somewhere comfortable and clean?'

'You got somewhere in mind?'

'I might have. I need to check first.'

'I dunno. The house ... they'd be upset if they knew I was looking to split. We're all mates, you know.'

'I'm sure they'd get over it. And what sort of mates steal from you to buy smack?'

'That's just two of 'em. Well ... three.'

'How many of you live there?'

He stares into the middle distance. 'It changes. Prob'ly between twelve and fifteen at the moment. But a lot of people crash there. One morning I woke up and found a couple sleeping next to me in bed! They must have snuck in, like, middle of the night.'

'Who were they?'

'Some girl and a bloke, never seen 'em before. I asked them if they'd mind leaving, and they were fine about it . . .'

'Oh no! I'm getting you out of there. You can't live like that, Robbie.' She fixes him with a serious stare. He looks away, and takes out the film script he has kept rolled up in his canvas messenger bag. He smooths out its curling pages.

'Should we get back to this?' he says meekly.

They have another go at it, but the noise of the café and their self-consciousness stall them. After ten minutes they decide to call it a day. Billie is still wondering what the real attraction of the squat might be.

'The girl I met back there – are you and she . . . ?'

He looks baffled for a moment, then smiles. 'You mean Mara? She's great, but she ain't my girlfriend. Why d'you ask?'

She shrugs. 'Oh . . . curious. D'you have a girlfriend?'

He then pulls an expression she hasn't seen on him before: slyly amused. 'Nope. You interested?' he asks, and they both laugh. 'How are things between you and your feller?'

'All right. He's probably going to move back in. Give it another try.'

'I hope – Bryn, is it? – I hope he's learned his lesson.'

She looks at him, startled. 'What would you know about it?'

'It was in the papers.' He pauses. 'Actually, Mara told me. The way he behaved . . . I'd never treat a girlfriend of mine like that.' *Loik tha'*.

'Well, he wasn't entirely to blame. I could have been more supportive. Possibly I became a bit boring – I'm more of a stay-at-home than he is.'

Robbie shakes his head. 'You could never be boring,' he says simply.

She smiles at him. 'I dunno, I think I've learned something during this separation.'

'What's that?'

She considers for a moment. 'That marriage requires you to be vigilant. I don't mean checking up on each other. I mean vigilant about yourself . . . When you get married you invite someone into your life, so you're always under scrutiny. As one half of a couple you have to hold on to a sense of yourself – of your privacy, your identity. You can't surrender that to someone else. Marriage is like a mirror, it will show you who you are, the good and the bad.'

She looks at him to see whether he's taking any of this in. His doe-eyed gaze is steady but unreadable. For all she can tell he might be thinking of something else altogether, like Mara, or his next band rehearsal.

'Anyway,' she continues, 'that's a long way down the line for you. And marriage can be a happy experience, of course. What about your mum and dad?'

He stares off again. 'They were happy. I think. My dad died eight years ago – heart-attack – and Mum was proper cut up. She's got someone else now, but she told me she still thinks about him – dreams about him. I dunno about marriage . . . Bit of a lottery, ain't it?'

Billie nods slowly. 'You could say.' They smile at one another.

6

Nell pays off the cab on Portland Road and walks towards the restaurant, its lights hushed and romantic against the dark of the street. This is one of Billie's places, and the first time the family has met with Bryn since his disappearing act of last year. Nell's mood is one of reluctance mingled with dread: she hopes she can behave herself. Even though she dislikes Bryn she understands his masculine allure; it reminds her of Johnny, and those years when she was in helpless thrall to him, when it still seemed their marriage – their family – might be saved.

She's the last to arrive. Gil, her grandson, is the first to spot her, and waves from their table across the room. He's seated between Chris and Tash, both dressed up for the night, which causes Nell a pang because she hasn't gone to much trouble beyond brushing her hair. Opposite them sit Billie and, with an air at once sheepish and grand, Bryn, who does the old-fashioned thing of standing to greet the lady.

'Nell, welcome!' he cries, pulling out a chair. He's wearing a dark suit and white shirt with a patterned tie. He has grown his hair a bit, she notices, as he brushes a hank of fringe away from his face. Next to him Billie looks on, smiling, though her eyes are anxious.

A waiter moves in to uncork a bottle of champagne. 'I told them we mustn't open it till you arrive,' Bryn explains over the pop. He takes the bottle from the waiter and makes a point of pouring the first glass for Nell.

She smiles at him on receiving it, and says, 'Cheers, lovely to see you all.' She is aware of Bryn's charm, as insistent as cheap aftershave. Her instinct is unyielding. Like Mrs Dalloway, when someone enters a room she either arched her back like a cat, or else she purred. In Bryn's company she has never purred. They all clink glasses, and Gil wants to know why he hasn't got one.

Nell asks the waiter, 'Can we have a Fanta for this little fellow?'

The waiter says they've got freshly squeezed orange juice, and Nell smiles her assent. She makes a rueful face at Gil. 'Sorry, love, they've just got the Holland Park Fanta.'

The room is lit with candles whose honeyed flicker lend the diners' faces a painterly drama. Billie looks around the table as they consult the menus. She has planned this evening as a way to rehabilitate Bryn without making a big deal of it, more 'normal service resumes' than 'return of the prodigal husband'. She knows Tash is on her side; even though she's not fooled by him Tash understands the attraction and certainly rates him above any previous boyfriend of hers. Chris gets on with almost everyone, that's his nature, and he greets Bryn as if there's been no hiatus at all; they're already stuck into blokey talk about the cricket World Cup that starts in a couple of weeks. Nell, seated next to her, is the gathering's potential firecracker. She's only spoken to her on the phone so far about Bryn's return to the marital fold; now that it's a fait accompli she's ready to face her.

'This is nice,' says Nell, though her smile is unconvinced, no brightness in her eyes. Billie feels the mood could tip either way.

'I'm glad we could get together,' she replies. 'I've been reading that book you lent me, the Merrymount daughter's journal.'

'Oh, what's it like?'

'Fascinating. I've just come to an awful moment – Laura's in love with this famous musician in Bath, he's encouraged her, then she comes back from a holiday to find that he's got off with her sister.'

'Sounds like a twerp,' says Nell.

'Mm, that's what her father thought. Unfortunately, the sister, Molly, is getting married to him. I've a suspicion it's not going to turn out well.'

That's a risky remark in the circumstances, but Nell mercifully lets it go. 'What about Joseph Rothwell? Hilary told me no one knew for years that Merrymount was his father ...'

'Mmm, I haven't come to that yet. The most interesting thing so far is the relationship between Laura and Lizzie Vavasor, the actress. You sense this deep affection between them and all the time a bomb's ticking away underneath.'

Tash, tuning in, says that Gil has started his ancestry project at school and has told his teacher about their famous forebear. 'I'm afraid he got a bit muddled about the detail. Gil, when Miss Garner asked you how William Merrymount was related to us, what did you say?'

The boy's eyes are downcast. 'I said he was my grandfather.'

They all laugh, and Nell says to him kindly, 'Well, you're right in one way – your grandfather *was* a painter. His name was Johnny, so you can put him in your project, too. I can help you with the dates.'

Billie looks over at Tash, who shrugs.

Gil says, 'So what was William Merry – Merrymount? – then?'

'Ooh, let's see,' says Nell, squinting. 'If he was my great-great ... he's your great-great-great-great-*great*-grandfather. How about that!'

The evening gathers in jolliness as the food starts to arrive. Bryn entertains them with an account of his am-dram debut in a tiny village hall somewhere in North Wales. It's an overlong story but he's a skilled raconteur, peppering the narrative with digressive bursts of parody and impersonation (his stage-Welsh voice always sets them off). Punchline to the tale is the local paper's verdict on his performance, the last half-hour of which required him to lie dead on the floor – 'In the role of the eventual victim, Mr Bryn Parish plays more convincingly as a corpse than he does when endowed with the advantages of speech and movement.' Billie's heard it before, of course, but she's laughing along with the others, delighted to see him being droll and self-deprecating, like he's working a crowd.

'For the record, I intend to feature that story when I write my memoir, in the chapter headed "Dai the Death".'

'You should go on *Wogan*, mate,' says Chris.

'I still aspire to a slot on *Nationwide*, to be honest,' Bryn says, glancing across the table. 'That's the ultimate accolade.'

Nell returns a smile. Billie says, 'You'll have to be quick about it, love. Friend of mine at the Beeb says they're taking it off in the summer.'

'No!' Bryn pretends to look deflated. '*Nationwide*, gone! It's like the ravens leaving the Tower. What next – *Top of the Pops*?'

'Oh yeah,' says Tash, reminded, 'we saw the Robbie Furlong video last week. He's very good-looking, isn't he?'

Billie nods. He's better looking in the flesh, but she will keep that to herself. This isn't the moment she intended to broach her plan, but seeing that they're all in a good mood she might as well offer it for discussion. 'Actually, I'm trying to find him – Robbie – a place to live. At the moment he's sharing this horrible squat in Fulham with a load of junkies ...'

There follows a general exclamation of disbelief, it being widely assumed that he would be living in a penthouse or a posh hotel. The idea of him rooming in a drug den shocks them – except for Bryn, who argues that it's perfectly natural for a pop star to slum it.

'You might almost say it's *de rigueur*. Musicians and drugs go together like babies and vomit.'

'Robbie's not like that,' says Billie. 'He doesn't even drink. I just want to get him somewhere safe, and clean.' She pauses, and turns to Nell. 'So I was wondering if you might put him up for a while.'

Nell is startled. '*Me*? I don't ... Whatever makes you think he'd want to live with me?'

'Well, you like having young people around, you have a big house with no lodgers at the moment, and I really think you and Robbie would get on – he's a good kid.'

Billie looks to Tash, whose expression is veiled, noncommittal. Without her support this could flop. She ought to have consulted with her first so they could present a united front. Nell, meanwhile, is stacking up the pros and cons. It's true she's missed the company since Sue and Simon left, and she does rattle around that house on her own. But can she cope with a musician for a lodger, bringing back his hairy friends and making a racket till all hours – not to mention the groupies? Billie says he's a good kid, but she's only known him for ten minutes ... There is also the rule she imposed on herself after the living nightmare of Roy.

'You know I promised you not to take in any more single men,' she says.

Billie draws in her chin sharply. 'Mum, Robbie's twenty-one, twenty-two tops. No offence, but I think we can discount any romantic intrigue here.'

'Oh, I don't know,' says Bryn. 'Nell's a very attractive lady, and a young feller with his sap up ...' He tilts his head meaningfully. Billie fires him a look that says, *Don't be a creep*. Nell is unmoved by his flattery, and lights a cigarette. There's a call for more wine.

Tash says, 'Chris, what do you think?' Billie knows this is the moment, since Tash only makes a point of asking Chris's advice when she feels the stakes are high.

Not one to be panicked, mild-mannered to a fault, Chris stares thoughtfully across the table. 'Nell probably knows what's best for her,' he begins (*I doubt that very much*, thinks Billie), 'but it sounds to me like this boy could do with some stability, a friendly influence, home comforts – who better than Nell to provide all that?'

Billie turns to Nell. 'I could bring him over one evening. Just to test the water.'

Nell, feeling a strange inward lurch, says, 'Fine. Why not?'

*

Later, getting ready for bed, Billie is deep in thought. During these weeks of rapprochement they have talked – she has talked – about the possibility of starting a family. She's been putting off the idea for years, mostly on account of her career but also because she doubted if she wanted to be a mother. In her late teens she had an abortion, which Nell paid for. A few years later she had another one (it was legal by then) but out of an obscure sense of shame she didn't even let Nell know. She wasn't ready to have a child then, that was all. But lately she's felt a change, a prompting that's just short of a yearning, and she's realised it must be time. Bryn, put on the spot, has admitted he's not crazy about the idea of kids but if that's what it takes to get back with her then he's in. Billie decides that this will do as a pledge.

A few minutes later he walks into her bedroom – *their* bedroom – and his steps slow up as he says, 'You're looking like – what's that phrase the Victorians used? – *in a brown study.*'

'What's that?'

'I think it just means "lost in thought".'

She looks up. He's in a good mood; the dinner *en famille* has passed off without incident. They've had some laughs. This might be the moment to revert to the subject of kids, to put him on notice, as it were. At least to let him know she's serious about it. And yet she hesitates: why risk a dampener after all the fun? It's late, too; maybe it's one for the light of day.

'Oh, I was just thinking ... we should do something with that spare room.'

She realises just as it's out of her mouth that this could be construed as a nudge, though it's quite involuntary. The room and its redecoration have been on her mind. She waits for Bryn's reaction. He pauses, gives a nod and continues undressing. The hint has passed him by completely.

It's a bright morning at the end of May and Nell is at the picture-framer's on Kentish Town Road. She's been coming here for years, decades, knowing that the shop's owner, Horace, will do a good job, though he's getting on now, in his seventies, with wonderful gnarled hands that remind her of the old woman's in the Velázquez painting. Nell can remember Horace's father, who ran the business before the war.

On the wall hangs a small framed photograph of Fortess Road in the early years of the century. She often stares at it. Dark-fronted houses on one side, stern shops with awnings on the other, while a horse-drawn bus and a tram can be seen pulling away in the distance. Her eye fixes on a boy in knee-britches and cap crossing in the foreground, unheeding of the camera's scrutiny. Everyone else in the photo must be long dead, but this fellow could still be alive, possibly in his late eighties. And still living round here? Then it comes to her that he would have been of an age to enlist in 1914 and gone to France, never to return. But the dead do return, in photographs like this.

She's had a natter with Horace and is about to leave when the little bell above the door pings and Gerald Leck, a neighbour of hers in Fortess Road, sidles in. On seeing Nell he booms a greeting. 'I've been hoping to run into you!'

Gerald, large and lumbering, blinks at her through heavy, squar-ish spectacles. He's a literary man, a former publisher, widowed some years ago and now in semi-retirement. They would often see one another at parties held among the artistic bohemia of Camden and Kentish Town, now dispersed with the years. One of the advan-tages of having lived in the same area all your life is that you get to know a great many people. And the drawback is that you find it quite hard to avoid them.

'How are you, Gerald?' Nell asks.

'Very well! But first I must ...' He's come to collect a picture, and once reminded Horace goes out the back in search of it. Left together, Gerald beams at her. 'Did I tell you I'm putting together another volume of the memoirs?'

'Yes, the third, I think you said.' It's become clear from the way he talks that Gerald believes she's read the first two, and she's kind enough not to disabuse him of that.

'Well, I'm up to the nineteen sixties and – extraordinary thing – I find I can remember far less about them than I could the nineteen thirties!'

'You know what they say about the sixties,' says Nell, who conversely recalls them quite well and fears what Gerald has in store.

His next words confirm it: 'So I was wondering if I might tap your – ha, ha! – far more retentive memory for my purposes. Just the *names* of people I struggle with ... We could do it over a bottle of wine one evening, if that would be ...'

Gerald has been alone since his wife's death, and with his children grown up and gone he craves company. Nothing wrong with that, but Nell suspects an ulterior motive here – because Gerald is also sweet on her, and the get-together he's proposing is likely a pretext for chancing his arm. She's sensed his interest before, from the way he stands a bit too close to her at gatherings, and his clunky attempts at flirting: he's an overgrown boy of the old school, and refers to women as 'fillies' and 'goers'. In truth, she feels rather sorry for him, and so puts herself out to be nice, but it doesn't change the fact that she's not keen. His myopic gaze and parade-ground bray do not light her fire. There's also his slightly offensive assumption that because they're about the same age they must also be in the same league. Nell likes attention, but not indiscriminately, and she draws the line at Gerald.

'Well, I'll bear it in mind, but at the moment I've got my work cut out with this retrospective ...'

Which are the words that Horace, reappearing at that moment, overhears, and pipes up, 'Ah, looking forward to that, Nell, thanks!'

Gerald looks round at her enquiringly: she's caught cold. 'You must come too, of course,' she says immediately. 'My dealer's just about to send out proper invitations.'

Horace is preparing to show Gerald the handiwork on his picture, and Nell sees her chance to escape. 'I'll be in touch,' she says, backing away.

'Don't go,' Gerald calls peremptorily. 'I'll walk back with you.'

So while Gerald and Horace fuss over the framing and sort out the payment, Nell, martyr to politeness, waits and waits, more or less ignored, all for the pleasure of accompanying her neighbour back up to Fortess Road.

Shooting has begun on *Heaven and Earth* at Twickenham. This afternoon's scene is set backstage at the theatre where Billie's dancer has just come out of rehearsal and finds Horatio, played by Robbie, mooching around. She doesn't yet know that he is the angel sent down to protect her. The short passage of dialogue they're filming runs thus:

GEMMA   Oh, are you the new call-boy?
HORATIO (*amused*) You could say so . . .
GEMMA   What do you mean? Are you or aren't you?
HORATIO I mean, I'm accustomed to people
               calling on me.

Robbie keeps flubbing the words, simple though they are, and with every crack of the clapper-sticks a mood of impatience builds. 'Scene eleven, take fifteen,' calls the assistant cameraman, and off they go. Robbie stumbles over the word 'accustomed' again, and they cut. An audible groan goes up. Billie draws Robbie aside for a moment. She gets him to say the line, which he does. 'OK, now I'm going to say my line and you take a deep breath, then say your line.' He does it as specified, and she gives his arm a squeeze.

They do the next take without a hitch. Vernon Sparks calls a break and asks Robbie over for 'a quick word'. Billie is about to wander off when she spots Maurice, eyes hooded, arms folded, leaning back against a wall. He's not on call for this scene, but he's been observing it from the sidelines.

'Enjoy that?' Billie asks drily.

'It boggles the mind how he might have fared *without* your coaching assistance.'

'Don't be nasty.'

'Vern's going to lose it. I could hear him grinding his teeth from here.'

'Robbie'll be fine. He just needs encouragement.'

'Mm. He's certainly getting that from his latest admirer.'

Billie looks at him. 'Admirer?'

'Kezia's been getting awfully friendly with him.'

Kezia Wilton plays the company's rivalrous prima ballerina in *Heaven and Earth*. She is a russet-haired, green-eyed beauty of about Robbie's age. Billie, who hasn't noticed the smallest scintilla of attraction between them, snorts a laugh. 'You're such a stirrer, Maurice.'

He makes a face of injured innocence. 'Just keeping an eye out for your protégé, dear. You know how these young people are ...'

'My *protégé* ...'

'Oh, how would you describe him?'

'He's my co-star,' she replies shortly. 'And he's perfectly capable of looking after himself.'

He's a master of the wind-up, old Maurice. She excuses herself to go to the loo, thus escaping a further dose of his insinuation.

In the late afternoon she's crossing the studio foyer when ahead of her she sees Robbie deep in conversation with – it takes a moment to recognise her – Kezia Wilton. There is a stillness in their body language; something has been said; she stands looking up at him intently. Billie halts, hesitates, then continues towards them. 'Hi!' she says, putting as much breeziness as she can into the salutation. She senses she has interrupted 'a moment' between them. Kezia flashes her social smile, and glances at her watch – she'd better be off, she says, giving them each a little wave goodbye.

Robbie turns to Billie, who waits for him to speak. The space into which she's moved seems to reverberate still with Kezia's presence. *Is* there something going on between them?

'Everything OK?' she says.

'Yeah, it's all cool.'

There's nothing there for her, so she presses on. 'You remember we talked about the house with the room to rent?'

'Uh-huh.'

'Well, I've checked, and it's available. I could take you to see it one day next week if you're interested.'

He nods, thoughtful. 'Where is it? D'you know the landlord?'

'It's a landlady, as a matter of fact. Are you going to the station? I'll explain to you on the way . . .'

7

Soave sia il vento
Tranquilla sia l'onda
Ed ogni elemento
Benigno risponda
Ai nostri desir

A late afternoon in early June. Nell, in her painting-room, is feeling the Mozart at full blast. The purling, gliding sweetness of those three voices in harmony is so intense it can force tears to her eyes. She's humming along, absorbed in her painting of the back elevations of Fortess Road, working on the colours that will bring out the subtly variegated brickwork. She would usually keep her ears pricked for the dainty tapping of the woodpecker, but in the last few weeks it's gone quiet. The bird has flown, perhaps found another tree, and in mourning she has cranked the volume high on her cassette player.

So high, in fact, that she doesn't hear the footsteps coming up the stairs, or the voices, and happening to turn almost jumps with fright on seeing a young man framed in the doorway, watching her; it takes a fraction of a second for her to realise that standing just to his side is Billie, who says, 'Bloody hell, Mum, you sure you've got that on *loud* enough?'

Nell tweaks it down as they sidle into the room. The first thing that strikes her, that would strike anyone: how beautiful he is. Not handsome – that word doesn't convey the distinctly feminine aspect of his pulchritude, the arch of the cheekbones, the plush mouth, the eyelashes you could ski off. Girlish, but boyish, too, with his skinny white limbs and the faint shadow of stubble on his jaw.

He half-lurches into the room, hand extended. 'Hello, Mrs Cantrip. I'm Robbie.'

She likes his politeness. They shake. 'Call me Nell.'

Beneath his unbuttoned check shirt she reads the name on his T-shirt. '"The Flowers of Romance". What's that – a band?'

'Yeah. Also a record. Have you heard of Johnny Rotten?'

'Course I have,' she says, offended. 'Just 'cos I'm ... I listen to pop music, you know.'

'She likes Prince,' Billie supplies.

'Sorry, I didn't mean ... Flowers of Romance were a punk band that never played live but became a bit of a legend – Sid Vicious was the singer. Rotten came up with the name.'

'I see,' says Nell. 'Shall I make us a cup of tea?'

While she goes down to the kitchen Billie shows Robbie around the house. Design-wise it is stuck in a 1960s time warp, lots of early Habitat furniture and swirly rugs and potted palms, but it's clean, and after Gunter Grove you could probably call it de luxe. On the top floor there are two bedrooms, the front one larger, the back one cosier. Billie says he can have either one; after some deliberation he chooses the back. She smiles.

'You've gone for my old room.'

He looks at her. 'Is that a bit weird? D'you mind?'

She shakes her head. 'I moved out when I was nineteen. Feels like a lifetime ago. Mum's had lodgers here ever since.'

He wanders around the room, stares out of the window. Then he plumps himself down on the bed. 'I wonder what you were like at nineteen.'

'Poor. I was at RADA and living in a grotty basement in King's Cross.'

'Cute-looking, I'll bet. Were all the blokes after you?'

'If they were I had no idea. I was madly in love with someone at the time.'

He looks at her appraisingly. 'I wish I'd known you then.'

'Why?'

'Well, I would have asked you out.'

The bald way he says this makes her laugh out loud, at once flattered and unnerved. 'Unfortunately when I was nineteen, you were . . . ?'

'Four. But I was quite advanced for my years.' He leans back on the bed, propped on his elbows. 'How are things going with Bryn? Has he moved back in yet?'

'This week. My mum's a bit –' she pulls a face – 'so best not to mention it. She's not a fan of his.'

'Nobody's good enough for her daughter . . .'

'Mm. So you like the room, then?'

'Yeah. It's gert lush,' he says with a wink.

'*Gert lush*?' She's heard him say this before and ignored it. 'What's that?'

He smiles. 'Bristol, innit? Just means, "really nice" . . .'

Down in the kitchen Nell has got Radio 1 playing, possibly in reaction to being asked if she's heard of Johnny Rotten. Billie and Robbie sit either side of her as she pours tea from the stripy blue-and-white pot. Nell asks him about his life in Bristol, and he talks about his mum, who's a supply teacher, and his sister, awaiting her A-level results. He goes back when he can, but this year he's been that busy touring and preparing for the film he's not had a free weekend.

'Has she been looking after you?' Nell asks, with a nod to Billie.

Robbie's reply is instant and earnest: 'Oh, been my saviour, she has . . .'

Billie smiles, then says archly, 'Though you're also thick as thieves with Kezia, I've noticed.'

She has disguised her uncertainty as a tease. He looks at her, frowning. 'Well, she's a nice girl, but I don't really know her.'

He's not being defensive, just straightforward, and Billie feels an unexpected surge of relief. She'll *kill* Maurice next time she sees him. Robbie asks Nell about her painting – he had a peek into her studio on his way down – and she mentions her upcoming show. In fact, she's just had an idea and makes a mental note to call Véro this evening.

'So how d'you like the idea of living here – not too quiet for you?' she asks him presently.

'Quiet is what I want,' he says. 'You'd better let me know if there are any ... house rules.'

Nell considers for a moment. 'Not really, apart from the eleven p.m. curfew, no women in the evening and no music after ten.'

Robbie stares at her, his expression frozen, then looks at Billie, who manages to keep a straight face.

'I'm joking, love,' says Nell.

'Gah, you had me worried for a sec!' he says over their laughter.

'Seriously, though, I don't want groupies camped out in the front garden.'

'They won't know I'm here, honest. You don't have to worry.'

Billie's right about him, she thinks, he's not how you imagine a pop star at all. Albeit on slight acquaintance there's nothing spoilt or arrogant about him, none of that unthinking entitlement that the young and famous throw on themselves like a magic cape. He's probably not as innocent as he looks – they seldom are – but she senses an amiability in him and a warmth: his attachment to Billie is almost puppyish.

'More tea?' she asks, taking up the pot.

'We'd be better be off, Mum,' says Billie, who's just noticed a stack of leaflets on the kitchen dresser. 'What are those?'

Nell rolls her eyes. 'Flyers for our MP. Tash bullied me into it when I said I wouldn't canvass. I'd better get them off before Thursday.'

'Are you even voting Labour?' says Billie. 'Last time we spoke you seemed all in for the Alliance.'

'I dunno. I'll decide on the day.'

'Tash is your other daughter, right?' asks Robbie.

'My big sister,' says Billie, standing at the door. 'Come on, we're going. You've got packing to do.' They've agreed that he'll move in this weekend.

'How are you going to move your stuff, by the way?' asks Nell.

He gives an embarrassed grin, looking at Billie.

'Muggins here has offered her pick-up service,' says Billie. 'Good job I got my car fixed.'

'See you Saturday.'

Later, Nell is on the phone to Véro for their now almost-daily call. 'I've got a title for the show, by the way.'

'At last! Go on . . .'

'"The Flowers of Romance",' she says, and waits. She can hear Véro turning it over in her head.

'Where have I heard that before?'

'It doesn't matter,' says Nell, who's not going to reference punk rock or Johnny Rotten because she knows that will find no favour with Véro. 'It just feels right to me. And the flower paintings are the main event, after all.'

'"The Flowers of Romance",' Véro says pensively, testing it on her dealer's ear. 'Well, I still like "A Maverick Eye". Or "Nell Cantrip: A Life's Work".'

Nell doesn't reply. She knows she's found her title, it's just a matter of waiting for her to come round. The silence lengthens until Véro says, in a slightly narked tone, 'Where did you come by this?'

'Have you heard of a singer called Robbie Furlong?'

'No.'

'He's a friend of Billie's, they're working on a film together. He was here this afternoon and happened to be wearing a T-shirt with this name on it. The Flowers of Romance. I knew practically from the moment I saw it.'

Another pause, and Véro sighs. 'All right ... I suppose it'll do. The catalogue is going to the printers on Monday. Are you sure about this?'

'Positive.'

After she rings off Nell goes into the kitchen and opens a beer. She has a title for the show. She has delivered the Labour Party flyers for Tash. Her painting of the backs is coming along. And the flowers she planted in March are peeping through in the garden. She goes up to the top floor where she's left the window open to give Robbie's bedroom an airing. While she changes the bed linen she considers her new lodger. That first sight of him in the doorway gave her a jolt ... Nice to have someone gorgeous to look at around the house. But there's something else about him she responds to, a sort of unworldliness, like he's just got off the boat. It goes with that funny West Country accent of his with its rolled 'r's and *ain't*s. He and Billie look like they've known one another for years.

Pity about their difference in age – they might have been boyfriend and girlfriend. He'd be so much better for her than Bryn. Just bad timing, isn't it?

Billie looks up from her book. She's sitting in a canvas-backed chair waiting for the next set-up, which is taking for ever. Around her continues the ceaseless to-ing and fro-ing on the sound stage where they are shooting *Heaven and Earth*, a cavernous hive of electricians and chippies and grips and camera assistants and script wallahs and make-up artists and wardrobe consultants and production runners. It still amuses her that so thickly peopled a space, with so much expertise at play, should generate so little of consequence: maybe three minutes of film squeezed out per day. Thank God she likes reading.

'Good book?' says Maurice Venning, appearing at her side with his unnerving soundless stealth.

'Mm. Diaries aren't my thing, but I'm hooked on this.' She holds it up for his inspection. 'Did I tell you that she's a distant ancestor of mine?'

'Merrymount ... not the painter?'

'The very one. Laura was his older daughter. She wanted to be a painter herself. You ever heard of an actress named Lizzie Vavasor?' Maurice shakes his head.

'Hugely famous in her day. Friend of Laura's. They live in this lovely whirl of parties and musical evenings and first nights at Covent Garden. And then the worst thing happens – can you guess?'

'They die horribly in a fire.'

'All right, second worst – Laura discovers that Lizzie and her father have been having an affair for years.'

'Oh dear. Those randy Georgians,' says Maurice, taking up the book and leafing through it. He stops at the section of monochrome plates, and a light sparks in his eyes. 'Hmm, look at *this* handsome dog.' Billie leans over to have a look.

'Ah, that's him, Joseph Rothwell – Merrymount's illegitimate son, and our great-great-whatever. That's the portrait once attributed to William but now known – because of this book – to be by Laura. Wonderful, isn't it?'

Maurice is nodding. 'Looks as if he might just lean out of the picture and shake your hand.'

'I wanted to get a print, but it seems to be in a private collection.'

'Shame,' he says, handing her back the book. 'How did it go with Roberto and your mother?'

'Fine. All gert lush.'

'What?'

'Bristol slang – means really good.'

Maurice wrinkles his nose. 'Gert Lush? Sounds like a char lady in a Noël Coward play. I'm rather alarmed by your protégé's influence on you. I notice you've been saying "Gah" a lot lately.'

'Have I?' she says, and grins. 'Well, it could get worse. He's moving in to my mum's place on Saturday.'

Maurice's expression shifts from disapproval to disbelief. 'You're joking.'

'Didn't I tell you? He's been living in this squat with a load of junkies. I had to get him out of there, and my mum's seemed the safest and easiest place to move him.'

His look is now one of gimlet-eyed penetration. 'Do you really know what you're doing?'

Billie stares back at him, uncomprehending. 'I'm not sure what you … The place this kid lives, he'd either be robbed blind or catch some horrible disease, or both, so I wanted to protect him – that's the meaning of *protéger*, isn't it?'

'It's not *his* protection I'm worried about, dear. I have a feeling this kid, as you like to call him, might not be as guileless as he looks. You seem to have gone gooey just because he talks like a Wurzel and stares at you with his big Bambi eyes. But he's been around the block. He's been in a band, for God's sake, so he knows plenty about how the world works.'

'I'm not gooey about him,' she says in surprise. 'I mean, he's good-looking, he's charming, he's got nice manners. But Maurice, he's *twenty-two*, and like most twenty-two-year-old men he's not that interested in women like me. Which is fine. Right now I'm trying to get my marriage back together – or didn't you know?'

Maurice doesn't reply, not in words at least. He does that thing Billie finds really infuriating – nods in knowing silence, as if to say, *Your defence is pathetic, but I refuse to argue*. It could be part of his wind-up routine, like the other day when he told her that Kezia was cosying up to Robbie. He loves to wrong-foot, to provoke, so she mustn't rise to the bait. On the other hand, she knows he's very beady in his social observation: he attends to people, closely, and he's unsentimental about the truth. *Has* she misjudged Robbie?

8

After clearing out of Gunter Grove Billie has to drive them to another tumbledown squat a few streets north where Robbie has stored his LPs. He says he has them boxed up but will need a hand carrying them to the car. She has envisaged a stack of maybe fifty or sixty, rather like her own collection; in fact, there are five huge cardboard boxes which fill up the back seat of her old Mercedes and block the rear-view mirror. *I'm like his mother picking him up from university*, Billie thinks. All that he owns, it seems, are clothes, records and a Ferguson music centre. He keeps his guitars in storage, apart from the peacock-blue acoustic, in its case, which he has propped between his knees in the well of the passenger seat. This is surely not the typical life of a 1980s pop star. Unworldly as he is, Robbie must be earning a packet from his royalties and his tours, yet he lives like some itinerant, of no fixed abode – until today.

As they navigate the back streets of West London she says, 'You do have a bank account, don't you?'

'Course,' he replies. 'What, is your mum worried about me paying the rent?'

'No, that's not why I asked. You always seem to have just a wodge of cash.'

'It's how my manager arranges it. I prefer it in cash.'

She wonders about this manager and his arrangements. Maybe the next thing she ought to do is fix him up with an accountant.

They arrive at Nell's about noon. It's a sultry June day, traffic booming down Fortess Road, the leaves thick and dusty on the trees. The blare of an ambulance siren knifes the air somewhere in the distance. Billie lets them in, and they walk through the house to the garden where Nell and Tash sit together on the garden bench; they're watching Chris bowl slow over-arm to Gil, who's wielding the dinky Gray Nicolls scoop bat he got for his birthday. Billie performs the introductions, feeling slightly managerial herself as she leads the getting-to-know-you chat – she has gone from playing his mum to his PR. But she is pleased to see that Chris and Gil quickly warm to him, and even Tash relaxes her guard.

On the table lies this morning's *Guardian* confirming the Tory landslide, like a death notice.

When Nell slips off to make a salad Billie suggests to Robbie they unload the car now rather than wait till after lunch: she's worried that a passing thief might drive off with all his worldlies.

'D'you need some help?' Chris asks.

'Nah, you're fine,' says Robbie, 'just a load of clothes and LPs.'

Billie quietly curses this unthinking refusal as she's wrestling a ton-weight of vinyl up the several flights of stairs. She does the trip twice, three times, and by the fourth her arms are aching, her shirt damp. The temperature in the bedroom, now Robbie's room, has become close, as it always does at the top of the house in summer.

Boxes and piles of clothes lie heaped across the floor and the bed as Robbie heaves the last lot through the door. The two of them stand there for a moment, sweating like racehorses. 'Well, that was fun,' Billie deadpans, and in silent thanks he wraps his arms about her. Through his shirt she feels the compact muscle and warmth of his body and gets a not-unpleasant whiff of what she recognises as Boots hair gel (it's called 'Country Born', and smells of chemicals). With his hands on her, a tingling bolt of lust shoots from the soles of her feet right up into her groin. She realises at this moment she'd be entirely amenable to his throwing her down on the single bed and ravishing her.

'You're a pal, you are,' says Robbie, releasing her. She finds no answering look of possibility in his eyes. For the rest of the afternoon she feels an ache of useless longing, and a terrible relief that she pushed it no further.

In the kitchen Nell is surprised when her new tenant slopes by and hands her a hastily wrapped gift. She opens it to find a cassette of *Chain Lightning*, his current record.

'Gosh, that's really ... Thank you, Robbie.'

'I know you like pop music. I mean, not sure it's exactly your thing ...'

'I'll have to listen and find out, won't I?' she says, waggling it in her hand. 'You all settled in up there?'

'Yeah, thanks. Dead cosy.'

When she asks him to carry some plates out to the garden he jumps to it. He's pliant as well as polite. Over lunch there's a post-mortem on the election, though no one really has the appetite for it apart from Tash. Nell, who's brought out beers with her salad, raises her glass in welcome to Robbie, 'who arrives as our lodger but already feels like our friend'. He thanks her in turn, and adds that this is by far the nicest house in London he's ever been in. Billie points out that's not saying much given the dosshouses he's been through.

Later they get on to music. Robbie talks Gil through some elementary guitar picking, and Gil puts on *Off the Wall* so he can exhibit his moonwalk.

'Are you named after Gil Scott-Heron, by the way?'

Gil nods brightly, and Chris says, 'I think you're the first person who's ever got that.'

'I saw him in concert a couple of times. He was amazing. Did you know that his dad played for Celtic?'

Asked to play something, Robbie makes only a token demur before taking up his guitar again. He tunes it in the faintly neurotic way Billie has observed before, grimacing and frowning as he makes tiny adjustments on the keys, then he feints to start before a supplementary round of fine-tuning. At last he plays a chord and sings:

Jagged jigsaw pieces
Tossed about the room

It's a slow ballad called 'Pieces of a Man', one of Scott-Heron's early songs, narrated by a boy witnessing his dad in a moment of shock, and shame – the old man has just opened a letter notifying him of redundancy. The original is piano-led, but Robbie has transposed the chords to his guitar, putting a new shade on the plangency. At the end, over their clapping, Billie asks him to do his song from the film, so he plays them 'Black-eyed Boy from Cloudy Fields'. He glances at her once or twice as he's singing, and smiles, as if they're both in on a little secret.

Later, as Billie is washing up at the kitchen sink, she says to Nell, 'You have to read the Merrymount book, by the way. Did you know that Laura and her sister lived round here?'

'No! Whereabouts?'

'A little villa in College Lane. This is early nineteenth century, when Kentish Town was still outside London. According to the footnotes it was all paddocks and flower gardens and skittle-grounds – people used to make excursions here.'

'College Lane . . . that *is* near,' says Nell, and waits a beat. 'What are skittle-grounds exactly?'

'Dunno. Somewhere they played skittles?'

'I thought you told me they lived in Cavendish Square.'

'They did, for years. Then the younger one who went soft moved out here with her pet macaw. Back then Kentish Town was known for its clean air.'

Nell half-snorts a laugh. 'That dates it.'

'Once Merrymount dies the two daughters seem forgotten about. Spinsters growing old together. But they've just been discovered again by Edmund, the illegitimate son – which is where I'm up to.'

'They may have known people on this road.'

'Mmm, I don't think these houses had been built yet. But think of all the times we've walked down College Lane, probably stepping on the same pavement they did. Just think, Mum – *our relatives*.'

'You should get in touch with Hilary,' says Nell. 'She'd love to talk with you about them.'

'I'm also going to see the Merrymounts in the National. I've never had a proper look at them before. I feel sort of possessive about him now I know we're related.'

Nell picks up another plate to dry, and lifts her eyes towards the ceiling. 'How's his nibs getting on up there?'

'He's unpacking his record collection – should be finished about next Friday, I expect. Oh, and he does have a bank account, says he'll pay you by cheque at the end of each month.'

'Right. He seems to have a fan here, anyway. Gil's face while he was playing guitar!' She lowers her voice for a moment. 'He's so good-looking, isn't he?'

'I suppose he is.' Nell smiles.

'Like the young Alain Delon. Bet you'd fancy a knock with him, eh?'

'*Mum . . .*' Billie puts on a disapproving face, though she's alarmed by the accuracy of her conjecture. She stares at Nell, wondering, but sees only lascivious good humour.

In the first weeks of Robbie's tenancy Nell barely claps eyes on him. He's up by seven for the car to take him to Twickenham, and he's not back from the day's filming until late, usually after she's gone to bed. Sometimes she hears from his room a loud blast of music, which suddenly cuts out. Has he just remembered he's not in the squat any more? She wouldn't mind if he did play it loud, she often does so herself, whether it's opera or something torchy by Dinah Washington or Sarah Vaughan. She's played the cassette he gave her a few times and quite likes it, though his singing voice spooks her a bit – it doesn't sound like his speaking voice at all. He sounds Scots, or Irish; you'd never know he was from Bristol.

When Madge, her cleaner, arrives Nell uses her as an excuse to visit his room and see how he's settled in. The long dressing-rail that was sent on from his last place is packed end to end with his clothes, most of which she's never seen him wear. Jackets in creaking black leather and buckskin and gold lamé – for stage wear? – plus combat fatigues, army greatcoats, suede blousons, drummer-boy tunics, tartan bondage trousers (hello?), fur-collared pea coats, jeans in every shade from white to indigo to black, shirts without number. His T-shirts fill up two large drawers in the dresser. There's a single book on his bedside: *Gertrude* by Hermann Hesse.

One morning a parcel arrives at her door. Inside: half a dozen copies of the catalogue for her show, with a handwritten note of congratulations from Véro.

The Flowers of Romance
Nell Cantrip
Paintings 1941–1981

She sits at the kitchen table staring at it. Véro's people have done a good job, the colours of the reproduced paintings have a clarity and definition against the white of the page. The title of each painting in sans-serif, with materials and measurements noted in a smaller font beneath, is pleasingly austere. Some have been dated, the ones Nell can remember. Inserted at the back is a loose sheet of A4 listing the titles, and their prices. She can hardly believe what they are charging for them – outrageous, really, though Véro brushes aside her misgivings. 'There's so much money sloshing around out there, darling, you have no idea.' Véro also adduces the Tory election landslide as promise of a new free-spending ethos. Can it be true? Nell, who had to scrimp and borrow as a young mother – for years she never had a pound extra to spare, or even a comfortable bed – is still quietly amazed by the prosperity of her later years. She doesn't feel guilty about it but she can't help feeling its precariousness. She comes of a time when livelihoods could disappear overnight.

When Billie stops by the following weekend – she's promised to show Robbie around the neighbourhood – the catalogue is there on the dresser. She picks it up, frowning.

'*The Flowers of Romance* ... did you get that from ... ?'

'Yeah,' says Nell. 'From the T-shirt he wore that day you first brought him round.'

She's still staring at it, unsmiling. 'You never said ... ' Is there just the tiniest hint of displeasure in her eyes? Nell is alert to nuances of mood, but she can't imagine why Billie might object.

'I liked the sound of it, I suppose.'

'You know it's just some punk band nobody's heard of?'

Nell nods. 'That's not why I ... Véro had been on at me for a title, for ages, and that just popped into my head. It sounded right.'

Robbie enters the room, and checks what Billie is looking at. 'I saw that earlier,' he says, smiling. 'Love it!'

Nell could offer Billie a challenging look at this point, but instead she catches her eye and shrugs as if to say, *Each to their own* ... It occurs to her that Billie is rather proprietary in her attachment – that Robbie is exclusively *her* friend, not Nell's or anyone else's. And what's with this weekend get-together anyway? Haven't they seen enough of one another at the studio?

She says, 'How's Bryn, by the way?'

'Fine. He's watching the cricket today.'

Some mischievous instinct prods at Nell. With studied careless-ness she says, 'Have you introduced him to Robbie?'

Billie looks at her mother sharply. 'Not yet. Things have been so busy I haven't had a chance.'

Nell waits a beat, then says to Robbie, 'Well, you'll meet him soon enough anyway, at my show.'

He gives a little twitch of surprise. 'Am I invited?'

'Of course. I've put you on the list.'

She can feel Billie bristling at that, at the familiarity of it. And yet there's not a thing she can say in objection. Robbie, unaware of these cross-currents, is poring over the catalogue himself, murmuring approval. Nell can see that he's pleased to be invited. That's partly why she likes him so much. Other men – Bryn, say – have the charm of confidence; Robbie has the charm of uncertainty.

Still, she doesn't want to alienate Billie, and as they're about to leave she says to her, 'I was wondering if you'd both like to have dinner here next week.'

Billie clicks her tongue in regret. 'Sorry, Mum, we can't – we're on location all next week, on the south coast.'

'Eastbourne,' says Robbie, pulling a face.

'A seaside jaunt. I'll expect a postcard, then.'

Five minutes later, as they're walking up Fortess Road, Billie turns to Robbie. 'Newsflash: my mum fancies you.'

He halts, frowning incomprehension at her. 'She does not.'

'Listen, I know her. Flirty Gertie's on the lookout.'

'Doesn't mean anything; you told me she flirts with Chris, too.' When she doesn't reply he adds, 'Anyway, she's attractive, your mum – why shouldn't she have a bit of a flirt? Doesn't bother me.'

'It bothers *me*,' she snaps. 'As for that "Flowers of Romance" business – you know she's just done that to please you?'

Robbie shrugs. 'Didn't seem like that. She really liked the title ...'

'Just don't encourage her. She'll give up after a while.'

Now he looks confused. Billie shakes her head, and they walk on. She's annoyed with Nell, and annoyed with herself for moaning about her in front of Robbie. But why does it bother her? It's not as if *she* has anything going on with him; they're just mates. Maybe she wants to keep him to herself. In which case, why did she singlehandedly contrive to move him in to Nell's house?

At her side Robbie is keeping quiet, aware that something is up. He looks about him as they walk, admiring his new neighbourhood. There's a feeling they ought to change the subject, and eventually Robbie makes the effort.

'My mum told me there's a music pub round here called the Tally Ho where Dad used to play,' he says brightly. 'On Fortress Road, I think.'

Billie huffs loudly in irritation. 'It's not Fortress, Robbie – it's For*tess*. *Fortess*. How many times have I got to tell you?'

'Sorry, I'm always ...' He tails off, mumbling.

Now she feels worse: she forgot about his dyslexia. They continue down the road in silence.

9

Billie stands at her open wardrobe, hesitating. She holds up for appraisal a little black dress with spaghetti straps. To take it or not? The prospect of wearing such a thing in Eastbourne is vanishingly slight – they'll be filming most days, often well into the night. But then they are staying at the Grand, and they might get an evening off ... She slips it from the hanger and folds it carefully into her suitcase. Over its lid she sees Bryn, propped up in bed, his attention divided between *The Times* and watching her pack.

'Expecting a bit of action down on the coast, then?' he says, peering over his reading glasses.

She laughs, a bit too eagerly. 'Not the sort of action you mean. What will you be doing while I'm gone?'

'Not much. Reading a script. A dinner in Soho on Tuesday.'

'Will Jenny Daunt be there?'

'Maybe, I don't know. Anyway ... Are you sure you don't want me to come with you? I wouldn't get in the way.'

She shakes her head. 'Darling, you'd be bored stiff. Eastbourne?! I don't understand why you'd want to.'

'Because I've barely seen you. I thought you might like it if I was there. Dinner together, late-night stroll along the esplanade, back to the room for some proper nooky.'

'Proper nooky? Wasn't that what we had last night?'

'Yeah, it was great,' he says, 'but this would be different – sex in a hotel is always different.'

'How?'

Bryn pulls his lopsided grin. 'Well, it's do with ... anonymity. You check in, go to a hired room, knowing you won't be there for long – and look, there's a double bed right there, and a bathroom that's just been cleaned. Then you lock the door, secure your privacy with a "do not disturb" sign, take your clothes off ...'

'Is there someone else with you at this point?' Billie asks, returning to her packing.

He pulls a face. 'Of course there is. But it might not be someone you know. Or it might be someone you know who's pretending to be someone else ...'

'Not sure I—'

'Come on, you know all that stuff about role-playing. It's like the number-one fantasy – the couple who check in under different names, then meet at the bar pretending to be strangers. Maybe the lady is pretending to be, I dunno, a prostitute. Adds a bit of spice to the encounter.'

Billie nods. 'So that's proper nooky?'

'You must see the attraction? In a hotel room you're temporarily relieved of your identity, free of responsibility, of duty ...'

'Ah. I'm beginning to understand. You can get your end away without feeling bad about it.'

'No, it's not about cheating – not necessarily. I like to imagine you and me checking in somewhere, under false names, then seeing where it leads ...'

'Hmm. Not for me. You see, I spend all day on set playing someone else. The last thing I want to do once I throw my togs off is play *another* part.'

'Oh well, if that's how you feel.' A long pause. 'To be honest, I was just hoping you might want to see me.' She hears something

333

hurt in his voice. She leaves the suitcase and goes to sit on the bed next to him.

'I do want to see you. How about you come down on the Friday evening? As long as we finish on time we can have dinner somewhere.'

He grabs hold of her and buries his head against her shoulder in a parody of a forties melodrama, whispering, 'Oh, thenk you, *thenk you*, darling.'

'All right. Very funny,' she says, pulling out of his needy embrace. Outside the flat she hears a car horn parp twice. 'That'll be my car.'

She quickly closes her suitcase, heaves it towards the door.

Bryn says, 'I'll be down there Friday afternoon. The Grand, isn't it?'

'Yeah. Don't worry, I'll make sure they put you in a nice room.'

He nods, then wakes up to what she's just said. '*Hey*—'

'Bye, darling!' she shouts from the hall, laughing.

As she fixes her make-up in the back of the car, Billie wonders why she has just given in to Bryn. She hasn't seen much of him since he moved back in, it's true, mainly because of the filming: the budget on *Heaven and Earth* is so small they can't afford to overrun. But it's also to do with keeping her life with Bryn separate from Robbie. They've been filming for six weeks and she still hasn't introduced them. She can't explain why.

The car has left behind Marylebone and entered the tattier outskirts of Kentish Town. Not yet nine o'clock and already the sun's burning up the sky. When they arrive at Fortess Road she asks the driver for five minutes while she nips inside to collect her passenger. Robbie is at the kitchen table eating a cooked breakfast, served to him by Nell. He sees the expression on Billie's face and says, 'I'll just finish this – gimme two minutes.'

She spreads her arms, incredulous. 'I said last night – be ready at nine o'clock.'

'Let him finish his breakfast,' says Nell. There's a fond look on her face that makes Billie want to throw something at her.

'Mum, we've got to go! There's a filming schedule – the meter's ticking.'

Robbie obediently rises and says, through a slice of toast jutting from his mouth, that he'll just fetch his suitcase. Nell, relaxed at the table, lights a cigarette and offers one to Billie, who shakes her head.

'Got the weather for it,' Nell remarks. 'It'll be lovely down on the coast.'

'You make it sound like a holiday. It's ten days straight of filming, with a nine o'clock start every day.'

'Still, you'll have sun and sea whether you're working or not. What's Bryn going to do while you're gone?'

Billie shrugs. 'He's got a script to read. And he's going to come down on the Friday – I don't know why he wants to ...'

'Don't you?' Nell's tone is speculative, which makes it hard to know what she means. Billie decides not to answer, and checks her watch. It's been a long time since Nell has seen her daughter in this uneasy skittish mood; it feels like something in her has been wound too tight.

From the hallway comes a sudden thump, a creak and Robbie's strangled 'Gah!' They find him on his hands and knees repacking his sprung-open suitcase.

It takes them an hour to get out of London. Once they're whizzing through the Sussex countryside Billie starts to relax; she puts aside the *Guardian* and turns to Robbie, plugged into his Walkman.

'You seem to be getting on all right with the landlady,' she says, with a half-smile. 'Don't recall her making cooked breakfasts for her previous lodgers.'

He pulls down the headphones so they make a collar around his neck. 'Yeah, she's great, your ma. We had some fun last night ...'

Billie stares at him. 'What d'you mean?'

'Well, I was flicking along that shelf of videos in your living room and – guess what – I found a cassette of *Eureka*. When I told Nell I'd never seen it she said, "Right, let's put it on" – and we watched it together.'

Eureka is the first film Billie ever made, in the summer of 1967. She hasn't watched it herself in years.

'So ...?'

'I loved it! I didn't *understand* it ... but I loved the look, and the clothes, and the music! Amazing. And as for you ...'

'I wasn't very good in it,' she says, knowing it for the truth but hoping to be contradicted.

'No, no, you light it up. I couldn't get over how young you looked ...'

'I was twenty-two. Same as you are now. I was fifth on the cast list, just after Vere Summerhill.'

'That the old guy? Nell was right gone on him – said she fancied him for years.'

Billie, cast upon the distant shore of '67, ponders her companionship with Vere, the faded matinee idol; with Nat, the writer; and Reiner, their director. London, in the June heat, and the just-released *Sgt Pepper* playing everywhere. She had a lot of luck back then, outrageous luck, really, given the circumstances in which Nat had discovered her ... Has she been as kind to Robbie as they all were to her? It's getting harder with him to draw the line between friendly assistance and possessiveness. She feels unsettled, petulant – like a teenager.

Robbie is eager to know more, especially about the music, and Billie tries to oblige with what she remembers from sixteen years ago. The actual filming went fine and the week's location shoot in Portofino was marvellous. Unfortunately that time is also mixed up with the end of her relationship with Jeff, a disappointed artist who couldn't cope with her success, and later went nuts. What happened between them is too bound up with misery and shame to revisit now, and Robbie in any case wants to hear about Dox Walbrook, the legendary horn player who did the score, and how Apple nearly sued the film company for plagiarism: the script had 'borrowed' without permission from the fugue sequence of The Beatles' 'A Day in the Life'. Strange, she's made a dozen features since then, some of them pretty good, and yet the one they always want to talk about is *Eureka*. When she tells Robbie that it's not even that great he looks at her, disbelieving – he doesn't understand that some films are never quite so enthralling as the stories attached to them.

Nell takes out her lemon drizzle cake from the oven and puts it on the counter to cool. She hasn't baked anything for ages, but she has a guest on the way who'll appreciate it. Hilary's phone call yesterday took her by surprise – after their meeting last month they've corresponded, in tacit agreement that they might not get together again for a while. That's why you're *distant* cousins, isn't it? But Hilary said she was in London seeing her daughter and would it be all right to drop by next morning? Nell looks forward to seeing her. She's wistful, too, thinking of all the years they've lived in ignorance of one another.

She goes out into the garden to inspect the flowers. It's a bright morning, a bit fresher than yesterday, with a slight haze in the air. She lights a Player's and mooches around the lawn until she hears the doorbell go inside. On the step she flings her arms around Hilary. Her back feels damp with sweat – she's rather overweight – and her arms are white and wobbly in the shapeless summer dress she's wearing. As she sits down at the kitchen table she gives out one of those extravagant groans of fatigue you'd expect from someone quite ancient, which Nell realises comes of carrying all that bulk around. Maybe she oughtn't to have baked a cake after all.

'Mmm, this is lovely,' says Hilary some minutes later as she's seeing off her first slice. She beams in her friendly way. 'And what's going on with you – have you taken up the guitar?'

Nell, puzzled for a moment, realises she must have seen the guitar leaning in the hallway. 'Oh, no – no, that belongs to my lodger, Robbie – Robbie Furlong?'

The name provokes no look of recognition from her cousin, so she explains how a young actor-friend of Billie's needed somewhere to live, and since Nell has a whole house available ... It later occurs to her that even if she had decided to take up the instrument she would be unlikely to begin her lessons on a cherry-coloured flying-V.

'They've just gone down to the coast for a week's filming,' she explains. 'Billie's very eager to meet you, actually. She's been reading the Laura Merrymount book you brought – telling me all about Mrs Vavasor and her father's affair and the sisters' moving to Kentish Town. You know they lived on College Lane?'

'Is that near here?' Hilary asks.

'You mean you ... It's five minutes' walk. I can take you there, if you're interested.'

From the light that snaps on in Hilary's eyes it's clear that she would be. Though first they must have another cup of tea, and perhaps another slice of cake. As they continue to chat, Nell senses in her cousin a certain distraction, a want of focus she didn't notice when they first met. This time she's done more of the talking, Hilary the listening – but fitfully. A couple of times she seems to check out of the conversation and then apologises for not paying attention. Nell hopes she isn't boring her.

Outside, the late-morning traffic swooshes on unnoticingly. They walk past the ramshackle run of shops that line the west side of Fortess Road, Nell occasionally catching their reflection in the plate-glass windows – two middle-aged women, fat and thin. She senses the strain in Hilary's movement as they go, and in her stertorous breathing (though unlike Nell she doesn't smoke). They double back up Highgate Road until they come to an alley off the main drag. At the next turn they enter the cobbled backwater of

College Lane, most of it late eighteenth-century cottages whose air of seclusion has more in common with a cathedral close.

Hilary is counting off the numbers on each door as they pass, until she stops outside the largest house in the row, white plaster walls, its door overhung with a handsome fanlight.

'I think this must be it,' she says, staring upwards. 'Molly and Laura's home.' Nell peers at windows that give nothing back. 'Pretty. Like something out of Jane Austen. How long did they live here?'

Hilary says, 'Molly moved here in the seventeen eighties when it was still a rural neighbourhood – the stage coach only stopped once a day. When their mother died I think that's when Laura sold up in Cavendish Square and came here.' They talk a little about the change it meant for Laura, who had lived a busy life hitherto and enjoyed company.

'Billie told me she gave up painting, too,' says Nell.

'Yes, though she went back to it later. Whenever I think of her life here' – there's a catch in her voice – 'I can only imagine how lonely it was ...'

Nell gives a sideways glance at Hilary, who has gone quiet, a moisture gleaming in her eyes. Her emotions are very close to the surface. Affecting not to notice so as to give her a moment, Nell takes up the conversational slack, speculating on the sisters' life in Kentish Town as she recalls it from Billie's report. When Hilary's head drops and a stifled sob escapes her it's clear there are quite other troubles preoccupying her.

'Oh, love ...' Nell places a tentative hand on her shoulder and her face crumples in distress. Through the gasps of her crying jag it comes out: Des, her husband, has just broken the news that for the last six years he's been having an affair. Of course, she has had her suspicions – who wouldn't? – but for most of the time they had rubbed along quite happily together. She says that he has been a kind and considerate man, and a good father to their two children.

'What did your daughter say?'

Hilary turns her piteously blotched face to her. 'I haven't told her. I couldn't. She loves him so much I – I felt ashamed.'

'Has he told you what he's going to do?'

She shakes her head, and half-whispers, 'I think he wants to leave me.'

The sobbing starts again, and Nell puts her arms around her. She sees now why Hilary has sought her out, even though they're practically strangers. Nell knows about unfaithful husbands, and what it's like to be abandoned. She will have lessons from this harsh school. She also recalls something Billie told her about Molly Merrymount and her marriage that ended in calamity – he turned out a proper rogue. Could it be that unhappy marriages run in the family? They have been standing in front of their ancestors' house for ten minutes, Nell still holding close her distraught cousin. No one has passed them on the street in that time; it seems they might continue there unobserved, invisible, for the rest of the morning. The sudden melancholy of the place makes Nell want to leave.

'Let's go and get a cup of tea somewhere,' she says.

Hilary nods like a stricken child and follows her out of the lane on to the high road. They find the life of Kentish Town going about its business, heedless of broken marriages and breaking hearts. Nell, passing along the street, sometimes glances at a face and wonders what secrets might be locked behind it – to think of all these tens, hundreds, thousands of individuals over-spilling this tiny pocket of the world, and each consciousness believing itself the very centre.

At a little café opposite the tube station they settle at a table. When the waitress brings them their pot of tea Nell pours, lights a cigarette and smiles across at Hilary. She has no idea what advice she can give. She has never met the husband and probably never will. She knows only how to listen, which may be the greatest kindness of all.

'Right. You'd better tell me all about it.'

10

Eastbourne, a sweltering day in the middle of July. The sun glints on the blue-green sea. Along the parade of flaking hotels and penny arcades, holidaymakers boil in the cauldron, like lobsters. Pink candyfloss, pink faces, pink sunburn. It's lunch-hour for the cast and crew of *Heaven and Earth*. Billie, edging through the fleshy hordes, sees a single-decker bus pulling to a stop just ahead. She turns to Robbie.

'Let's get this.'

They climb onboard and find themselves a space at the back. The vinyl seating is hot against her bare legs. The bus proceeds in fits and starts along the front. Robbie looks through the window at the sun-maddened bustle outside.

'Where are we going?'

'I don't know. I just wanted to get away from that lot.' She takes out a Chinese fan and wafts herself languidly. 'It's unbearable, this heat.'

They pass the pier, the adventure playground, the lines of parked cars; they are almost out of town when Billie spots something and jumps up to ring the bell. As they are alighting Robbie calls over his shoulder to the bus driver, 'Cheers, drive!'

On the pavement Billie is shaking her head. *'Cheers, drive ...'* She's got his Bristol accent to a T. 'What's that?'

'Just polite, ain't it?' says Robbie. He follows after her obediently. Billie is making for a fish-and-chip van parked by a grassy verge. There's a bit of a queue, so they have to wait. She asks him what he's going to have, and he peers at the menu chalked up next to the window.

'Erm ... fillet of cod, I s'pose.'

'Plus chips and mushy peas?'

He shakes his head – just the fish for him.

'Gah, no wonder you're so thin ... you don't *eat* anything.'

'I do so! I had an egg for breakfast this morning. And a piece of toast.'

Billie clicks her tongue in reproof. Unlike him she helped herself to a full English in the Grand's breakfast room earlier, as did Maurice and the rest of them. As ever, she's always starving when she's at work.

Once served they go to sit on the grass verge. Billie uses the dainty wooden fork to spear her fish, while Robbie just eats with his fingers, like a child. She wants to tell him to stop, but she's also aware of her habit of correcting him all the time. She feels like a bossy older sister, which isn't how she wants to be with him. Today he's wearing a white V-neck T-shirt, black jeans and Adidas trainers, his plainest and most attractive ensemble. She finds herself staring at him.

'When did you last have a girlfriend?' she says, out of nowhere.

He looks up, stops chewing. 'What?'

'Mum told me you had a visitor the other night – that Spanish-looking girl – Martha, is it?'

'Mara. Yeah, she came over; we had a bite to eat.'

Billie nods slowly. 'Very beautiful, as I remember ... '

'Yeah,' he says, with a thoughtful look. 'And still ain't my girlfriend.' She hopes he will continue, but he merely reverts to eating.

'So when *were* you last in a relationship?' She gives an arch emphasis to this last word.

He stares off. 'I was going out with a girl from home – I mean, Bristol – last year. It ended just before Christmas.'

'Did you give her the heave-ho?'

He half-laughs. 'Nah. She dumped me. She reckoned I was more interested in touring than I was in her.'

'Was she right?'

He shrugs. 'Maybe. But I gotta earn a living, ain't I?'

This is not really helping her to get a picture of Robbie's inner life. The songs he writes indicate a romantic sensibility, yet it seems nowhere apparent in his everyday manner. If he has a muse he's keeping it – her – well out of sight. One of the things Billie liked on first meeting him was his friendly openness, his lack of side. But since then she has made no headway, either because she hasn't asked the right questions or else because he's more private than she realised.

They have finished eating. She balls up their fish-and-chip papers, translucent with grease stains, and drops them in a bin. It's twenty minutes before they're needed on set, so they walk back along the beach. The sun hammers down fiercely. She slips her arm through his, and wonders if other beach-walkers take them for a couple. With her shades and sun hat on she doesn't look much older than him. Does she? Something is not right with her. At first she thought she might be ill with something, though she has no temperature and her appetite is plainly in working order. It's a bit like the sick feeling when she's waiting to hear about a part she wants, a nervous anticipation that hollows out her stomach. It will pass soon. She hopes it will pass soon.

Finished with shooting on the esplanade, the filmmakers have moved down the beach for the big rescue scene. Billie's character Gemma thinks she has seen a child being pulled out to sea, crying for help – in fact, it's a deadly illusion created by her evil angel, who knows this part of the shore is treacherous with riptides and will carry off swimmers to their doom. Gemma plunges in, because she's brave like that, and soon enough realises there is no drowning child – only a tide about to overwhelm her. But help is at hand, for her guardian angel Robbie, piloting a speedboat, sees her flailing figure and makes a beeline towards her. The crew, filming from a sailboat alongside, are setting up the scene in which Robbie will plunge into the water and save Billie from the waves.

The scene should be straightforward, so long as Robbie knows how to make a convincing dive. 'No problem,' he says to the director. Billie senses his anxiety as they set out in the boat, but when she asks what the matter is he shakes his head and says, 'Just make sure you grab hold of me soon as I hit the water.'

The sea in mid-afternoon, if not quite as smooth as a millpond, won't trouble the cameraman, who's an old hand. Now in the water, Billie gives Robbie a reassuring wave as he waits poised on the stern of the lolling speedboat. The assistant checks that they have a clear shot, the camera starts rolling and Vernon calls, 'Action.' A second's delay, and Robbie pulls away from his jump. 'Cut.'

'Are you all right, love?' Vernon calls to his actor, and Robbie nods wanly.

After another round of checks they go again, and again he backs out of the dive. He's muttering to himself, which Billie knows isn't a good sign. She calls to him, jokingly, 'Come on in, the water's lovely,' and he returns a tight smile.

On the third take Robbie dives, but goes in so quickly and awkwardly she doesn't have time to grab him. When he claws his way to the surface she realises immediately what's up, though it hasn't occurred to her, to anyone, till now. He makes a desperate panicky effort to reach her, and misses, disappearing below. 'He can't swim!' she cries out. Within seconds one of the crew throws a lifebuoy into the water. Billie did her swimming badges at school, but her memory is hazy as to life-saving beyond a few diagrammatic drawings. Robbie surfaces again, gasping, thrashing, calling her name. She puts her arm through the ring buoy and pulls it behind her. At that point instinct takes over, and she knows what to do. He's wearing a loose shirt, so instead of risking a front hold that might drag both of them under she circles behind him and seizes his collar, tugging him towards her. Then she lifts the ring and flips it over him.

Later she has trouble trying to reorder the sequence of events. The adrenalin of the moment seems to have wiped her memory clear; apparently the whole thing lasted no more than fifteen seconds, though it felt much longer. Hauled to safety Robbie sits on the deck, shivering under a blanket. He's going to be fine, but he's too shaken to continue this afternoon. As they return to the shore, Billie overhears the director of photography mutter, 'He couldn't even manage a decent dive.'

That evening Vernon Sparks takes Billie and Maurice out to a bistro in the old town. Robbie has gone off to a club with some of the younger lot; it soon becomes clear why he wasn't invited to dinner. The bistro is small, candlelit, housed in a row of former fishermen's cottages on a quiet road – most roads are quiet in Eastbourne. Vernon, a bluff, benign, shaggy-haired Lancastrian in his early fifties, has been looking rather harassed of late, his good humour in short supply. Once drinks arrive at the table he comes straight to the point.

'You know this film's heading straight for an iceberg.'

Billie, slightly defensive, says, 'It's not as bad as all that.'

'I'm not having a go at you. If anyone's to blame it's me. I've been in this game long enough to know you should never cast someone on looks alone.'

It is immediately understood who he's talking about. Maurice sighs. 'Quite old-fashioned, isn't it, not being able to swim.'

Vernon makes a *pfft* noise. 'Swimming's the least of it. This lad can't even *read*. I've just been told he's got severe dyslexia.' Billie doesn't dare glance at Maurice lest she gives them away. 'We should have dumped him end of the first week and recast. But I stuck when I should have twisted, and then it was too late.'

'I think he's doing OK,' Billie says loyally. 'I mean, he was never going to be Gielgud, but he's got presence.'

'I look at the rushes every day and I'm not even sure about that.'

Even Maurice sounds a supportive note. 'He must have impressed you when he auditioned . . .'

Vernon shakes his head. 'All he did when he came in was play us a couple of songs. He sounded great. He looked great. I thought, well, Bowie had never acted before Nic Roeg cast him in *The Man Who Fell to Earth*. We'll be fine.'

Just then their food is served – scallops flambé, fish mousse with lobster sauce, a silver platter of *fruits de mer*. Vernon orders a second bottle of Muscadet as he reminisces grimly over his misadventures in the film world. He's been involved in stinkers before and describes them with the relish of a battle-hardened pro. But Billie can only think of the disaster in waiting. Are they really about to go down with all hands? Maurice's thoughts must be bending the same way, for he now says, 'Vern, there must be something we can do to get out of this . . .'

The director pulls a Delphic expression. 'As a matter of fact there is, which is why I've got you two here. Most of what we've shot so far is useless. But,' he raises a stubby finger, 'I've asked an old friend of mine, Ivan, to write us some new scenes, most of 'em starring you two. The good news is that Ivan's got funny bones – so we up the comedy.'

'What's the bad news?'

'We're short of time. So that means a lot of rehearsals, hard work, late nights. I just need to know that you're both up for it.'

'Of course we are,' says Billie. 'But what's Robbie going to think when Maurice and I are on the call-sheet and he isn't?'

Vernon frowns. 'Who cares what he thinks? He's getting paid just the same. We can fiddle with his scenes in editing while you two give the performances of your life.'

Maurice gives Billie a look. 'No pressure there, then.'

'Don't fret, love, the new material's dynamite,' says Vernon, picking up the menu. 'Now – another bottle, I think, and maybe a Tia Maria parfait to finish.'

On returning to the Grand they find the hotel bar in a late-night buzz. The French windows are open to the sultry evening. She sees Robbie in the corner amidst a large knot of crew members – some actors, the hair and make-up team, a couple of wardrobe people. Vernon has slipped off to his room, Maurice gone to chat up the runner he's taken a fancy to. Billie, only a bit tipsy, feels too agitated to go to bed, and when Kezia Wilton gives her a wave she goes to join her.

'Heard there was some drama at sea today . . . and you played the hero,' Kezia says, widening her green eyes.

Billie shrugs. 'I did what anyone would've. I just happened to be closest to him.'

'Weird, isn't it? I mean, didn't his parents ever see those Rolf Harris teach-'em-to-swim ads?'

'I think Robbie's dad was more concerned with teaching him how to play the piano and trumpet and banjo.'

'Yeah?' Kezia bugs her eyes again – she doesn't know Robbie that well and appears eager to find out more. Can he really play all those instruments? Was he close to his dad? Does he talk much about his mum? Given that he is sitting only a couple of tables away from them, Billie wonders why Kezia doesn't simply ask him herself. He's really quite approachable, she almost starts to say, until another question indicates where Kezia's thoughts are tending. Has she met his girlfriend?

'What girlfriend?' Billie asks, frowning.

'Oh, I just assumed he had one,' she replies.

'Why?'

'Well, look at him! Guys like that usually have *at least* one.'

Billie realises, with a sudden stab of panic, that this girl has got Robbie in her sights. Kezia is smart(ish), good-looking and probably about the same age he is. She keeps glancing over at him, in an appraising way, and Billie senses danger.

'Shall we shuffle over and say hello?' she suggests, and Kezia follows. Robbie greets his saviour by flinging an arm around her shoulder. He's clearly emotional about what happened. Billie knows that her part in the incident has been exaggerated – there were others around who would have saved him – but she's happy to accept his affectionate display of gratitude. Robbie does flirt with Kezia a little, but then he flirts with everyone, including Neil, the crew's bearded, sixteen-stone chippie. It's just his way of charming people. Billie, partly relieved, glugs down another huge glass of white wine. When she gets up to go to the loo she feels the floor tilt sideways and has to steady herself. Stumping back to the bar she meets Robbie coming out: he squints at her.

'I do believe you're smashed,' he says, not disapproving, but worried.

Without warning she feels hot tears bulge at her eyes. The strange exhaustion of the last few weeks has finally undone her. 'I'm sorry,' she half-gasps. 'I think I should go to bed.'

He folds her in his arms, which only makes her sob the more. 'Come on, I'll take you to your room,' he says, guiding her towards the lifts. He talks to her on the way in a low, solicitous tone, his hand at her back as if she's a convalescent. Emerging from the lift at their floor they turn down the hushed empty corridor, pass through swing doors, following the numbers. Billie wonders if she's not merely drunk but sickening; her brain feels fogged-up, her limbs heavy. They reach her room first, and she unlocks the door.

'Will you come in for a minute?'

Inside, he goes to the bathroom and fills a glass with water. He brings it to her, and they sit together at the foot of the bed. She takes deep breaths, calming herself.

'What's been up with you?' he says, laying his hand on hers.

She sips the water and says, 'I don't know ... This film, working down here, the heat – what happened today, with you nearly ...' She's also stressed about Vernon and his recent appraisal of Robbie's performance, but of course she can't mention that. 'It's weird having Bryn back. I'm still not sure what we're ... Plus I'm not really getting on with my mum.'

Robbie is watching her intently, anxiously. 'Is that to do with me being there?'

'No. Yes. I mean, I'm not sure ...'

She looks at him, trying to decide if he understands what's really going on. She half-wishes he would take the initiative, but it's quite possible he hasn't a clue. Before she has time to stop herself she's bumped her face up against his, and once he absorbs the surprise of her mouth pressing on his he returns her heat; they hold one another in a stiff pose of ardour, as if a sudden movement might break the spell. Billie is adjusting herself to the improbable closeness of his face, feeling the voluptuous detail of it – the pillowy give of his lips, the shape of his nose, the liquid doe eyes she admired from the start yet never dared linger upon. Slowly, like a tree starting to topple, they fall back on to the bed, their mouths not letting go, and once horizontal he senses permission – no, invitation – being offered to explore the rest of her with his hands. So it begins. All she hears is his breathing in her ear. As her skirt rides up over her hips she recalls someone talking about sex in hotels and its particular illicit thrill – and abruptly she stiffens, breaks away from him. Bryn. It was Bryn.

Robbie is looking down at her, panting, startled. What's he done wrong?

'Sorry. I'm sorry,' she says, turning her face away.

He rolls off her. 'No, it's my fault. You've had a load to drink and you're upset. I shouldn't even be here.'

He's sitting up now, and she's a little taken aback by his responsible tone. She was expecting him to be so turned on that he'd coax her out of her hesitation. Instead, he's become gallant and given her an excuse to back off with dignity. Is he perhaps not as overcome by her as she imagines? Or is he aware that she has much more to lose, and wants to save her from herself? To think of getting a lesson in self-restraint from a pop star ...

Neither of them says anything as he rises from the bed and straightens his clothes. He trudges to the door, and as he opens it she calls his name. Her voice comes out quiet but urgent: 'Don't go. Please.' He looks back at her, caught amidships, and stops. She reads something sorrowful, possibly regretful, in the hang of his shoulders. When she says 'I don't want you to go' it's as if she's replying to something he's said.

But he hasn't said anything; he only waits. Then with some deliberation he pushes the door closed again and turns to face her. His expression seems to say, *We've gone and done it now.*

11

They will have to be very careful. Film sets are notorious rumour factories, and if a whisper of what's going on reaches the others it will also reach Bryn. It's now Wednesday morning: he is due in town in a little over forty-eight hours. Having telephoned room service to ask for breakfast, Billie suddenly leaps out of bed to stop Robbie answering the knock. 'Just leave it there, thanks!' she nearly shrieks through the door in panic. 'What did I just say about being careful?' she asks him, and receives a bewildered look that rather shames her. She can't help bossing him about. But having worked in a hotel once, she knows how much the staff gossip about their guests. It only takes one unguarded comment to spark the machinery into life.

'I'm sorry,' she says once they're back in bed. 'But we've got to be discreet.'

He nods, munching on a piece of toast. 'Mum's the word.'

'No. *Bryn*'s the word.'

The sun peeps through a gap in the heavy drapes. Lying there she feels an exhilarating compound of delight and foreboding. Even the fog of her hangover seems to have lifted. To think she had been persuading herself all that time that she was ill ... unless love itself is an affliction. The symptoms were there – she just misread them. After last night's intervention it seems her condition has improved.

She watches Robbie as he gets up and pulls back the curtains on a postcard view of the seafront. He moves with the unconscious grace of youth, drinking the last of his coffee and scooping up the clothes he dropped on the floor some hours ago. He slips on his pants and jeans.

'Oy, what are you up to?' Billie asks, hoping for a quick reprise of last night's action.

He looks at her. 'I'm being careful, like you said. Liz from wardrobe's dropping by my room for a fit-up at eight thirty.'

When he's gone she finishes her breakfast and steps out on to the shallow balcony. It's a glorious summer morning, wide veils of blue sky torn by the screeching gulls. Out at sea boats look tiny, toylike. She lights a Silk Cut and takes a meditative drag. So it's done; no going back. The timing, she has to admit, is unfortunate. If this had happened two months ago there'd be no cause for dismay – two single friends tumbling into bed. But now Bryn has moved back in she's officially cheated on her husband. She *could* say it's revenge for what he did to her back then: one in the eye for the 'love rat' (*Daily Mail*). It doesn't feel right, though. She holds herself to a higher standard than he does. Even when she had the chance of getting her own back (there was never a shortage of interested men) she refused it. Bryn's infidelities didn't force her to 'seek comfort' in the arms of someone else; she just wanted Bryn, as he used to be.

This is the promise on which she has taken him back – their marriage, as it used to be. As of last night, that dream is over.

Hampstead on the same midsummer morning. Nell parks her car halfway down Heath Street and gets out. The sun glimmers through the lattice of the trees, like light through a cathedral window. It's so tranquil she can hear birdsong as she walks down to the gallery. Through the plate-glass front she watches Véro, arms folded, directing a young man in T-shirt and jeans who is holding up a canvas against the wall.

She taps on the window, and Véro turns a cross face towards the sound until she sees who it is, and smiles. She strides over to the door and unlocks it.

'Darling,' she says, wafting a strong scent of Fracas as she plants a kiss. The cream walls and stripped pine floors of the gallery make a reassuringly plain setting for Nell's paintings, many of which she has not seen framed before. The framers have done a good job, even if it has taken the work away from Horace, her old familiar. 'This is Ryan,' says Véro, introducing the youth, who dips his head to Nell in greeting. 'Go and get us coffees, will you, darling? The petty cash box is on the desk in my office.'

Ryan jumps to it, footsteps clattering across the wooden floor.

'So what do you think of this?' says Véro, sweeping a queenly arm around the walls. 'I thought we should start with the main room and then work backwards.'

'It's all – gosh – a bit overwhelming.'

'OK with the height? I've decided to hang them at eye-level, instead of making everyone look up. More intimate, hmm?'

Nell nods absently. Her eye is drawn to the portrait of Johnny, in 1946, still with the lean and hungry look of the war years. She steps up to examine it. God, how in love with him she was. The young woman who painted it, one among the varieties of herself, was then all passion and anxiety. A young mother, a wife. She has gone now, that woman, and yet part of her continues to this day as someone else – Nell Cantrip, utterly changed, and the same.

She turns to Véro, who's watching her. 'You remember I said about this . . . '

'NFS. I've marked it on the list.'

The sound of the telephone calls Véro to her office, leaving Nell to wander the room alone. Some of the paintings she remembers very well; others she stares at and wonders how *she* could have created them. Why that mark, that stroke? She feels somewhat amazed by her younger self, by the energy, the ambition. She's glad to be on her own at this moment: if people could see her admiring her own stuff they'd think her a proper conceited cow!

Eventually she retreats into the back where she can hear Véro on the phone. She sits down on the little sofa in the ante-office where a stack of glossy magazines sit alluringly on a table, like in a posh waiting-room. She flicks through *Tatler* – nothing there to detain her – and takes up a Christie's catalogue, *Georgian, Victorian and British Impressionist Art*. She's hardly even noticing what's in there (the money involved is absurd) and is about to toss the thing down when it falls open on a painting she recognises – and a cry escapes her.

25

LAURA MERRYMOUNT (1752–1820)
Portrait of a Young Man
oil on canvas 29¾ × 24½ in.
£15,000–20,000

PROVENANCE:
Mrs Margaret Evenlode, then by descent to her granddaughter.

LITERATURE:
Letters and Journals of Laura Merrymount 1785–1809, Hamish Hamilton, London, 1960

For many years the provenance of this lively and beguiling portrait was unknown. Neither the painter nor the sitter could be identified, although a brief reference to it is found in a memoir by the artist Denton Brigstock (1864–1936). He recalls buying the painting at auction in London some time during the 1880s; it was at that time still anonymous, and Brigstock admits that he knew almost nothing of its origin: 'A rumour going about that it was an unknown work by William Merrymount proved groundless' (*Recollections* p. 76). He later made a gift of it to a friend, probably the Chelsea painter Paul Stransom (1863–1909), from whom it passed to his sister Margaret (Maggie) Evenlode. At that point the picture might have faded into obscurity had it not been for a remarkable discovery in the 1930s. Colonel Thomas Burlingham was researching a history of his forebears when, on a visit to Umberley Hall in Wiltshire, he happened to open an old toy chest and found loose pages of correspondence and a journal written by Laura Merrymount (1752–1820), older daughter of the great painter. An entry written in August 1809 establishes that she completed the portrait at her home in Kentish Town, and that the young man is in fact her half-brother, Joseph Edmund Rothwell (1788-1853), a theatre manager. He was the illegitimate offspring of William Merrymount's affair with the actress Elizabeth Vavasor.

Considered purely in artistic terms, the portrait is one of the most striking of its era. The refinement of the brushwork brings the sitter's face into vivid relief, contrasting with the bold impasto brushstrokes of his burgundy velvet coat. It conveys a powerful sense of affection between brother and sister, though such is the elegance of its composition one begins to understand why certain Victorian scholars attributed it to 'the Master' himself. In fact, we now know from Laura's journal that Merrymount had encouraged his daughter to paint and even held an exhibition of her work at the family home in Cavendish Square. Regrettably, aside from the present portrait and two drawings of William Merrymount on his deathbed, none of it has survived.

There is yet one more tantalising aspect to this picture. That we may be reasonably certain in confirming *Portrait of a Young Man* as a work by Laura Merrymount derives from an internal detail within the painting. Behind the young man's head, situated above the fireplace, can be seen a painting of two young girls, identified as Laura and her younger sister Molly. This is a celebrated lost masterpiece, *The Merrymount Sisters at Night*, to which Laura first makes reference in her journal in October 1785:

> *[My father] holds that his Landskips are his most accom-*
> *plished work but that his favourites are 'Portrait of the*
> *Painter's Daughters' & the earlier 'The Merrymount Sisters at*
> *Night' — which we all know as 'Molly & the Captain'. Visitors*
> *to the house are apt to comment upon the latter, such is its*
> *renown as a Conversation-piece. It was painted in the year of*
> *I think 1763, when I was eleven & Molly nine, as we stood in*
> *the Drawing room amid the encroaching dark of the evening*
> *(Pa still likes to paint at night).*

The painting's chequered history may be traced through her journal. Merrymount himself refused all offers to sell it, insisting that it should be handed down to his daughters after his death. When Laura went to live with her sister in 1797 among the paintings she took with her was this family favourite, 'Molly & the Captain', though its possession was troublesome.

Several times it became the target of swindlers and once it was stolen (later recovered) from the Royal Academy. Its unfortunate fate was sealed after Laura decided to move it from their dining room to the parlour. An accidental fire there in which Molly Merrymount perished also consumed the painting. Thus the tiny reproduction above Joseph Rothwell's head is the only visual evidence that remains of *The Merrymount Sisters at Night*. That Laura included it in her painting possibly signifies a belated wish to compass all three siblings within a single frame. It enhances the charm and freshness of *Portrait of a Young Man*, not to mention its value as the single extant work in oil by a lesser-known Merrymount.

Nell continues to stare at the reproduction of the painting, the first time she has seen it in colour. (The plates in the book are all black-and-white.) Her immediate urge is to tell Billie, and then Hilary, her cousin, whose entry into their life set off the whole shooting-match. The coincidence of it almost spooks her. Six months ago she would have looked upon this and remained absolutely unaware of its connection to her.

When Véro re-emerges from her office Nell holds open the page for her inspection.

'That young man, believe it or not, is my great-great-grandfather,' she says, 'and the painter is my great-whatever-aunt.'

Véro takes the catalogue from her to scrutinise. 'How do you . . . ? Are you sure?'

'You remember the morning I got that phone call from a cousin who you thought was a fortune hunter? Well, she told me about it. It's all in the essay on the facing page.'

Véro skim-reads the text, frowning, somewhat impatient: she's only prepared to show an interest because Nell's her artist. She glances quickly at the date of the catalogue and her brow lifts.

'The auction's in the middle of September. You could bid for it.'

Nell pulls a face on checking the details. 'Don't think so. Have you seen the estimate?'

'Fifteen to twenty's not bad, darling. And you'd easily be able to afford it once we're through here.'

'I've never spent twenty grand on anything! In any case, it might go for much more – it's one of a kind.'

'That's why you should go for it,' says Véro, whose curiosity is piqued now that the issue concerns money. 'I'd say it would be pretty hard-hearted of you *not* to bid, given the family angle. It will probably never come to auction again.'

At that moment Ryan returns bearing coffees, and Véro is once more all business as she hustles him back to the main gallery. As Nell remains on the sofa, half-listening to her instructions ('No, that's all wrong') she thinks seriously about what she can afford. She's got about ten thousand in savings, and the show will bring in funds, though perhaps not as much as her dealer envisages. Maybe she could take out a bank loan. She's still thinking about it as she drives home, not just the fact of their kinship but of Laura's obscurity as a painter. The struggle for acceptance is long, and for a woman sometimes impossible. All the years it has taken Nell to get here. But then the future is always hard to reach.

That painting will never be offered for sale again, Véro's right. Is she mad to consider it?

It's Friday morning and Billie, lying in bed at the Grand, feels a sickly unease. Bryn arrives later today. They talked on the phone last night and she tried, ever so subtly, to put him off – Eastbourne's just a giant old people's home, the hotel isn't any great shakes, hardly get a minute off from filming. But no, he's coming, *can't wait* to see her, getting in around seven. Billie tries to insert a note of TV brightness into her voice ('Lovely!') and just about succeeds. Three nights with Robbie and still nobody on set has twigged yet. They sometimes hold hands when they're alone. Only once have they come close to being rumbled, when a unit photographer surprised them as they canoodled in a doorway. Billie leapt away from him like a scalded cat.

Across the room Robbie, in his undies, holds up a pair of her jeans – Jordache, she bought them in New York a couple of years ago.

'I love these,' he says, 'the cut of 'em.'

Before she can say anything he pulls them on and goes to look at himself in the wardrobe mirror.

'What are you doing?'

'Look, see ...' He does a profile turn in the mirror, admiring. They are indeed an excellent fit. 'Mind if I wear 'em?'

She stares at him incredulously. 'Yes, I do mind.'

'Really? I often swapped clothes with girlfriends.'

'Well, isn't that dandy?'

'Mara used to lend me this great fur coat ...' He's smiling as he recalls it.

'I don't care who lent you what, you're not at the Blitz Club now – so get 'em off.'

He looks over to check if she's serious (she is) and making one of his faces he reluctantly shucks them off. The unit is due to meet, as usual, downstairs at 8.45, so Robbie sneaks off to get fresh kit from his room. Billie quickly dresses, and as she's fixing her make-up realises with horror something she's left undone in preparation for Bryn's arrival. Taking a half-full cup of coffee she tips it over an incriminating stain on the bedsheet. Then she phones reception to ask if housekeeping would kindly change her bed linen today – she's just had a bit of an accident with a coffee cup, so sorry . . .

She goes to the mirror again. She's had more sex over the last three nights than she's managed in total over the last three years. It's a wonder to her that nobody can see it from the glow on her skin – nobody except Maurice, who *has* been shooting her odd looks. He may suspect, but he couldn't possibly know; her dedication to secrecy has been Masonic. That she and Robbie are often together on set is actually the perfect cover, the double-bluff to end them all. For who would credit that dog-eared cliché of co-stars having an affair?

The forecourt of the Grand is thronged with the crew, there's a coach waiting to take them up to Beachy Head for today's filming. Sun hats and Ambre Solaire are in evidence. Billie is sharing a cigarette with the Bermuda-shorted cameraman when Robbie sidles up, taking her aside for a quiet word: he's left his sunglasses in her room and needs to retrieve them. She checks nobody's watching and slips him the room-key, like a secret agent. The coach is almost full by the time Robbie emerges hurriedly from the hotel and climbs aboard. He's got his Wayfarers and – Billie double-takes in disbelief – he's also wearing her jeans. *Of all the nerve* . . . She's seated towards the back, surrounded, so they'll be kept apart on the short journey. Which is just as well for Robbie, who's plumped down at the front chatting to one of the hair-and-make-up girls. She fumes privately as they drive west along the front and up towards the promontory.

Why is she so irritated? If he'd asked her nicely back in the room she might have been amenable, but instead he just puts them on and starts vamping in front of the mirror. Maybe it's the whole easygoing, squat-sharing, nouveau-hippie attitude that gets her back up. There are boundaries to observe!

Once they disembark she has to wait until she can get him on her own. While they're setting up the cliff scenes – an angel is about to disappear over the edge – she collars him behind one of the lunch trailers.

'Oy. What is it with you? You asked me if you could borrow those jeans and I said no.'

He seems taken aback by her hostile tone. 'Well, I didn't think you'd mind *that* much . . . They're just jeans, babe.'

'Don't "babe" me. Why do you assume I wouldn't mind? I'd told you not to, but you took 'em anyway. It's fucking annoying – and disrespectful.'

He looks at her rather solemnly. 'It ain't disrespectful,' he replies. 'I didn't take 'em just because I thought they looked cool. I wanted to have something of yours next to my skin.'

That's thrown her. She will have to make a recalibration: it's hard to make a fuss now. She doesn't really know what to say.

'I'm sorry if I've upset you,' he says. 'I won't wear them again.'

'No, it's all right, I didn't . . . If you really want to that's fine.'

He takes her hand lightly. 'If you were my girlfriend I'd be wanting to swap clothes with you all the time.'

She returns a quick smile. 'Well, that's sweet. And weird. I've never been with someone who's wanted to do that. Anyway . . . '

'We're still friends, aren't we?' he says. He's asked her this before, and she makes the same reply.

'Best of.'

*

Nothing in all the world lifts the heart like knowing there is someone out there who feels intensely about you. Billie won't call it love – she isn't that moony – but the awareness of being desired is the next best thing. Vernon, meanwhile, has been shooting the new scenes between her and Maurice, which are appreciably more dynamic than anything in the original script. So far Robbie seems not to have noticed his exclusion. Though they haven't had much time to rehearse it, the dialogue is written to allow them some latitude, and Vernon likes a degree of improvisation. There's an unspoken feeling that the scenes play more fluently without Robbie slowing them down. She feels disloyal thinking it, and at the same time knows it's true.

Around five they break for the day – it's the weekend – and begin to pack up. Maurice, who hasn't said much to her today, draws her apart. He has a strange look on his face.

'I notice Roberto's been modelling your jeans . . .'

'Yeah', she replies, 'he's got a thing about them. Jordache. Cult New York label, hard to get over here.'

'Is that so?' This polite phrase is at odds with the curl of his lip. When Billie offers a shrug in return he says, 'Pull the other one, dear. Are you sleeping with him?'

She laughs at that. 'He's a child! We're friends, that's all.'

Now he narrows his eyes. 'I can tell there's something going on. You've got that funny bow-legged walk, and I know it's not from horse-riding.'

'That's a bit crude, Maurice, even for you,' she says, and coolly walks off towards the coach. She fears Maurice's disapproval; in normal circumstances she'd tell him everything. But she's jumpy as a kitten with Bryn coming down tonight. For now, outright denial is the safest option.

Arriving back at the hotel Billie walks into the foyer, and there, grinning like Mr Punch, is Bryn. It's not yet six o'clock.

'You're early!' she manages to say before he wraps her in a bear-hug.

'I know, it's a bit keen.' He's beaming at her.

Her smile shields her panic. Cast and crew are ambling by in ones and twos, shooting a sideways look at them. Robbie is going to come through the revolving doors any second, wearing her jeans. She has to get Bryn away and up to the room before a nightmare unfolds – too late, here he comes right now, not yet sensing the danger. Robbie spots her, starts to approach, failing to read the frantic message in her eyes, *Keep walking*.

From somewhere she finds her voice and introduces them to one another. Bryn, as the senior, holds out his hand rather grandly. 'We meet at last. The pop star!'

Robbie gives a modest reflexive shrug, says hello. Something now in Billie's body language warns him not to linger, but Bryn is being friendly, ready to chat.

'Is it always this quiet here? I just walked from the station and didn't see a single person under seventy. I thought, *Welcome to Sin City!*'

'It's all right,' says Robbie, in his easygoing way. 'We're filming most of the time so we don't notice the old folk.'

Bryn listens, smiling. Billie can tell he's amused by Robbie's West Country accent. He'll be doing impersonations of him by the time they get to the room.

'So how's filming been?' Bryn continues, looking from one to the other. 'Any gossip for me?'

Billie, forcing a laugh, shakes her head, and at that moment there comes a blessed deliverance. A lady from reception sidles up to Robbie to say a telephone message is waiting for him, and off he goes. Billie and Bryn stop at the bar for a sharpener and a catch-up. He is evidently delighted to see her, which only tightens the screw on her guilt.

'It's been that lonely without you,' he says, taking her hand.

'We only talked on the phone last night ...'

'You don't know how uxorious I've become. In fact, I'll prove it to you once we get upstairs.'

That's another thing. She knew Bryn would arrive frisky from their week apart. But after three nights of Robbie in her bed she feels strange – a bit trampy – about the immediate resumption of what Bryn charmingly calls 'the conjugals'. Once they do repair to her room he's diverted by the sea view, so she quickly nips off to have a bath, locking the door in case he gets any ideas. As she soaks in the steaming tub, minibar gin and tonic to hand, she considers the mess she's got herself into. She's never cheated on Bryn before, or anyone else, as far as she can recall. That he has not the faintest suspicion isn't much relief, nor does she feel the intoxicating thrill of power that friends who've had affairs speak of. For her it's a dilemma. She likes being married: she also likes being desired by a young stranger. In other words, she wants it both ways, like everyone else.

She spends the evening distracted, and drinks too much. Vernon is hosting a dinner for twelve in the hotel restaurant, and Billie's placement at the table is purgatorial, opposite Maurice (glowering), with a producer (droning) on one side and Bryn (pontificating) on the other. Robbie, seated further down, listens to Bryn's expansive advice on acting with every show of politeness. They seem to get on well. At one point she overhears Bryn riffing again on the town's elderly population and his line 'Dover for the Continent, Eastbourne for the incontinent' gets a general laugh. They've never heard that one before?

She's had enough of surprises for today, but there's one more in the offing as *digestifs* come round. Having moved further down the table, Bryn has found a captive audience in Robbie, out of Billie's earshot. She finds out what they've been talking about when Bryn sits up and raps out – *duh-duh-derdah-duh, duh-duh-derdah-duh* – the first bars of 'New York, New York'. He explains to his nearest neighbours that Robbie here has just been asked to play a month of club gigs in Manhattan. The big time! (It was the message he picked up at reception earlier.) Robbie, along the table, catches her eye and pulls a face somewhere between delight and embarrassment – he obviously wanted to tell her himself, in private. *Wow!* she mouths, and tries to smile.

12

Nell has got a new song on the brain. She's been hearing it a lot on Radio 1 and can't shake the refrain.

War baby – this means
War baby

She hasn't bought a single in about thirty years, though she'd like to now. They've probably got it at Woolworths down the road. This morning she's in the garden singing when Robbie comes out in his tartan dressing-gown. He's not been on call at the studio this week and has just got out of bed.

'Heard you from upstairs,' he says, whistling a few bars of the song. 'You a Tom Robinson fan?'

'Is that who it is? I dunno, I just like the song. *Whatever it is you keep putting me through*,' she sings, and they laugh.

After all the weeks of preparation her show opens tonight. Tash called round earlier with an Ossie Clark blouse to lend her, and this afternoon she's going to have her roots done at the hairdresser's. Robbie asks how many are expected this evening, and she thinks about a hundred. Véro has a number of rich clients she means to get her claws into. Nell has rounded up most of her friends, plus a few hangers-on like her neighbour Gerald.

'Thanks for letting me bring Mara,' Robbie says.

'That's all right, love.'

'It's just 'cos she's a fan of yours ...'

'Yeah, you said. But even if she wasn't a fan you can bring who you like.'

A pause, then he says, 'Ain't seen Billie lately.' Nell senses trouble brewing; since Eastbourne she hasn't seen much of her either.

'Is everything all right between you?'

A little twitch of pain passes over his face. 'We had a row, nothin' serious. I think she's still getting used to having Bryn back.'

'Maybe she realises it's a mistake,' she says, and then wishes she hadn't.

'Why do you dislike him?'

'Oh ... He reminds me of my first husband. A liar, and a bolter.'

He blinks his surprise at the baldness of that. 'He seemed OK to me ...'

'He's always charming. And he likes men more than women.'

Robbie gives a short, unprovocative laugh at that, as if there's nothing else left to say. From his dressing-gown pocket he fishes out a wilted joint, and sparks up. She watches him, amused; when he offers her a toke she declines.

'I'd better not. Can't turn up at the hairdresser's stoned.'

'Best thing for it, you ask me.' He looks about the garden for a few moments, thoughtful. 'Your woodpecker ever come back?'

She smiles, shakes her head, surprised he remembers. 'I think it's gone for good.'

The evening is so warm they keep the gallery door propped open; Véro's puttering desk fan is no match for the body heat generated within. Guests seek refuge on the pavement with their drinks. Every so often a taxi chugs down Heath Street and deposits a few more into the soupy throng. Nell's private views of old were modest affairs in gallery bookshops – she remembers an early one at Zwemmer's in Litchfield Street – whereas this feels like a Big Deal. The party divides along social and sartorial lines. Véro's moneyed clientele are mostly men, old-school patricians in bespoke from the Row and younger entrepreneurial types in double-breasted jackets, plus a scattering of primped matrons and super-tanned divorcees eager to spend their settlement cash. These significantly contrast with Nell's rackety crowd of ageing hippies, art-scene eggheads and pioneering gentrifiers from the Camden–Kentish Town hinterland. A pinch of glamour is present among certain actor friends of Billie's, whose faces the other partygoers squint at, thinking, *Don't I know you?*

Billie arrives early with Bryn, who makes a beeline for the temporary bar. She scans the room in search of Robbie. She's barely seen him all week, since they're shooting the scenes that might rescue *Heaven and Earth* from disaster and therefore don't involve him. Impossible to spend a night together now they're back from location. Nor have they really discussed his impending flit to the States. Robbie's manager thinks it's likely to be a longer engagement: the solo LP is doing well over there. Billie is disconcerted. Has she risked her marriage for someone who's about to scarper? But here comes Tash, pulling an amused-dubious face as she edges her way through the crowd.

'Bloody hell, the *people* Véro knows,' she says in an undertone. She's never at ease amid conspicuous affluence.

'Yeah. More Sloane Rangers than you could shake a stick at,' says Billie. 'But who cares? Just count the red dots. Is Chris here?'

'He's coming straight from work.'

A dumpy, bespectacled lady who has just smiled at Billie for no reason now approaches them. She's sweating profusely, and haloed in such an air of meek goodwill that Billie thinks she must be a fan.

'Hello, you're Billie, aren't you? And you must be ... Tash?' They stare at her for a moment, both perplexed. 'I'm Hilary – your mum invited me – your cousin. Rather a distant one.'

'Hilary – yes!' Billie cries, and pumps her moist hand. Two

things about their cousin become quickly apparent: she is quite as loquacious as Nell described, and – what touches Billie – turns out to remember almost everything she's been told about them. She knows that Billie has been shooting a film in London and Eastbourne with Vernon Sparks, and has just recognised 'that very good-looking man over there' as Bryn, her husband; she knows that Tash teaches at Central, was formerly at Hornsey, and that she's married with 'a little one' named Gil. She looks across the room at Nell, mobbed by admirers, then beams at them: 'She's a remarkable person, your mother.'

'We've always thought so,' says Tash, with a rare smile of her own.

They talk for a while about the Laura Merrymount journals, which Billie can quote from, to her cousin's delight. 'I suppose you've heard about the portrait coming up for auction?'

Hilary nods. 'Nell phoned me. Do you think she's serious about bidding for it?'

Billie glances at Tash, who says, 'It's a crazy amount of money. But she seems determined.'

'It *would* be rather wonderful to own it, though ... I gather it's been in private hands for years – presumably the owners had no idea who it was by.'

Since they've been talking she looks increasingly uncomfortable under the gallery lights. Sweat is beading across her pink brow, and Tash suggests they could all do with a drink. As they shoulder through the press of bodies Billie spots Robbie over in the corner deep in talk with Mara. Nell has already warned her about this, and still she feels a ridiculous flash of jealousy at the sight of them.

Nell, meanwhile, hasn't had a breather since she arrived. Friends and well-wishers pop up in front of her, one eager face after another, and the carousel she stepped on seems to be running, dreamlike, out of her control. She smiles, projects an interest in everyone she meets. Apart from 'thank you', she can't remember a single thing she's said all evening. She hasn't felt this overwhelmed since she stood next to Johnny in the reception line at their wedding. If only she could cool down: the blouse is damp on her back, and God knows how her make-up's coping. Véro appears at her elbow again to introduce some art-world grandee she's never heard of, and then she's plucked away by someone else. At one point Bryn catches her eye, and she flags up a smile even for him.

It did her heart good to see the girls chatting with Hilary a few moments ago; she'd like to have joined them, instead of standing here like a totem pole danced around by strangers. And, oh heavens, here's Gerald lurching towards her, as tall and implacable as an old wardrobe. He grins, blinking through his heavy owlish spectacles and stepping so close she has to shuffle backwards.

'Nell! Many congratulations,' he booms ripely. It is a voice that was once used to being listened to. 'Never knew you commanded such high prices!'

Nell glances up apologetically. 'I don't set them, Gerald. That's my dealer's department. Are you having a nice time?'

'Mm. Good to see the old faces again – some looking rather older than others,' he adds, with a complacent chortle.

'We're all getting on, I suppose,' she says leniently.

'Indeed.' He pauses as something occurs to him. 'I spotted you recently, by the way, on Kentish Town Road. You and a young chap. I gave you a shout but you didn't hear.'

Nell claims innocence of his call (though how one could miss it at Gerald's stentorian volume is remarkable). 'That was probably my lodger.'

Gerald, not a master of nuance, makes an exclamatory *ooh* at this revelation.

'You looked, if I may say, *engrossed* in his company. My initial thought was, Nell's done all right for herself, though I didn't know she liked 'em that young!'

Does he mean to offend her, or is he simply being gauche? 'Robbie's a musician, and a friend of Billie's. I'm just the landlady.'

'Lucky fellow!' he says, attempting a gallantry. Which he then goes and ruins by adding, 'Best be careful – he may be one of those who's looking for a mother figure.'

'How's the writing?' she says.

Gerald, taking her curiosity for granted, launches into a quite thorough account of his new memoir, repeating things he's forgotten he told her last time. There's a column in *Private Eye* that Nell sometimes reads, called 'Great Bores of Today', essentially an unpunctuated monologue of male blah. She always hears it in her head as Gerald's voice – self-assured, drawling, somehow inescapable. If it were anyone else she could tune out while maintaining the pretence of listening, but Gerald is so emphatically *in her face* she feels herself a kind of hostage.

' . . . and then there's the biography of Cyril Connolly I still mean to write,' he's going on, ready for his next mini-lecture.

She must be emanating some invisible signal of distress because at that moment Robbie interposes himself, his pretty, dark-eyed friend in tow. Nell, more grateful than she can say, introduces him and Mara to Gerald, who might now see that his jokey insinuations from earlier were not appropriate. He hangs around for a moment before excusing himself.

'Sorry for the interruption,' Robbie says.

'Don't be,' she replies in an undertone. 'You bloody saved me.'

'Hi,' says Mara, with a shyly raised hand, 'so nice to be here.'

'You're welcome, love. Robbie says you're a painter, too?'

The girl makes a demurring expression, mumbles a modest denial. They look fantastic together, these two, and Nell wonders if they're actually sweethearts. The question takes on a new impetus as Billie approaches, her smile not quite hiding the tension.

'Hello,' she says to Mara, 'we met at Gunter Grove, I think.'

Billie hasn't misremembered Mara's quiet, feline allure. She's still on the alert for their spark of erotic connection, despite Robbie's insistence otherwise. Conversation between the four of them amid the boiling throb of the party becomes disjointed, desultory; only when Mara engages Nell one-on-one with a question about her painting does Billie seize her moment.

'I'm going outside for a breath of air,' she says. 'Mind keeping me company?'

Robbie knows from her tone that this isn't a request. A couple of minutes later he emerges on to the street and sees Billie standing apart from the knots of pavement guests. Arms folded, she has a cigarette alight, and releases a brooding jet of smoke from the side of her mouth.

'Hello, stranger,' she deadpans.

Robbie steps up toe-to-toe, smiling. 'All right?'

'Careful. He's within spying range.'

He glances back at the gallery, its picture windows aquarium-like against the encroaching dark.

'So you brought her along after all.'

He shrugs. 'She's a fan of your ma's. D'you really mind?'

'Why should I mind?' she says, a bit snappishly. 'I'm not your keeper. You can do as you please.' She can hear in her voice a brittleness. *Start again.* 'I've missed you.'

He takes her hand lightly. 'How's it been on set? I feel kind of . . . forgotten.'

'Just a few scenes Vern's mate has written to "punch up" the comedy.'

He looks rueful. 'I dunno, I wish I'd never . . . Acting just ain't me. Vern knows it. I think that's why he gets so agitated.'

'Don't say that. They all love you on set.' *At least that much is true*, Billie thinks.

'The only good thing that's come of it is meeting you.'

She stares at him, moved. With a quick look up the street she gives a sideways nod, signalling him to follow. There's a turning just past a row of shops where she lingers, stepping into the shadows of a doorway in the gable end. As he comes near she catches hold of his waist and pulls him against her.

371

'God, I've missed you. Have I already said that?' Not waiting for him to speak she clamps her mouth on his, and for some moments they're lost in each other. The sky might fall in and she wouldn't care so long as her body can press against him, his mouth swamped in hers. When they at last come up for air she gasps, 'If only we could go off right now and fuck each other's brains out.'

Robbie laughs. 'Nice way of putting it.'

'You're bloody lucky to have me doting on you.'

'I know. Shocking, ain't it?'

It jolts her to think how helpless she is. There have been too many misalliances in her past to feel safe about this one. Another phase of smooching is underway when footsteps suddenly come near on the hitherto deserted pavement; then they slow. Billie looks round, partly curious, and jumps in fright at the enquiring face of Chris, her brother-in-law.

All three of them freeze.

'Chris,' murmurs Billie, in greeting or in pleading, she can't tell. The insoluble wrongness of the scene has momentarily undone them. Chris falters, ambushed, and his gaze falls away.

'I'm just on my way . . .' He wafts an arm in the direction of the gallery, as if they don't already know. It's too embarrassing to hesitate a moment longer, and with a barely perceptible nod he moves on, disappearing around the corner.

In the stunned aftermath Billie is rooted to the spot, a hand covering her mouth. She is making wild conjectures about what might follow, and begins to hyperventilate. 'Oh Jesus, oh Jesus,' she moans.

Robbie has his hands pressed together and fitted against his mouth, as if in prayer. He mumbles, 'Gah. That was . . . *awful*.'

Billie is spooked. She senses a vortex stirring darkly in wait, ready to engulf her.

Robbie has the air of a schoolboy who's been stood in the corner. She wants him to say something to alleviate the pressure, but she knows he's not capable of it.

She has to calm herself. It's horrible to be caught in flagrante, but at least it was by someone unlikely to make a fuss. Chris isn't a blabbermouth. Like Tash he's steady, self-contained, a creature of common sense. Unlike Tash, he's not the sort to give her a bollocking, however much deserved.

'We'd better get back,' she says to Robbie. As they walk she does her thinking aloud. 'It's possible Chris won't say anything to Tash. He's quite reserved. For now let's act like everything's cool. If it comes up let's just say ... something happened at the studio ... I got upset and you were trying to comfort me.'

Robbie steals a glance at her. 'Comfort you – with my tongue in your mouth?'

She doesn't seem to hear that. 'Oh shit, I've just remembered.' She stops dead on the pavement. 'There's some dinner Véro's organised after the show tonight – Mum, Tash and Chris, plus a load of Véro's boring clients. I'll have to cry off—'

'Don't cry off,' says Robbie. 'That'll make you look guilty.'

She looks at him – maybe he isn't as unworldly as she thinks. 'All right. In the meantime, we'd better keep a distance. Make sure Bryn sees you with Martha.'

'Mara.' He leaves a beat, then says, 'Maybe you should think about tellin' him.'

'What, Bryn – about us? Are you mad?'

'He's going to find out sooner or later.'

'No. No, he isn't. Robbie, listen to me – that can't happen. I'm trying to put our marriage back together. Because I love him, d'you understand?'

He seems stung by that. 'So what are you doing with me?'

She looks away. 'I don't know.'

They are back at the gallery, the lights blazing and a drone of voices through the open door. They don't say another word to each other for the rest of the evening, though Billie keeps a furtive watch, conscious that she may have hurt him. But she can only put out one fire at a time. When the party begins to thin out and Véro rounds up her dinner guests, Billie makes sure she's not in the group that leaves with Tash and Chris; once they're in the restaurant she arranges that she and Bryn are seated at the other end of the table. Monitoring their faces she reckons that her secret is safe for now and, by degrees, her panic of earlier recedes.

'Are you all right?' Bryn asks her at one point. She responds with her perkiest smile, assures him she's fine, and he winks back at her, unsuspecting.

At the end of the night, as taxis are prowling in wait and guests linger on the pavement with last cigarettes, Billie accidentally catches Chris's eye. She has her arm through Bryn's at that moment, which possibly makes it worse. Chris's gaze isn't hostile, it's flat and unillusioned. He knows, and that's enough. She burns with shame, and a dreadful relief, because she also interprets in his look a proud dismissive note: *I'm no snitch.*

13

Buoyed by a phone call the next morning from Véro, who sounds cock-a-hoop about sales, Nell goes up to Robbie's room to offer him breakfast. His door is slightly ajar. She taps once and leans around: the bed is unslept in. She goes back down to the kitchen, lost in thought. At the party she saw Billie sneaking off with him, and noticed that both of them returned with funeral faces: they've had a bust-up, she's not sure about what. Maybe he's told her that he's seeing Mara – in whose arms he perhaps lolls at this moment.

She has started priming a canvas when the phone rings – Billie. They get down to a post-mortem on the party and the dinner, Nell carefully avoiding any mention of Robbie.

'I saw you talking to Hilary, by the way. What a nice woman.'

'Isn't she?' says Billie. 'Did she tell you any more about the husband?'

Nell sighs. 'He's gone. Moving in with a younger woman, someone at his work. Thirty years of marriage down the Swanee.'

'Poor her.' Mother and daughter are thinking the very same thing: they don't fancy Hilary's chances of meeting someone else. Nell hears background noise at the end of the line.

'Are you at the studio?'

'Yeah. It's our last day tomorrow.' She leaves a beat before saying, 'I wonder if I could have a word with Robbie.'

'He's not here, love.'

'What, he's gone out already?'

'No, he's . . . he didn't come in last night.'

Another pause. 'Oh. I see.' Nell can almost hear her brain whirring. Ought she to say something? Billie beats her to it. 'I suppose he's told you about New York.'

'Mm. End of September. I haven't asked him whether he'll keep the room.'

'He'll probably end up staying over there,' she says, with a trace of asperity.

'Is everything OK?' asks Nell. 'I get the feeling—'

'It's fine,' she says, cutting her short. 'I just need to talk to him about something. Can you ask him to call me?'

She is trying to be honest with herself. Was it just a holiday fling? No, she was falling for him from the start, that day they met at the Savoy. Call it a passionate misadventure. Easy to fancy him, of course – how could you not? – but it's something else that got to her. His vulnerability. His oddness. Even his way of thanking a bus driver. For someone so adored he has so little swagger. If you'd just met him off the street you'd never guess he was a pop star. Then there is his youth, which has the effect of making *her* feel young.

Being on location gave them the opportunity. Yet even without Eastbourne she would have found a way. It's surprisingly easy to pull the wool over someone's eyes. Bryn once knew that; now she does, too. Can she bear to keep on doing it, though? The encounter with Chris was a warning shot. When Robbie eventually phones she thinks first of meeting him at the Savoy (a nostalgic reprise) but then realises that hotels constitute a risk: she might weaken. Which is why she's heading right now for Kensington Gardens, on a Saturday afternoon. Bryn hasn't asked where she's going. Why would he?

The sun that came out in the morning has ducked behind the clouds by mid-afternoon. It's still warm, though, and around the

Pond it's becoming crowded. The weird bleating notes of an ice-cream van crinkle the air. She spots Robbie on the other side, in bowling jacket and a red baseball cap pulled over his brow.

He looks pleased to see her. 'All right, my lover?' he says, amping up his West Country accent to amuse her.

She considers what he's wearing. 'Looks like you're halfway to New York already. Let's get away from the crowd.'

They walk towards the parkland shadowed with trees. The crowd thins out the deeper they move into shade. In one little copse she sees a man seated, head bowed in concentration, sketching. Robbie wants to know if Chris has said anything to her; he blows out his cheeks in relief on hearing the all-clear. Billie looks at him.

'I phoned you yesterday morning. Mum told me you didn't get home on Thursday.'

He shrugs. 'I went back to Gunter Grove with Mara.'

'Oh. And slept with her, I suppose.'

He frowns at her. 'You sound a bit snippy.'

'Well, did you?'

A pause. 'We slept in the same bed, yeah.'

A huffy snort escapes her. 'This is what it's come to – me being a paranoid bitch because I can't trust you.'

'What? I ain't about to run off with someone else.'

She halts, incredulous. 'You're about to "run off" to America, last I heard. Which makes me wonder what the hell I'm doing.'

'It's a couple of months,' he says, protesting. 'I'm coming *back*.'

'We just met at the wrong time, that's all. You're at the start of something, and I'm ... I'm at a different stage altogether. Thirty-seven. I want to have a baby before it's too late. Bryn may or may not commit to that, but I'm damn sure *you* don't want anything to do with it.' Her gaze narrows critically. 'Will you please take that cap off? Makes you look like a half-witted teenager.'

Robbie slowly removes the cap and folds it into his pocket. He stands there in silence, seeming to order his thoughts. 'I didn't know that you wanted . . .' he says quietly. 'I ain't thought about it myself. But if that's what it took for us to be together then . . .'

'Look, I'm not trying to force your hand. It's mad to think of being a father at your age.'

He gives her a searching look. 'Well, what is it you want? Just tell me, an' I'll do it.'

'Nothing. There's nothing you can do. I got myself into this mess. It was stupid of me. I'm a married woman, for God's sake.'

Another long pause as Robbie weighs her words. 'You said the other night you loved him. Does that mean you want to stay with him?'

She hears a batsqueak of fear in his voice. 'It's not that I want to,' she says, sensing the door about to swing shut. 'But I think I have to. If you were here it might be different, but you're going away – as you should—'

'You make it sound like I'm going off to the South Pole. It's only New York! Gah, you could come *with me*, if you wanted. What about that?'

The awful thing is that he's being serious. He probably wants her to go with him, but he hasn't thought it through. That's the impetuous side of youth. You love the idea now, but there's every chance you won't love it down the line.

'I can't. I can't just chuck everything in.' It cuts at her heart to see him looking so hurt. She needs to go, now; a moment longer and she might crumble. She has to steel herself. 'We can't see one another again. Next time I come to Fortess Road I'll make sure you're out. When you go to the States, I'd rather you gave Nell your notice. You should buy somewhere anyway.'

'Billie,' he says, dazed by her decisiveness. 'Ain't we friends even?'

She feels tears about to come. They will come if she doesn't get away this minute. 'I'm sorry, Robbie, I've got to go.' She leans in to kiss his cheek, and turns away, hurrying. She doesn't dare look back.

*

The night sky has gone mauve. Swallows dart around skittishly. Down in her garden Nell has just lit a cigarette, the tip glowing red like a firefly against the dark. On the table lies a salad bowl and plate, a hunk of cheese she's been paring, curl by curl, for her supper; some water biscuits, and a bottle of Pilsner. She's been reading today's *Guardian*, but the light is too grainy for her to continue. Across the backs here and there a square of electric light blazes out of the gloom: someone else alone on a Saturday night?

Véro called again this afternoon. She hasn't processed all the payments yet, but she reckons that Nell is set to make, before tax, about twenty-five grand. That's more than she used to make over five years. 'Are you sure?' she asks Véro, who laughs. Yes, and by the way she's booked their places for the auction at Christie's. 'Nothing to stop you buying it now, darling.' The catalogue, bookmarked at Lot 25, *Portrait of a Young Man*, has taken up residence on her kitchen table. When she first took it back to the house Nell would stare at the picture for minutes on end.

She's read the accompanying essay on its provenance at least half a dozen times and still can't get over the happy accident of its coming to light. She wonders about that previous owner, someone named Margaret – 'Maggie' – Evenlode, sister of a painter she's never heard of.

After clearing up the plates she slumps in front of the news but finds herself yawning helplessly before it's over. She's getting ready for bed when she hears the front door go. Robbie – on his own. No voices drift up. He'll probably be off to bed himself: he doesn't really watch telly. She's got the bedside radio on low when from downstairs comes the tactless jangle of glass breaking. Nell gets out of bed and pulls on her dressing-gown. At the bottom of the stairs a crack of light gleams from under the kitchen door. 'Robbie?' she calls, and pushes it open. Lit by the open fridge, Robbie has his back to her, kneeling: water pools on the tiled floor from the jug he must have dropped. As he picks up the broken shards of glass his shoulders shake, triggered by strange honks of laughter. Is he stoned? 'Oh dear,' says Nell mildly, taking this in, and opening a cupboard for the dustpan and brush. Barefooted, she makes a careful circuit around the blast area in case there's a stray splinter.

'Here, let me do that,' she says, waiting for him to move. He turns his head, and she sees, to her horror, that he's not laughing but sobbing. An involuntary *Oh* falls from her mouth. Stunned for a moment she drops to her knees beside him, puts an arm around his shoulders. 'What is it, love? What's the matter?' She gets a glimpse of his face, damply pink and puffy-eyed – even he looks a bit ugly in tears – and her petting of him can't staunch the flow. 'Can you tell me what's the matter?' she asks again, and this time he chokes out, in a thick, gluey voice, 'Please don't ask.'

'All right,' she says softly, and somehow coaxes him from his knees to sit at the table – she'll make him a cup of tea, the all-in-one remedy.

'Sorry about the jug,' he mutters, but she only replies *Shh* and makes a quick sweep of the broken glass with pan and brush. She tips the fragments into the bin, puts the kettle on; when she looks round Robbie has rested his head on folded arms, the sobbing quieter but still unconsoled. *Oh Christ, what's happened?* she thinks, in a sudden panic. She puts his tea (two sugars) on the table. Every time she's touched him has made it worse, so she decides to wait until he's ready. When he lifts his head he doesn't catch her eye.

She says kindly, steadily, 'Darling, I'm not going to pry, but just tell me this. Has someone died?' His mum, maybe, or his sister? She can't conceive of anything worse than that.

He does look at her now, and gives an unhappy half-laugh. 'No. No one's died.' For some moments he sits motionless, then drags a hand across his smudged face. He has recovered command of himself. 'I've just been ...' he begins, then looks at Nell, his eyes glistening. 'An affair of the heart.'

His smile seems to say, *Can we leave it at that?* And she nods.

They drink their tea, Nell filling the silence with a desultory account of her day. She presumes that something has happened between him and Mara – handed him his coat, given him the elbow, called it a day. Well, if it's fellow-feeling the boy needs he's come to the right place. After what she went through with Johnny she could talk out the rest of her life with 'affairs of the heart'. But what comfort will that bring?

Around midnight Nell, swallowing a yawn, says, 'I think it's past my bedtime. You're not staying up, are you?'

Robbie shakes his head, and rises from the table. 'Don't they always say things'll look better in the morning?'

'That's occasionally true,' she concedes.

She turns off the kitchen lights and begins up the stairs just in front of him. On the landing she turns. 'Goodnight, love. Get some sleep.'

He holds out his arms and she moves towards him. But what he does next surprises her – he leans in and kisses her flush on the mouth. She lets him linger a moment and then pulls away, with a disowning laugh.

He looks at her very earnestly for a moment, and says, 'You're a beautiful person, Nell. I mean it.'

She doesn't know what to say to that. 'Yeah, well ... 'night then.'

Sleep refuses to come, despite her tiredness. Faintly, very faintly, she can hear Robbie strumming chords in his room. She pictures him there on his bed with the blue guitar, starting early on his break-up song. Her heart makes a little stutter. She thinks about the kiss, and his calling her 'a beautiful person'. She wishes he'd said a beautiful *woman* rather than person, which is only a compliment on her character, like 'noble-souled'. A woman always prefers her desirability to be noticed before her goodness.

As she turns over she feels a needle-sharp pain in her foot (*ouch!*) like a wasp sting. She puts on the light and throws back the cover. Spots of blood tattoo the sheet. She bends down to scrutinise the ball of her left foot; there, pin-cushioned in the soft flesh, is a superfine sliver of glass, unnoticed till now. She thought she'd been so careful.

Billie does her grieving in private, necessarily. She can't let Bryn see her upset, and there's no one else on whom to offload her misery. She hasn't even the satisfaction of knowing she's done the right thing: maybe she and Robbie could have made a go of it, if she'd been braver. Meanwhile, an awkward evening looms, the wrap party for *Heaven and Earth*. It's being held at a members' club in Berkeley Square. She doesn't really want to go, not just because Robbie will be there; she's been feeling under the weather – depleted. But it would be a terrible snub not to show up. The club is in a Georgian building that's been partly converted from a family house, its cramped staircases and sloping floors glazed with charm but hardly practical for a party of two hundred or more.

She arrives with Bryn. He will be her shield for the evening, though she doesn't tell him that. Bryn is in his element, of course, just as he was when he came down to the Grand for the weekend. He's already so chummy with the cast it's as if he's been starring in the film himself. When Kezia comes over to say hello she and Bryn hit it off instantly, and for once Billie doesn't mind; it excuses her from having to be sociable. She wanders off. She hasn't seen Robbie but she senses he's in the building, the way you can with someone who's been on your mind. Vernon Sparks takes her aside, full of praise for her performance – he believes the film will be saved after all. 'Remember that night at the bistro I told you we were heading for the iceberg? Well, we'd already collided with it, to be honest. Holed beneath the water. The extra scenes we did with you and Maurice stopped us sinking.' Billie smiles at him. He loves a seafaring metaphor, does Vern.

'So we got away with it?'

Vern snorts. 'Oh, it's still a piece of shit. But at least it floats.'

Not a trace of that verdict is detectable in his address from the stage half an hour later. He says *Heaven and Earth* is destined to be a hit, and for him personally it's been one of the happiest shoots he's ever worked on.

A voice confides in Billie's ear: 'You know what they say – Where there's a happy shoot, there's bound to be a turkey.'

She turns and smiles: Maurice. 'Hello, darling.' To judge by his demeanour he has thawed from their little *froideur* of recent weeks. Such is her relief she almost bursts into tears.

He seems to read something concerning in her face. 'Are you all right?'

'Not in a party mood. Can we go and get a drink?' she asks him, and they head for the bar. Over double vodka and tonics it all comes out – Robbie, their affair, Chris catching them, her decision to end it. Maurice listens, gravely, without any expression of surprise. She's no longer sure why she resisted telling him in the first place. She feels miserable still, but unburdened.

'Have I done the right thing?' she asks quietly.

He pauses. 'He's *very* young. And clueless. It's bad timing, as you say. Then again ...'

'What?' She doesn't want to hear the counter-argument.

'It does sound like he was mad about you.'

'Oh God,' she says, and feels despair rising to the brim again. 'I wish I hadn't ... I wish we'd never—' The sentiment goes unexpressed, for at that moment there's a roar around the room and shouts for Robbie to come to the stage. They're demanding he play for them. Vernon introduces him as 'the boy wonder' (one of his kinder epithets, if Robbie only knew). From the corner of the room he appears, the first time she's set eyes on him tonight. He has a reluctant air, though it's notable he's remembered to bring along his guitar. He fiddles with the tuning for some moments – his nervous tic – before leaning into the microphone. He plays 'Black-eyed Boy from Cloudy Fields', the one he played for her all those weeks ago at Gunter Grove – and they whoop with their applause.

They want an encore. Robbie stands there in his performer's trance. Then he mumbles something about a new song he's written, it doesn't have a title yet. He plays a chord.

At dawn I left my boots at the door
And those jeans I borrowed from you
A songbird's lament at my heart it tore
I wonder if you heard it too

She is heading for the exit by the time the second verse kicks in.

14

Billie takes a deep breath and tells herself not to panic. She's been to the bathroom and found spotting on her sanitary towel. In the last few days she's also felt a burning sensation down there, like peeing molten silver. It might be nothing. A small infection. But she's heard too many stories about STDs to feel quite safe. She remembers Tash getting an awful dose of chlamydia years ago, and in normal circumstances would seek her advice, but she's been avoiding her (and Chris) since the party. She can't go to her mum for fear of bumping into Robbie.

Unfortunately the pain isn't going away; it's getting worse. She rings her GP, who recommends making an appointment at Praed Street. On another blazing August morning she sets out for the clinic, not far from where she lives. Yet it's far enough in her condition, and tramping through streets frazzled by the heat and roaring with buses and taxis she begins to feel faint. Noisome vapours of fried food waft across her face, mingling with the bad breath of London drains. Sweat patches darken her shirt, and her bladder already feels like it's aflame. If decency allowed she would squat in that alley she's just walking past and piss there. Billie can't help regarding this interior assault as a personal injustice. What has she done to deserve it?

In the waiting area she takes a seat and tries to calm her fevered brain by clamping on her Walkman. She's got Laura Nyro's *Gonna Take a Miracle* loud in her ears when, from the facing row of plastic chairs, a middle-aged lady leans towards her as though eager to speak. She wears horn-rimmed spectacles and cardigan in a style faintly redolent of a kitchen-sink drama from the 1960s. Billie, despite longing to be left alone, politely lifts her headphones in response.

The woman smiles, with a hopeful tilt of her head. 'It's Lizzie, isn't it?'

'I'm sorry?'

'You were in *The Marchioness of Malden*, yes?' She has named a recent period drama on TV.

'I'm afraid not,' she replies. She's never seen it, let alone starred in it.

The woman continues staring, her smile almost incredulous, as if it's Billie's misremembering, not hers. Then with a little shake of her head she says, 'Where do I know you from, then?'

'I really can't imagine,' Billie replies, her own smile fixed. This seems to conclude the exchange. She's about to restore her earphones when her interlocutor suddenly narrows her field of enquiry.

'What are you in for?' she asks eagerly.

Billie stares back, blank-faced. 'Malaria.' The woman's mouth falls open, and she rears back in her seat.

'Cantrip?' a nurse calls out. *Thank Christ.* Billie stands and, widening her eyes at the woman, trips off towards the surgery.

Nell's plan for dinner has gone to pot. Billie for some reason hasn't returned her calls, and Bryn doesn't appear to know where she is. Robbie, deep in rehearsals for his tour, has been away for three days; he's probably forgotten all about it. Now Tash has rung to say that Chris can't make it either – something to do with work, sends his apologies.

Nell sighs. 'Looks like it might just be you, me and Gil.'

It's a shame, because she's made a fish stew that could probably feed ten. She's dolled herself up, too, in white slacks, a purple
skinny-rib top and a silk scarf tied into her hair: the Riviera look,
as she thinks of it. On arriving, Tash looks startled: 'Is this a special
occasion?'

'Not really. I just wanted to get you all together.'

They lay the table in the garden. It's late August, still warm,
but you can feel the turning of the year approach; the evenings are
shorter, autumn in the air like a warning rumour. Nell fetches them
a beer each from the fridge. Gil is in the living room, glued to *Top
of the Pops*.

'Have you spoken to Billie lately?' she asks Tash.

'Not since your party. I left a message but she didn't call back.'

'I thought she might be avoiding me, but if you haven't either . . .'

'Chris reckons it's not working out with Bryn. He says you only
have to look at her to see she's not happy.'

'I still don't understand why she took him back . . .'

'Well, you know she's desperate for a kid. Maybe that was one of
the conditions she made with him.'

Nell feels something tear at her heart; Billie hasn't talked to
her about this. They were always close. When she had an abortion
years ago Nell took her to the clinic. (Paid for it, too.) Tash is busy
dressing the salad; in her phlegmatic way she doesn't notice the
effect this revelation has on her mother. For a few moments there's
a lull in their talk. The tinny roar of *Top of the Pops* drifts out from
the living room.

'Well, fine, if she wants to have a baby,' says Nell, almost to herself. 'But it's not the way to save your marriage.' She resists the urge
to add, *Speaking from experience.*

Tash, oblivious, says, 'Are we ready to eat?'

She goes inside to fetch Gil. When she returns she's got the boy
in tow, and – hello – Robbie, just through the door.

'Sorry I'm late,' he says, with a mock-grimace. 'Rehearsal overran.'

'It's fine!' Nell cries, nearly giddy with delight. 'We haven't even started.'

As she serves up the food Robbie tells them about the wrap party last week, and how all the cast and crew felt the sadness of it coming to an end. He'd never been on a set before, and the intensity of the twelve weeks they'd been together had brought them close. 'Like a big family, really,' he muses. 'It was a struggle for me – acting, I mean – but to be part of the film was lush. I'd never have got to meet Billie otherwise' – he looks at Nell, and Tash – 'or you.'

'Or me,' Gil says, and they laugh.

He seems much happier than he did last week, Nell thinks. Perhaps he's made it up with his girlfriend. Or found someone else?

Only the very young and the very beautiful can be so aloof

The line has been running in her head for days. It makes her think of him. Robbie's very young and very beautiful, but he's not aloof, he's actually rather a warm person. But he's detached from the world, somehow, as if he might be visiting from elsewhere. He doesn't seem to have that many friends. When she agreed to let him move in she worried that he might turn the place into a den of dope-heads and groupies and what-have-you, but aside from Mara and the occasional floppy-haired youth like himself, he's been here more or less on his own. Maybe he's not someone who needs much company.

'So, you're off to America, then,' says Tash presently.

'Yeah. Got some club dates in New York – heard of CBGB? Then Boston, Chicago, few other cities. I dunno what's in store, to be honest. The Dead March – my old band – had a real following over there. My new stuff's quite different, more jazz and blues.'

'Perhaps they'll like it even more,' says Nell with prompt loyalty.

'Will you come back from America?' This is Gil, who's been listening intently. 'I mean, back to this house?'

'I dunno. Depends if Nell will keep the room for me.'

He shoots a glance at her. Tash chimes in: 'I think Gil's asking because you promised to teach him guitar.'

'I haven't forgotten,' he says, with a little laugh. He turns to the boy. 'What d'you say about a quick lesson, after we've cleared this table?'

They carry off the plates, leaving Nell and Tash to have another beer and a smoke. The night sky has a voluptuous purple-black depth, setting the stars in relief like tiny stones on a jeweller's cloth. The long hot summer is winding down, and what lies beyond seems to Nell too sad for words.

From inside the house the telephone starts to ring, and slowly she gets to her feet. In the living room she can hear Robbie and Gil talking in low murmurs against the strum and twang. She picks up the phone.

'Mum, it's me.'

'Darling! Where have you been?'

'I'm at Maurice's. I need to talk to you ...'

She can hear something constrained in Billie's voice.

'Why don't you come over now? Tash is here.'

'And Robbie?'

'Yeah. He's in the living room playing guitar with Gil.'

There's a pause, and she says no, not tonight. She'll come over at the weekend. 'Has something happened with Bryn?'

A faint but audible sigh. 'I'll explain when I see you.'

She rings off. Nell is at a loss. What's she doing at Maurice's, for heaven's sake? He lives in some godforsaken suburb of south London. Returning to the garden she relays the call to Tash, whose unemotional good sense has a calming effect on her mother. It might just be a 'bump in the road', she reasons: Billie has always had a combustible temperament. If it's really serious then they'll get together and deal with it.

When they call it a night and Tash goes to collect Gil from the living room they find him clutching an acoustic guitar, its body so wide he almost has to peer over the thing.

'Been trying out a few chords,' Robbie explains. 'Done pretty well, eh, Django?'

'Why d'you call me that?' Gil says, wide-eyed.

"Cos Django's my new name for yer.'

Gil asks if he can play for a bit longer, and Tash shakes her head. 'Way past your bedtime, mister.'

They say their goodnights on the step. Back in the kitchen Nell tidies up before joining Robbie on the couch, haloed in smoke. The burnt ropey smell of weed pinches the air. Without a word he holds out the thin joint to her.

'If I was a proper landlady,' she says, taking a short toke, 'I'd sling you out for bringing drugs into the house.'

Bong! The strength of the next hit is like a clapper tolling behind her eyes. It goes shuddering through her cerebral cortex, leaden circles rippling to the top.

'God almighty,' she mutters. She leans back, trying to relocate her centre of gravity. Slowly, slowly, the reverberation fades: better not try that again. Next to her, Robbie has a look of benign, puzzled concentration, as though he's totting up a sum in his head. At last he says, 'You all right?' He places his hand lightly on her knee.

After a moment she manages to say 'Mmm,' and hands him back the doobie.

She giggles. 'Don't let me touch that again.' Her voice has gone slightly croaky.

He takes it from her. She's righted herself, though she has that curious sensation of floating, drifting above it all. His other hand, she notices, is still on her knee. She's quite happy to leave it there.

'Is there something I could do for you instead?'

There's a catch in his voice that makes her look round. He's staring at her. Is he asking her what she thinks he is or – before she can take another breath the kiss she has imagined is now startlingly upon her. The urgency of it winds her; she needs to come up for air. But she doesn't want to stop just yet, because his hands are suddenly all over her, too, under her top and running up her stomach to her breasts.

How can this be happening? she wonders. She needs to put the brakes on before things run away from them.

'Oy,' she gasps, holding him by the shoulders. She looks at him closely. 'How much of that have you smoked?'

His dreamy expression changes. 'I ain't stoned, if that's what you're thinking.'

'So ... what's this about?'

Now he looks slightly offended. 'I'd've thought it was obvious. Didn't you realise when I kissed you the other night ... ?'

'You were upset. About Mara.'

He shakes his head. 'Nell. I've wanted to do this, like, from the very first time we met. D'you remember it? You were in your painting-room. You had Mozart on really loud. I just thought – What a *beautiful woman*.'

She half-laughs. 'You've known loads of beautiful women. All of 'em a lot younger than me.'

'Shut up,' he mutters, sealing her mouth with his own. This time the kiss lingers, meltingly, and she no longer resists his hands, unclasping, uncovering, unzipping. In his haste he hasn't even turned off the lights – and if he doesn't mind why should she?

Billie wakes from unrestful sleep. She's been dozing since about seven this morning when she heard the milkman's step outside the window. The sofa bed in Maurice's living room isn't the most uncomfortable she's ever slept on, but it's a close thing. The fireplace is flanked by bookshelves on either side. In the small hours she got up to browse them, looking for something to send her off. Shakespeare, her staple, requires a concentration which her poor fagged brain can't muster. Poetry, likewise. In the end she finds a Penguin of La Rochefoucauld's *Maxims*, and spends a half-hour grazing on his nuggets of wisdom: 'We are so accustomed to disguise ourselves to others that, in the end, we become disguised to ourselves.'

I must remember that, she thinks, yawning extravagantly.

A tap at the door, and Maurice enters carrying a mug of tea and a matronly air. 'How's the patient this morning?' he asks.

'Bit groggy,' she admits, accepting the tea. 'And my arm's still aching.'

The arm in question has been recovering from a jab, administered on the day she visited the Praed Street clinic. The scene won't be forgotten. 'I'm afraid you have a serious infection,' says the woman doctor who examines her. 'What?' says Billie, fearing, and now hearing, the worst. 'Cervical gonorrhoea. There has been a lot of it about lately,' she adds. Billie searches her expression for disapproval, or sympathy, and finds only professional straightforwardness. 'The good news is that we are treating it with an antibiotic, spectinomycin, which has been very effective.' The bad news? 'The treatment is by injection. It may be a little bit painful.'

'Little bit' doesn't strictly tell the truth.

Maurice sits down on the edge of the bed. 'You've talked to your mother?'

'I'm going to see her on Sunday. I'll ask her about Robbie – whether he ever . . .'

'Brought someone home? Why don't you just ask *him*?'

'Because he'll lie to me. He probably picked it up while he was at Gunter Grove. Listen, he told me he woke up there once and found two complete strangers in his bed.'

'Lucky him,' murmurs Maurice. There's a beat, then he says, 'Have you told Bryn yet?'

She shakes her head. 'I don't dare. After everything I said to him, about sneaking around and how it had to stop . . . Now here's me with the clap.'

Maurice's expression is ambiguous. He seems poised to ask another question, then holds off, perhaps waiting for Billie to speak. She too perceives something unsaid, but she won't go there. The moment passes.

'Thanks for the tea,' she says.

*

Nell has been mooching in front of a canvas, her progress on it stalled for the last hour. Her head is too busy with what's happened – what's still happening. Twice this morning, on her own, she has burst out laughing. It's like being a moony teenager again; she deserves a proper telling-off. And yet after a long solitude it feels so extraordinary to be desired that she wants to hoard every glinting image in her memory bank, like a miser with his gold. He left early yesterday morning for another band practice in west London, said he'd be staying overnight at Gunter Grove, where most of his mates seem to live.

Nothing from him since. *Only the very young and the very beautiful* ... How unsettling a new relationship is; exhilarating, and fretful. You need to be reassured at the start, even in small things like a glance, or a tone of voice. At the moment even a phone call from him would be a relief. They didn't know one another well before, it felt like trying to sing a duet without quite knowing how the tune goes. Now sex has created an intimate new layer of strangeness. The next morning he didn't slink off or look embarrassed. He made her a cup of tea and got back into bed and talked. This is the best time of all, she thinks, when you conduct that delightful investigation into what the other person was feeling, thinking, and so opens up the longer perspective of first impressions, of what they got wrong about you and you got wrong about them.

Just a phone call would do.

It's getting on for midday when she hears Billie let herself in downstairs. Since they last spoke on the phone events have accelerated beyond them. Nell has no idea what she's going to tell her. Is there even the slightest possibility she could keep the thing with Robbie a secret? Anticipating some revelation about Bryn, she vaguely hopes that Billie will be too preoccupied to twig what's been going on at Fortess Road.

On descending to the hallway Nell feels an immediate pricking of alarm. Billie looks awful. Her eyes are raccooned with fatigue, her hair looks dull and unwashed; despondency vibrates from her like a force field.

'Darling,' she says, wrapping her in a hug. Has she lost weight too?

'Mum.' Her smile is forlorn – but at least it's a smile.

They go through to the kitchen and Nell makes them tea. Yes, she'll stay for lunch, though she doesn't feel that hungry. Billie lights a cigarette, rubs away a tear with the heel of her hand.

'What's happened, love?' asks Nell, staring at her, sick with foreboding.

'Nothing good.' Her voice is quite calm. 'I've got … I've contracted an STD. Cervical gonorrhoea, to give it the full name.'

'Oh thank God! I thought you were going to tell me you had *cancer.*'

She half-laughs. 'Well, I suppose every cloud …'

'Bryn. That rotten—'

'Mum, before you say anything, I have to tell you – it's someone else.'

'You mean … Who?'

Billie closes her eyes. 'Robbie. When we were in Eastbourne. I shouldn't have got involved, but … it was over almost before it had begun.'

She looks across at Nell, who has gone white. There is no name that could have confounded her more. She must try to command herself, but at the moment she can't get her voice to work. Billie is staring at her, unsuspecting. Still nothing comes.

'Mum, please say something.'

'I'm – I don't know what … Are you saying that you caught this from him – from Robbie?'

'I think so. That girl Mara he hangs out with – or someone else I don't know about. That's the risk with people who live in a squat—'

'But how can you be sure it's not Bryn?'

'I can't, not until I … Only given the promises he made, it's just not … It's just much more likely to be Robbie. He's young, and he knows loads of women.'

Nell, trying to keep a lid on her panic, says, 'He doesn't strike me as the sleep-around type, to be honest.'

Billie shrugs, impatient of her mother's doubts. It's easy to see why she would sooner point the finger at Bryn – she's never liked him. Both of them sit at the table brooding, cast adrift on their own wrecks. The talk moves on to her treatment at the clinic, and the jab that's left her arm sore. She'll have to go back there in a few weeks to get the all-clear.

'In the meantime,' she adds, 'you'd better tell Robbie to get himself checked out. When will he be here?'

'I don't know,' replies Nell distantly. 'I haven't seen him for a few days.'

She gets to her feet, in a kind of daze, and starts to prepare lunch. Billie, meanwhile, needing to pee, goes upstairs to the bathroom. She's squatting uncomfortably on the toilet seat when her eye catches on something hanging over the radiator: a T-shirt, emblazoned with THE FLOWERS OF ROMANCE. Robbie's. What on earth is it doing here? *He* wouldn't have left it there, since he has his own bathroom on the next floor. A thin shadow flits, bat-like, in the furthest reaches of her consciousness, a glimpse of the inconceivable. It *is* inconceivable, and she dismisses it.

When she returns to the kitchen Nell is decanting gazpacho into bowls. The radio isn't playing, which may be a sign of trouble. She sits down, pours herself a glass of water.

'There's a T-shirt of Robbie's in your bathroom.' Her tone is breezily inquisitive.

Nell, ladling out the soup, still has her back to Billie. 'Mmm. He gave it to me.'

'Oh. Why?'

She turns, and pulls a face. 'I suppose he knew I liked it – you know, naming the show after it ...'

Billie nods but doesn't say anything. Nell carries the bowls over and sets them on the table, one each. Strain peeps from behind her eyes. They begin to eat, talking in low voices – how long she's going to stay at Maurice's, whether she's going to take a holiday before the next job. Billie can sense her mother's distracted mood, and the effort she's making to engage in the conversation.

They have cleared up lunch and moved on to coffee when the front door opening sounds through the hallway. There's a clunk of something being set on the floor – a guitar case – and Nell calls out, 'Hello?'

Robbie walks in, his smile vanishing on the instant he sees who's at the table. 'Hi ... sorry to interrupt.' He looks uncertainly from Billie to Nell, who for this last hour has been in such turmoil with Robbie's changing identities – lodger, seducer, betrayer, infecter? – she hardly knows what to make of him. The room is suddenly bristling with imminence, the sense of a grenade about to be unpinned. Nell adopts an air of fatalistic calm.

'Would you like a cup of coffee?' she says. He looks at her, shakes his head. He seems unsure whether to stand or sit.

Billie, without a greeting, says, 'I hear you've been at Gunter Grove.' Robbie admits it with a barely perceptible nod.

'Well, you'd better tell whoever you've been sleeping with there that she needs to get to a clinic. And you should, too.'

He frowns, confused. 'D'you mind telling me what you're on about?'

Billie snorts her contempt. 'What I'm *on about*' – there's a sour mimicry in the words – 'is that I've got a nasty infection, which you gave me.'

'I ain't given you nothin', he says indignantly. 'I ain't been sleeping with anyone and I ain't infected.'

'Thanks, Doctor! You can be infected and not show any

symptoms. Jesus, what a fool I was to—' She stops herself: that line of argument can go nowhere useful. 'There's no way I could have got it from anyone but you.'

'Oh yeah? What about your husband? Sounds a more likely candidate than me.'

This counterattack flings petrol on the bonfire. 'I think you should pack up your stuff and get the fuck out of this house. Like *now*.' Her voice quivers with hostility.

Robbie is shocked into silence. A look passes between him and Nell. Both of them know there must be a reckoning, but not like this. Dismissed, he takes a step backwards, then Nell says, 'Stay where you are.' She turns to Billie. 'This is my house. I'll tell him when he has to leave.'

Now it's Billie's turn to be momentarily dumbfounded. 'What? Why are you defending him against me?' Her expression goes through a sequence of rapid changes as the answer to that question dawns on her.

'Oh my God,' she says, a hand flying to her mouth in horror. She looks from her mother to Robbie. *Yes, there's the penny dropping*, thinks Nell. 'Oh, Mum, you didn't – *you didn't*.' Nell's silence tells her otherwise. Billie hangs her head, emitting little gasps of distress. 'How could you?' she whimpers. Then without warning she steps across the room and slaps Robbie's face, again and again, crying and screaming at him.

He cowers against her flailing fists. 'Stop, *stop!*' he pleads over her shrieked obscenities. Fury drives her on. When he manages to grab hold of her wrists to defend himself she kicks him, in the shins, then in the groin. He yowls in pain.

Nell is shouting too, and as she tries to drag her off him Billie's elbow recoils from his grasp and catches her flush in the eye. Nell briefly sees stars, and staggers back against the table. When she tries to sit down she misses the chair and collapses on the floor. That brings the brawl to a sudden halt.

Robbie hurries over to help her but Billie interposes herself. 'Don't you fucking touch her!' she nearly spits, and Robbie shrinks away.

Billie gets Nell up and on to the chair. Sitting down she mutters an apology, still trembling, face smudged and swollen. The hysteria has blown itself out, but the tears keep coming. *How could you?* is the question that Billie can't get out of her head. She stares at her mother for some moments in a muddle of disgust and shame and pity. *How could you?*

Later she remembers that it was her idea to move him in here.

She gets wearily to her feet. 'I'm going,' she says to Nell. There is no kiss, no goodbye hug. Out in the hall she passes Robbie sitting at the bottom of the stairs. A wild scratch-mark is scored down his cheek.

As she goes to the door she stops, turns back. 'Tell me when you get your result. And then we won't ever have to speak again.'

15

Nell is lying on the couch, her throbbing eye hidden by the bag of frozen peas Tash holds against it. It's late afternoon on this explosive Sunday. Billie went from Fortess Road to Tash's, where she poured it all out – a second wave of hysteria which Tash has just finished mopping up. The cold compress of peas has become uncomfortable, and Nell removes it.

Tash scrutinises the damage. 'Mmm. Bit nasty.'

'Oh God. I'm going to look like one of those battered wives who say they just walked into a door.' She thinks about getting up to look in the mirror but then can't quite face it. 'So ... what did you say to her?'

'Well, I was listening, mostly. But I did ask her why she's so convinced it's Robbie and not Bryn who gave her ... it.'

'She can't bear the idea it might be Bryn. She invested too much in getting back with him.'

Tash looks at her levelly. 'You realise that if Robbie is the culprit *you'll* have to get checked too.'

Her tone is matter-of-fact. This is Tash's wonderful side. She might be doctrinaire about politics and causes, but in the matter of human behaviour she is one of the least judgemental people Nell has ever known. She is not the sort to give her a lecture on sexual conduct even if she felt like it. People will do what they must.

Nell thinks back to the night Robbie came home late and broke down in the kitchen. Her mistake was to assume he'd been jilted by his girlfriend – Mara, or whoever – when he was distraught at losing Billie, and couldn't tell anyone about it. So in his fragile state he had turned to Nell, for what better reminder could he have of the woman who'd just given him up?

'You don't think I'm a freak, do you?' she says to Tash abruptly.

'Oh Mum.'

'Billie does – she used that word. Where sex is concerned middle-aged women are bloody pariahs, have you noticed? Fine if you're an older man, you can cop off with an eighteen-year-old and no one'll bat an eyelid. But a single older *woman* with a sex drive, people are up in arms – you're unnatural, disgusting. Or else you're a joke.'

'That's not what Billie thinks. In fact, she's always been worried that you haven't got someone. It was just unfortunate you ended up with . . . the someone she was still in love with.'

'If you could have seen the look she gave me when . . . She's never going to forgive me, Tash.'

Tash lights a cigarette and blows a pensive stream of smoke from the corner of her mouth. 'She'll come round. It might just take a while. Whether she'll get over Robbie . . . Where is he, by the way?'

'In his room. I told him you were coming. He won't come down – to get beaten up twice by a woman is more than his pride can stand.'

'Well, thank God he's off to America . . .'

Nell nods, and something clutches at her heart. She doesn't feel allowed to say that she'll miss him.

A few days later Billie is reading on the sofa in Maurice's living room when the phone rings. He picks up, and after a brief exchange holds the receiver towards her: 'Nell.' She gets up, pads across the room and puts the phone to her ear, as if she's in a play.

'Hello.' Her tone is flat to the point of unfriendliness.

'Darling . . . Are you all right? I've got some news.' Billie feels her heartbeat accelerate sickeningly. 'Robbie just got his results from the clinic. He's clean.'

She takes a moment to digest this. 'Are you sure?'

'I've got it written here in black and white. So I think you owe him an apology.'

'He can whistle for it,' Billie replies.

'Why are you so mad at him? It takes two, you know.'

'I'm very well aware of that. You obviously think it's OK to get involved with someone you're forty years older than. I don't.'

'Why? Can't I have a life too?'

'Yeah, but not by stealing my friends.'

'I didn't – why were you so determined to move him in here?'

'Because I thought he'd be safe! The last thing in the world I imagined was you getting your claws into him.'

'That's a nice thing to say to your mother.'

'It's *because* you're my mother we're in this fucking mess.'

There follows a hurt silence. Nell eventually says, 'My eye's fine, by the way. It's gone the colour of an aubergine.'

'Sorry. I meant to ask ... I just ... Tash said she's been over to see you.'

'Least I've one daughter who still respects me.'

'Well, you should try not to alienate her, then. I'm glad your eye's better. Oh, and tell Robbie I want my jeans back. Bye.'

She hangs up, in every way unsatisfied. Irritation nips her, like a crab. Across the room Maurice is looking at her steadily.

'That was the medical bulletin,' she says. 'Robbie's clean.'

'Pure as the driven slush,' Maurice says, with a slow blink: he's doing his 'quiet disappointment' face. 'I don't know why you're being like that to your mother,' he adds.

'Don't you?'

'I never had you down for a prig.'

She feels winded by that. 'Maurice, *please* don't turn against me. I don't mean to be a ... I just feel let down.'

'I know you do. And I'm on your side. But think about it from her point of view. I'm guessing Robbie just tried it on with her one night. If you're a woman who's been lonely for years and misses being touched, why wouldn't you respond? She's got needs like everyone else.'

'Yes, but why with him?'

'Nell didn't know about you and him—'

'So she says.'

'Isn't it really that you're revolted by the idea of your mum with a twenty-three-year-old?'

'Well, yeah, maybe I am. Wouldn't you feel the same if it was your mother?'

Maurice gives a worldly shrug. 'I don't think that kind of thing happens much in Petts Wood ... but I'd try to keep an open mind.'

'Would you really?'

'Yes, because I love my mother, as you know, and however improbable the idea of her meeting a "young man", I'd want her to be happy.'

'Improbable's one word for it. Grotesque might be more accurate. She's in her sixties!'

'She's a *woman* – who happens to be getting on. Like you will one day.' When she fails to reply he continues. 'You know, there's something Oscar once said that strikes me as very true. "The tragedy of old age is not that one is old, but that one is young." Nell doesn't feel old, whatever appearances to the contrary. She wants to be loved, still. You shouldn't despise her for that.'

Billie, no argument left in her, silently curls up on the sofa, foetal position.

Some moments later the phone rings again.

'If that's my mother ringing back tell her I've gone to bed.'

Maurice picks up: then he muffles the cupped ear of the receiver with his hand. 'You might want to take this – it's Bryn.'

*

September has seen August out the door and settled itself in the air, turning the leaves gold, cooling the sun. Nell has got Sinatra on in her car, driving south towards the West End. In the passenger seat Tash is flicking through the auction catalogue, pausing here and there, whistling at the estimates. She has rolled the window down while she smokes; the honk and grind of steaming London traffic competes with The Voice and 'Last Night When We Were Young' as they wait at the lights. She suddenly notices Nell staring at her, half-smiling, half-appraising.

'Something the matter?'

'Just admiring your profile. I'm going to get back to portraits.'

'You mean – of me?' Tash frowns.

'Both of you. I used to draw you a lot when you were small.'

'Why did you stop?'

The traffic starts moving again.

'I just got out of the habit. So that's my next thing – you, and Billie. If I ever get to see her again.'

It's nearly four weeks since she and Billie last talked. They've never had a falling-out as serious as this. Tash, their go-between, knows them well enough not to push for a peace summit. This is a cold war that may require waiting out.

'Has Robbie collected his stuff yet?'

Nell shakes her head. 'He's gone home to see his mum for a week. Then he'll be off, end of this month.'

Before he left for Bristol they had a long talk, in Nell's kitchen. They hugged each other with relief. She asked him what he intended to do once he got back from the States. 'You can leave your stuff here if you want,' she said. 'It's not like I need to rent your room out.'

He looked at her uncertainly. 'Thanks. But I don't think I should stay here,' he said. 'As long as Billie's mad at me she's not gonna come round knowing . . . I can't be the reason you don't see each other.'

Quite mature behaviour, that, she thinks, to remove himself from the picture. He's a good kid, really. He's got his life to live, all those songs to write, there'll be women throwing themselves at him. What place could she possibly have in it? *Old enough to be ...* She must try not to think about it; any of it.

Outside Christie's Hilary is waiting by the steps. She has dressed up, in mother-of-the-bride frumperie. She's so grateful to have been asked, though as Nell points out, it's only because Hilary gave the family tree a shake that they're here today. Up the slow-ascending stairs they go and into the great octagonal room, where Véro is already seated amid the filling rows. She's also dressed for the occasion, in one of her hard-as-nails businesswoman suits, boxy, with shoulder pads. Before Nell introduces Hilary as her cousin, she notices Véro eyeing her, possibly wondering who's the podgy matron tagging along. Nell, remembering her own first impressions, has been chastened: appearances may deceive. She tactfully places herself and Tash as a buffer between them.

It's years since Nell has been to a big auction. They were dingy affairs back then, most of the lots unloved furniture and paintings not much above Piccadilly-railings standard. Christie's is smart, or at least likes to pretend it is. Nell senses a strong spiv element at large, even among the blazer-and-signet-ring types who hang around art sales. Véro surveys the other dealers with professional disdain ('Like caterpillars on a salad,' she whispers to Nell), wary of anyone else scoring a success here. The auctioneer, a prim young man with foxy hair and small eyes, brings the house to order with some boilerplate instructions on the sale. Bidding begins, with white-gloved assistants carrying in one painting after another, holding them up impassively for inspection. A quick-quick-slow rhythm governs the proceedings. A couple of lots will be summarily dispatched, followed by another that stirs up a buzz in the room as the bids fly in. The regular crack of the hammer sounds like judgement coming down.

Nell is daydreaming when Tash gives her a nudge, indicating the row behind. 'Look who's here.'

She turns around to see Billie, who's just taken a seat. She's wearing a tobacco-coloured velvet jacket and dark jeans. A tiredness around her eyes. She doesn't say anything, just raises her hand. A rueful smile creases her mouth, which Nell understands instinctively: peace, at last. She ought to have known that Billie wouldn't miss this.

Lot 25 comes up, and Nell catches her breath as *Portrait of a Young Man* is placed on the stand. The first time she's seen it in the flesh. The painting seems to glow from the frame, like a thing alive. Joseph Edmund Rothwell, their kinsman, face to face. Her connection to it feels almost glandular. While she's been staring at it bidding has begun, and at a brisk pace, the auctioneer almost gabbling to keep up. Increments of five hundred pounds leapfrog one another. Nell, holding her paddle, hasn't plunged in yet, though her heart's already at a gallop. 'The bid is at twenty-six thousand pounds . . . twenty-six five hundred . . . twenty-seven, thank you, sir . . .'

Véro is looking at her, expectantly. *Twenty-eight thousand pounds? This is madness*, thinks Nell. Whatever money she made on the show last month will be gone at a stroke (and even that won't cover it). She has the natural wariness of her interwar generation, the ones who shied away from extravagance because they had known austerity and feared debt almost as much as death. And why must she have the painting anyway? There is the romance of its history, of course; a history intimately entwined with her family. This young fellow, Rothwell, bursting into the lives of two middle-aged women, his energy crackling through their house. He made them feel noticed again. That's the effect youth could have. Still has – she should know.

But must one *own* a thing just because one loves it?

'Darling, are you going to bid?' Véro's urgent whisper comes. The bid now stands at thirty thousand. The auctioneer gazes over the room enquiringly, his hammer poised. She looks at Joseph Rothwell again, and slowly, diffidently, she raises her paddle. He points at her: 'Thank you, madam, thirty thousand five hundred ... Against you, sir ...' A man on the other side of the room is ready to fight her for it. The bidding escalates, like the remorseless numbers scrolling up a petrol gauge as you fill the tank. *Stop, stop,* she wants to beg, nodding through another five hundred. They are now at thirty-four. Nell feels herself tremble, desperate to get off this horrible ride but clinging on anyway. She can take out another mortgage perhaps ... and sell the car? At thirty-five her rival in the room hesitates. Is he done? Her heart sinks as he nods to continue, and the bid comes back to her. A hush in the room.

At that moment a hand touches her shoulder. It's Billie. 'Don't stop now. We'll go halves on it,' she says, *sotto voce.* Mother and daughter hold one another's stare. They will complete this vertiginous climb together. Nell turns back to the auctioneer, and raises again. Thirty-five thousand, five hundred. This time their competitor pauses briefly before he shakes his head.

'Going once. Twice ...' The hammer thunks down. 'Sold.'

The hum in the room starts up again, and the next lot is carried on.

Outside, at the top of the staircase, a strange euphoria grips them. Véro is almost singing her congratulations – she loves a big spender – while Hilary beams her delight: 'It's back in the family at last!' she cries. Nell smiles, properly trembling with a mixture of relief and incredulity. She cannot yet come to terms with the stupendous sum she has laid out. And there is Billie, who up close looks ill as well as fatigued.

'Are you all right, love?' She instinctively takes Billie's hand in hers.

'I'm fine. Just a bit drained from ...'

'How are things with ...?'

'He's moved out. For good this time.' Then, as Hilary approaches, she says, 'I'll tell you about it later.'

Back on King Street the afternoon sky has gone the colour of slate. The women perform their minuets of departure. Tash has to hurry off, so too does Véro, who will send her assistant to collect the painting for them next week. She gives a wave before she folds herself into her dinky silver Porsche parked along the way. Moments later they hear its insolent clattering roar from the end of the street.

Nell needs a cup of tea, Billie knows a little café up on Jermyn Street; so together with Hilary they make their way through the sober brick labyrinth of St James's, talking in hushed voices of the hour just past.

Some days later Billie sits at the bar of the Pineapple, a pub just round the corner from Fortess Road. She used to hang out here in her mini-skirted youth, drinking Pernod and blackcurrant. The long hot summer has swooned to an end; she noticed a distinct chill in the air as she was walking here. Quite a year. It's only six months on since the afternoon she first met him at the Savoy. For some reason the Hermann Hesse paperback sticking out of his pocket remains vivid to her. She wonders if he ever finished it.

The door swings open and there's Robbie, in a zipped leather jacket and black cargo trousers. He still wears the Ray-Bans, the famous person's bid for anonymity – or possibly for attention. His smile is tentative. They haven't seen each other since she was smacking him around the head in Nell's kitchen. Without kissing her he takes the stool adjacent.

'Don't know this place,' he says, steering his gaze around the room.

'Old haunt of mine,' she replies. 'Coke?'

He nods.

'Mum tells me you're all packed up. Excited?'

'Sort of. Flying tomorrow afternoon. I got a phone call this week from one of the club promoters in New York, told me he was a big fan ...'

'That's good.'

'Only thing was he called me "Roddy" the whole time. I couldn't bring meself to correct him.'

She laughs, and picks out a cigarette to light. 'They'll know your name soon enough.'

They look at one another appraisingly. His cheek still wears the faint trace of a scratch-mark she gave him.

'Wasn't sure I was gonna see you before I left.'

'Nor was I,' she says. 'I'm sorry about . . . ' She lightly touches her hand to his cheek. 'A case of mistaken identity, honest.'

He shrugs. 'Nell got the worst of it – that shiner . . . '

'I suppose Bryn can count himself lucky. Ironic that the guilty man somehow managed to avoid physical harm.'

'Did you scream at him?'

'Actually, when it came to it I was amazed at my calm. I decided to tell him about you and me, so that ruled out taking the moral high ground.' She smiles to herself. 'I just hope the penicillin jab hurt him.'

'Nell said you had to go back to the clinic for an all-clear.'

'Mm . . . to tell the truth, that didn't go quite to plan.'

'Gah, you ain't ill?'

A little muscle tweaks the side of her mouth. 'I wasn't sure if I should tell you this. You see, the doctor told me that my tests came through fine, the infection's cleared, but it seems . . . ' She takes a fortifying drag of her cigarette. 'It seems that I'm pregnant.'

Robbie's expression freezes. 'You mean . . . ?' His hand moves questioningly to his chest. At that moment Billie feels a dreadful compassion for him.

'Of course I got it wrong before, so best not to . . . but I'm pretty certain it's yours.'

He is stunned into silence, which she decides to wait out. Eventually, he says, 'So you're going to keep it?'

She nods. 'Look, I'm not telling you this because I expect

something from you, because I don't. I'm going through with it no matter what. I just thought I should let you know.'

He stares off again, lost in thought. She thinks for a moment it might have been kinder to keep this to herself. Kinder to him. Her romantic record is pretty awful – a goons' parade. She has picked wrong with a consistency bordering on wilfulness. Bryn wasn't by any means the worst. With Robbie there hasn't even been a honeymoon period. What began in furtiveness quickly degenerated into suspicion, misunderstanding, violence ... and nearly all of it her fault. It occurs to her that sometimes it might be wisdom to let go of the loved one instead of holding them to account. Why do we need to possess?

She picks up her cigarettes from the bar. 'I'm going to leave you to think this out. It's obviously a shock—'

'Don't go,' he says, staying her. The colour appears to be coming back to his face. 'If you're sure it's mine, I'm in. I want to be involved.'

'Robbie, honestly, I can do this on my own. You can walk away and I won't think badly of you—'

'I don't see that as a choice. I could have gone off today and been none the wiser. But you've told me now – so how can I walk away?'

'I did consider not telling you. You're young, you're ... going places. Why would you want to have a kid in the way, spoiling the fun?'

He looks at her with a tender, almost pitying expression. 'It wouldn't be just a kid. It'd be *our* kid. That's the difference.'

What does his commitment even mean? she wonders. That he'll be a proper father and help out? She holds her gaze on him for what feels like an age. He maintains a poker face, until without warning he raises his brow enquiringly, and she laughs.

'What did Nell say?' he asks her.

'I haven't told her. One step at a time. God knows how she's going to take it.'

He looks at her quizzically. 'If I know your mum she'll be ecstatic. There ain't a woman who's got more love in her than she has.'

A few weeks ago she would have snarled in his face for saying that. Now it makes her only slightly uncomfortable.

'America, though,' she says, suddenly anxious now that hope is in play. 'What if you don't come back?'

He shakes his head, smiles. 'You've got to have a *bit* more faith in me than that.'

The garden is taking on a faded look, the flowers going bald, their colours leached out. The laburnum seems to be in mourning. It hasn't hosted her woodpecker in months, though she still finds herself listening out for it. She misses that chiselling sound.

Nell wanders to the far wall and turns around, her gaze uptilted to the roofline of the houses. Her painting of those backs is the best thing she's done this year. Véro has suggested she turn it into a series. It might not be a bad idea. The way the bricks change colour in the light, their patterning, feels transcendent; they have been witness to a city as it rises, falls, rises again. The sight of them moves her. Even in her loneliness – especially in her loneliness – there is always the urge to work.

Inside the house the phone is ringing. When she answers it takes her a moment to recognise the voice at the other end; north Londoner, creaky like an old gate. It's Horace, her picture-framer. He's currently in possession of her *Portrait*, which needs an overhaul now they've found woodworm in the frame. Nell has considered the risk of entrusting her precious picture to a modest little shop on Kentish Town Road – Véro would be horrified – but she likes the idea of Horace seeing it, working on it, and she'd rather the repair money went to him than one of Véro's high-end associates.

Horace wants to consult her about the reframing, says he's found something that's confused him. She'd better come down and take a look for herself. So Nell finishes her cigarette, puts on her navy mac and sets off. As she walks down the road she's thinking about Robbie; he'll be in New York by now. He was in an odd mood when they said goodbye. She noticed an acoustic guitar he hadn't packed, and asked him if he wanted it to be sent on. When he said he'd collect it on his return she was stumped. 'You mean you're coming back here?' He hesitated, seeming embarrassed, and mumbled that he hoped to 'if all goes well'. Then something occurred to him. He tore a page from his notebook, wrote a few words and folded it under the bridge of the guitar. She examined it later. It read:

This one's for you, Django! Good luck. R

As he waited for the cab he said to her, 'You don't regret it, do you?'

'What?' she asked, disconcerted.

'It's just that you've never said anything – about what happened.'

'I don't regret it. At all. Do you?'

He shook his head, seeming relieved. After a moment he said, 'Can we still be friends?'

'Isn't that a song?' She half-laughed, and kissed his cheek. 'I hope they're nice to you over there.'

She's not convinced she'll ever see him again.

At the framer's Horace calls her into his workshop at the back where he's been dismantling the picture. He reckons the carved frame is an original, early nineteenth century, with some later bodged repairs. But there's something odd he's found beneath the stretchers.

'You see the edges here, all these nailheads – something's been tacked to the reverse. Might just be a hessian backing, to strengthen it. But it could be something else.'

'Can you prise it off?' she asks.

'Well, I can ...'

'I mean, without damaging it.'

Horace pulls a face, as if his craftsmanship has been impugned. 'I can do it now if you want to wait.'

Nell watches as he makes busy with his pliers, plucking one black tack after another from the perimeter of the frame. A few have stuck fast with age, and he switches to a thin screwdriver to loosen their hold. She watches with trepidation lest his hand slips and pierces the canvas, but Horace, despite his years, has the steady precision of a Swiss watchmaker. Whatever lies pressed to the reverse is slowly coming away. The last couple of nails are pulled, and he lifts off what is plainly another canvas and turns it over.

Nell draws in a breath sharply. It is a portrait of two young girls, sisters by the look, the older one staying the hand of the younger one as she reaches towards a candle flame. It has been painted at night, and by a masterly hand. A rich dark harmony of colouring is at work, the silk dresses of the girls appearing to glow from the shadows. Nell's startled gaze drops to the painting's edge, where the initials WM are inscribed.

'Blimey,' says Horace, frowning.

Nell cannot find her voice for a moment. She knows what it is, though it can only be here by a miracle. She picks up *Portrait of a Young Man* and places it alongside the picture of the sisters.

'See this, it's a double,' she says, pointing to the picture that hangs behind the young man. 'Laura Merrymount placed her father's painting of his two daughters just behind the figure of her brother, Joseph. Its formal title is *The Merrymount Sisters at Night*. She called it *Molly and the Captain*, and it was supposed to have been destroyed. But here it is. Laura must have hidden it away . . . and she painted it in miniature as a clue. It's been here all along.'

The old man looks at her uncertainly. 'Why would she do that?'

Nell shakes her head. 'To keep it safe? I think it had a strange history – stolen, rescued from a fire and . . . Well, I don't know why.'

They stand in contemplation, without speaking. Nell feels brought up short, the distant years suddenly concertinaed, collapsed inside this little room, the present. What was lost, improbably found. Only it was never lost; it was waiting for the future. She looks at the unblemished faces of Molly and Laura, their dark liquid eyes innocent of fate, of decay, of time's vicissitudes.

'These girls are family of mine, Horace,' she says, and moves her hand lightly towards the canvas, as though she might be going to greet them.

Credits

Acknowledgements

My thanks to Richard Beswick, Zoe Hood, Nithya Rae, Alison Tulett, Jon Wood, Peter Straus.

Blessings on Catherine Smith, Amy Hough, Ryan Gilbey, Simon Hopkinson, Jenny Uglow.

A special thank you to Tom Robinson for allowing me to quote from his song 'War Baby'.

The prompting for this book I owe to the exhibition *Gainsborough's Family Album* at the NPG in November 2018. No artist in my experience has ever painted family, or children, more beautifully. I was also much absorbed by *The Letters of Thomas Gainsborough* (2001) and Claire Tomalin's biography of Dora Jordan, *Mrs Jordan's Profession* (1994).

For 'The Flowers of Romance' section I am indebted to Viv Albertine's *Clothes Clothes Clothes Music Music Music Boys Boys Boys* (2014), and to Gillian Tindall's magnificent history of Kentish Town, *The Fields Beneath* (1977).

My greatest debt, as ever, is to Rachel Cooke, a peerless companion and encourager during lockdown, when most of this book was written.